Plato stumbled away from the earth sciences exhibit, past the service elevators, and back to the dinosaur skeletons. Thankfully, the place ███████ ed. He felt sick to his stom███ ███████████████████ forehead.

He finally s███████████████████████████ lyptodon. The thing lo█  and ungainly as befo██████████████████████████

Even more so ████████ ████ was something especially unnatural about the two objects sticking out from beneath the shell, back near the bony tail. Two objects that almost certainly weren't part of the display. A pair of human feet, jutting from beneath the dome like the Wicked Witch of the East's after Dorothy's house fell on her.

Except that these feet weren't wearing ruby slippers. They were wearing snakeskin boots. Near the head of the weird creature, a tiny river of blood was trickling across the floor. Plato leaped over the ropes, scrambled to the back of the glyptodon, and burrowed underneath. He already knew what he would find.

The back of the victim's head was completely caved in. His misshapen face grinned at Plato with a ghastly rictus, as though he had just realized his fondest wish. The murder weapon was lying nearby.

The victim, Marvin Tucker, a famous hematologist, had finally discovered a dinosaur bone.

SKELETONS
IN THE
CLOSET

Bill Pomidor

A CAL & PLATO MARLEY MYSTERY

A SIGNET BOOK

SIGNET
Published by the Penguin Group
Penguin Books USA Inc., 375 Hudson Street,
New York, New York 10014, U.S.A.
Penguin Books Ltd, 27 Wrights Lane,
London W8 5TZ, England
Penguin Books Australia Ltd, Ringwood, Victoria, Australia
Penguin Books Canada Ltd, 10 Alcorn Avenue,
Toronto, Ontario, Canada M4V 3B2
Penguin Books (N.Z.) Ltd, 182–190 Wairau Road,
Auckland 10, New Zealand

Penguin Books Ltd, Registered Offices:
Harmondsworth, Middlesex, England

First published by Signet, an imprint of Dutton Signet,
a division of Penguin Books USA Inc.

First Printing, March, 1997
10 9 8 7 6 5 4 3 2 1

For my parents, Bill and Jeannette,
who taught me to believe.

ACKNOWLEDGMENTS

A great deal of the research for this novel was performed at the Cleveland Museum of Natural History, where I made a very fortunate discovery of my own: The museum's curator of physical anthropology was none other than Dr. Bruce Latimer, who had been my anatomy lab instructor during medical school. Bruce provided a wealth of facts, details, and inside information about the fantastic Hamann-Todd skeletal collection, the nature of physical anthropology, and the often unusual life of a physical anthropologist. Dr. Mike Williams, curator of vertebrate paleontology, answered some very unusual questions about the structural integrity of dinosaur skeletons. Lyman Jellema gave me a behind-the-scenes tour of the museum, and Jan McKay, communications manager, helped with many details about the museum itself.

Cathy Aingworth contributed some very important information about her field of expertise—a field which unfortunately I cannot describe here without spoiling the plot. Ubelaker and Scammell's nonfiction work, *Bones: A Forensic Detective's Casebook,* furnished the details for some plot elements in the story. Mark Gottlieb's *Northern Ohio Live* article provided some background on the Hamann-Todd Collection. And finally my parents—Walter (Bill) and Jeannette Pomidor—have provided ongoing guidance, support, and research and editing help. This book is dedicated to them.

Trifles light as air, are to the jealous confirmations strong as proofs of holy writ.

—William Shakespeare, *Othello*

CHAPTER 1

"It's hideous, Cally." Plato Marley took another bite from his prime rib sandwich and grimaced at his wife. "It's killing my appetite."

Cal smiled fondly at the object parked between the sugar and the ketchup bottle. "Pretty accurate, isn't it?"

"Pretty loathsome." Plato swallowed heavily and forced his gaze away from the table. He stared across the Cuyahoga River instead, watching the ponderous mass of an iron ore barge slowly blot out his view of Cleveland's skyline. They were lunching at Shooter's today, celebrating Cal's appointment as an assistant professor of anatomy at Siegel Medical College.

Despite the warmth of the late October afternoon, the restaurant's vast outdoor deck was all but deserted. The only other diners were a glitzy couple seated near the door. The waiter had offered the pair a table nearby, with a better view of the river, but they had glimpsed Cal's prize and politely declined. They were huddled over their small table, whispering and darting occasional glances at the grisly object.

Cal speared a radish into her mouth, then hefted the human head with her free hand and demonstrated its virtues for Plato while she crunched away at her salad. "I'm testing it for a company in Maine. Three guys—a sculptor, an anatomist, and a plastics engineer."

Half of the skin was already peeled away, exposing a tapestry of muscles and nerves. A marvelously realistic eyeball rested atop the A.1. bottle, glaring down at Plato's apple cobbler. Cal peeled the other skin away, along with the ear and most of the tousled brown hair, and handed the mess across the table.

"Feel that," she urged. "They call it Plaskin. Just like the real thing, huh?"

Reluctantly, Plato slid his fingers over the flayed latex. Cal was right. He could feel little surface irregularities, a few wrinkles in the skin of the forehead, and he could *swear* he felt a five o'clock shadow. His stomach flip-flopped. "God! How do they *do* that?"

"Don't ask me." Cal draped the skin over the sugar bowl and started peeling muscles away. "Their plastics engineer tried to explain it, but I don't understand it all myself. They start with a cast of someone's face—" She gestured at the head. "This one's based on Harold Hawkins—the president of the company. Handsome guy, when he's got all his skin on. Anyway, they use some kind of computer modeling to get the proper textures for different kinds of skin, for the surfaces of organs, muscles, brain, whatever."

She detached Harold's temporalis muscle and handed it across to Plato—a limp scallop-shaped piece of tissue with the look and feel of raw flank steak. After handing it back, Plato instinctively wiped his fingers on his napkin.

"A lot of companies make peel-away models," Cal continued. "But these Plaskin models feel just like the real thing. It's that plastics engineer—he's got this stuff down to a science."

She undid a pair of hidden catches and started to swing the now-bare skull open at the midline, affording Plato a glimpse of the dura mater, the outer covering of the brain. He quickly grabbed her arm and showed her his watch.

"Sorry, dear." He feigned disappointment. "I'd love to see more, but I've got to make rounds at the hospital this afternoon."

Cal glanced at the watch and sucked in her breath. "And *I've* got to lecture in the anatomy lab in half an hour." She swung the skull closed again and pressed a salivary gland into place, then paused. "But what about our desserts?"

"Let's take them home," Plato suggested. "We can have them tonight."

The waiter boxed their desserts and handled their check with record speed. Reassembling the model took much longer. When Cal finished, she still wasn't satisfied. "Only problem with this stuff," she observed as she pressed the half-nose into place, "is that it just doesn't stay *on* very well. There! How's that?"

Plato frowned as the nose slipped away again, revealing the septum and ruddy turbinates of the nasal passages. The tousled brown hair was askew, as though trimmed by a drunken barber. The eyeballs stared in opposite directions. The tongue wouldn't quite fit inside the mouth.

All in all, the model looked far more like the victim of some horrific crime than an anatomy lab teaching aid.

"I think Harold could use a little Velcro," Plato observed.

"You may be right," Cal clucked. She gently slid the head into an oversized Ziploc sack and stuffed it into her canvas book bag, then handed him the dessert box. "You can carry this. We'd better hurry."

Luckily, Siegel Medical College wasn't far away—just up the road on the west bank of the Cuyahoga. Plato swung the ancient Rabbit into the school's parking lot with ten minutes to spare, pulled up to the curb, and reached across to open Cal's door.

She treated him to a long, lingering kiss, then frowned.

"What's the matter?" Plato asked.

"I wish you had time to walk me to the door," She sighed. "I get so tired of being ogled."

"Ogled?" He frowned. "Someone is *ogling* you?"

"You don't have to sound so surprised." Cal grimaced, then pointed to the sidewalk leading from the parking lot to the entrance. Siegel Medical College had finally raised enough money for a much-needed research wing, along with repairs to the crumbling back half of the building. A barbed-wire fence lined the edge of the sidewalk. Beyond lay a vast rectangular pit, roughly the size of a football field. The construction site was packed with equipment from a sandbox of dreams: excavators, backhoes, cranes, dump trucks, a cement mixer or two, all bearing the familiar Windsor Construction Company logo.

"The female medical students call it 'running the gauntlet'," Cal explained. "Every time a female staffer or student walks in from the parking lot, those construction workers start whistling and hooting, carrying on like a pack of lovesick coyotes."

Plato rolled his eyes. "You're kidding."

"They're always drooling over my legs," she continued, smoothing her tan slacks. "That's why I haven't worn skirts to work for the past couple of weeks."

He switched off the motor and set the parking brake. "Come on—I'll walk in with you. I've got a few minutes to spare."

Not that it was likely to do much good, Plato knew. Even if his presence kept the workers quiet today, he couldn't escort Cal inside every time she came to lecture at the college. Maybe they could complain to the administration—Dean Fairfax owed them a favor or two.

But as they strolled past the building site, Plato saw no sign of the construction workers.

"Maybe they're at lunch," he guessed.

"No such luck," Cal replied. "They eat on-site. Otherwise the women could sneak in and out. See? There they are."

Cal pointed past the barbed-wire fence to the far side of the enormous hole. An excavator was down in the trench, its shovel resting on the lip of the ditch. A crowd of yellow hard hats was clustered around the scoop.

Nearby, the main entrance to the medical college burst open. One of Siegel's finest flew through the doors. He spotted Cal and jogged over.

"Dr. Marley—thank goodness you're here." Officer Henry Douglas smiled with relief.

"Why?" Cal asked. "What's wrong?"

"I don't know." The young security guard rocked nervously on the heels of his patent leather shoes. "I just got a call from the building foreman. Their shovel hit something—he thinks it's a bone."

"Bone?" Cal frowned. "Human?"

Henry shrugged. "Don't know. I had no idea who to call. This isn't exactly covered in the Security Officer's Handbook, you know. I tried the anatomy lab, but nobody answers the phone."

Plato nodded approvingly. Not many people would have thought of calling the anatomy department, but Henry was pretty bright. He'd helped Cal out of a tight situation once before.

"Let's go." Cal turned on her heel and marched toward the gate. Plato and Henry followed close behind.

As he swung open the gate, the construction foreman shot a questioning glance at Cal.

"This is Dr. Marley," Henry explained. "One of our anatomy professors."

The foreman wasn't much taller than Cal, but he was a foot or two wider. He grinned broadly and shook hands with Plato. "Nice to have you along, Doctor. This little lady your assistant?"

He gave Cal a wide smile, touring his eyes over her honey-blond hair and trim figure, then frowning at her slacks.

Plato shook his head and pointed to his wife, pretending he wasn't a physician himself. "*That's* Dr. Marley—over there."

The construction foreman gave a wide-eyed grunt, like he'd just caught a wrecking ball in the solar plexus. He slowly lifted his gaze to Cal's face. "Oh. Uh, sorry, lady."

But he recovered quickly, turning to the security guard. "Don't you think maybe we ought to call the police in on this or something? Get somebody *official* involved here?"

"Dr. Marley is a deputy coroner," Henry explained patiently. "That's about as official as you can get."

The foreman gave a dubious shrug. "It's your call, buddy."

"So where's this bone?" Cal asked.

"Over there." The foreman sighed, pointing back toward the excavator. "But you'd better get some hats on first."

He led Cal and Plato to a rack of hard hats beside the gate, then walked them around the back edge of the crater. Henry had headed back to the security office, but a dozen construction workers filed behind the trio. The foreman stopped at the excavator scoop. The rest of the machine was still down in the pit, its long arm outstretched like a giant fiddler crab about to heave itself free of the ocean.

Standing several feet away from the scoop, the foreman pointed to a dirty ocher shaft poking up from the fresh clay. "See it?"

Cal set her bag down, pulled the bone free and gave it a cursory glance, then passed it over to Plato. "Fibula."

Plato glanced at the long thin bone. He, too, recognized it as a leg bone. But he hadn't the foggiest notion whether it came from a human or a hippopotamus. The foreman backed away quickly when Plato offered him a look.

"I can see it just fine from over here," he called. "Looks like a cow bone. We get a lot of those. Found a whole cow skeleton last year, when we were digging for a new wing at Case Western."

"Could be," Cal agreed. "The fibula isn't a very distinctive bone—this could have come from a cow, or a deer, or maybe even a bear. Are there any more?"

"You'd have to look down in the hole." He waved his arms in front of him, palms out. "We stopped digging when Jamahl hit this. Didn't want to mess up any police investigation."

"Didn't want to mess up your hands," one of the workers teased, then grinned at Cal. "Don't let Ernie fool you—he almost lost his lunch when we found that cow skeleton last year."

"That's bullshit, Jamahl." The foreman's face lit up like pink neon.

"Sure, Ernie. Sure." The wiry black man shook his head and chuckled. "Whatever you say."

"I want to climb down there and take a look," Cal said. "Do you have a small shovel I can poke around with?"

"Yeah," Ernie replied. "But the hole's too deep for climbing." He jerked a thumb back to a large steel box perched on the rim of the excavation. "You'll have to go down in the cage. I'd better go down with you."

"You better behave yourself, boss," Jamahl cautioned.

The foreman whirled around. "Don't you have some work to do?"

"Nope." He grinned broadly. "This is my excavator—remember?"

Cal frowned down at the huge excavator scoop. It was full of clay. "There could be some more bones in here, too, I suppose."

"Sure could, ma'am," Jamahl agreed. "How about if I get another shovel and check through it?"

"That would be wonderful." She turned to Plato. "Would you mind helping him while I check down below?"

"No problem." Plato nodded eagerly. Hospital rounds would run late today, but he didn't mind. For once, he was just as curious as Cal.

He and Jamahl spent a good half hour sifting through the clay with their hand shovels, gently prodding the soil, shaking and slicing it into tiny pieces, and finding nothing but pebbles. While they worked, Jamahl filled Plato in on his boss.

"Ernie's a moron, but he's the owner's nephew or second cousin or something." He gathered another shovelful of clay and squinted at it. "He's worse than usual today, though."

"Why is that?" Plato squinted at a wrist bone for several seconds before deciding it was a rock.

"We had the whole foundation dug and ready for pouring the footers, all on schedule," Jamahl explained. "Then this morning, the building inspector comes and says the ground is still too soft here by the river. Says we need to dig down another two feet. I thought Ernie was going to kill him."

"Why'd you tell Ernie to behave himself?" Plato asked suddenly.

The construction worker chuckled. "Ernie likes pretty ladies. Thinks he's God's gift to women—can't keep his hands to himself. But if that gal's really a doctor, she just might burn his ass to the ground." He glanced up at Plato and grinned. "I wouldn't mind seeing that. I'm next in line for his job."

"She's really a doctor," Plato assured him. "And you're right—he'd better not mess with her."

"You know her pretty well, huh?"

"You could say that. She's my wife." Just then, Plato's shovel struck something hard. "Hey, I think I've got something here."

Together, they probed the boundaries of the object, carefully lifted the surrounding block of clay free, and placed it on the ground. Using their fingers, they scooped away the mud and dirt until Plato got a firm handhold on the bone. Jamahl scraped off the last of the clinging clay as Plato plucked the bone free and held it aloft. Camped around the edge of the pit, the other workers saw it and cheered.

"Distal femur," Cal pronounced from behind him. She had approached while Plato and Jamahl were wrestling with the lump of clay.

She took the bone from Plato and studied it carefully. The shaft was long and straight, but the jagged edge of one end suggested that the other half was still buried somewhere in the pit.

"Did you have any luck down there?" Plato asked her.

"Not much." She reached into her sack and pulled out a familiar-looking bone. "Nothing but the other fibula. Not that it matters now. We'll have to get a crew from the coroner's office to come and dig up the rest of the skeleton, very carefully."

"What do you mean, 'rest of the skeleton?' " Ernie wedged

himself between Plato and Cal, squeezing them aside with his vast abdominal girth. "I'm not letting you throw this whole project off schedule just because of a stupid cow skeleton."

"It's not a cow skeleton," Cal assured him calmly.

"Deer, bear, whatever. The point is, you can't—"

"The *point*, Ernie"—Cal jabbed the bloated paunch with her finger—"is that this is a *human* skeleton."

The foreman backed off and rubbed his belly nervously. "There's no way you can be sure about that. You just said—"

"I said I couldn't tell for certain from the fibula," Cal admitted. She brandished Plato's find under the foreman's nose. "But the *femur*, now—that's a whole different story."

Plato had to grin as Cal adopted her lecturing tone and led the crowd of construction workers over to the flat edge of the scoop. "Aside from the skull, the distal femur—or thigh bone—is one of the most distinctive bones of the human body."

She propped the base of the bone on the flat surface. Rather than standing straight upright, the long shaft took a fifteen-degree angle to the left.

"It's all a question of mechanics," Cal began. She tapped the level surface of the scoop. "Pretend this scoop is the top of the tibia, the lower leg bone. It's flat in all animals—like a shelf. Has to be, or the thigh bone would slide off, right?"

A dozen hard hats nodded.

"Now think about the back legs of a cow, or a deer, or a horse. They come down straight from the pelvis, don't they? Their thigh bones are like two pillars, dropping basically straight from the hips to the ground." She leaned the thigh bone over so that its shaft stood straight upright while the base angled up from the shelf beneath. "Like this—so they can support the weight of the body. That's the way it is with four-legged animals. Same thing with bears—they have a very wide stance, right? Their feet are about the same width apart as their hip joints."

The audience nodded again. Like the medical students, Cal had them hooked.

"Of course, bears don't move very fast when they're standing. Having their feet so far apart means they have to swing their hips each time they take a step. So if a bear wants to move fast, he drops down on all fours."

"She's right," a voice in the crowd agreed. "Last time I went hunting in the Alleghenies, I—"

Someone shushed him.

But Ernie was growing impatient. "So get to the point, missy. What's all this got to do with human bones?"

Cal rested the base of the femur flat again, so that the shaft angled away from vertical. "In humans, the feet are placed closer together than the pelvis. The lower leg bones rise pretty straight, but the upper leg bones have to angle outward to meet the pelvis at the hip joint. We're the only animals that have such an outwardly angled femur—that's why we can run fast on two legs."

Most of the workers nodded their understanding, but Ernie wasn't convinced. "I still don't see how you can tell all that from one busted piece of bone."

A younger fellow with a sunburn and a ponytail spoke up. He placed his feet together and pointed to his hips, smiling earnestly. "See, Ernie, the thigh bone angles out like this, so—"

"I know *that*, Jimmy." The foreman rolled his eyes in disgust. "I'm not a *complete* idiot. I'm just saying, maybe this came from a girl bear—girls have bigger hips, right? Or maybe it came from a gorilla. Or maybe a cow that broke its leg."

"There are other indications," Cal persisted. "The lateral edge of the patellar groove, for instance—"

"What I'm saying," Ernie interrupted, "is I'm not going to shut down this job site until I get some kind of official word."

Cal's voice hardened. "I assure you I'm the only official you need. As Deputy Coroner for Cuyahoga County—"

"Listen, lady." Ernie gave a patronizing smile. "I enjoyed your little talk, but we've got a job to do here. I can't let some hysterical female march in and shut things down without getting some kind of official backing." He turned to Jamahl and jerked a thumb at the excavator. "Get digging again. We've wasted half the afternoon as it is."

Jamahl shook his head slowly. The other workers shifted uncertainly.

Plato saw Cal reach into a coat pocket for her ID badge from the coroner's office, then change her mind. A faint smile tugged at the corners of her mouth.

"I have *other* proof that these are human bones," Cal said quietly.

"Forget it." Ernie sneered. "I don't need any more lectures."

"This proof speaks for itself," she assured him. "I hadn't wanted to bring this up, but since you insist—" She yanked the Ziploc pouch from her book bag and pressed it into Ernie's grasp. Before he looked down, she continued. "I dug it up down there, while you were waiting back in the cage. It's remarkably well-preserved. Sure, a little bit of the skin has peeled away, and the nose keeps falling off, but—"

Realization of the bag's contents slowly dawned on the foreman. He stared at Harold's head with a sick, horrified fascination. Like a center fielder realizing he's just caught a live hand grenade instead of a baseball.

A greenish pallor spread over his face as he swiveled his gaze up to Cal, swallowed heavily, and dropped the sack. It landed with a ghastly *squish*. Legs shaking, the foreman tottered off to the trailer parked in the corner of the building site. He didn't quite make it.

"Ernie always did have a weak stomach," someone muttered. The others chuckled.

Cal retrieved the bag, dusted it off, and dropped it back into her book bag. She turned to Plato. "I'm going to give Harold the highest recommendation I can. An absolutely *splendid* reproduction."

He grinned. "That wasn't very nice, Cally."

"It wasn't meant to be." She rubbed the back of her coat. "Silly bastard *pinched* me—twice. In the cage. I told him if he did it again, I'd cut his fingers off."

She patted her breast pocket, the one that held her dissecting scalpels, then turned to the other workers. "As Deputy County Coroner, I'm closing this construction site for today. I need you all to get your things and step outside the fence. The police will be here soon and they'll let you know what to expect."

As the hard-hats shuffled off, several flashed admiring glances at Cal. She drifted off toward Ernie's trailer.

Standing beside Plato, Jamahl grinned. "That's one *fine* woman you got there."

"I know."

They both watched Cal approach the trailer. In response to

her knock, Ernie reluctantly poked his head out the door. As Cal talked, the foreman nodded vigorously, eagerly, to her every suggestion.

"Bet she makes *you* behave yourself," Jamahl mused.

Plato sighed. "You got that right."

CHAPTER 2

"This pelvis offers us some interesting information, hmm?"

Ralph Jensson was cradling a broad circlet of bone in his bare hands. The Cuyahoga County Coroner gazed over his half-moon glasses at Cal, dark eyes glinting like obsidian. The pelvis in his hands was stained a mottled brown from the riverbank clay that had formed its grave.

He and Cal were facing each other across a stainless steel gurney in the main autopsy room at the Cuyahoga County Morgue. Between them lay the products of the afternoon's excavation: a collection of dirty brown bones neatly arrayed in precise anatomical position. The arm and hand bones were splayed to the sides, while the shoulders were raised in a perpetual shrug. Disjointed ribs leaned against one another for support, and twenty-four bones from the spinal column tilted toward the sacrum and coccyx like a parade of fallen soldiers.

Jensson passed the bony circlet to Cal like the Archbishop of Canterbury handing over the crown. She hefted its weight and studied it from every angle.

"Obviously female," she began.

"Quaite," Jensson agreed, a hint of Scotch brogue creeping into his voice. The county coroner had come to Cleveland as a boy, but he spent every August in Aberdeen and rolled his R's until Christmas. "The broad sacrum, the wide angle of the pubic arch, the low degree of sacral curvature—all make that intuitively obvious. But the structure has other stories to tell, hmm?"

Cal smiled inwardly. Ralph Jensson was one of the main reasons she had come to Cleveland after spending most of her life in Chicago. Jensson was one of forensic pathology's pioneers. He had performed his first autopsy before Cal was born. As a Life Fellow of the American College of Forensic Examiners, he had helped distill the coroner's art into a science, eliminating guesswork, standardizing procedures, and applying computer and chemical analyses to forensic detection. Over the past four decades, he had trained many of the top names in the field.

Jensson was a full professor at Case Western, but he was also a visiting professor at Chicago's Northwestern University—Cal's alma mater. He had impressed her during the few lectures he delivered there when she was a student. During her residency and fellowship in Chicago, Jensson had been something of a long-distance mentor, a guiding light for her career. His invitation for Cal to join the coroner's staff in Cleveland had seemed a natural extension of a relationship that began during medical school.

Cal had excelled during her training, but she wanted to be even better. So she had gladly accepted the half-time position. And gladly learned to put up with Jensson's nasal twang, his persistent questions, his way of always eking out just a few more facts from a body or a bone or a bullet fragment.

"She was probably more than twenty years old at the time of death," Cal observed. She pointed to the four faint lines between the so-called "sacral vertebrae" at the back of the pelvis, which had fused to form the solid bone of the sacrum. She traced her fingers along the wedge-shaped bone, which had knitted to join with the other bones of the pelvis. "Judging by the complete fusion here, along with the slight calcification of the symphysis pubis, I would estimate this woman to be twenty-five to thirty-five years old."

"Excellent, Cal. Excellent." Jensson reached across the table to run his finger along the pelvic rim. "Any other—hmm—indications?"

The county coroner loved to play guessing games with his clients—deducing habits and occupations, as well as ancient and long-forgotten injuries. Cal ran her fingers along the iliac crests, felt the sharp nub of the iliac spine, the ischial tuberosity. The points where the muscles inserted on the bones were remarkably prominent.

"These areas," Cal concluded with a gesture, "suggest that

she had muscular, well-developed lower extremities. Perhaps the victim was an athlete."

"Victim?" Jensson raised a feathery gray eyebrow. His mottled, freckled head was pale and completely hairless, making the furry brows even more conspicuous, the dark eyes seem even larger. Jim Cartwright, another deputy coroner, had once compared Jensson to a barn owl with alopecia. He wasn't far off the mark.

The old coroner squinted at Cal. "You have evidence that a crime has been committed—hmm?"

"Sorry." Cal reddened. "Slip of the tongue."

"Quaite." Jensson took the pelvis from Cal and gently planted it at the center of the skeleton. "Otherwise, I think you've drawn some excellent conclusions. Judging by the rest of the available bones, I would place this woman's age at approximately twenty-five years. The prominent ridges on the pubis as well as those of the lower extremities indeed point to an athletic lifestyle."

He retrieved a shoulder blade from the table and closed his eyes, passing his fingers over the vertebral border like a fabric merchant sampling silk. "And yet, the development of the upper extremities is relatively normal. She may have indeed been an athlete—a cyclist, a runner, or a skier. Or perhaps her occupation required a good deal of walking—something like a mail carrier, perhaps."

"Or a migrant farm worker," Cal added. "Or maybe just a drifter. Someone who spent a lot of time on the road, walking or hitching rides."

"Exactly." Jensson nodded and slid the shoulder blade back into place under the collarbone. "Of course, we have several more obvious indications. She was of average height, five-five or five-six. Her weight at death is uncertain, though the apparent development of her bones argues against malnutrition. On the other hand, the muscular development apparent in her lower extremities makes it unlikely that she was physically inactive or tremendously obese." He patted one of the lower leg bones and ran a finger along its length. "The platymeric shape of her tibias also suggests a great deal of muscularity. The slope of the flattening—"

Staring at the large bone, he broke off suddenly, then picked it up. "Strange. I can nae *see* anything, but—" He handed the bone to Cal. "Here. What do you feel?"

Cal brushed her bare fingers along the smooth surface of the tibia. Halfway down, she found it. A hint, a whisper of a ridge running diagonally across the curved lateral surface of the lower leg bone. Cal traced the ridge with the tip of her index finger.

"Exactly." Jensson sighed. "Your tactile sense is excellent."

"It must be a healed fracture," Cal concluded. "It's too low to be the insertion point for the tibialis anterior muscle."

"We'll have it x-rayed," the coroner said, then gave a hopeless shrug. "But I'm afraid it won't do much good."

Cal nodded, gazing at the table. The digging crew from the coroner's office had done a marvelous job of recovering the menagerie of bones buried beneath Siegel's future research wing. Several construction workers had also stayed behind to help with the spadework and sifting. They had found most of the bones—even the other half of the broken femur. The skeleton was missing only two finger bones, the sternum, and a heel bone. And one other very critical piece. Cal's eyes traveled past the tibia and pelvis, up the spinal column and ribs, to the cervical vertebrae.

Uncrowned by the skull, the neck seemed elongated, distorted, and somehow obscene. The workers had dug a deep trench, spaded over the surrounding area, and sifted through piles of excavated dirt. But the missing skull was nowhere to be found.

Without it, identification of the body would be extremely difficult. The coroner's office would be unable to make comparisons with dental records, to attempt a facial reconstruction for publication in the newspapers, or even to guess the owner's race.

Jensson's finding of a healed break in the tibia increased the odds of identification, but only slightly. Still, if anyone found a likely match, and if the missing person's medical records included an X ray of the healed leg fracture, the image could be compared with this bone to give a positive identification.

Jensson gently placed the bone on a shelf and filled out a pink slip of paper. The Cuyahoga County Morgue housed its own X ray unit—for detection of bullets or knife fragments, for determining the extent of skull fractures and other types of

bony injuries, and for recording unique findings in John or
Jane Doe cases like this one.

"Any theories?" Cal asked with a smile.

Jensson was always warning her to steer clear of theories, to
avoid speculating on the backgrounds of her cases. He had
taught her that objectivity was the coroner's most important
tool—more valuable than scalpels or microscopes or computers. He was imperturbable in court, sticking to observations,
limiting his judgments to only the most certain of conclusions,
and offering deductions only when asked.

But after forty years of forensics work, he had an uncanny
knack for sensing the circumstances of each death, leaping
from observation and deduction to inference and intuition, and
almost always making the right call. Always off the record,
though.

And off the record, the prosecutor's office had learned
about Jensson's hunches, and learned to trust his intuition. So
had the coroner's staff.

Jensson crossed the room to the sink. Beside it, a drying
rack held an assortment of surgical steel knives and three fine
pipes. The coroner selected his favorite, a billiard pipe with a
cherry wood bowl. He rapped its contents into the sink, re-
loaded the pipe and puffed it to life, then leaned against the
countertop and closed his eyes.

"The first conclusion is rather obvious," he began. "Based
on the brownish discoloration and low density of the bones, it
seems likely that the body was buried several months ago, or
more probably several years ago."

Jensson was right. The bones felt *old*—they were remarkably light despite their dampness, and their tan surfaces were
etched and sandpapery rather than smooth.

Cal nodded. "Assuming that the body decayed where it was
buried."

"Precisely." Jensson's eyes slowly opened. "The possibility
always exists that the body decayed to a skeleton elsewhere,
and for some unknown reason it was moved to its ultimate
burial site. Of course, that is rather unlikely. Since the bones
were found twenty feet below ground level, whoever buried
them would have either needed to dig a twenty-foot grave in
full view of Siegel Medical College, or dig a much shallower
grave at the construction site once the excavation had begun.

The latter possibility would have required the gravedigger to leap an electrified barbed-wire fence with a sackful of human bones slung over his shoulder—a sort of Santa Claus of Death. Laying his finger aside of his nose and a' that."

Cal chuckled. "Maybe the reindeer helped."

"Perhaps." Jensson shrugged. "A simpler explanation is far more likely. I believe the body was buried quite a while ago. At least forty years ago."

"Why so long?" Cal asked.

"Because of Siegel Medical College's flooding problems." He puffed on the pipe until a pall of smoke circled his head. "Not long after the school was built—back in the twenties, I believe—a big chunk of Siegel's riverbank washed right into the Cuyahoga. The lower level of the medical school was flooded. After that, the surrounding area was built up with dredged soil from the river bottom. They stopped doing that in the mid-fifties."

"So the body was probably buried before that." Cal nodded her understanding. "At least forty years ago."

"Right." Tobacco-stained teeth gleamed as Jensson's lips parted in an expression that was half smile, half grimace. "But it more likely happened around sixty years ago."

Cal cocked her head curiously. The old coroner sounded pretty certain.

His eyes twinkled. "You're not from the area, so I wouldn't expect you to know. Anyway, it all happened long before you were born. Back when Eliot Ness was Cleveland's safety director."

"Eliot Ness?" Now Cal wondered if he was pulling her leg. "In *Cleveland*? Give me a break."

"You Chicagoans think Ness spent his whole career there— the Untouchables and so on." Jensson picked up the tibia and led her down a long corridor to the X ray unit. He left the bone in a box outside the door with the pink slip wrapped around one end. "After Prohibition was repealed, Ness came to Cleveland. Spent most of his life here—even ran for mayor in the fifties."

The coroner led her up a flight of stairs to a dingy conference room. He stood just inside the doorway, contemplating a set of battered steel bookcases in the far corner. "Ness was good for the town. Took on police corruption single-handed, and cleaned up the streets."

He crossed to one of the bookcases and selected a volume, thumbing through its pages. "But there was one case he never solved. It haunted his life."

Jensson handed the book to Cal—Steven Nickel's *Torso*.

"Cleveland's first and only serial killer," the coroner explained. "Twelve confirmed victims, and probably several others. The killer did his work in the thirties—between 1935 and 1938."

Cal glanced at the book, still puzzled. "So why do you think this is another case?"

"Victims of the Torso killer—or the Kingsbury Run killer— all had one thing in common." Standing near the bookcase, the old coroner—with over four decades' worth of experience— could not repress a shudder. "Their manner of death."

Cal glanced at the cover of the book and quickly understood.

"All apparently were beheaded," Jensson continued. "Neatly, surgically, skillfully."

She frowned. "That was how they were killed?"

"Quaite." The coroner sucked air from his now-lifeless pipe. "And in several cases, the heads were never found."

CHAPTER 3

Plato was sneaking out of Riverside General's main lobby that evening when his pager burst to life with an earsplitting screech. Swallowing his heart back into his chest, he fumbled with the controls and finally managed to shut the damned thing off. It was a new model that chirped ever more loudly as the battery wore down. Plato hadn't replaced the battery in months; his pages now sounded like the death wails of a demented rat.

He took a deep breath of cool autumn air, gazed mournfully at the parking lot beckoning in the distance, and turned back to the hospital. The clock in the lobby read six-thirty. He and Cal had both been on call for the past ten days running; he was hoping to get home early enough to cook something besides Budget Gourmet. Cal would probably get home on time tonight, but her culinary skills were limited to hard-boiled eggs and microwave popcorn.

Plato found a telephone and dialed the number. With luck, it would be a routine question—a ward secretary who couldn't read his orders, a nurse asking permission to use Tylenol for a patient's headache, or maybe a disgruntled records clerk who needed a signature. He'd take care of it, then head home and throw that turkey breast in the oven. Or break out the olive oil and fry up some chicken Parmesan; the freezer still held an emergency supply of marinara sauce.

But luck wasn't with Plato today. A breathless nurse answered the telephone from the 2100 unit.

"Dr. Marley?"

"Yes."

"Dr. Hoffman asked me to call you." Her voice quivered

slightly, like the page operator's did when she announced a
code blue. "He thinks Mrs. Leighton is having a stroke."

Plato hung up the phone and dashed for the stairs; 2100 was
only one flight up from the lobby. Agnes Leighton was Plato's
very first patient—she had joined his practice when he was a
lowly family medicine intern, stuck with him during his geriatrics fellowship, and followed him into his private practice
when he joined the Riverside faculty. Agnes had always insisted that Plato would be her last doctor, that her next referral
after Dr. Marley would be to Saint Peter himself.

Pounding up the steps, his footfalls and gasps echoing in the
empty stairwell, Plato reflected that Agnes hadn't quite gotten
her wish. Her three-year bout with colon cancer had brought
its share of consultants—the oncologist, the general surgeon,
the rehabilitation specialist. But she had always depended on
Plato for her general medical care. And throughout the long,
weary fight, she had kept her perspective, her biting sense of
humor, her sharp intelligence undulled by the disease that
surgery had barely slowed.

Plato jogged down the hall but drew up suddenly outside
Agnes's door.

If Agnes Leighton had really suffered a stroke, it certainly
hadn't affected her vocal cords. She was railing at Sam Hoffman—the geriatrics fellow—in no uncertain terms.

"Of course I can spell 'World' backward, you big lummox."
Her shrill voice carried from the room and echoed down the
hall. "I can also spell 'Idiot' backward—let's see—T-O-I-D-I.
How's that?"

Standing in the doorway, just out of view, Plato smiled to
himself. Young Dr. Hoffman was testing Agnes with a mental
status exam. The only trouble was, Agnes hated mental status
exams with a passion. She considered them an insult to her intelligence, and she was right.

"That's very good, Mrs. Leighton," Sam continued in a patient, reassuring voice.

"Why the hell do you have to be so patronizing?"

A plump nurse's aide pushed a med cart past Plato and
smiled. "Mrs. Leighton sure does like to speak her mind."

Plato nodded and edged closer to the doorway. Sam Hoffman was sitting in a chair at the foot of the bed. Agnes
Leighton was propped up in bed, arms crossed over her chest,

pressing her attack on Sam's intellect and only rarely pausing for breath. As a retired Cleveland policewoman, she had a very straightforward—and very loud—delivery. And as one of the first woman detectives on the force, she resented insults to her intelligence. She had made that clear to Plato very early in their relationship. She was making it clear to Sam as well.

"I'm sorry you feel that way," Sam said as Agnes finally wound down. "Just a few more questions. Do you remember those three words I told you to remember for me, at the beginning of our chat?"

"Yes."

"What are they?"

"If you can't remember them yourself, *I'm* certainly not going to tell you. Maybe you should have written them down." She frowned quizzically. "How in heaven's name did a forgetful person like you ever graduate from medical school?"

"*Missus* Leighton." Finally, a hint of irritation crept into Sam's voice. "I'm only trying to help you. I'm asking these questions because—" He glimpsed Plato in the doorway and sighed. "Please excuse me, ma'am."

Sam shuffled into the hallway, mopping his glasses on his long white coat and looking tired. But then, Sam Hoffman always looked tired. He had a long, droopy bloodhound face, rheumy eyes, and a ragged mop of brown hair that hung down over his forehead like wilted spinach. He and his wife had three children in diapers and a set of twins on the way. Their fertility was the stuff of hospital legend.

Sam sighed at Plato and shook his head in bewilderment, like a bloodhound that had lost the scent.

"Thank goodness you're here," he finally groaned. "I think Mrs. Leighton had a stroke, but I can't get a straight answer out of her."

"What kind of symptoms is she having?" Plato asked.

"Facial asymmetry, mostly. Her mouth is slack on the left—like this." With his droopy cheeks, Sam gave a very good impression of a stroke victim. He let the left side of his mouth sag down while he smiled with his right. "And her hand is a lot weaker on that side, too."

Plato nodded. Weakness in the hand and face could certainly point to a stroke. The only trouble was that Mrs.

Leighton already had some very good reasons for her face and hand weakness.

"Did you ask Agnes about her facial droop?" Plato asked.

"No." The geriatrics fellow shook his head. "I wanted to test her thinking ability first. But she's so irritable. . . . Of course, irritability could fit with a stroke, too."

"That's true." On the other hand, Plato knew, it could also fit with Agnes Leighton's personality. "Strokes *can* cause mood changes."

"Should I order an emergency CT scan?" Sam asked.

"How about if we hold off a minute, Sam." Plato smiled gently and put his hand on the geriatrics fellow's shoulder. "Maybe Mrs. Leighton can explain her facial droop for us."

Agnes Leighton grimaced when Sam entered, but she spotted Plato and quickly flashed a lopsided grin. "Nice to see you again, Dr. Marley. I thought you'd gone home for the night."

"Not yet, Agnes." Plato pulled up a chair and gestured for Sam to sit. "Dr. Hoffman was wondering about your facial weakness."

"Oh, this?" Agnes patted the left side of her face. "Bell's palsy. Had it for twenty years or so now."

At the foot of the bed, Sam Hoffman wrinkled his jowls and blinked with surprise, like a bloodhound who'd just sniffed his way into a nest of skunks.

"Bell's palsy?" he finally croaked.

"Yup."

Of course, Sam Hoffman knew that Bell's palsy was a common problem caused by damage to the facial nerve rather than to the brain itself. Agnes Leighton's facial droop had nothing to do with a stroke.

Sam blinked a few more times, then turned his tired eyes back to Plato. "But her hand weakness—"

"Came from a nasty wrist fracture," Plato replied. "You'll find that in the chart, along with a note about her Bell's palsy."

Agnes beamed her crooked smile again and shook her head sympathetically.

The geriatrics fellow shook his head. "I'm really sorry about all this, Dr. Marley. I should have checked—"

"That's okay, Sam." Plato shrugged. "I'd been meaning to have a chat with Mrs. Leighton anyway."

Sam's pager made a meek mewling noise, like a croupy kitten. Apparently his batteries were fresher than Plato's. He thumbed the button and stood. "I'd better get that. I'll see you tomorrow, Mrs. Leighton."

"Of course you will, dear. Have a nice day." She watched him leave, then scooted over and patted the bed beside her. "Come and sit down, Dr. Marley. What did you want to talk about?"

"About you, Agnes." Plato sat down and touched his patient's shoulder. "You've got to start treating my assistants a little better."

"I'm *training* him, Dr. Marley." Agnes Leighton's broad smile erased the lines and wrinkles on one side of her face. With her prominent cheekbones and wide gray eyes, Plato imagined the policewoman had captured almost as many hearts as she had criminals. "Teaching him to be more patient."

Her grin was contagious. Plato smiled and squeezed her hand. "Just go easy with him, okay? Like you did with me. Good geriatrics fellows are hard to come by."

"Of course." Her gaze drifted over to the empty bedside table, and the corner of her mouth turned down. "Anyway, Dr. Hoffman started it."

"Started what?"

Agnes sighed. "All I told him was that I wanted him to take these damned tubes out of me and ship me back to the nursing home." She gestured at the two IV machines standing sentry beside the bed, the green plastic oxygen line creasing her face, and the nasogastric tube taped to her cheek. "Well, he looked at me like I was *crazy*. And then he finally noticed my droop. Checked my muscle strength and started firing all those stupid questions at me."

"Wait a minute, Agnes." Plato shook his head. He was starting to feel like Sam Hoffman. "Slow down. *Why* did you ask him to take your tubes out?"

Agnes gave a tired sigh. The past year had been a downhill slide for her—a long losing battle with cancer, an orderly retreat from the field of life. She'd lost forty pounds in the past six months. Years ago, Plato had fretted over her weight, warned her about the risk of heart disease. Now her skin was two sizes too large. Beneath the saggy wrinkled parchment she was all angles and hollows, elbows and knees.

"It's simple, really." She raised gaunt shoulders in a scarecrow shrug. "I just want to die."

Right then, Plato's pager shrieked again—in a lower key, like a tormented soul.

"Good God!" Agnes cried. She grabbed Plato's arm. "I thought it was Satan himself, coming for me out of your pocket." She squinted at the pager and shot Plato a pitying look. "Is that some kind of punishment, your having to wear that thing?"

"Something like that, yes." Plato grimaced at the beeper and tried to gather his scattered thoughts. The page had come from Coronary Care. It was probably important, but he didn't want to leave Agnes.

"Something urgent?" she asked.

"Not really." He dropped the pager back into his pocket and frowned at his patient. "What makes you think you want to die?"

"I don't *think* I want to die. I *know* I want to die." Her face grew set and solemn. She reached down for his hand. "I'm serious about this, Plato. I'm tired of fighting. Tired of feeling sick. Tired of being *tired* all the time—like I just finished running a dozen windsprints."

"Maybe your potassium is down," Plato suggested quickly. "I should order a P–6—"

"Tired of that cancer blocking and twisting my guts," she continued. "Tired of upchucking every time I think about food."

"Your surgeon said another operation could—"

"No." She squeezed his hand, hard. "No more operations."

Plato stared at the floor and searched for something to say. Beside Agnes's bed the two IVACs ticked relentlessly, counting the drips flowing into her veins, the drips that kept her alive. Agnes's intestinal tract was completely blocked, just beyond her stomach. Plato had seen the X ray—a new ringlet of cancer was squeezing down on her small intestine like a hangman's noose.

She could take no food or drink by mouth. The vacuum unit hissing on the wall constantly pumped her stomach dry, just to keep her from vomiting. Agnes was right. Without the IV, she would certainly die.

"Listen," Agnes continued. "I just finished talking with that

surgeon before Dr. Hoffman came in. He says he could oper-
ate and clear the blockage, but there's no way he can get all
the cancer. Even with another operation, I'd only have a
year—and probably less."

"But at least you'd be able to eat," Plato pointed out. "To
get rid of those tubes and things. You'd be more comfortable,
and you'd almost certainly live longer."

"That's just what *he* said." She crossed her arms again. "But
supposing I even make it through the surgery—I'd probably be
just as bad again in a few months. Right?"

"Right." Plato swallowed heavily. "But if you—"

"And what kind of life is this?" Her eyes were steady and
clear and determined. "I'm going to die soon, anyway. I want
to go back to the nursing home—back to Wyndhaven. That's
my home now. I want to die at home."

Plato shook his head. From deep within his pocket, the
pager howled in torment. "Damn!"

"You'd better get that."

"I know." He stood. "I'll be right back."

"No, you won't." Agnes reached out to slap his thigh. "You
just get out of here. We can talk about this some more tomorrow." She flashed her crooked grin again. "*I'm* not going anywhere."

Plato hurried down the hall to telephone the coronary care
unit.

"Dr. Marley? This is Cindy, down in CCU." The ward clerk
had the nasal whine of a fall allergy victim. "Remember those
orders you wrote this afternoon? I'm checking them off and I
can't read one of the drugs . . . You're not still in the hospital,
are you?"

"I'll be right over."

He hopped the elevator to the third floor, jogged over to the
coronary care unit, and found Cindy sniffling over the chart.

"Right here." She pointed a finger at a long word beginning
with a "T."

Plato grabbed the chart and held it up to the desk lamp. The
unit's lights were always dimmed shortly after dinner, to help
the patients get at least a little bit of rest during the night. He
squinted and rubbed his eyes. He traced the letters with his fin-

gers, as though they were Braille. Finally he picked out the second letter—a "y."

"Tylenol," he pronounced proudly.

"Tylenol?" Annie echoed.

"Yes. One gram q. six hours p.r.n. pain. See?"

Annie squinted at the scribbles. "I thought it said Tegretol. But that didn't make any sense—you don't give Tegretol for pain."

"Right."

She sighed. "Dr. Hoffman's handwriting is even worse."

"I know."

"Plus, you forgot to sign it." She gestured at the page.

"Sorry." He scribbled his signature.

Sneaking out of the hospital again, Plato glanced at his watch. Quarter to eight. He had just enough time to get home and defrost some Budget Gourmet.

CHAPTER 4

"So what happened then?" Cal asked.

"I got paged to the CCU." Sitting at the kitchen table later that evening, Plato shot a glance at the Salisbury steaks sizzling inside the microwave. Cal had decided to surprise him by starting dinner herself. He *was* surprised—nothing had caught fire yet. "No big deal. Just a few orders they couldn't read."

"So you didn't talk with Mrs. Leighton again?" She dumped a sackful of frozen broccoli into a bowl and doused it with salt.

"No. I stopped by her room on my way out, but she was already asleep." Plato squinted at the microwave again. "Are you *sure* you're not supposed to turn those steaks?"

"Quit fussing." Cal rolled her eyes. "The box doesn't say anything about turning."

"That doesn't mean—"

"And this new microwave cooks pretty evenly." She turned from the broccoli and faced him, hands on her hips. "Listen, buddy. You're not the only person in this house who can cook, you know." She cocked her shoulders and gave him a haughty glare. "*I* once worked in a restaurant."

Cal *had* worked in a restaurant, Plato knew. A year in high school flipping burgers at McDonald's. But from the way she acted, she might have spent the year in Paris studying at the Cordon Bleu.

"Anyway, nobody can screw up a TV dinner." Cal donned oven mitts and retrieved the chopped sirloin from the microwave.

Now, Plato really *was* impressed. The steaming patties were done perfectly, swimming in gravy, filling the kitchen with a rich aroma. Food always smells better when someone else cooks it, he reflected. Even frozen dinners.

"There!" Cal smiled smugly and reached for the bowl of broccoli. "See? It's not so hard."

She put the broccoli, uncovered, into the microwave. She set the timer for fifteen minutes.

Plato winced, but held his silence.

Cal sat down across the table and doffed her oven mitts. "So what are you going to do about Mrs. Leighton?"

"I don't know." Plato shook his head slowly. He had been worrying about Agnes all evening. The more he thought about her situation, the more depressed he became. Whenever the old detective made up her mind about something, she almost never budged. Criminals had learned that, to their dismay. Now Plato was finding it out, too. "I can't just let her die."

Cal reached across the table and squeezed his hand. Her soft brown eyes were gentle with concern and sympathy.

"I know she's one of your favorite patients, Plato." She squeezed his hand again. "But why *can't* you just let her die? It's what she wants, isn't it?"

"It's what she *thinks* she wants." He shook her hand away and stood. "But she's not being rational about it. She's not *ready* to die. Not yet."

"How can you tell?" Cal asked softly.

"What do you *mean*, how can I tell?" For no reason at all, he felt a sudden flare of anger. At Cal, at himself, at no one and everyone.

"What do *you* know about it?" He shook his head angrily. Cal just didn't understand. She didn't know anything about Mrs. Leighton—she'd never even *met* the woman. Who the hell did she think she was, questioning his judgment?

"I just wanted to—" she began.

"Forget it." He waved his hand. "I'm *sorry*."

But he didn't really mean it. He set the table, slamming cabinets and cupboards and drawers, sending dishes and cutlery clattering across the Formica. Behind him, Cal played goalie, nabbing a knife, catching a cup, bagging a butter dish before they flew to the floor.

How can I tell?

He swung open the ancient Frigidaire and throttled a two-liter bottle of diet Pepsi. He brandished it at Cal and growled, "You want some?"

"Yes, please." Her voice was meek, humble. She accepted the full glass from him like Oliver Twist receiving a second bowl of gruel.

How can I tell?

He sat down again and took a few deep breaths to calm himself.

"Mrs. Leighton hasn't checked out all her options yet," he explained. "The radiation oncologist thinks he might be able to buy her another year."

Cal raised her left eyebrow skeptically—Plato *hated* when she did that. She frowned. "But her intestines would still be obstructed, right?"

"Probably," Plato grudgingly agreed. Actually, they might even get worse. But he wouldn't admit that to Cal. "Even without surgery or radiation, she might last a year."

"But what would that year be like?" Cal's voice was soft, soothing, controlled. Like she was talking a lion back into its cage. Or a jumper down from a bridge. "It *is* Mrs. Leighton's decision, isn't it?"

Plato jumped to his feet again, paced back and forth in the kitchen, peered through the window at the gathering gloom outside. And took a few more deep breaths.

Cal was only a pathologist—a *forensic* pathologist. Aside from the occasional lab work at Riverside, all of her patients were dead. What did she know about taking care of living, breathing, feeling human beings?

Why was he so *angry*?

"Of course it's Mrs. Leighton's decision," he told the window.

Cal rose from her chair, tucked her head under his arm, and slid her hand around his waist. Together, they stared out at the darkness of the night.

"And I'd go along with her decision—if she were suffering horrible pain, or losing consciousness, or if she were sure to die soon." Plato sighed. "But Agnes doesn't seem *that* uncomfortable. And she's sharp as a tack."

"Maybe she wants to quit while she's ahead," Cal pointed out. "While she still has the power to decide. Before things get any worse."

But Plato wasn't listening. "Maybe she's depressed." He rubbed his forehead. "I might start her on an antidepressant. Too bad Agnes doesn't have any family . . ."

A shot rang out from the counter behind them. They both spun around as a fusillade of angry reports sounded from inside the microwave. Behind the mesh window, the broccoli was exploding, rocketing from the bowl like a dozen green Roman candles.

"*Damn!*" Cal dashed over and stopped the microwave.

Slowly, cautiously, she swung the door open, leaned closer, and peered inside. "Looks like the Hanging Gardens of Babylon in here."

Plato crossed the kitchen and looked over her shoulder. Every single sprig of broccoli had detonated, plastering the floor, walls, and ceiling of the unit with a fine spray of adhesive green mush. "Looks like the bottom of a lawn mower."

Cal ran her finger along the ceiling and tasted.

"Creamed broccoli." She stole another taste and smacked her lips. "Not bad. Not bad at all. Needs a little salt, though."

Plato felt his anger slowly fading, like a bad dream. He put his arm over Cal's shoulder. "Okay, Escoffier. Let's eat."

Halfway through dinner, he finally slowed down enough to talk again. Aside from the broccoli fiasco, the meal was fabulous. The frozen Salisbury steaks were done to perfection, the Potato Buds were just the right stiffness, and the can of creamed corn topped everything off perfectly.

"Excellent repast, my dear."

"Thank you." Cal smiled. "It was nothing, really."

"So how did your little fossil hunt go today?" Plato asked. "Did you find the rest of Siegel Man?"

"Siegel *Woman*," Cal corrected. She set her fork down and patted her stomach happily. "And yes, we found most of her."

She told him all about the excavation, the recovery of the skeleton, and the missing skull.

"You couldn't find it *anywhere*?" Plato asked.

"Nowhere." Cal sighed. "Believe me, we tried. Several of the workers hung around to help out with the dig. Jamahl even poked through the piles of dirt with his excavator scoop." She smiled. "He's an artist with that thing, Plato. I swear he could open pop cans with it."

"I wouldn't be surprised." He plunged his fork into his

mashed potato dam and watched gravy spill across the plate. "But you couldn't even find a piece of the skull?"

"Nope." She tipped her head back, guzzled the last of her Pepsi, and stifled a burp.

"That's weird." Plato shook his head. "Doesn't make any sense."

"Ralph's got a theory about it." Cal grinned. "You ever heard of the Kingsbury Run murders?"

Plato scratched his head. "Those killings back in the thirties?"

"Right. Do you know anything about them?"

"Not really. I wasn't around then, you know." He shrugged. "The *Cleveland Post* ran a feature about the Kingsbury Run killings a few months back. Some reporter tried to claim that the killer might still be alive, in a nursing home somewhere. Or maybe a mental hospital."

Cal grimaced. "Sounds like *A Current Affair* or something."

"You know the *Cleveland Post*. Cleveland's answer to the *National Enquirer*. Quality journalism." He smiled sardonically. "Hell, the killer would have to be eighty years old by now, right?"

"At least. You still have the article?"

Plato shook his head. Living halfway between Akron and Cleveland, they subscribed to two newspapers—the *Plain Dealer* and the *Beacon Journal*—but not to the *Post* tabloid. "I read that article in the doctors' lounge, while I was waiting for you to finish an autopsy."

Cal pursed her lips. "I'll have to look it up in the library, then."

"Why?" Plato chuckled. "You really think Siegel Woman might be another victim? Just because it's an old skeleton doesn't mean—"

"There are other reasons," she insisted. "Did the article mention how the Kingsbury Run murderer killed his victims?"

"I can't remember exactly." He frowned. "Didn't the killer strangle them or—"

"Beheading," Cal pronounced.

"Pardon me?"

"He cut their heads off." Cal drew a finger across her throat and made a loud snipping sound. "While they slept."

"Yech." Plato rubbed his neck, covered his jugular veins with his hands.

"Apparently he became quite skilled at it," she continued. "Or maybe he was very proficient to begin with."

Beneath his hands, Plato could feel his carotid arteries pulsing like small contained fountains, measuring the rhythm of each heartbeat.

Cal stepped over to the counter and grabbed a book. She slid it to his side of the table. "I read most of this before you came home. Fascinating stuff."

"For *you*, maybe." He pushed the book back. "I think I'm losing my appetite."

One hand still covering his neck, he forked another bite of sirloin into his mouth. It tasted like shoe leather in gravy. Animal flesh. He could feel his jaw muscles clenching, his neck muscles tightening in counterstrain, his tracheal cartilage sliding up and down as he swallowed. He imagined a knife cutting, cutting—

"Most of his victims were drunks or addicts," Cal continued, opening the book. "Homeless people. Down-and-outers who lived in a cardboard shantytown near the Cuyahoga or down in the Kingsbury Run area. Cleveland's Skid Row."

"So I heard."

"The killer apparently befriended drunken hobos, or just murdered them while they slept." She flipped through the pages. "Either way, his victims showed remarkably few signs of struggle. The authorities assumed he either drugged them, or they were too drunk to resist."

Plato watched the gravy on his plate puddle and congeal. The Salisbury steak had lost its appeal.

She closed the book and stared up at the ceiling. "Of course, he may have used something like chloroform or ether. Those drugs were certainly around in the thirties."

Plato pretended not to hear. He whistled loudly. "Here, Foley!"

The blind and half-deaf Australian shepherd padded in from the living room. Plato cupped a bit of meat in his hand and held it to the animal's nose. But Foley simply turned away.

"Wonder what's gotten into him?"

"He hasn't touched his food at all today," Cal noted.

"But he *loves* Salisbury steak." Plato scraped his plate into Foley's bowl. "There. That should do it."

"Where was I?" Cal asked. She pulled a slip of paper from the book. Apparently, she had taken notes. "Oh, yes. The killer beheaded his victims quickly, and with a great deal of skill. After death, he often dismembered the bodies entirely, using a very sharp instrument like a butcher's knife or a scalpel."

Plato felt his neck again. It was still intact.

"The victims showed little in the way of messy cuts or hesitation marks." She frowned at her slip of paper. "The heads were often buried separately from the bodies."

Plato scrunched his chin down beneath his shoulder blades. "I'm enjoying this little history lesson, really I am. But what does all this have to do with the bones you found today?"

"*That* woman's head and body were apparently buried separately."

"You don't know that," Plato argued. "The skull probably got carried away in one of the truckloads of dirt they use for landfill. Next year, somebody out in Medina County will find it in their front yard when they plant their tulip bulbs."

"There were no knife marks on the bones," Cal observed. "And we found them in several different piles of dirt—as though the body parts had been scattered. Just like the Kingsbury Run killer would have done."

"You're reaching, Cal." Plato chuckled bravely. Whistling in the dark. "Jamahl probably took a few scoops to dig the whole thing out. *That's* how the bones got scattered."

"Maybe," she agreed. "Why are you all scrunched up like that? With your hands on your neck?"

Reluctantly, Plato sat up straighter. "It's cold in here."

"Right." She glanced at her notes. "There's another aspect about the Kingsbury Run case that makes these new bones interesting."

"What's that?"

"From the way he worked—the neat killings, the precise dissections, the police thought he was either a butcher or a doctor."

"A doctor?" Plato swallowed heavily.

"Right." Cal nodded. "They also thought he might be someone connected with a laboratory. A place he could carry on his dissections and disarticulations without being seen."

"A mad scientist, huh?" Plato's laugh sounded hollow, even to himself. He was afraid he knew where all this was leading.

"He may not have been a *scientist,* but he was certainly mad." Cal shrugged. "Samuel Gerber—the county coroner back then—claimed that the murderer's skill pointed to someone with dissecting experience and an excellent understanding of human anatomy. So the police chased down a bunch of theories—that the killer was a butcher, or maybe a doctor who lived or worked in the Kingsbury Run area."

"A doctor?"

"The *ideal* suspect would have been someone affiliated with a medical school." Cal tugged her blond hair back behind her ears. "But the police could find no evidence pointing to Case Western or Siegel."

"Cally—"

"Until now." She gave a little smile, folded the paper, and tucked it back into her book.

"Weak, Cal. Definitely weak." He sniffed. "Know what *my* theory is?"

"What?"

"That you need a vacation. With this new position at the medical school, and your deputy coroner post, and your work at Riverside General, you have *three* half-time jobs. Something's got to give, and I'm afraid your brain is going first."

"Get serious."

"I *am* serious." Plato sighed. "You know what will happen if you breathe a *word* of this to anyone."

Cal considered, then nodded slowly.

"Quick as a flash, Siegel Medical College will be splashed all over the papers again." Plato grunted. "You'll lose your new faculty position in anatomy, because there won't be any cadavers. No one will donate. They'll be afraid a homicidal anatomist will come to claim their bodies before they're finished with them."

"Who said anything about anatomists?"

"It's the obvious choice, isn't it?"

Cal shrugged.

"Anyway, I think you're way off track with that skeleton."

She sat back in her chair and folded her arms across her chest. "So where do *you* think it came from?"

"I bet it was a medical student prank."

"A *prank*?"

"I'm sure of it." Plato leaned forward and folded his hands on the table. "Siegel has a big skeleton collection—a couple of hundred skeletons, in a storage room near the dissecting suite. They use the skeletons for research."

Cal ran her fingers through her hair. "I didn't know that."

"You didn't go to school there. I did."

"You think one of the students broke in and stole a skeleton from the collection?"

"Yup."

"Why?"

"Who knows?" Plato asked. He flapped his hands. "Why do medical students do *anything*? Medical school makes you crazy. You know that."

"Yeah, but why steal a skeleton, and then bury it again? And where's the skull?"

"I don't know. Maybe it got hauled away, like I said." He snapped his fingers. "Maybe *that* was the prank. Some medical student wanted a skull—to play a joke, or scare someone. Or maybe just for a souvenir. So he kept the skull and buried the other bones."

Cal smirked. "Weak, Plato. Definitely weak."

"I know." He shrugged. "But it's better than your crazy idea. Anyway, I think you should talk with Sergei Malenkov tomorrow, and ask him to check his skeleton collection."

Sergei Malenkov was the anatomy lab director at Siegel. A fossil in his own right, he had joined the faculty decades ago, not long after the medical school opened.

"Maybe so. I'm lecturing there again tomorrow—I can ask him." She eyed Plato's empty dish. "You having dessert?"

Plato thought about Harold the Head, and the bones they'd found, and the Kingsbury Run killer. "Somehow, I'm not very hungry anymore."

"I'm not surprised," Cal replied, completely missing the point. "You really went to town on those Salisbury steaks."

She walked over to the sink and sighed wearily. They hadn't done the dishes in days. A pile of dirty plates teetered on the counter like a California mudslide waiting to happen. "Who's doing the dishes?"

Plato carried his plate over to the pile and balanced it on

top. "Just leave them. Maybe some elves will come by in the middle of the night and wash them for us."

"Or some mice will." She turned away and headed for the hall and the stairs. "I'm not choosy."

Following her out of the kitchen, Plato glanced down at Foley's dish. The Salisbury steak still rested atop the mound of stale dog food, untouched. Foley lay on the floor nearby, staring at the treat with the dull gaze of a hangover victim eyeing a full bottle of Jack Daniel's.

Plato knelt and scratched the old Aussie's belly. Foley responded with a sluggish lick.

"You don't look too good, old boy."

Foley the Wonderdog turned his head and fixed his cloudy eyes on Plato's face. His cropped tail thumped the linoleum.

"Maybe we should get you to a vet."

"It won't do him any good," Cal said gently. She was standing in the doorway, watching them. "Foley's fifteen years old. That's a hundred and five, in people years. He's got cancer, liver problems, and kidney trouble. I don't think vets do liver transplants."

She took the Salisbury steak from Foley's bowl and placed it in Dante's empty cup.

Instantly, the flame-colored tabby beamed into existence beside Cal's ankle, purring and arching its back. Plato watched the disgusting creature devour Foley's dinner.

"Are you going to tolerate that?" he asked his dog.

Foley watched apathetically, then gave a little shrug and let his head sink back onto his paws. Might as well let *someone* enjoy it, he seemed to be thinking.

"Foley's probably got the flu again," Plato insisted. "It's the season, you know."

"Maybe." Cal lifted that skeptical eyebrow again—the left one—and let it slowly fall back into place. Like a signal flag running up and down a pole. Clearly, she was humoring him.

"Anyway, he's going to the vet tomorrow."

"Whatever you say, dear."

Dante finished his meal, padded over, and licked Foley's face. The dog closed his eyes and let out a grumbly little sigh.

After Plato and Cal's wedding, the two animals had hated each other. Over the next year or so, the animosity had subsided to an uneasy truce. Eventually, they tolerated each other, then developed a grudging respect. And now, with Foley's slowness and ill health, Dante seemed positively affectionate, pampering him like a doting parent with a sick child.

The cat sketched a circle on the linoleum, stretched its legs, and curled up between Foley's head and forepaws. The old dog closed his eyes.

"He'll be just fine," Plato repeated. He followed Cal to the foot of the stairs. "Just a little flu. He had the same thing last year around this time. He'll be just fine."

"You're probably right," Cal agreed. She nodded her head firmly.

But turning the corner to climb the stairs, Plato caught a glimpse of Cal's face in the mirror, and spied that left eyebrow just before it came down again.

CHAPTER 5

"Plato."

In his dream, he was running. Sprinting away from something. A horrible, animal something, with huge sharp fangs and claws, ragged fur, and frenzied bloodshot eyes. And a terrifying, heartrending howl.

"Plato."

A whispered voice was calling to him, from somewhere in the darkness. Calling him to safety.

Except the whisper sounded terrified, too.

"*Plato!*"

He opened his eyes. Beside him, Cal was sitting bolt upright in bed. The cream-colored shirt made her body almost invisible against the pale bedroom wall. Lately, she had started wearing Plato's old long-sleeved dress shirts as nightgowns—they hung practically to her knees.

He wished she wouldn't. With her invisible torso, Cal looked like a disembodied head floating in the darkness, three feet above their bed. The head was tilted, elfin ears twitching beneath the long blond hair.

"Did you hear that?" she finally hissed.

"Hear what?" He reached out in the darkness, to assure himself that her body really was there.

It was. She smacked his hand. "Don't you *ever* think of anything else?"

"I was just making sure—"

"*Listen!*" she urged.

He shook the sleep from his head, then sat up beside her to listen. For a long moment, the decrepit house was silent. Except, of course, for the sighing of the wind in the eaves, the settling of the old timbers, the gurgling of money disappearing down the drain.

And then he heard it. From somewhere off in the darkness, deep in the bowels of their century-old money pit of a home, the sound came again.

Plato hadn't dreamt it. The sound was even more hideous, more grotesque, than when he had been asleep.

"What is it?" he finally asked Cal.

"How should *I* know?" Her nose twitched thoughtfully. "Sounds like some kind of animal."

Plato had a horrible thought. "*Damn!*"

He hopped out of bed.

"Where are you going?" Cal asked anxiously.

"Downstairs." He pushed his feet into the ridiculous duck-shaped slippers Cal had bought him last Christmas. "Foley's probably sick. I'm going to check on him."

"It doesn't *sound* like a dog, Plato." Cal clutched his hand. "It sounds almost human. You know?"

"I only heard it once." He paced beside the bed.

"I thought I heard words," she continued softly. "Or maybe it was Dante. You know how he sounds when he's upset."

"You were probably dreaming."

"Maybe." She turned away, reached under her side of the bed, and pulled out a long, slender object. A twenty-six-inch Easton aluminum T-ball bat. She'd bought two of them last year, when Plato went to New Orleans for a family medicine conference. She carried the other one in the trunk of her car. "All the same, you'd better take this along."

It fell into his hands with a metallic thud.

Plato handed it back. "Thanks anyways. But I don't think this'll help much."

"You never know." She swung it back and forth, testing its weight. "I was the top hitter on my high school softball team. I always feel safer with a bat in my hands."

"Good for you." He walked across the room and girded his loins with a flimsy terry cloth robe. "Coming along?"

The sound came again. A low, mournful wail, half human and half animal.

Cal dropped the bat into her lap and hugged herself—a head and a pair of interlocked hands floating in the darkness. "I'll stay here, in case you need help. I can surprise them."

"Them?"

"Them, him, it." One of the hands flapped. "Whatever."

Plato realized he was stalling. He strode bravely to the door, face set with determination, duck bills flapping on the bare floor. Quietly, he opened it and slipped into the hallway.

Marley Manor was built in the shape of a U, with a large central foyer flanked by the living room and dining room. The kitchen and "servants' quarters" were off in the east wing, and a library, conservatory, and bedrooms were housed in the west wing. The three sections flanked a central courtyard full of weeds, broken fountains and birdbaths, and crumbling stonework.

In the decades before the former owners had found a young couple foolish enough to buy it, most of the house had fallen into a horrible state of disrepair. Plato and Cal had stopped most of the leaks in the sagging roof over the east wing and salvaged much of the ancient kitchen equipment, but the servants' bedrooms upstairs were still full of algae and pigeon droppings. The central area was reasonably livable. In the west wing, the library and conservatory were stuffed with secondhand furniture, boxes of medical textbooks, and mice. Upstairs were three empty bedrooms, plus Plato and Cal's room at the very end of the hall.

Plato guessed that the unholy screech was coming from the living room. To reach it, he had to negotiate thirty feet of ancient, squeaky floorboards, a rickety staircase, and another few yards of hallway. Moving slowly, carefully, Plato slipped along the edge of the hallway, where the floorboards were less prone to squeaking.

He paused at the top of the stairs, and heard it once again. A high-pitched wail followed by a low, throaty growl.

It *couldn't* be his pager. For one thing, it had never growled like that. For another, he was almost certain he'd taken it upstairs to the bedroom.

The scream came again—shrill, insistent. Then the rumbling growl. And something else. A high-pitched mewling sound, with almost human inflections.

Foley and Dante. They were fighting with some animal.

Plato sprang into action, stumbling down the stairs as the scream came once more. A hellish squeal, like a gutshot pig on PCP. Then Foley's authoritative bark and snarl, a scrabbling, clawing sound, a frightened yelp, and a few frantic crunches.

Silence reigned again.

Plato burst into the living room and peered around.

As always, he and Cal had left the living room light on before locking up and going to bed. Dante was perched atop the bookcase, back arched, orange fur standing on end, claws sunk deep into Cal's copy of Robbins's *Pathologic Basis of Disease*. Like a fuzzy basketball with ears and claws. Foley was down on the hardwood floor, still wrestling with the intruder. Clearly, though, the old Aussie had victory in his paws.

Bits and pieces of Plato's two-hundred-dollar pager were scattered across the rug, the chair, and the coffee table where he now remembered leaving it before dinner last night. Part of the black plastic case and a few wires dangled from Foley's mouth. The gray LCD display hung from his left ear.

The dog glanced up at his master and smiled proudly, triumphantly.

Plato squatted down and patted him on the head. "Good dog, Foley. Good boy."

A hundred and five years old, but Foley still had some fight left in him.

"Hello, this is Dr. Marley. Could you find out if someone was trying to page me?"

Plato was sitting on the living room sofa. Foley was curled up at his feet. Dante had descended from his perch to spring onto the coffee table and sniff tentatively at the dead shards of silicon and plastic.

"Certainly, Dr. Marley." Despite the hour—three a.m.—the page operator sounded brisk, efficient, and alert. Far better than Plato felt. "Shall I try an overhead page?"

"That would be fine."

At the doorway to the stairs, the T-ball bat appeared, sniffed the air, and withdrew. Slowly, Cal's blond head emerged around the corner. Both hands were clutching the rubber grip, the barrel stretching out before her like a broadsword blade. She hurtled across the room in a quick flèche, then lunged, parried, and riposted. Finally, she sketched a bow to her imaginary opponent.

Still waiting for the page operator, Plato silently applauded.

Cal flapped a hand in question.

Plato gestured at the pile of rubble he had gathered on the coffee table.

She made a moue, then shooed Dante away from the wreckage. She disappeared into the kitchen, returned with a Ziploc bag, and scooped the debris inside. She dropped the mess into his lap with a slight smile.

"Maybe they can fix it," she whispered.

"Hah, hah." Plato wasn't amused. "Look at me, I'm laughing."

"Plato?" The voice on the phone sounded familiar. "This is Tom Brunelski, down in the ER. We've been paging you for an hour."

"Sorry. My dog ate my pager." How lame that sounded.

"Hah, hah." Tom's laughter was genuine. "You're a funny guy, Plato."

"Thanks." He hadn't expected Tom to believe him.

"Anyway, we've got a transport coming in from the nursing home. A patient of yours—Albert Windgartner."

Plato's heart sank. "You're kidding."

"Nope." Tom paused, bit into something, and made chewing sounds. He was probably on his lunch break. "They tried paging you direct to get permission to transport. But like you said, your pooch ate your pager."

"He really did," Plato insisted doggedly. He fingered the Ziploc bag in his lap. "I'll bring the pieces in so you can see."

"Sure, Plato. Sure." He chuckled again, and took another bite. It sounded like a sub sandwich. "You ever thought about going on TV? Doing *Improv* or something like that?"

Plato sighed. "When's Albert due to arrive?"

"Any minute now." Crunch, crunch. "He's got a fever again—the nurse practitioner there thinks it might be another pneumonia. You coming in, or you want the resident to give you a call?"

"I'll come in." He glanced over at Cal. She was already

curled into a ball on the other side of the sofa, snoozing under a lap blanket. Dante was half hidden beneath her hair.

Plato sighed again. "Give me twenty minutes."

"You can have thirty."

"Thanks, Tom. You're all heart."

He hung up the phone, scribbled a note for Cal, covered her with his robe, and headed upstairs to dress.

"What the—hell are—*you* doing here—Dr. Marley?"

The question was punctuated by gasps. Albert Windgartner was propped up on an emergency room gurney, a green plastic oxygen mask strapped to his pale face, an intravenous line hooked up to his left arm. Even with the extra oxygen, he was still short of breath and as white as his bedsheets, almost cyanotic. Behind the mask, his lips puckered and sucked at the air, like a fish out of water.

His shortness of breath came from chronic lung disease, from a hundred pack-years of smoking. And from something else—a deeper, more insidious ailment. One which would almost certainly kill him, even sooner than the smoking would have.

Albert reached out a hand as big as an excavator scoop. Plato shook it, startled at the strength of the old man's grip. He shouldn't have been. Albert Windgartner had started a fledgling construction company back in the '40s, working alongside his men and leaving the accounting and bookkeeping to a trusted office crew. But even after he moved on to develop office towers and shopping malls and a string of luxury nursing homes, he maintained his blue-collar roots—and blue-collar muscles. Albert's face was thick with wrinkles, like sun-bleached leather. His balding scalp was covered with sun freckles. But his shoulders and arms were still heavy with muscles. And his blue eyes were hard as ice.

"They told me you were sick, Albert." Plato frowned. "I wanted to come in and check you out."

"No need—to trouble—yourself." Each word fogged the green plastic mask. "I'm just—fine."

"No trouble at all." Plato approached the bed and pulled out his stethoscope. "You just lie back and relax, now. No talking, okay?"

Albert nodded wearily, and let his head fall back to the

pillow. He went through the motions of the examination with the practiced ease of the chronic patient, pulling up his shirt so Plato could listen to his heart, leaning forward and breathing slowly so Plato could check his lungs, even opening his mouth and sticking out his tongue before Plato pulled out the tongue depressor.

After the exam was over, he waved a giant hand. "See? Like I said—I'm just—fine."

"You could be better, Albert." Plato washed up and returned to the bedside. He rested his hands on the rail and looked into his patient's eyes. "It's pneumonia again. I think we'll need to keep you here for a few days."

The mall mogul's face fell. Like so many of Plato's elderly patients, Albert hated the hospital. He was afraid of it. He was certain he would die there. And with that certainty came the completely illogical conviction that he would stay alive as long as he stayed out of the hospital.

Well, maybe not *completely* illogical. In Albert's case, the hospital was a very dangerous place. But then, so was Wyndhaven Colony—the posh nursing home where Albert lived. Virtually all hospitals and nursing homes harbor sick patients suffering from highly toxic, drug-resistant infections. Infections that could easily spread to a person as susceptible as Albert.

Albert Windgartner suffered from aplastic anemia—bone marrow failure. His blood cell factories had largely shut down, leaving him short of red cells, white cells, and platelets. As a result, he was highly prone to oxygen shortage, infections, and bleeding problems.

But whether it was dangerous or not, Albert had to be treated in the hospital. The X rays taken at the nursing home had shown an obvious infiltrate—a white opacity—in the lower lobe of the right lung. Plato's exam confirmed it. When Albert breathed, the right side of his chest sounded like a bubbling aquarium.

Plato patted his patient's shoulder. "Just a few days, Albert. I promise."

The old man nodded, pushed the mask against his face, and sucked air. He closed his eyes and settled deeper into the pillow, finally too tired to speak.

"I'm going to check on your room. I'll be back in a few minutes."

Albert's daughter was waiting for him just outside the curtain. Erica Windgartner's face lit up when she saw her father's doctor.

"Plato! I'm *so* glad you're here." She clutched his arm. "How's Dad?"

"More of the same." He shrugged. "Let's find somewhere we can talk."

Plato led her to a private conference room just outside the automatic double doors leading to the hospital proper. Like many rooms at Riverside General, the door bore a small brass plaque that read "In Loving Memory of Cora Windgartner." It was a cozy little room, with a plush overstuffed sofa, a few framed prints of city scenes, a coffee table, and a wing chair. Plato was tempted by the sofa, but he took the chair instead. As tired as he was, the sofa wasn't a good idea. And he wasn't sure he wanted to sit beside Erica Windgartner.

Despite the hour, and the fact that her father was gravely ill, Erica Windgartner looked as fresh as a sunny summer morning. Her eyes were blue like her father's, but not quite as chilly. Her soft, full lips were pursed. Long blond tresses hung down past the shoulders of her charcoal gray melton jacket. Beneath the jacket, she wore one of those black lacy camisole things that were so distracting for Plato. Especially when they were worn by gorgeous females.

It didn't help that he and Erica had dated seriously for several months before he'd met Cal.

Sitting on the couch, she seemed to read his mind. "How's your wife?"

"Just fine." Plato stirred uneasily. "She's teaching part-time at the medical school now."

"I know." Erica smiled. "I've seen her in the hallway there a few times."

"You're getting a medical degree after all?"

It had been a running joke between them, back when they were dating. Erica had done everything right, everything her father wanted. She had attended an Ivy League school, majored in business administration, and returned home to help pilot the family business. But after only a couple of years, she'd found herself shackled by a self-doubt that came from having things too easily, and had longed to prove herself on her own. When Plato teasingly suggested medicine, Erica considered it seriously. She applied to Siegel—and was easily accepted.

But she changed her mind at the last minute—when her father suddenly became ill. She had been playing the devoted daughter ever since.

"A medical degree?" Erica smiled sadly. "Hardly that. I've been attending the trustees' meetings here and at the medical school ever since Dad got sick. And giving him full reports, of course."

"Of course." Plato nodded.

Besides owning Wyndhaven Colony—and half the other nursing homes in Cleveland—Albert Windgartner was on the boards of trustees at both Riverside General and Siegel Medical College. He maintained an office at the nursing home where he kept a firm hand on his business despite his illness. Plato imagined that Erica's decision-making powers were very limited.

"Speaking of your father," he continued, "I'm afraid he's doing worse."

Erica's mouth tightened. "His blood count is down again?"

"Way down." Plato stared at his hands. "Even more than before."

She bit her lip. "Will he need another transfusion?"

Plato nodded slowly. "I think so."

"You know how he hates them."

"I know." Albert Windgartner was—justifiably—worried about hepatitis and AIDS and all the other bad things that could come from transfusions. But it was another necessary risk—just like the hospitalization itself. Plato shot an appraising glance at Erica. "You'll probably have to talk him into it. He listens to you, if he listens to anyone."

"That's the catch—'if he listens to anyone.' But I'll try." She leaned forward and touched Plato's knee. "I really appreciate your coming up here, in the middle of the night. Dad always says he doesn't want special treatment, but—"

"This isn't special treatment, Erica." He shook his head

slowly. "I would come in for any of my patients who were as sick as your father."

Her blue eyes sparkled wetly. "He really needs that transfusion, doesn't he?"

"Yes. He really does."

Erica Windgartner leaned back in her chair, put her hand over her mouth, and took a deep breath. She stared at the ceiling for a long moment, then brought her eyes down to Plato's again. "There's no cure for this." It wasn't a question. "He's not going to get better."

"We don't have a cure," Plato admitted. "For cases like your father's, we don't even know the cause. As for his getting better, though, that's not impossible. The experimental drug he's been getting might help."

"He's been on it for six months."

Plato nodded. The drug being tested at Riverside worked in only a small percentage of cases. "Some people recover on their own, given enough time."

She swallowed heavily. "But they have to be pretty lucky, don't they?"

"Yes." Lucky enough to survive infections, to avoid bleeding to death from lack of platelets, to miss being transfused with infected blood, to dodge the thousand and one bullets nature throws at all of us daily—bullets our natural defenses help us to avoid. "Yes, they do."

"Daddy's been pretty lucky already." She pulled a Kleenex out, folded it neatly, and pressed it to the corners of her eyes. "I'm starting to wonder when his luck is going to run out."

She stood, and Plato followed her to the door. On an impulse, he put his arm over her shoulder. It felt strange, awkward. Erica was almost as tall as he was. She leaned into him, cried on his shoulder for a minute or two, then pulled away.

"Thank you," she sniffed. "And thanks again for coming in like this. You probably didn't get any sleep."

"That's okay." Plato stuck his hands into his pockets and encountered the Ziploc bag. "I needed to come in early anyway."

"Really?" She tucked her Kleenex into her purse. "Why's that?"

He pulled out the wreckage of the Motorola. "My dog ate my pager."

She glanced at the bag, then burst out laughing until her shoulders shook. "Oh, Plato. You've got *such* a sense of humor."

She kissed him on the cheek. Still smiling, she walked out the door and left him alone with his pager and his confusion.

CHAPTER 6

"Aside from the head itself," Cal intoned, "the neck is probably the most complex part of the human body."

Staring around at the glassy-eyed anatomy students, Cal found herself wishing she had brought Harold the Head with her today. Not that he would have helped much, really. Harold stopped just below the chin. His neck was a mere stump, a clumsy plastic stand designed to hold his head upright.

The Plaskin developers were counting on Harold's success to provide enough capital for models of every region of the body. *Including* the neck.

But even a full-scale Harold would never substitute for actual dissection, for touching real bones and arteries and veins, for grasping muscles and nerves and understanding their strengths and failings, for feeling the finality of a scalpel cutting into flesh.

As Cal was doing now.

The cadaver on the table before her was lying prone, or facedown. A dozen first-year medical students were clustered around the table, craning their heads over each other's shoulders to observe Cal's handiwork. For the past few weeks, they had dissected and studied the superficial structures of the head and neck. This morning, she would teach them how to delve into the deeper areas of the neck, to study the esophagus running from the mouth to the stomach, and the deep arteries connecting the heart to the brain.

"If you aren't careful, you can damage some important landmarks," Cal warned. "I'll show you the best way to do today's dissection. Then you can go back to your tables and teach the other students in your groups."

She patted the cadaver's neck with a gloved hand. He had broad, muscular shoulders, gray hair, and a mole behind his left ear. His head was slightly turned, as though he were listening to her lecture. His back was bare, and the shroud was pulled down to his waist.

Lying there on the table, arms stretched out before him, the demonstration cadaver might have been waiting patiently for a massage. Except that most of the skin of his face had already been dissected away, and the gray-haired roof of his skull was lying beside his waist. At the center of his neck, a large rectangular flap of skin had also been removed.

"Before you start with your own cadavers, you'll want to check their ranges of motion." She clutched the head beside the ears and pivoted it from side to side. "I can't twist it very far. Why is that?"

"Rigor mortis?" suggested a gangly red-haired fellow.

"Not a bad idea," Cal answered gently. "Except rigor mortis is only a temporary condition."

A short girl with dull eyes and a sleepy voice spoke up. "Doesn't the cruciform ligament have something to do with it?"

"That, plus another one," Cal answered. She was pretty sure the girl's name was Nancy. "Do you remember the name of the other ligament, Nancy?"

The student bit her lip and stared at her feet. Her answer was barely a whisper. "The . . . umm . . . *alar* ligament?"

"Excellent!" Cal praised. Nancy was much smarter than she looked. "The cruciform and alar ligaments limit rotation of the head."

Nancy sighed with relief.

"Getting back to the dissection, you'll see that Sergei Malenkov has already removed the posterior arch of the atlas," Cal explained. Earlier that morning, the lab director had made his rounds with a bone saw and performed several cuts on each cadaver, to make today's procedure easier. "So our first move will be to cut through the *dura mater*."

Cal slid her fingers into the rectangular hole Sergei had made near the base of the skull when he had cut away the arch of the first neck bone. The floor of the hole was carpeted by the dura mater, a tough fibrous sheath that encases the brain and spinal cord. She cut through the dura and the tectorial membrane beneath, and folded the flaps back. Then she gestured to her audience.

"It's very important that you all see this," she said. One by one, the students paraded past the cadaver, peering into Cal's excavation while she explained.

"As Nancy mentioned, the neck features a very effective defense against damage to the spinal cord." She pointed to the cruciform ligament at the bottom of the hole. The cross-shaped fibrous band connected the base of the skull to the first and second neck bones. Beneath it, the alar ligament stretched across the base of the skull to check the pivoting motion of the neck. "Aside from these important ligaments, we have the atlas and axis themselves—the first and second cervical vertebrae. They lock together like a peg in a hole, to further limit motion of the neck."

After she had explained their significance, Cal snipped through the ligaments and showed how the cadaver's range of motion had changed. Rather than halting at the right or left shoulders, the head could easily be twisted completely backward, like Linda Blair's in *The Exorcist*.

Cal continued her cuts and snips, freeing up this ligament and that, cutting through muscles and tendons and blood vessels, and touring her students through the structures as they dove deeper toward the center of the neck. Finally, she turned the body over and severed the *longus capitis* muscle, then tilted the nearly detached head forward onto the chest.

"There, now. Wasn't that easy?" Cal set her scalpel on the table and grinned at her audience. "Now you all can do it on your own cadavers."

Several students groaned before shuffling off to their own dissecting tables. It promised to be a long morning for them. The entire procedure had taken Cal—a forensic pathologist— over an hour. The medical students would probably take much longer.

She stared down at the severed head, and wondered how the Kingsbury Run killer had ever managed it.

After the dissecting session was over and the students had left for lunch, Cal made the rounds of the lab with Sergei Malenkov. Most of the students were quite faithful about carefully packing away their cadavers, but the old anatomist still fretted and fussed over his charges like a nervous mother putting her thirty-six children to bed at night.

"Here, now." Sergei trotted over to one of the cadaver boxes and pointed a long bony finger at the lid. A flap of plastic was caught between the folding metal doors. "You see this? Rothman's group always leaves their cadaver this way." His reedy voice carried just a hint of a Russian accent. "Very sloppy. Just like their dissection."

Cal helped him lower the doors open. Inside, the shroud was loose, the plastic was barely wrapped around the body, and the tissues were dry.

"And Rothman wants to be a surgeon. Pah!" He grabbed a spray bottle and anointed the body with oil, shaking his head and gnawing his lower lip with his huge yellow teeth. Cal smiled to herself, remembering the medical students' perennial nickname for their anatomy lab director: The Giraffe.

It perfectly suited his teeth, his height, and his long thin neck. With his gangly legs, Sergei even *trotted* like a giraffe—prancing from table to table during dissecting sessions, quizzing students on landmarks and structures, nibbling on their answers, and scattering seeds of knowledge across the lab.

"Now, here is something we see but rarely." Sergei's hands fluttered as he lifted the shroud toward the head. He pulled the oily cloth back again and poked at the cadaver's neck, near the Adam's apple.

"An anomalous right recurrent laryngeal nerve," he mused. "Very interesting. We must point it out for the students."

Cal was impressed. The nerve was hard enough to find, even in its normal distribution. Yet Sergei had noticed it with the ease of a veteran bird-watcher spotting a cardinal on a treeless lawn.

On the other hand, The Giraffe had spent a lifetime down in the anatomy lab. Even the origin of his nickname was shrouded in legend—rumor had it that a former surgeon general had thought it up, back when he attended Siegel in the 1940s. But no one really knew.

"Might I interest you in a cup of coffee?" Sergei asked as they swung the doors closed. "I have a full pot of French vanilla, my favorite."

"That sounds wonderful." Cal was pleased. As an associate

professor now, she was technically Sergei's superior—the lab director's formal education was supposedly limited to a bachelor's degree in biology and a funeral director's certification. But he was a self-taught prodigy, a wizard at human anatomy. As Plato had once put it, Sergei Malenkov was a walking encyclopedia—*Gray's Anatomy* with legs.

And besides, this was Sergei's lab—and had been, for fifty years or more.

Despite her medical degree, her pathology training, and her academic appointment, Cal still felt a bit intimidated by the old anatomist.

She followed him out of the lab and over to his office near the students' lockers. The dusty little room was hardly more than a storage area with a couple of chairs, a coffeemaker, and hundreds of anatomy texts and journals and specimen jars. A door in the far wall led to Sergei's inner sanctum—a vast laboratory with a large dissecting table, pumps and solution bottles, and racks for fresh cadavers.

Sergei filled a pair of coffee mugs and led Cal through the doorway into his lab. "I often take my breaks here, rather than in my office. This place is much more private, and far roomier."

He was right. The lab was occupied by only one cadaver—a freshly prepared body lying spread-eagled on the stainless steel dissecting table.

The woman might have been a model. Long, lithe limbs, a slender figure, and a face that was pretty even in death. A semicircular ring was stamped across her bare chest, a dusky blue-gray smear across the pale flesh.

"Automobile accident," Sergei clucked. "A tragedy. My assistant has not yet had time to pack her away."

Holding his coffee in one hand, Sergei approached the body and gently lifted a lock of soft auburn hair from the woman's forehead. A faint patch of blue was visible at the hairline. "Aside from this, and the stamp of the steering wheel on her chest, she has no visible external injuries." The old anatomist shook his head sadly. "Massive internal injuries, though. Bruising of the heart."

He shook his head again and sighed, as though his own heart was bruised. "She was not wearing her seat belt, of course. A mother of two. I think she did not expect to be with us so soon."

He sipped his coffee and slumped into a swivel chair beside the counter. Cal sat on a plastic folding chair nearby. They both eyed the new cadaver sadly.

"Those are the upsetting ones," she agreed. "The old and sick ones, you expect to see them. But when their lives are cut so short . . ."

"You must see a great many of those," Sergei murmured.

"We do." Cal thought of the gunshot victims, the stabbing victims, the drug overdoses. The wrecked lives. "We certainly do."

"And yet, there must be some unusual cases as well." The Giraffe's eyes twinkled. "Like your discovery yesterday, here in our own backyard."

Sergei had been busy with meetings and classes yesterday afternoon, but he had eventually broken free to come outside and observe the final stages of Cal's dig.

"Have you made any progress toward identifying the victim?" he asked.

"A little bit." Cal shrugged. "We can't do much without the head."

Sergei frowned. "You could not find her skull?"

"No. She—" Cal broke off suddenly. She was *sure* she hadn't mentioned the sex of the victim.

"I observed the pelvis when I was outside, of course." The Giraffe's yellow teeth flashed in a grin. "Sexing skeletons is not limited to forensic pathologists, you realize."

"Certainly." She smiled. "Speaking of skeletons, Plato mentioned that the medical school has quite a collection."

"Oh, yes. We certainly do." His head bobbed. "Or I should say, we *did*."

"Did?" Cal frowned curiously.

"Of course, they still belong to the college." He took another sip of coffee. "But they are on semipermanent loan, in order to join a much larger collection."

"Larger collection?" Cal echoed again. She was confused. "You mean, in a cemetery?"

"Hardly that, Doctor." The old anatomist chuckled. "Preparing over two hundred skeletons from cadavers involved much arduous work over many years. I would not bury such an effort."

"Then where *are* they?"

Still chuckling, he flapped a hand. "At the museum, of course. Where else?"

"The Natural History Museum?"

"Yes." Sergei sat up proudly. "I have been trying to move our collection there for years. The Cleveland Natural History Museum has a fantastic skeleton collection—more than three thousand humans, and more still from other primate species. For the purposes of teaching and research. You have heard of the Hamann-Todd Collection, I presume?"

"Certainly," Cal replied. She had heard of the collection, but she knew very little about it.

"I began my own small collection here many decades ago." He set his coffee cup down and stood. "Taking skeletons from the remains of unclaimed or permanently donated cadavers. A process long and tedious. But over four decades, we gathered quite a significant number. Nothing like the Hamann-Todd, you must understand. But significant nonetheless."

He led her around the body to a small steel door in the back of the lab. It opened into a large windowless room, narrower than the laboratory but still quite spacious. And empty, aside from a few plain cardboard boxes stacked at the far end.

"All that remains of our magnificent skeleton collection," Sergei said with a wry smile. "Only five skeletons, praise God! For years, I have worked to persuade Dean Fairfax to donate our collection to the museum."

"You didn't want to keep it here?" Cal asked.

"At first, I thought it was a good idea," Sergei explained. "To have our own private research collection. But no one used them. The boxes were stacked in this big closet, floor to ceiling. It became difficult even to open the door. The bones will be much more useful at the museum, joining with the magnificent Hamann-Todd collection."

"Why didn't Dean Fairfax want you to donate the skeletons?"

"Pride. He is quite jealous of Case Western, you know. Our dean sometimes misses the—what is the phrase? Ah, yes—the *long view*." The anatomist grunted. "Harlow Fairfax was a nearsighted dissector, too. Always slicing through the finer nerves and arteries."

Sergei really *was* old, Cal mused. Dean Fairfax was nearly ready for retirement himself.

"But he finally agreed." Sergei stepped to the center of the room and waved his arms in a grand circle. "And so, finally, I now have space for a proper office."

"When was your collection sent over to the museum?" she asked.

"Just this past weekend. Saturday morning. I came in myself, to make sure that the workers loaded the bones and records properly."

"Records?"

"Yes, of course. I only made skeletons from cadavers which had proper medical records listing illnesses, causes of death, and so forth—and only when the hospital and family agreed to donate the medical charts. Such records are extremely useful in medical research."

"I see."

He gestured to a battered gray file cabinet gathering dust in the corner. "We had medical charts for all the cadavers which I made into skeletons." He opened the top drawer and riffled through the remaining files. "I only kept charts for these last five skeletons. They show some interesting diseases of the bones—rickets, osteomalacia, and so forth. I plan someday to mount them, and set up a display for the students."

Cal took a deep breath, and nerved herself to ask the question she'd been holding inside for ten minutes. "Sergei?"

He glanced up from the file drawer. "Yes?"

"When you sent the skeletons to the museum Saturday, did you happen to count them?"

"Whatever for? I had set aside the five I was keeping, along with the records. The remainder were simply—" He broke off, and his face clouded. His voice grew hard. "Of course. I see now why you are asking this. You think perhaps one of our youngsters may have placed the skeleton outside, as a prank."

"Sergei, I—"

"Such things have been known to happen, at *other* medical schools." He crossed his arms and glared at Cal.

"I'm sorry if I offended you," she said. "It's only that—"

"No." Just as quickly, the anger disappeared. He shook his

head, and his gaze softened. "You have not offended me. You are simply using your wits, as I am not. I was a fool not to see it sooner." He sighed. "Your suggestion is entirely possible— even plausible."

"I hope I'm wrong," Cal murmured.

"So do I." He flipped through the files. "It should be simple enough to check. I made one file with a master list of names, dates, chart numbers, and box numbers. We need only compare—"

He lifted his head and squeezed his eyes shut, massaging his forehead with one huge palm. "Strange."

"What is it?"

"I was *certain* I placed the master file in here." He thumbed through the manila folders. "But now I see only the files from these five skeletons."

"Maybe you sent it to the museum with the other files," Cal suggested.

"Perhaps." He pushed the drawer closed and drummed his fingers on the cabinet. "Though I had no reason to. I clearly recall checking through the master file and setting it here, in the front of the top drawer."

"When was that?" Cal asked.

Sergei sighed. "A month ago, at least. When I made the arrangements to donate our collection. I have not looked at the master list since then."

"Maybe I could check at the museum," she said. "I'd like to go over there anyway, to see the collection."

And to count the skeletons from the Siegel donation, Cal thought to herself.

CHAPTER 7

"Don't be such a wet blanket," Cal chided.

She and Plato were heading south on Martin Luther King Drive, the long winding boulevard that snakes across Cleveland's near east side to link University Circle with Lake Erie. They were munching on takeout chicken sandwiches and fries while Plato piloted the Rabbit to the museum and grumbled about his lost afternoon.

"I had a whole *hour* free today to catch up on my chart work," he complained. "And what am I doing instead? Gobbling my lunch while my wife drags me to a dusty old museum to look at dinosaur relics."

"Not *dinosaur* relics," Cal corrected patiently. "*People* relics. The Siegel skeleton collection."

She had explained all this before, not that it helped. Dr. Alice Devon, curator of physical anthropology at the Cleveland Museum of Natural History, had been only too glad to talk with Cal. But the curator already had several appointments scheduled for this afternoon and tomorrow. The only free slot she had was early this afternoon, right after lunch. Or perhaps Cal would rather set something up for later this week?

Cal had agreed to drop by after lunch. The only trouble was, her preowned Chevrolet Corsica was in the shop, again. That left Plato's Rabbit as the only alternative.

He didn't *have* to come along. The doctor's lot at Riverside was only a block from the medical school. Cal could have simply walked over and taken his car. But Plato had insisted on picking her up.

"I wouldn't be checking this angle out at all, if you hadn't suggested it," she reminded him. "Anyway, I could have driven myself."

"The shift on this car is tricky, Cal. You know that."

Cal hid a smile behind her sandwich. Plato would never admit that he was just as eager as she to discover the origins of Siegel Woman.

Traffic was light today; they hit the museum's parking lot with minutes to spare. A trio of yellow school buses was docked beside the front entrance, disgorging a swarm of first and second graders who clogged the sidewalks, buzzed over and around the life-size stegosaurus statue, and assailed the group entrance doors with the joyful frenzy of a plague of locusts chancing upon a backyard garden.

At five feet two inches tall, Cal didn't have much of a height advantage over the group. She put her head down and waded through the crowd as Plato ran interference for her. Near the entrance door, she glimpsed a fellow sufferer—a petite teacher struggling helplessly against the tide of small heads like a drowning victim about to go under. As Plato finally wrestled the door open wide enough for Cal to squeeze inside, she caught a last glimpse of the teacher, her voice shrilling to a frantic bleat—*"Please*, children. Single file. *Single file!"*

Inside, the museum was cool and dark and blessedly quiet. Across the alcove, a huge Foucault pendulum swung its gleaming steel bob in a tireless arc. Off to the right, a wide doorway led to the Sears Hall of Human Ecology with its stuffed snakes, birds, and mammals from every continent of the world. To the left, the Murch/Fawick Gallery led to the gigantic moving dinosaur show—doubtless the main attraction for the horde milling outside the doors. And nearby was a small registration window for museum guests.

Cal signed in and told the volunteer about her appointment with Dr. Devon. A minute or two later, a tall woman with long brown hair and a wide smile emerged from a nearby stairwell. She swept across the alcove to them, her long white coat flapping behind her like a pair of wings.

"Cal Marley?" Her handshake was warm and firm. "Alice Devon. Nice to meet you."

After Cal had introduced Plato, the museum curator turned and gestured toward the stairwell. "How about if we chat in my office downstairs? I've got a nice little cubbyhole right next to the bone lab."

They followed her down a flight of stairs, along a short corridor, and into a spacious room featuring a vast central lab bench, black counters along two sides, and a rack of cabinets against the far wall. Several young men and woman were clustered at intervals along the central table, huddling over bits of bone or rock, a skull here, a rib there, studying and chiseling and measuring.

"Our bone lab," Alice Devon explained. "We do some of the fine cleaning here, cataloguing and measuring. And entering data for statistical analysis."

She pointed to a computer perched in a corner of the room. "We're putting the entire Hamann-Todd collection into a database. Users will be able to research any number of questions with the click of a button."

"Sounds impressive," Cal offered. Alice Devon seemed very proud of her department.

"Thank you." The curator flapped a hand. "But I'm getting ahead of myself. Let's go into my office and start at the beginning. Then, if you want a tour, I'll be glad to take you around."

A door to their right led into a small anteroom, presumably for Alice Devon's secretary. Beyond, the curator's office was far more than a little cubbyhole. The room was big enough to contain a dozen crowded bookcases, a round table, a wide teak desk, and a few display cases variously filled with bones, fossils, shells, and semiprecious stones shimmering under an ultraviolet light. In one corner, a meticulously labeled human skeleton in a bow tie and cuffs lounged against a stack of journals. High up on the wall behind the curator's desk, a gleaming white moose skull was mounted, rack and all. Beside it, a tiny skull grinned with enormous front teeth.

"Rocky and Bullwinkle," she explained. "Unclaimed hunting trophies that a taxidermist friend of mine mounted and sent from Montana last winter. Some Christmas present, huh?"

"Better than getting Pepe LePew," Plato noted dryly.

"Much better." Alice chuckled. "Have a seat, folks."

She slid into her own chair and almost vanished. The desk was piled chin-high with papers and articles and files. She cleared a space to rest her elbows, propped her chin in her hands, and waited for Cal and Plato to take the pair of chairs across from her. "Now, then. What can I do for you?"

Quickly, Cal recounted the story of yesterday's bone hunt at Siegel, Plato's theory about a possible connection with Sergei's skeleton collection, and this morning's discovery that Sergei's master list was missing.

Alice Devon was a good listener, sitting with her head tilted and her eyes narrowed to slits, like an eagle taking its sights on a mouse. Or maybe an archaeopteryx eyeing a juicy dragonfly. Cal found herself saying more than she had planned—fleshing the story out with her own hints and ideas and intuitions, as though the museum curator were an old friend. And already, that was how she seemed.

At the beginning of Cal's story, Alice Devon smiled and gave several confident nods. But as the tale continued, her smile melted into a mask of puzzlement. Finally, when Cal finished, the woman shook her head.

"I thought I had answers for both you and for me," she began. "But I'm sure my answers are only going to make things more confusing."

She sifted through the upper strata on her desk, found the right mound, and excavated a manila folder from the depths. She opened it and ran her fingers down a sheet of paper.

"One of the anthropology grad students surveyed the collection as soon as it arrived Saturday," she explained. "It was pretty easy work; Sergei kept his records in very good shape. But here"—she flipped a page and tapped the paper—"four of the skeletons appear to be extras. No medical records or dissection findings whatsoever."

"Extras?" Cal was flabbergasted. She had come to the museum hoping to find that one of the skeletons was missing. Now it seemed that the museum had four skeletons too *many.* "Extra skeletons?"

"Exactly." Alice turned the folder around and slid it across the morass of her desk. Sure enough, four of the entries on the list were simply marked NO RECORDS SENT.

"But Sergei insists that he had medical records for every skeleton he made," Cal told her. "He was very adamant about that."

"All I can say is, they didn't turn up on this end." Alice

Devon shrugged helplessly. "The movers packed the medical records in three separate boxes. We checked all three."

"Was Sergei's master list in one of the boxes?" Cal asked hopefully.

"I didn't even know there *was* a master list." The curator folded her hands and touched her index fingers to her lips, staring at the chart. "We got two hundred and six skeletons Saturday, all carefully cleaned and neatly packed. We got three boxes of file folders, with only two hundred and two files." She shook her head. "There was no master list. I was planning to call Sergei this week to ask about the missing files. I assumed he had simply overlooked them—that perhaps they were in the wrong drawer. But I don't suppose it could be that simple, could it?"

Cal shook her head. "Sergei looked everywhere for his master list. I'm sure he would have noticed four extra medical charts."

Beside her, Plato was still staring at the open folder. He shifted his gaze to Alice. "Why don't these extra skeletons have catalog numbers?"

"*None* of them should have catalog numbers yet. We haven't—" She pulled the folder over and scanned the list again. "Oh, yes. These numbers on the list aren't ours—they're Sergei's. They were written on the boxes and the files. He started with a very simple but effective labeling method—just a date, expressed in numbers. Like this first entry—052662. That probably means the cadaver arrived on May 26, 1962. Or maybe that's when the person died. Later on, when the hospitals started listing patients by number, he simply used those."

"But none of those four extra boxes have catalog numbers," Plato persisted.

"Don't they?" She ran her fingers down the chart and frowned. "You're right. That's strange."

"Maybe the numbers *are* on the boxes," Cal suggested. "Your assistant might not have marked them unless he had both the chart and the box."

"I think he would have written down the box numbers anyway. But I suppose anything is possible." Alice slid her chair back and stood. "There's only one way to find out—we'll have a look at them ourselves."

"You still have Sergei's boxes?" Plato asked.

"Of course." She flashed a grin. "And most of the skeletons are still inside them. My staff does great work, but they'll need a few weeks to unpack, measure, and catalog all those skeletons."

She led them back out to the bone lab and gestured at the table. "I think they're working on Number Ten right now. We *might* be finished by Thanksgiving. Right, Jerry?"

A gaunt fellow with long black hair and an underfed goatee looked up from the scapula in his hands. "Right, boss. Could be sooner. This Malenkov guy does good work—most of the measurements are already written down. And very accurate." He eyed the shoulder blade in his grip like a card shark studying a winning hand. "Mostly, we're just double-checking."

"Great." She led them through the lab to a door in the back wall, near the rack of cabinets. "How about if I show you the Hamann-Todd collection first, so you have some idea of what's going on here?"

"I'd like that," Cal said. Plato nodded agreeably.

The curator led them into a huge room behind the lab—a thirty by thirty space dominated by banks of floor-to-ceiling storage units. Each unit stretched nearly the entire width of the room. Alice walked down the corridor formed by the ends of the storage units on one side and by simple file cabinets on the other. She paused to press a button on one of the units. The vast wall of storage units—each twice as thick as a library bookcase and twenty-five feet long—glided silently to the side on tracks in the floor.

In seconds, an aisle was created between two of the massive storage units.

"Like Moses parting the Red Sea," Plato observed.

Alice chuckled. "Yes, sometimes it feels that way."

She led them halfway down the aisle and pulled open a drawer at random. Inside the rectangular plastic compartment was a collection of dusty brown bones—like those of Siegel Woman, but much cleaner and drier. She picked up a spinal vertebrum and handed it to Cal, then handed a collarbone to Plato.

"You'll notice the skull isn't in here," she pointed out. "We keep them in a separate set of properly sized drawers, in order to save space."

Cal hefted the disk-shaped vertebrum in her hand. It was dry and weightless as a piece of balsa. "These are awfully light."

"That's because they're awfully dry," Alice explained. "We keep the humidity quite low in here, and most of these bones have had years to dry out."

She looked closer at the bone Cal was holding. The flat surfaces were dotted with tiny holes. "Looks like this fellow's bones were light for another reason, too. See?"

Cal squinted at the holes. "Pott's disease?"

Alice nodded. "Tuberculosis of the bones."

"You two are talking way over my head." Plato handed back the collarbone and poked at the other bones in the drawer. "Hey—what are these little things?"

Clustered in the corners of the drawer were dozens of tiny beige granules that looked like bits of dried rice or the husks of some grain.

"Dermestid beetles," the curator answered. "Or what's left of them."

"Beetles?" Plato sounded incredulous.

"Sure. That's how we get the bones so clean."

He smiled uncertainly. "You're joking, right?"

"Nope." She replaced the bones and slid the drawer closed. "Dermestid larvae will eat almost *anything*. Sergei has a colony of them over at Siegel—just like ours. Or he did. I suppose he'll get rid of his dermestids, now that he's not maintaining a collection anymore."

She noted the number on the drawer and led them up the aisle again. At the main corridor leading back to the doorway, she consulted the old fashioned file cabinets and found the chart whose number matched that of the drawer they had opened.

The medical record was from the 1940s, and featured physicians' notes, measurements, and drug dosages, all written in an antique, feathery hand.

"Cornelius Updyke," Alice read aloud. "Died of massive tuberculosis in 1937, at the age of twenty-one. A schizophrenic—he lived down at the old Gladbrook Asylum."

She handed the chart to Plato.

He flipped through it, stopping at a page near the back. "What's this? It looks like German."

"It probably is." The curator studied the document. "This is

an old Martin form. They filled it out after Cornelius died. It
has eighty-six different observations collected during the post-
mortem—from hair and eye color to the length of the great
toe. Kind of a shotgun approach to collecting data. Some of
the information is worthwhile, and some isn't."

She leafed through the folder again and found a pair of
black-and-white photographs mounted on the same page. They
both showed the subject lying on the dissecting table, from
slightly different angles. Cornelius Updyke's face was pale
and emaciated, and his eyes were sunken. The landmarks of
his skull showed clearly in his cheekbones and forehead and
jaw. His arms and legs were mere sticks, with round swellings
at the joints. The sharp edges of his ribs threatened to slice
through the skin of his chest.

The origin of the word "consumption" was obvious.

"Stereoscopic photographs," Alice explained. "Two pictures, taken from slightly different angles. Gives the illusion of
three dimensions, when you use a viewer."

Plato flipped through some of the other files in the drawer.
"Typhoid fever, syphilis, *apoplexy*. Good heavens—some of
these are really old. I've never even heard of most of these
drugs."

"We had a medical historian in here just last week," the curator told them. "He was researching pneumonia in the
1930s—just before the antibiotic era."

"How many skeletons do you have?" Cal asked.

"Over three thousand—humans, that is. And we have hundreds from other primates—mostly gorillas and chimpanzees."

Cal wished she had been able to use such a collection during
her pathology residency back in Chicago, when she had written a paper on skeletal changes from vitamin deficiency.
"They must be very useful for research."

"They are." Alice slipped the file back into place and closed
the drawer, then led them back toward the lab. "The collection
has already had a number of different applications—from the
latest computer modeling of prosthetic limbs, all the way back
to Johansen's analysis of 'Lucy'—one of the earliest ancestors
of man." She stood in the doorway and gazed proudly across
the bone lab. "The Hamann-Todd Collection is the largest of
its kind in the country."

Standing beside her, Cal's mind was racing. Something

Alice said earlier had suddenly clicked. Something about
Sergei's collection at Siegel. And dermestids.

And the extra skeletons here.

"You mentioned that Sergei has a dermestid colony at the
medical school?" she asked.

Alice nodded. "I've seen it—he keeps the bugs in a small
outbuilding near the parking lot."

"How do the dermestids work?" Plato asked. He shot a
glance at Cal, apparently following her train of thought. "Do
you just take a dead body and throw it in with the bugs, and
end up with a skeleton a few days later?"

"It's not *quite* that simple." She grinned. "But it's close.
Like I said, the dermestid larvae will eat almost anything. But
the process goes much quicker if the body is dismembered
first. So for big animals—like humans or gorillas—we remove
the limbs and do it in stages."

"They clean the bodies right down to the bones?"

She nodded. "They're hungry little devils. They'll eat hides,
cotton clothing, and probably our furniture if we let them.
That's why our colony is kept separate from the rest of the
museum. And why Sergei keeps his in a different building altogether."

"Is there anything they *don't* eat?" Cal asked.

"Neural tissue." Alice shrugged. "They're very finicky
about that. So we have a different procedure for extracting the
brains. It's rather interesting." She smiled graciously. "If
you'd like, I could—"

"That's okay," Plato interrupted quickly. "Thank you."

"Maybe we could see Sergei's collection," Cal suggested.

"Of course." Alice led them to the outer corridor again, but
rather than heading for the stairs, she followed the hallway to a
large double door. Walking a few paces behind the curator,
Cal met Plato's gaze again.

"Should we tell her?" Plato whispered.

Cal needed only a moment to consider. Alice Devon was
obviously quite intelligent and competent. And Cal trusted her,
instinctively.

To learn how a skeleton had been buried at Siegel—and
how four extra skeletons had somehow found their way into
Sergei's collection—they would need Alice Devon's help. As

she herself had put it, things were getting more confusing rather than less.

But the museum curator had no idea how confusing things really were.

Alice unlocked the door and flicked a switch. Fluorescents lit the room with a dull greenish glow. The bare concrete floor was covered with stacks of plain brown boxes. It looked more like the receiving station of a post office than the tomb of over two hundred human skeletons.

Alice walked across the room and gestured at the piles. "You see that Sergei used the same system for packing skeletons that we use here—small cubical boxes for the skulls, and longer, flatter boxes for the other bones."

In one corner of the room, a small pile of eight boxes was separated from the other stacks. Alice, Cal, and Plato walked over and sifted through the boxes, but they found no tags.

"Unmarked, just like the entries on my assistant's chart." Alice lifted a box from one of the other piles and pulled at the tag. The label peeled back easily. "The tags might have simply fallen off. Some of these boxes have been sitting around for decades."

"It's awfully coincidental that labels are missing from four boxes of each size," Plato observed. "The same boxes that didn't come with charts."

"There's another possibility," Cal finally pointed out. "Maybe the labels were never there at all."

Plato nodded.

Alice Devon set the box down and shook her head slowly. "I don't think I'm following you."

"I'm not sure I understand it either," Cal said. She leaned against the doorjamb and sighed. "But we were starting to wonder if these four extra skeletons might not really be part of Sergei's collection. If perhaps those bodies were donated against their will."

Alice frowned.

"I know it sounds crazy," Plato told her. "But what if someone knew about Siegel's skeleton collection and decided to use it?"

Her face gradually cleared, and she gave a quick nod. "I get it. What better place to hide a book than in a library?"

"And what better place to hide a dead body than in Siegel's skeleton collection?"

They were all silent for several moments. Cal rubbed her chin and stared at the pile of bones, thinking furiously. None of it made any sense.

"Listen to us," Plato finally said. "We're talking about someone killing people, turning their bodies into skeletons, and dumping them into Sergei's collection. It's crazy."

"Crazy, but entirely possible." The curator's eyes slitted again—the archaeopteryx spotting another dragonfly. "It wouldn't be hard. You'd probably need to know something about anatomy, and have access to a lab. Dismembering a body is tricky work, and kind of messy. After that, you'd just dump it into the dermestid colony and wait."

"How long would it take?"

"Four weeks would do nicely." She shrugged. "Then you brush off the bones, do a little cleanup work, and slip them into a couple of Sergei's boxes."

"You'd have to take care of his master list," Plato pointed out.

"Not necessarily," Cal said. "At least, not until you found out the collection was being moved. Once he made the skeletons, I doubt Sergei kept very close track of them."

"You're probably right," Alice agreed. "That room had gotten awfully crowded. I doubt if Sergei would notice a few extras. And I *know* he kept a stack of unused boxes in the same room."

Cal nodded. "So you think it's possible that these skeletons were planted in the collection?"

Alice paused to consider, then gave a firm nod. "Yes, I think it's possible. Anyway, it's worth looking into. We have no evidence to the contrary." She covered her mouth and chortled. "Listen to me—'no evidence to the contrary.' I'm starting to sound like one of those cop shows on TV."

"You'll get used to it." Cal smiled. "Your assistant didn't happen to find an extra skull lying around in this collection, did he?"

"To go with the skeleton you folks found?" Alice shook her head. "I'm afraid not. It would have been on the list."

"Too bad." Cal hadn't expected Siegel Woman's skull to be here, but it was worth a try.

"Come to think of it, we may have trouble matching these four skulls with their corresponding skeletons." Alice grimaced. "After all, none of these eight boxes are marked. I might be able to make some guesses, based on size and age and so forth. But that's all it would be—a guess."

"Looks like you two are in the same fix," Plato observed.

"Trouble is, I don't even have enough information to make a guess." Cal shrugged helplessly. "Maybe some of these skeletons belonged to murder victims, but we can't even *begin* to identify them. With no records, no charts, and not even a rough idea of when they died, I don't know where to start. I'll bring it up with Coroner Jensson, but—"

"I have a suggestion," Alice interrupted. "About where to start, I mean."

"I'd love to hear it."

The anthropologist patted one of the cube-shaped boxes in the unlabeled pile. "How about having a facial reconstruction made, from one of these unidentified skulls, and running it in the newspapers? An artist's sculpture of what the face probably looked like. If you get an identification, you might at least find out whether the person died a natural death, or was missing, or whatever."

Cal nodded. It was a good idea. "I agree. We've done that kind of thing in the past. But our resident sculptor has moved to Florida. We'd have to send it down there, and I'm not sure if she would do it."

Alice grinned. "You've got another resident sculptor right under your nose."

"What do you mean?"

"I started out as a sculptor—got a master's degree in three-dimensional art forms. I've done representations of humans using everything from Carrara marble to wire and cloth." She brushed a lock of hair back from her forehead. "I finally realized I was more interested in the mechanics of the body than in the art. So I went into physical anthropology."

"You're comfortable modeling faces from skulls?" Cal held her breath.

"Very. This won't be the first time, by a long shot." She shrugged. "When I was getting my doctorate in Michigan, I did a few reconstructions for the Detroit police. They had a lot of this kind of thing going on. I got positive ID's on three out of five skulls."

Cal was impressed. Three out of five was very, very good.

"A few labs have moved to computer modeling, but I like to use my eyes and hands." Alice Devon reached into one of the cube-shaped boxes and pulled out a skull. "Take this fellow, for instance. Almost certainly a male. Square jaw, and a prominent zygomatic arch. High cheekbones—probably Nordic, by the look of it. So go with blond hair, but pick a more neutral color anyway just in case we're wrong." She lifted it closer and peered at the eye sockets. "Deep-set eyes, rather far apart, and a long, low brow. . . ."

Cal listened patiently and smiled at Plato. The mystery of Siegel Woman was turning into a tangled mess, with no end in sight. But Alice Devon was proving to be a godsend.

CHAPTER 8

Alice Devon's facial reconstruction made the Friday papers. The *Plain Dealer* ran it at the head of the metro news section, and the *Beacon Journal* put it on the front page.

Alice hadn't chosen the Nordic fellow after all. The sculpture showed an older Caucasian woman with wide eyes, a generous mouth, and a perfectly shaped oval face. The hair was neutral gray, and a neutral length—just above the neck, with a slight wave.

Cal admired the *Plain Dealer* photo over her bowl of Froot Loops Friday morning. Alice Devon really was an artist. Where most reconstructions simply looked like mannequins or lifeless generic people—like anyone or nobody at all—Alice had managed to mold life into her sculpture. The woman's bright eyes stared out at the camera, and her full lips were pursed ever so slightly, as though smiling at a secret only she and the photographer knew.

And in a way, she was.

"She's pretty good, isn't she?" Plato asked. He passed the *Beacon Journal* across the table and reached for the *Plain Dealer*.

"Sure looks that way," Cal agreed. She studied the *Beacon Journal* photo. It was the same picture, just a bit larger and sharper. Because three of the four skeletons were male, Alice had chosen to represent the woman. That way, she knew which skeleton the skull matched, and could make inferences about size and build.

Both photos had run with the same brief story—a press release sent out by the Cuyahoga County Coroner's office saying that the bones had been found in an undisclosed location near downtown Cleveland, that the subject was roughly five feet three inches tall and of slender build, aged fifty to seventy years, and that a small reward was being offered for information leading to her identification.

No mention was made of Siegel Medical College or the Natural History Museum.

The *Cleveland Post* had telephoned Cal late last night—at home, of course—wanting more information. Where exactly were the bones found? Was there any link with the alleged recovery of a skeleton at a building site near Siegel Medical College? Had the skull from that skeleton been found yet—and had this facial reconstruction come from that skull?

Cal had politely refused to comment. Presumably the *Post* had published Alice's reconstruction as well, though she hated to think about the suppositions and inferences that had probably accompanied the picture.

The microwave dinged. Plato dropped his paper, hurried across the kitchen, and pulled a plateload of pizza from the little oven. He sat down again and sampled one of the pieces like a vintner tasting a fine Bordeaux.

"*Recherché!*" He smacked his lips.

Cal stuck out her tongue. "You're disgusting."

"What." He donned his innocent, wounded expression. But with his cheeks bulging with sausage, pepperoni, onions, and jalapeño peppers, he looked more like an over-grown chipmunk with indigestion. "What."

"Pizza for breakfast?"

"I didn't have any supper last night." It was true. Plato had been hammered with admissions yesterday evening. He hadn't escaped from the hospital until after midnight. At that point, he was too weak and tired to think, to eat, to climb the stairs to the bedroom. He'd squeezed in beside Cal on the sofa and woken at sunrise with a stiff neck, a sore back, and a stomach that had shriveled down to an unhappy little prune.

"Poor baby," Cal clucked. "Maybe you'll fit into your suit tomorrow night. If you don't eat too much pizza."

"Froot Loops aren't nature's most perfect food either," he shot back. "Little gobs of colored sugar."

He tore into the pizza again. His stomach made contented noises and got down to business. Foley padded over and licked Plato's pantleg. He handed the dog half a slice of pizza. It disappeared, instantly.

"He's looking better," Plato observed.

Cal grinned. "That visit to the vet Tuesday scared him."

Plato sighed, remembering. The vet had poked and prodded and listened for over half an hour before deciding there was nothing he could do, and billing them for eighty dollars.

"At least I'm not on call this weekend," Plato said. He reached down to scratch the dog's neck. "Maybe I'll take Foley for a second opinion tomorrow."

"Dan is back from Grand Cayman?"

"Yes. Finally." He pulled his new pager from his pocket and glared at it. "I'm turning this thing off at five o'clock sharp."

Dan Homewood was Plato's partner. Every October, he spent two weeks at a rented house on some obscure Caribbean island. Still single, with no student loans and no house payments, he could easily afford it. Even on a staff geriatrician's salary.

"Dan's flight came in last night. I—" Plato suddenly paused. "Tomorrow night? What's tomorrow night?"

Now it was Cal's turn to look innocent. "What do you mean?"

"You said something about me fitting into my suit tomorrow night."

She frowned. "I did?"

"Yes. You did." Plato folded his arms, leaned back, and smiled generously. "Must have been an innocent mistake. Because you know that the Ohio State-Michigan game is on ESPN tomorrow night. After we fix the roof tomorrow, you and me and Homer are going to eat chili, drink beer, and watch the Wolverines get stomped."

Plato's cousin Homer—an assistant county prosecutor— had graduated from Ohio State's law school. Plato had attended Kent State and, like many Kent State alumni, had quickly lost hope and adopted another university's football team as his own. But the Ohio State-Michigan rivalry transcended college allegiances anyway. The annual match was something of a contest between the states themselves.

Tomorrow night, it would be played under the lights and televised nationally.

"I have no intention of going to the medical staff dinner tomorrow night," Plato concluded haughtily. "They'll just have to get by without me."

"They'll have to get by without a lot of people," Cal agreed. "The planning committee didn't know the Ohio State-Michigan game was being played at night. By the time they found out, they'd already rented the museum."

"Museum?"

"The Natural History Museum." Cal smiled. "They're advertising it as *Dinner Under the Dinosaurs.*"

"That's better than last year," he observed. Last year's medical staff dinner was held at the Cleveland Metroparks Zoo. In the monkey house. It was advertised as *Dinner in the Wild*. The wild was awfully smelly. "You're right, though. I bet half the medical staff will stay home."

"I know." Cal poked listlessly at her Froot Loops and rainbow-tinted milk. "I guess I'll just have to go by myself."

"Why go at all?" Plato asked. Cal was a rabid football fan. As a Northwestern University alumnus, she couldn't seriously cheer for Ohio State—except on the day when they played Michigan. Then, she got almost as involved as Plato and Homer. "I thought you wanted to watch the game too."

"I do." She shrugged. "But we already paid for tickets to the dinner."

"So we lose a few bucks. What's that, compared to the Ohio State-Michigan game?"

"I *have* to go, Plato." The corners of Cal's mouth folded down. "I have to pick up my award."

"Your *award*?" His puzzlement turned to surprise. "*You* won an award?"

"Don't act so astonished. Yes, I won an award. They told me about it last week, when they noticed I hadn't signed up for the dinner. I was hoping to surprise you." She sat up proudly and waved her spoon in a grand flourish. "I won the First Annual Thaddeus Crumm Prize for Outstanding Resident Education."

"Who's Thaddeus Crumm?"

"I don't know." She shrugged. "I guess I'll find out tomorrow night."

Plato chewed his pizza slowly, washed it down with some

diet Pepsi, and burped thoughtfully. He had a tough decision to make.

Why was marriage so complicated?

"It's almost seven o'clock. We'd better get going." Cal's voice sounded hollow and distant, like she was talking from a deep, dark cave. She stood and carried her bowl to the sink, then turned. "Will you at least tape the game for me tomorrow? I don't trust that VCR timer."

Plato sighed. The moment of truth.

Was he a man or a mouse?

"Homer will tape it for us," Plato said. Doubtless, Homer would decide his cousin was a mouse.

"What do you mean?" Cal's brown eyes lit with a dim flicker of hope.

"I mean, I'm going with you." He walked across the kitchen and folded Cal into his arms. He leaned over, so she fit into the hollow just under his chin. Her blond hair smelled like lilacs. His clasped hands spanned her waist.

Maybe she would wear the black taffeta tomorrow.

"You can't just walk in there and pick up a Thaddeus Crumm prize all by yourself," he continued. "You need an entourage—like with the Oscars. Someone to take pictures, someone to hold your speech for you, someone you can thank for helping you get where you are today."

"Who's that?" she asked his breast pocket.

"Me."

"Oh, yeah." She tilted her face up, stood on her toes, and kissed him. "Thanks."

"Besides," Plato pointed out as they stepped onto the porch, "if Homer can keep his mouth shut, we might not find out who wins until we watch the tape."

Plato spent the morning seeing office patients, ran overtime because his receptionist had mistakenly double-booked two of his slots, skipped lunch, and headed over to the hospital to visit his patients. Now that Dan was in town, he only had to make half as many visits. Hospital rounds were going smoothly until he stopped by the Intensive Care Unit to see his last patient—Albert Windgartner.

Despite two blood transfusions and three days of high-dose antibiotic therapy, Albert was sliding downhill. The pneumonia was advancing; each successive chest X ray showed the fluffy white infiltrate growing, seeping across the radiolucent darkness of his lungs like some noxious cloud. His blood oxygen levels were dipping low enough that he might need the ventilator soon. He was spiking fevers at random, indicating that the antibiotics might be missing their target.

His poor immunity was Death's wildcard.

Plato spent half an hour sifting through a chart already plump with interns' notes, residents' notes, the ICU specialist's notes, the infectious disease consultant's notes, nurses' records, lab studies, and radiology reports. The hematologist—the blood specialist whose experimental drug was being used to treat Albert's aplastic anemia—had even stopped by.

But nobody had any answers.

It was a familiar situation. As a geriatrician, Plato had faced it many times before. The phenomenon came under a lot of different guises with a lot of fancy names—multiple organ failure, septic shock, adult respiratory distress syndrome—but for certain elderly patients, all the diagnoses added up to one simple fact: they were ready to die. You fought it with antibiotics and powerful heart drugs and ventilators and monitors, but the patient just didn't respond. The body simply seemed to give out, slipping away with all the inevitability of a freighter sinking in a hurricane.

Albert Windgartner seemed to be drifting into that kind of decline.

Plato snapped the chart shut and headed over to Albert's bedside. The old man was half hidden beneath a maze of tubing and wires. A Swan-Ganz catheter plunged into his chest just below the collarbone and threaded its way through his heart. An arterial line pierced his left wrist, providing constant information on blood pressures and oxygen levels. A nasogastric tube taped to his cheek led to a suction unit on the wall. Near the ceiling, an oscilloscope sketched every heartbeat, every breath, every little movement in the crowded bed.

On the wall television high up in the corner, the newest Geraldo-clone was teasing a jilted lover into a jealous frenzy.

Albert's eyes rolled over to Plato. His fingers fumbled with the television remote. The lover vanished into the ether.

"Trash."

Plato wasn't sure if he had heard the word, or just lip-read it. Albert's breathing was hardly strong enough to fog a mirror. His face was the color of weathered pine, his lips two thin cracks in the board.

But his eyes were still icy blue. He stabbed a button on the remote, waited patiently while the bed levered him into an upright position, and fixed his gaze on Plato. The lips twisted into a tight smile.

"Just the man—I wanted—to see."

"Hello, Albert." Plato approached the bedside and shook his patient's hand. The old man's grip was stronger than ever. "How're you doing?"

"Could be—better." Albert gave a half shrug, wincing at the Swan-Ganz catheter, and gently patted the shoulder bandage with one quivering hand. "Could be—a *lot*—better."

"We're still having trouble finding the right antibiotic," Plato explained. Since the admission last Tuesday, he had given Albert daily briefings on his condition, explained the latest test results, and described the treatments they were trying.

But each day, as Albert's condition worsened, Plato found it harder to find the thin line between reasonable optimism and complete fabrication.

Today, it was harder than ever. As Plato finished his exam and wrapped up his visit, Albert fixed him with that frosty blue gaze. He clutched Plato's arm with one massive hand.

"I'm not going—to make it. Am I?"

For the first time since Plato had met him, the old man's proud gaze melted. The blue eyes were pleading—not for a cure, but for the truth.

"I don't know, Albert." He reached down and squeezed the hand. "I don't know. We're trying everything."

"Sometimes—everything's—not enough." He paused to catch his breath. "Erica doesn't—see that. Talk to her."

Plato nodded quickly. "This doesn't mean that—"

Albert cut him off with a brisk shake of the head. He

winced again, and fingered the bandage on his shoulder. "No bullshit. Remember?"

Plato remembered. Albert had set the terms months ago, when Plato first diagnosed his aplastic anemia and explained the seriousness of his illness.

"No bullshit," he agreed.

"I'll talk with—her, too. I *have* to." Albert's eyes slid away from Plato's. He stared at the basket of flowers sitting on the bedside table. Above it, a Mylar balloon with a pink teddy bear and a heart proclaimed "I Love You."

"She always thought—she wasn't good—enough for me," Albert began. "After Cora died. You know—about all that."

He waved his hand absently.

Plato did indeed know about all that. Erica Windgartner had been trying to please her father for the past thirty years. Ever since her mother died. Trying to live up to his expectations, to fulfill the plans her father had made for the son he'd never had.

"I'm proud—of her." Albert's eyes lifted to Plato again. "I guess—I want her—to know that."

"I think she does," Plato replied softly. "I really do."

Albert nodded, but his eyes searched Plato's face for something more. And found it.

"But I know she'd love to hear it from you anyway," Plato suggested. He took a deep breath, and let his eyes drift up to the Mylar balloon. "And I bet you have a lot of other things you want to tell her."

Despite the hard boundaries of her relationship with Plato, Erica had once opened up enough to talk about her father. To tell Plato about the frustration and bitterness she felt. How he had seemed to see her first as a burden, then an asset, but never as a daughter. How he always seemed to push her away every time they started to get close.

Plato had understood her feelings perfectly.

The old man followed Plato's gaze up to the Mylar balloon. His forehead wrinkled slightly. Cold blue eyes whipped back to Plato's, the ice harder than ever.

But just as quickly, they melted again.

"No bullshit," Albert breathed, nodding slowly. One massive hand came up to rub his eyes. He stared at the teardrop in amazement, as though he'd just found a gold nugget.

He glanced up at Plato and smiled sadly. "Maybe you could—send for her?"

Plato squeezed Albert's hand once again before he turned to leave. Already, the grip was weaker.

He would tell Erica to hurry.

CHAPTER 9

Marietta Clemens recognized the face in the picture. She was sure of it.

Plato hadn't left Riverside General until early evening. By all rights, he should have gone straight home. He had been on call for the past two weeks. He had averaged four hours of sleep a night for the past five days. Nursing home rounds at Wyndhaven could certainly have waited until Monday. But as he followed Interstate 77 south from Cleveland, he found himself exiting early and following the winding country road over rolling hills and rusting bridges until he finally turned into the parking lot at Wyndhaven Colony.

He just wanted to get nursing home rounds over with, he told himself. That way, he'd have a clear weekend.

Monday would be so much less hectic if he stopped by Wyndhaven today.

Besides, it was on the way.

But he wasn't buying it. The *real* reason he was stopping here today was to check on Agnes Leighton. Despite Plato's arguments, pleas, and threats, Agnes had stuck to her decision. And so, yesterday, Plato had no other choice than to discharge her back to the nursing home to die.

He would just peek in on her today, he told himself. To see how she was doing, to make sure she was comfortable.

And, incidentally, to make sure that she hadn't changed her mind, that she didn't want to go back to Riverside General for surgery.

He parked the old Rabbit in the blacktopped main parking lot and followed a winding sidewalk through trees and gardens toward the central building. A sign beside the parking lot read

WYNDHAVEN COLONY—A FULL-SERVICE RETIREMENT COMMU-
NITY.

Wyndhaven was exactly that. The buildings were set in a
pastoral landscape of forests and hills and sprawling lawns and
winding, wooded paths. Three luxurious six-story apartment
buildings nestled among the trees just west of the parking lot.
Each building featured forty assisted-living units providing
meals, a centralized activity center, optional in-home nursing
services, and emergency contact systems.

The nursing home itself—Plato's destination—was a six-
story building with two large wings and enough beds for 200
moderately ill patients.

Despite its large size, Wyndhaven's nursing home had a
long waiting list. Aside from its reputation for high-quality
medical care and excellent service, the nursing home had its
own referral system. Many of the patients were former residents of the apartment complex who had grown too ill to live
independently.

And most of them still had a fair amount of money. In that
way, Wyndhaven assured itself of a steady flow of full-paying
customers, maintained a high level of care and service—and
remained very profitable.

Other Medicare-supported nursing homes drooled over
Wyndhaven's clientele.

As always, Elroy Nestor and his motorized wheelchair were
parked in the courtyard outside the nursing home. Elroy was a
retired stockbroker who had accrued a small fortune with his
own portfolio before a massive stroke had debited some of his
memory and left him crippled in the bargain. The stroke had
changed his personality as well, making him slightly aggres-
sive and very suspicious.

Plato smiled as he walked by. "Hello, Mr. Nestor."

Elroy glared back from behind his cataract glasses. With his
small, thin face, pointed nose, and enormous hairy ears, Elroy
Nestor looked like a bat with astigmatism. He stared at Plato
for a long moment, then snatched a clipboard from his lap.

"Name?" His nose twitched officiously.

"I'm Dr. Marley. Plato Marley."

"Right." The old stockbroker squinted at his watch, clicked
his pen, and jotted the name down. "Visiting?"

"One of my patients," Plato replied. "Agnes Leighton."

"Fine." Elroy looked up and gave a brisk jerk of his head. "Go on inside."

"Thank you."

Plato couldn't remember whether Elroy was delusional or just very suspicious—he was Dan Homewood's patient—but his routine certainly seemed harmless enough. Many visitors simply ignored the self-appointed doorman, but he still scribbled down their descriptions as they entered and left the building. Once last year when Dan was on vacation, Plato had examined Elroy in his room. After the visit, the stockbroker had proudly shown his log books to Plato—names, dates, and times for virtually every daytime visitor to Wyndhaven Colony during the four years he had lived there.

Plato left Elroy behind and headed inside. The reception area was spacious, brightly lit, and tastefully decorated. Chippendale sofas, comfortable recliners, and several assisted-lift chairs were carefully positioned throughout the room. Every square foot of the reception area was wheelchair-accessible, with three-foot gaps between most of the furniture, and convenient placement of lift chairs to make transfers easier. None of the furniture had sharp edges or corners. The carpet was rich and elegant, yet shallow enough to allow wheels and canes to move easily across the floor.

And the place was impeccably clean. Plato had never seen so much as a speck of dust on the furniture or a misplaced sofa cushion. Wyndhaven Colony even *smelled* clean—a constant scent of soap and cleaning solvents, as though the entire nursing home had just been scrubbed from floor to ceiling. And yet Plato had never seen a maid. He pictured *Jetson*-like robotic servants lurking behind the walls, coming to life each time a spot of lint or a dab of mud marred the furniture or carpets.

The patient care staff was even more efficient.

Plato moved farther into the room. One wall of the reception area featured a large bank of floor-to-ceiling windows, like those lining airport concourses. The windows looked out over the forest to the east of Wyndhaven Colony—ponderous oaks and wispy poplars, ragged elms and majestic maples, all decked out in their autumn finery. Fall had been warmer than usual this year, so the leaves were just at their peak. The window bank was a kaleidoscope bursting with color—rich reds and golds, vibrant yellows, flaming oranges. The scene could have been part of a picture puzzle.

A week from now, most of the leaves would have died and fallen to the forest floor, their beauty forgotten until next year.

Marietta Clemens was perched on a sofa in front of the windows, a cup of tea balanced on her lap. Her face was open and innocent and filled with wonder, like a child seeing fireworks light up the sky for the very first time.

And for Marietta, maybe that was how it felt. Her memory problems were far worse than Elroy Nestor's. She had come to Plato's practice a few years ago, when her dementia was already well advanced. At the time, Marietta had been very independent and very intelligent, living on her own and getting around her memory loss by papering her house with Post-it notes—to remind her what had happened that day, what she needed to do tomorrow, where the aspirins were, which medicines to take at what time, and when her daughter was coming by to visit. By the time she finally agreed to move to Wyndhaven Colony, her doors and mirrors and cupboards were drifted over with sticky notes, like the fallout from some bizarre yellow snowstorm.

These days, Plato could do nothing but watch and wait. Mrs. Clemens suffered from multiinfarct dementia—showers of tiny strokes had gnawed and worried away at her memory and intellect like a school of hungry piranhas setting upon a stricken deer. Ironically, the illness stole her short-term memory first, but hardly touched her recollections of a year or a decade or a lifetime ago.

These days, Mrs. Clemens only surfaced in the present for a moment or two before going under again, drowning in a pool of long-ago memories and half-forgotten times.

Still staring out the window, she sighed. "It's such a beautiful day. Don't you think so?"

"I sure do."

She gave a start of recognition, turned her gaze to Plato, and smiled. "Hello, Dr. Marley."

Her voice rose slightly, as if she didn't quite trust her memory. She probably didn't. Even Marietta Clemens had given up pretending.

"Hi, Mrs. Clemens." He sat down on the sofa beside her. "How are you doing?"

"Very well, thank you." She set her teacup on an end table. "It's nice to see you again. Do we have to go back to my room?"

"No." Plato shook his head. "I'm just visiting. I examined you last week, remember?"

"Of course." But her forehead wrinkled with confusion. She glanced out the window, and the wrinkles cleared. "I'm glad. It's such a beautiful day. Don't you think so?"

"I sure do."

"The leaves are just past their finest." Marietta pointed a liver-spotted hand at the windows. "Some of them have fallen already. It's too bad—you can almost see that ugly building next door."

Plato squinted through the glass wall and frowned. As far as he knew, there were no buildings next door. Not to the east, anyway. Wyndhaven Colony was set in the wooded hills of southeastern Cuyahoga County, where few businesses or industries had yet made their marks.

But Marietta's home in the city had sat beside a vacant, decrepit office building. With her poor eyesight and even poorer memory, the old woman probably imagined she was home again. Too bad that an old memory had to spoil her new reality.

Plato smiled at his patient. "How's your hip feeling?"

"My hip?" She frowned into her lap. "Fine, I guess. Why—is something wrong with it?"

Mrs. Clemens's hip had been replaced last year. In spite of the surgery, she still had trouble getting around. A walker stood beside the couch, a patient servant waiting to aid her on the long turtle-march back to her room.

"No—nothing's wrong with it," Plato assured her. "I'm glad you're feeling well."

"Thank you." Marietta was still staring at her lap, which was draped in the first section of the *Beacon Journal*. She smoothed the front page flat and lifted it closer to her face. She turned to Plato and smiled again. "My roommate was in the paper today."

She folded the newspaper in half and handed it to him. Her smile was downright beatific—as though she had just witnessed a genuine miracle.

"Right on the front page," Marietta continued. She shook

her head and sighed. "Louise always was a popular gal—even here in the nursing home. All the men loved her."

She leaned closer and lowered her voice to a conspiratorial whisper. "Just between you and me, there were some nights when her bed wasn't even slept in. I'd muss it up for her, so the nurses wouldn't catch on."

"You say she's in the newspaper?" Plato stared at the folded page. Only one picture was visible.

"Yes. Right here." Marietta stabbed a finger at the photo. "She's dyed her hair brown, but that's Louise all right."

"Louise?"

"Louise Higgins. But we always called her Lou." She eyed Plato suspiciously. "Why—didn't they print her name right?"

"Yes," Plato lied. He lifted the paper and pretended to scan the text. "Yes—here it is. Louise Higgins."

"I wish I knew what the article said." She rubbed her eyes and squinted at the page. "I left my cataract glasses in my room. Would you mind—?"

"Not at all." Plato lifted the paper in front of his face and frantically searched for a reasonable story. Mrs. Clemens tended to get very anxious and upset over small problems or changes in her daily routine. Hearing that her former room-mate's skeleton had turned up somewhere in Cleveland would probably set off a nervous breakdown.

Beside the story on the facial reconstruction, a column told of a benefit concert sponsored by one of the local banks.

"It looks like Mrs. Higgins helped organize a benefit for Children's Hospital." Plato folded the paper again. "The article just lists the performers who came. I guess there was a big turnout."

"That sounds like Lou. She was entertainment director here before she—" Marietta patted her silver hair and frowned. "Strange. I could have *sworn* Lou died last year. Some kind of blood problem."

"You must be thinking of somebody else," Plato suggested.

"I must be." She shook her head. "Lou couldn't organize benefits very well if she was dead, could she?"

"Not really." He rustled the paper. "Mind if I borrow your newspaper? I haven't had a chance to read it yet today."

"Not at all, not at all. I never read it anyway—I'm always

losing my glasses." She shrugged. "So I just look at the pictures. They're more interesting anyway."

"They certainly are." He took one more glance at the picture
before slipping the paper into his briefcase.

Marietta Clemens turned her gaze to the windows once
again. "It's such a beautiful day. Don't you think so?"

"I sure do."

Agnes Leighton frowned at the front page of the *Beacon Journal*.

"It could be her. Maybe." She lifted her reading glasses and
pinched the bridge of her nose. "The eyes are just right. But
the hair is way off."

Agnes was sitting in a vinyl chair in her room, holding the
newspaper up to the window. Plato had shown her the photo
soon after he arrived. Agnes had seen the picture in the *Plain
Dealer*, but she hadn't taken a good look at it.

"I know I'm supposed to ignore the hair, but I can't."
Agnes's lopsided grin looked more like a grimace today. The
past four days of starvation were already taking their toll. Her
eyes were sunken, and her cheekbones were jagged peaks in
the landscape of her face. She'd been dangerously thin before
her hospitalization. She now had very little energy reserve left.

"Louise always dyed her hair this brilliant red color," Agnes
continued. "And it was real frizzy, from too many perms. Like
she had a flaming porcupine sitting on her head."

"Cover the hair in the picture," Plato suggested.

She framed the face with her bony fingers and nodded
slowly. "You know, Marietta could be right."

"You think it's Louise Higgins?"

"At least fifty-fifty. But what the hell are her bones doing
popping up somewhere in Cleveland? I thought she died of a
blood problem. Something about clotting—she had all these
horrible bruises everywhere." Agnes cocked an eyebrow at her
doctor. "I bet *you* know more about this than you're letting on.
Your wife's with the coroner's office, right?"

"Right."

"So what's the big mystery about? I thought Lou died a natural death."

"She probably did."

Quickly, Plato told Agnes the story of Siegel Woman—the

headless skeleton in the construction site, Sergei's missing master list, and the four extra skeletons in the Hamann-Todd collection.

"So this face belongs to one of those extra skeletons from the museum?" she asked.

Plato nodded.

She drew a deep breath and let it out slowly. "You better not let the *Cleveland Post* hear about this."

"The *Post*? What do they have to do with it?"

"Haven't you seen the paper today?" Agnes riffled through a stack of magazines and newspapers on the walnut table beside her chair. She pulled up Friday's *Post* and handed it to Plato. "They're really pushing this Torso Murderer stuff."

The headline screamed TORSO MURDERER FEARS REVIVED! *Downtown Skeleton Find Points to '30s Mass Murderer*. A quarter-page photo of Alice Devon's reconstruction was featured on the front page. A few grisly photos from the original serial killings were thrown in as well.

Plato skimmed the article. Most of the details of the Siegel skeleton recovery were included, along with a few thinly veiled hints that Cleveland's notorious Kingsbury Run killer might have actually been based at Siegel Medical College.

"Lucky thing they didn't find out about your extra skeletons," Agnes commented wryly. "They would have had a field day with *that*."

Plato nodded.

"Then again, if this is really Lou's skeleton"—she tapped the newspaper photo—"it can't have anything to do with the Torso Murderer. He'd have to be at least eighty years old by now. Besides, Lou died from that bleeding problem. Or so they said."

"You know about the Torso Murderer?"

"Sure. Who doesn't?" She waved a hand. "Not personally, of course. I was just a kid when all that was happening—eight or ten years old. I grew up near Kingsbury Run—used to play under the tracks there. My mama got so frantic when the killing started, she practically grounded us for a year. I think that's when I decided I wanted to be a cop."

"You wanted to catch the killer?"

"No." She smiled shyly. "I just loved Eliot Ness. Read about him in the paper—every single article. After all, I was stuck inside all the time. That was before all those movies about him and everything. Ness was just an ordinary guy. But honest—you could see that." She rested her head on the back of her chair. "I met him a few times, after I joined the force. He didn't treat me like a woman, you know? Treated me like I was just another cop. I liked that."

"Must have been an interesting time."

"Nothing like *The Untouchables*." She closed her eyes, then opened them slowly. "Eliot Ness didn't always get his man. God knows he tried, though. They thought the killer was a bum, so Ness burned down that shantytown over by the river. He caught hell for that. But he never caught the Kingsbury Run killer." She shook her head. "Nobody did. And nobody ever will."

"You sound pretty sure."

"The *Post* has it all wrong. This skeleton business isn't the work of the Kingsbury Run killer. At least, not those extra skeletons at the museum." She frowned. "He wouldn't try to hide the bodies—he set them out in plain view. He left one of them right out near City Hall. I think he *wanted* to get caught. You know?"

Plato nodded.

"Anyway, if those extra skeletons are connected with the bones you dug up at Siegel, you've got something lots worse than a feeble old Torso Killer on your hands." She picked up the paper and eyed the photo once again. "The more I look at that picture, the more sure I am that Marietta is right. Lou only died last year. That makes this into a very current problem."

"I'll check it out, Agnes." He planned to show the picture to some of the nurses on Marietta's floor, to see if anyone else recognized Louise Higgins in the clay. "Thanks a lot. I'll let you know what we find."

"You do that." She grinned crookedly, and squeezed his arm. "But hurry up. I'm not planning on being around much longer."

Tucking the newspaper into his briefcase, Plato grimaced. "I wanted to talk to you about that, Agnes. I wondered if you were having any second thoughts."

"Nope." She shook her head firmly. "Other than second thoughts about keeping this damned IV in." She stared at the catheter in her hand. "What's it for, anyway?"

"For hydration," Plato replied quickly. "You'll be much more comfortable if you're getting fluids through your vein."

Agnes squinted suspiciously. "And I'll live longer, too, right?"

He squirmed. "Well, that depends. I mean, you could have a heart attack tomorrow, and—"

"You know what I mean." She jabbed a finger at the IVAC machine. "This thing will probably keep me alive a lot longer, right?"

"Not necessarily a *lot* longer," he insisted.

"I want it out. Please." She patted his arm gently. "I know this is hard for you, Plato. But I'm taking too damned long to die. I hardly feel any different than I did last Monday."

Plato opened his mouth, and closed it. Opened it, and closed it. Searched for something to say.

This visit wasn't going at all like he had planned.

"You may be thirsty," he warned her. But strictly speaking, he knew that wasn't necessarily true. He had spent yesterday evening studying the literature on death and dying, and the withdrawal of medical care. Many dying patients tolerated complete fasting better than hydration and IV nutrition.

The only trouble was, Agnes Leighton wasn't ready to die.

Was she?

"Your father was every bit as stubborn as you are." Agnes grinned. She had worked with Sergeant Jack Marley on one or two cases back in the '60s. She liked to remind Plato of the fact, when her doctor wasn't cooperating with her wishes. "But Jack wasn't half as stubborn as me."

"I doubt if anyone is as stubborn as you, Agnes." He stared at the ticking IVAC. "I'd hate for you to be uncomfortable."

But he wasn't sure that was the only reason for the intravenous fluid. In all honesty, he hated the thought of losing Agnes.

"If I get thirsty, I'll suck on ice chips—like I'm doing now." She jerked a thumb over her shoulder at the suction device mounted on the wall. "It all goes back in there anyway."

Plato shook his head. "I really don't see how I can agree to—"

"You don't *have* to agree," Agnes insisted. She fingered the tape that secured the line to her hand. "I could just pull it out myself, after you leave. And *keep* pulling it out, until you cry 'Uncle.'"

She smiled. "'Course, I'd end up bleeding all over the bedsheets. Which wouldn't make either of us any too popular with the nurses. You know how picky they are about keeping this place clean."

Plato sighed. "Has anyone ever told you that you drive a hard bargain, Agnes?"

"My late husband, God rest his soul." Her eyes drifted up to the ceiling. "A defense attorney, though he never won an argument with me. Died ten years ago." She sighed, and closed her eyes. "I'll be joining him soon, if my doctor lets me take this goddamned IV out."

Agnes Leighton's gaze met Plato's again. "You're holding up the reunion, son."

Plato nodded reluctantly, squeezed her hand, and shuffled off to write the order.

CHAPTER 10

Just like most Fridays, Cal worked late. Nothing interesting, just an urgent meeting at the prosecutor's office to go over the autopsy evidence for a homicide case that was slated to start next Wednesday. The prosecutor was going fishing in Canada this weekend, and he wanted to bring the file along. Just in case he had a little extra time to look it over.

So it was almost seven o'clock before Cal turned into their long driveway and rolled to a stop beside their sprawling, ramshackle century-old home. It had been beautiful, once. Back in the 1890s, Cal imagined. Half-moon windows, graceful turrets, sheltered balconies, and a huge wraparound porch. A Victorian dollhouse brought to life.

Except that it was dying of old age. The roof was a sagging hammock for water to rest on. The clapboards were literally rotting away from the walls. The brick-and-block foundation had horizontal cracks big enough for mice to stroll through with their loved ones. Birds and bats scuffled nightly in the eaves.

Nothing a little fixing-up money couldn't take care of, the realtor had assured them. A few months after signing their lives away on the mortgage, they learned that a little fixing-up money amounted to about a hundred thousand dollars. Maybe they could get a price break if they appeared on *This Old House*.

But even that would have to wait a few years. Until they made a little progress with another financial albatross—their quarter-million dollars' worth of combined debt in Health Education Assistance Loans—the federal government's answer to rip-off credit cards.

Picking her way across the rickety front porch, Cal tried to look at the bright side. She and Plato had just been on call for two weeks, so they both had a long stretch of free nights and weekends coming. They couldn't fix the house, but at least they had enough money to go out tonight.

Dinner and a movie would be just perfect. Crossing the threshold, she felt like a weary sailor making port after a long voyage.

But her calm serenity quickly dissolved.

From somewhere in the house, Plato was alternately shouting and woofing in some crazed doglike dialect. Foley was answering with horrible squealing barks, the same sounds he had made when his ear was half-bitten off in a fight with a stray and the vet had tried to stitch the shreds back together.

"Aye-Aye-A*yeeeeah*!" Foley screamed. "Aye-Aye-Ay-*eeeeah*!"

Cal ran down the hallway to the kitchen, expecting to find a rabid dog and husband.

It wasn't quite that bad. Neither were frothing at the mouth, and Plato even tossed her a quick glance before getting back down to the business of chasing Foley around and around the table while the dog screamed and Plato woofed. For a fifteen-year-old Australian shepherd who was supposedly dying of old age, Foley was still pretty nimble. Plato nearly caught him before Foley wormed his way under the table, hopped over a chair, and skittered into Dante's food, scattering the hard little pellets across the floor.

Squeezed into the crack between the stove and the counter-top, Dante hissed indignantly. But he stayed put.

Plato scurried around the table, danced across the cat food pebbles, and finally crashed to the floor beside Foley. He dragged the dog to him in a bear hug.

"Aye-Aye-A*yeeeeah*!" Foley squealed.

"*Plato!*" Cal decided she had had enough. She darted across the floor and glared down at her husband. "What are you doing? Can't you see you're tormenting the poor animal?"

Foley rolled his eyes up at her mournfully and hopefully, like a condemned prisoner meeting the governor on execution day.

"Thank goodness you're here," Plato said. He lifted a furry leg and waggled it at her. "Hold this steady, okay?"

"Why?"

"I've got to give him his digoxin."

For the first time, Cal noticed the syringe in Plato's hand. He'd been trying to hide it while he chased the dog around the room, but it hadn't helped.

"Poor fellow's got congestive heart failure," Plato continued. "I noticed it as soon as I came home. He looked half dead, just lying there in his basket."

"He looks pretty spry now." Still, Cal held the dog's leg while Plato injected the powerful heart medication.

"Aye-Aye-Ay*eeeah*!" Foley squealed again. But he held still.

"How did you get him to a vet on such short notice?" Cal asked.

"I didn't." Plato carefully capped the syringe and released the dog. Foley limped into a corner and frantically slurped his leg. "I tried to, but they were all closed."

"So how did you get the digoxin?"

"I called it into the drugstore," he replied. "How else?"

"Who did you prescribe digoxin for?" Cal asked apprehensively. "Me?"

She imagined the pharmacist's look of pitying concern next time she entered the drugstore. She wondered how she would explain her sudden return to cardiac health.

"Using your name wouldn't have been honest," Plato chided. "I prescribed it for Foley." He gestured at the vial of medicine sitting on the counter.

Cal picked it up. The label read "Foley Marley. Use as Directed."

"Good thing you didn't name him 'Spot,'" Cal observed.

"I had to pay cash for it—he's not on our insurance plan."

"Right." she shook her head. "**You**'re crazy, Plato. You know that?"

"Feel his leg," Plato insisted. "It's all swollen. And his lungs are full of rales."

Reluctantly, Cal edged close to the dog again and squeezed a furry leg. Pitting edema, sure enough. One of the hallmarks of congestive heart failure. Because of a heart attack, or old age, or any number of reasons, the heart can grow weak and begin to fail. Blood is pumped less efficiently, and fluid collects upstream from the heart—in the lungs and the tissues of the body. Fluid in the lungs makes crackly sounds called rales. Fluid in the tissues makes pitting edema—a dense, squishy feeling to the skin that leaves indentations after you press it.

Digoxin and diuretics were two mainstays of treatment. Digoxin helped the heart pump more effectively. Diuretics helped the kidneys work better to move the excess water out of the tissues and lungs.

If the drugs worked the same in dogs as they did in humans.

"Do dogs even *get* congestive heart failure?" Cal asked.

"Sure they do. That was one thing the vet told me to keep checking on." Plato shrugged. "He told me to feel his feet every day and see if it was getting worse."

"So now we'll have to torment this poor dog with shots every day."

"Not every day. I just want to keep him alive until we can get him back to the vet tomorrow." Plato put the vial into the kitchen medicine cabinet, beside the Tylenol and vitamins. "He'll probably put him on oral medication."

"I suppose that's all right, then. As long as we can make it to a movie tonight." Cal slipped her arm around her husband and waggled an eyebrow at him. "I heard that new Costner flick was pretty romantic."

"No problem." Plato rummaged in the cupboard and found another syringe. "Foley just needs his diuretic, and then we can go."

Cal groaned.

Through some primitive instinct, Foley seemed to understand Plato's words. He stopped licking his leg, turned his rheumy eyes toward Plato, and growled suspiciously.

Cal hurried over and trapped the dog in the corner. Hugging him to her hips, she grabbed one of the good legs and held it out for Plato.

"Another romantic evening." Cal sighed. She stroked the dog's snout fondly. "You and me, Foley. Together at last."

"Aye-Aye-Ay*eeeeah*!"

"*You* certainly have a flair for romance, Cal." Plato gazed about him and made an expansive gesture. "The setting sun, the fleecy clouds, the other young lovers holding hands and waiting for nightfall. And what's that?" He sniffed delicately. "*Eau de Van Exhaust*. Lumina, I think."

He was probably right, Cal reflected. At least half the vehicles at the drive-in were vans. A Chevy Lumina was parked in the row ahead, still running. Probably to generate some heat before the movie started. It was one of those clear, crisp October evenings, where the line between fading sunlight and looming shadow marks the distance between autumn's glow and winter's chill.

The kids playing on the swingsets beneath the giant movie screen were decked out in parkas and hats. Next week they'd be wearing mittens.

"Two weeks of call in a row is too much." Cal sighed. "Especially in the fall. Before we went on call, it was still summer." She reached across the seats to hold Plato's hand. "And we haven't been out together in a long time."

"We haven't done a *lot* of things together in a long time," Plato griped. He started the Rabbit and flipped the heater on high. "But at least you're getting to see your Kevin Costner movie." He grimaced. "Some romantic evening we're having here."

"We'll see," Cal murmured. But Plato didn't hear.

Before they had started their on-call marathon, the Costner movie had been showing in all the theaters. Two weeks later, it had been relegated to drive-ins and a few matinees. Plato had wanted to scrap the whole thing, to see the latest Schwarzenegger flick instead, or rent another video. But Cal had stood firm.

So here they were, at the Parkside Family Drive-In Cinema. Gathered, as Plato had said, among dozens of teenage lovers, who, by the looks of it, were already trying to start some families of their own. Up ahead, a disembodied hand appeared in the window of the Lumina, drawing the curtains together. Night had nearly fallen.

"We'll see," Cal repeated softly.

"Hmm?" Plato asked.

"Oh, nothing."

The lights suddenly dimmed. The projector flickered to life, casting a pale blue beam across the sky. A forty-foot-tall

Pepe LePew pranced across the screen in an old Warner Brothers short that Cal practically knew by heart.

Plato reached over to turn the volume down, then rummaged in the paper bag sitting between them. They had stopped at the On Tap in the Falls on their way to the theater. The bag full of cheese fries and half-pound burgers smelled delicious.

"Drive-ins may not be very romantic," Plato observed as he munched on a mouthful of fries, "but they're great places to eat. And you can talk all you want, without bothering anyone else."

"Right," Cal agreed. She plucked her Sicilian burger from the bag and gobbled half of it in a few quick bites. "So how was work?"

"Dull. Very dull." Munching his onion burger, he cocked an eyebrow at Cal. "Except for my visit to the nursing home. That was pretty exciting."

"What happened?" she giggled. "Did Mrs. Avery lose her teeth again?"

"Hardly." Plato sniffed. "You know, Cal, geriatrics isn't quite as boring as you seem to think it is."

"Especially when your patient's teeth turn up in your briefcase."

Plato scowled. Last spring, the Case of the Missing Teeth had baffled doctors, nurses, and patients at Wyndhaven Colony for nearly a week. Until Mrs. Avery's teeth had popped up in Plato's seldom-used briefcase. Apparently, he had left the case open on her nightstand, and Mrs. Avery had accidentally set her dentures there during her monthly physical exam.

"Especially," Plato pronounced grandly, "when one of my patients happens to recognize a certain photograph published in the *Beacon Journal*."

Cal nearly choked on her Sicilian burger. But then she eyed him skeptically. "You're joking, right?"

He put his hand over his heart. "May all my teeth fall out if Marietta Clemens didn't recognize that picture as her roommate at Wyndhaven."

During the second and third cartoons, he filled her in on his talk with Marietta and his visit with Agnes Leighton.

"Hopefully, Marietta's roommate was a patient at Riverside

General," Plato concluded. "Most of the Wyndhaven residents are. That way, I could just pop down to Medical Records at Riverside and pull her chart, and you could see if her records match up with the bones."

"It may not be that easy," Cal warned. "She may not have had any good X rays, or she may not have any medical records, period. After all, Sergei supposedly had the charts for those four skeletons, and they're missing."

But she was excited. Having the photo recognized was an incredibly lucky break. And having the skeleton's owner in Riverside General's record system would make things much easier. Even if the chart itself was missing, the computer might have some information. And the accounting department probably maintained decades' worth of archival records.

Porky Pig poked his giant head through the screen, stuttered his farewell, and faded away in a flash of blue captioned, "*Our Feature Presentation.*"

Cal frowned thoughtfully. "Maybe we could run up to Riverside tomorrow morning, and—"

"Shhh!" Plato turned up the volume and tipped his seat back. "It's starting."

Cal reclined her seat and helped finish the french fries while she watched the movie.

True to its billing, the film was thoughtful, intriguing, and very romantic.

Costner gave an excellent performance. But halfway through the movie, Cal realized she hadn't been paying much attention. For one thing, her thoughts kept drifting back to Plato's talk with Marietta Clemens, and the old woman's claim that the face in the *Beacon Journal* photo had belonged to her roommate.

What could it possibly mean? Who would abduct an old nursing home patient—however popular with the male occupants—murder her, and hide her bones in a medical school's skeleton collection?

If, instead, she had died from natural causes, Cal could simply check the woman's death certificate and determine where and how she had died. But then, why were her medical records missing from Sergei's files?

And what was the connection, if any, between the extra skeletons and Siegel Woman—and the Kingsbury Run Killer?

Surely the killer wasn't still around, living in a nursing home, as the *Cleveland Post* was suggesting.

Or was he?

Cal glanced across at Plato, wondering how he felt about the case. But he was a million miles away, totally enthralled by the movie. The flickering glow from the screen cast colorful shadows across his face; scenes and images registered in his eyes as his expressions and emotions shifted and merged with the action in the film.

Cal loved watching movies with Plato—as much for the shows themselves as for their effect on her husband. Oddly enough, that was one of the things which had attracted her to him. No matter how sappy, sentimental, or dimwitted the plot, he could ignore a film's shortcomings and be sucked into the characters' lives and stories. With the best of films, he became totally immersed. He was an empath—depressing films could bring him down for days, while uplifting movies could drag him up from the deepest gloom.

That same empathy attracted his patients to him as well. He had an honest listener's face, and a heart to match. He cared for his patients, deeply.

Maybe *too* deeply—like with Agnes Leighton. But he seemed to be learning from her. Learning a lesson he didn't want to be taught.

Learning to say good-bye.

Up on the screen, the characters were saying good-bye. Plato's eyes glistened in the pale blue light.

He glanced over at her. "This is kind of depressing, you know."

"I know." Across the bucket seats, they were holding hands. She leaned closer and nuzzled his neck. "But who says we have to watch it?"

"What do you mean?" He sounded appalled. "You want to leave, in the middle of the movie?"

"We don't *have* to leave." Cal sidled closer, hitched herself over the shifter knob, and pressed against him. She breathed in his ear, letting her hands roam across his broad chest. Casually, she unbuttoned his shirt and slipped her hands inside.

Breathing hard, he pulled away and stared at her. "You can't be—"

She silenced him with a kiss.

"Who would ever know?" she whispered. "We're in the last row, with nobody on either side." She pointed ahead to the Lumina. It was rocking slowly on its springs, back and forth, back and forth. "*They're* certainly not watching us."

"You're crazy." He scooted away again, pressing himself against the driver's side door.

She followed, a grinning Pepe LePew. "Ah, *l'amour*! My leetle dumpleeng, he wants to play zee hard to get, ees that eet?"

"I can see the *Plain Dealer* now." Plato shaped the headlines in big block type. "Front page—DEPUTY CORONER ARRESTED AT DRIVE-IN THEATER. PROMINENT GERIATRICIAN—"

He gasped. She had moved again, rearranged herself in the cramped seat, loosened some clothing, and made her point very convincingly.

"M-m-maybe we'd be more, uhh, comfortable in the back seat," he breathed.

The back seat was awkward and cramped, but very private. Especially after Cal draped two silk scarves over the two side windows.

Half an hour later, they reluctantly clambered back into the front of the Rabbit. Plato eyed her suspiciously.

"Pretty crafty, Cal. You planned this whole thing—the extra scarves in your purse, the way you wanted to park in the last row. So the screen wouldn't flicker, you told me. Hah!"

"Guilty as charged." Leaving over the gearshift, she nestled in the crook of his arm and smiled. "But you wanted a romantic evening, right?"

"Right. And I certainly got one." He squeezed her shoulders and let his arm drift down her back. Leaning closer, breathing into her hair, he whispered, "How about if we slip into the back seat for an encore?"

"I'd love to." Cal hitched herself up, wiped the heavy mist from the front windshield, and peered out. Up on the screen, the credits were rolling. Cars and vans were already clustering at the exit. "But I think we'd better not."

Plato sat up and squinted through the glass, disappointed. He turned up the sound and listened to the theme music for a moment. "I was hoping it would be a double feature."

"It *can* be," Cal pointed out. She tilted his head down and brushed his lips with hers. "We could go home and turn on the late movie. And not watch that either."

"Pretty crafty," Plato repeated admiringly. He dug the keys from his pocket, started the car, and headed for the exit. Glancing over at her, he flashed a LePew smile. "Thees time, your leetle dumpleeng *won't* play hard to get."

CHAPTER 11

"You need to get in shape," Homer Marley clucked critically. "You look like you just got clipped by a steamroller in the middle of the Boston Marathon."

"That's exactly how I feel," Plato groaned. "You lawyer types have a way with words."

Not that Plato agreed with his cousin about getting in shape. Homer hadn't just finished two weeks of grueling call, stayed up half the night imitating an amorous skunk, and woken with the sun to take his dog to the vet.

On the other hand, Homer *had* come to help work on the house today. And he would be keeping an eye on Foley tonight, and watching the house, and making sure their VCR actually taped the Ohio State-Michigan game.

And snarfing up the gallon of Plato's special chili that was defrosting on the kitchen table.

Sitting beside Homer on the edge of the newly finished section of roof, Plato eyed his cousin enviously. Plato was over six feet tall, but the assistant prosecutor was a full head taller and outweighed him by at least fifty pounds—all of it muscle. He was former running back for Willoughby South, and an almost-star for Ohio State.

In his spare time, Homer coached high school football in Shaker Heights. He'd helped lead the team to the playoffs for three years straight. In return, he had access to some of the finest weight-lifting equipment in town.

Plato hadn't lifted weights since high school. He hadn't been in serious shape since his freshman year at Kent State. Helping Homer drag the thirty-foot redwood rafters up the ladders paired beside the house, Plato's arms had quivered and shaken and threatened to give way. So Homer had moved the ladders closer together and shouldered most of the load, without breaking a sweat. Up at the top, he had heaved the rafters onto the bare joists like so much pine. He had handled the pine studs and collar ties like so much balsa wood.

Rebuilding the twenty-by-thirty section of roof had taken most of the day. Dismantling the sagging, dry-rotted rafters over the servants' quarters. Tossing the disgusting mess overboard, and trying not to picture the ground three stories down. Hauling the new rafters and studs and plywood up the ladders by hand, since Homer didn't trust the walls enough to use a winch. Measuring and cutting and drilling and hammering until Plato's arms were ready to fall off. Laying down the tar paper and shingles and trying hard to care whether they were straight.

And enduring Homer's patronizing concern for his lousy physical condition.

A tray of Sam Adams appeared at the edge of the roof, followed by a blond head.

"Beer, anyone?"

"Sounds great, Cal." Homer sprang to his feet, tightroped along the edge of the roof, and snagged the tray from Cal's grasp. Years of dancing along offensive lines and dodging hurtling tacklers had given him a grace that belied his size. He hefted the tray into the air, handed Cal over to Plato, and passed the bottles around. They all sat and dangled their legs over the edge of the roof.

Cal took a deep draught and sighed, smacking the foam from her lips. "That really hits the spot."

"Sure does." Homer belched loudly. "Pardon me."

Cal belched, even louder. The noise echoed back up from the ground below. "Think nothing of it."

She wrinkled her nose at Plato. "What's the matter? You look like you've been floating in Lake Erie for a couple of weeks."

"Thanks, Cal." Plato took a swig of beer and burped weakly. "Homer says I look like I just got clipped by a steamroller after winning the Boston Marathon."

"I didn't say *winning*," Homer corrected.

"I like your version better," Cal told the lawyer. She

squinted at Plato critically. "He's not bloated enough to be a floater. Not yet, anyway."

"Give him another few pounds." A grin creased Homer's wide face. "He'll get there."

"He's already *got* another few pounds." She poked Plato's belly and frowned. "Right here."

Homer and Cal chuckled together.

Their cheerfulness was downright nauseating. Cal had put in just as much work as Plato—probably more. Swarming up and down the ladders with tools and hardware, drilling pilot holes, driving screws and nails while Homer and Plato held the rafters in place, hammering the shingles down twice as fast as Plato and almost as fast as Homer.

Why was Plato so tired? They were probably right—he was sadly out of shape. That extra five pounds he'd put on since summer was edging up toward ten. His pants pinched his waistline. He huffed going up a flight of stairs.

He needed to eat right, exercise, lose weight.

Plato eyed his beer thoughtfully, then took another swallow. *Tomorrow.*

"So how's your Jane Doe coming along?" Homer asked Cal. "You got any leads on that skull you ran in the newspapers?"

"Not yet." Cal glanced at Plato, then back to Homer. "We got a few crackpot calls at the morgue, the usual stuff, but nothing has panned out."

"What are you bothering with it for, anyway?" He tipped his head back and drained the bottle in one long swallow. "I heard Jensson thinks those bones are really old. Ancient history. Maybe even something from the Kingsbury Run days."

Plato shuddered slightly, and patted his neck.

"There's more to it than that," Cal said quietly. She pulled her feet up from the edge and hugged her knees to her chest. "Maybe a lot more."

"Like four skeletons more," Plato said.

"What are you talking about?" Homer's dark eyebrows lowered suspiciously. "That picture in the papers came from the construction site at Siegel—right?"

"No." Cal shivered. "The Siegel skeleton didn't *have* a skull. Not that we could find, anyway."

Quickly, she explained Plato's theory that Siegel Woman

might have come from Sergei's skeleton collection. But she and Plato had learned that most of the Siegel skeletons were now at the Natural History Museum, joining the Hamann-Todd collection. Rather than showing that a skeleton was missing from the Siegel group, their interview with Alice Devon had disclosed four *extra* skeletons. Cal told Homer how none of the extra skeletons had charts or catalog numbers, and explained that Sergei's master list had disappeared.

Finally, she briefed him on the preparation of human skeletons for study and display. She told him about the dermestid colony at Siegel.

"The newspaper photo came from one of the four extra skeletons in the Hamann-Todd collection," Cal said. "Skeletons that came from Siegel."

"Blech." Homer eyed the foam in the bottom of his bottle as though it were a swarming mass of dermestids. He wrenched his gaze away and squinted at Cal. "So you think someone's been killing people, dumping them in with these bugs, and stashing their bones in Siegel's skeleton collection?"

"That's one possibility." Cal shook her head. "It sounds crazy, I know. But the other choice is just as crazy—who would want to steal a bunch of dead people's medical records? And why?"

Plato smiled slightly.

"What I don't get is, how did that other skeleton—your Siegel Woman—end up at the construction site?" Homer asked. "Why didn't the killer hide it in the collection, like the others?"

"I've been wondering about that." Cal pressed the half-full bottle to her forehead. "Maybe that skeleton was intended to join the collection, too. But it couldn't."

Plato nodded quickly. "Because the collection was already gone."

Homer's forehead wrinkled. "When was the Siegel collection moved to the museum?"

"A week ago," Cal replied. "Last Saturday."

"Wow." He absently peeled the label from his beer bottle. "That makes all this pretty recent, doesn't it?"

"Mmm-hmm." She frowned. "Only trouble is, the skeleton we found at Siegel really looked like it had been in the ground a long time. *That* part doesn't make any sense."

"You have any leads on identifying the skeleton from the dig?"

"A thin one. Very thin. Remember that girl who went missing from Case Western last spring?"

"The grad student?" Homer shrugged. "I thought she had psychiatric problems or something. They just decided she skipped town, right?"

"Yeah. She had a history of hopping from college to college, dropping out for long spells, and registering again somewhere else." Cal nodded. "She was a loner, and she supposedly had some psych problems, and nobody really pursued the case. You know how it is with missing persons." She sighed. "But she also had a history of a broken leg—the same type of fracture that we found in the skeleton at Siegel."

"You're kidding." The lawyer rubbed his forehead wearily.

"Afraid not. Anyway, Siegel Woman's skeleton looks like it's been sitting in the ground for a lot longer than a few months. But we're still going to track down that student's X rays and compare them with the bones we found."

"This case is getting too complicated for me."

"It gets even more complicated." She waved her bottle at Plato. "One of his patients thought the photo in the papers looked like her old roommate at the nursing home."

"Really?" Homer perked up a little.

"Only trouble is, the lady is pretty demented." Cal sighed. "She thought her roommate was still alive."

Homer frowned, and shot a glance at Plato. "Think there's anything to it?"

"Maybe." He nodded slowly. "Marietta was pretty bright, before all her memory problems started. Her judgment and thinking are *still* in pretty good shape, considering what she's been through." He took a long pull of beer and stared out across the bright trees lining the black asphalt of the driveway, remembering Marietta's wonder at the autumn colors. "She lived with Louise Higgins for a few years. Facial recognition is one of the last things to go. And Marietta seemed pretty sure of herself."

Even more sure than she had been of recognizing her own doctor, Plato reflected.

"Did anyone else think the photo looked like Louise Higgins?" Cal asked.

"I checked around with some of my other patients, and with a few of the nurses. Nobody was really certain." He sighed. "Trouble is, Lou died last year. A lot of the nurses float between units, so it's hard for them to recognize all the faces— especially a year later."

"Why not get a picture from the family?" Homer suggested. "That way, you could compare for yourself."

Cal winced. "Politically, that's a little tricky. If her skeleton is really one of the extras, and Siegel lost track of them, the family could get pretty upset." She shrugged. "Anyway, we don't need a photo. We're going to check Louise Higgins's medical chart. We can be much more certain that way."

"If she *has* a chart." Plato set his beer bottle in the gutter, leaned back on his elbows, and stared up at the tall clouds swirling overhead. "I called Medical Records at Riverside this morning—just before you got there, Homer. They said they'd check around for her chart and try to pull it for me by Monday."

"I wonder if they'll be able to find it," Cal mused.

Somewhere, far away, a phone was ringing. Plato glanced at Cal. Cal glanced at Plato.

"Your turn." She smiled sweetly. "I got the beer."

Reluctantly, he climbed to his feet, stretched a few of the kinks from his legs, and paced over to the ladder. Holding tightly to the rungs, he lowered himself slowly and painfully to the ground. He counted fifteen rings by the time he hobbled across the front porch. Over the door hung Homer's seven-foot-long Ohio State Buckeyes flag.

He pushed it aside and hurried in, snagging the phone on the sixteenth ring.

"Hello?"

"Hello, is Cal—?" The voice halted, embarrassed. "Oh, I'm sorry. I must have the wrong number."

The man's voice was high-pitched and hasty—a rapid-fire squeak, full of New England inflections. Like an anxious Boston chihuahua.

"Wait a min—" Plato protested.

But the caller had already hung up.

"What the hell?" He stared at the phone a minute before hanging up and heading back outside.

"Who was it?" Cal asked.

"Wrong number," Plato replied. He frowned at Cal, and sprawled beside her on the roof again.

"So you looked up Louise Higgins's death certificate," Homer was saying.

Cal nodded. "Bleeding ulcer. She died at Riverside General. I hope they can find her chart, but I don't think they will. After all, the chart *should* have been in Sergei's files."

They were all quiet for a long moment.

"I don't get it," Homer said finally. "If that lady died a natural death, and she's got a legal death certificate, why would anyone bother to hide her bones? Or steal her medical records?"

Cal shook her head. "I don't know. It doesn't make any sense."

"Malpractice," Plato said quietly.

She frowned at him. "What?"

"Malpractice," he repeated. "That would explain it."

"What does malpractice have to do with four—no, *five*—extra skeletons popping up at a medical college?" Homer asked. "You think some doc is screwing up, and turning his dead patients into skeletons so no one can sue him?"

Homer chuckled, but Cal was nodding thoughtfully.

"In a way," Plato said. "But the doctor didn't *have* to put the body in with the dermestids. Sergei already did that for him."

"Now you're saying that old anatomist is in on this?" Homer's eyes widened. "Some kind of conspiracy? Come on, Plato. You really *have* been working too hard."

"He doesn't mean Sergei is part of it." Cal took another sip of beer and rested her bottle in the gutter beside Plato's. "He's saying that the charts were stolen after the bodies were donated to Siegel. Right, Plato?"

"Exactly. If those people died because of a pattern of malpractice, their doctor may have destroyed the charts later on, to cover his tracks."

Homer spent a few moments digesting Plato's theory. Finally, he nodded.

"So all we have to do is get the medical records for those extra skeletons, find the common threat, and nail the doctor who's responsible." Homer waved a hand. "Simple, right?"

"Except for one thing," Cal said. "If those medical records really are missing or destroyed, we may *never* be able to identify those skeletons—let alone figure out who their doctor was."

Homer nodded. "And I just thought of another problem." He sighed. "If you do match those bones from the excavation site with that missing student from Case, where does *she* fit in?"

Cal nodded thoughtfully. "The student's death obviously wouldn't have been malpractice. She was healthy when she disappeared. But even if she had died at one of the local hospitals, the missing persons check would have identified her."

"That's assuming you get a match with the Case student," Plato protested. "But if that skeleton's really as old as Cal thinks—"

"Oh, my God!" Homer stared at his watch and leaped to his feet.

"What's wrong?" Plato sat up, alarmed.

"It's after six o'clock!" Homer raced to the ladder and slid down the rails like a veteran firefighter fleeing a collapsing high-rise. "I've got to shower and turn the game on!"

Plato poked his head over the edge of the roof. "But kickoff isn't until seven."

Homer paused for a moment at the bottom of the ladder. He windmilled his arms in wild exasperation and shouted up the side of the house. "Pregame! Started ten minutes ago!"

Cal frowned as she watched the lawyer retreat into the house. "I think Homer must have some serious money riding on this game."

"Homer doesn't gamble on football," Plato replied. "Just investments."

"But he's been awfully keyed up today," Cal observed. "Kind of *rabid*, you know? He's hardly talked about anything but the game all day." She sighed. "Of course, both teams *are* undefeated. Maybe that explains it."

Plato shook his head. He was thinking of those long-ago Saturday afternoons perched in front of the black-and-white TV with Homer while they watched Archie Griffin gallop over rushing records as Woody Hayes mixed it up with the media, remembering the years his cousin had trained and played and dreamed of making The Team, picturing Homer's sick despair when he missed the final cut at Ohio State.

The depression hadn't lasted long, though. Homer had turned his massive energies to his studies, eventually graduat-

ing fifth in his law school class. But at least a couple of weekends each year, he still made the three-hour pilgrimage down
to the shrine for a few of the home games.

"I thought *you* were bad," Cal concluded. "But Homer's
even worse."

"It's kind of a religious thing," Plato explained. "I'm just a
convert. But Homer's a True Believer."

From somewhere inside the house, the Ohio State fight song
was playing, loud enough to send vibrations up through the
new roof. The True Believer was singing in the shower, loud
enough to drown out the fight song.

"I sort of wish we could stay to watch the game," Cal said
wistfully. "Maybe if you called, and told them I was sick—"

"Shame on you." Plato frowned sternly. "Thaddeus Crumm
is probably rolling over in his grave."

"I doubt it—old Thaddeus went to Ohio State, too." Cal
paced over to the ladder. "Another True Believer. He's probably parked on a cloud somewhere, watching the pregame show
with Woody Hayes."

CHAPTER 12

"Don't even *dream* of turning that radio on."

Cal's voice slashed through the darkness like a surgical steel dissecting knife. Plato's hand jerked away from the tuner knob.

"What's wrong?" He frowned across the car at Cal. "I was just turning some music on."

"It's seven-fifteen," Cal pointed out. "The game started fifteen minutes ago. No matter what station we listen to, some goofy deejay is bound to shout the score between songs."

Plato nodded grimly. Before leaving the house, they had programmed the VCR with all the care and diligence of a pair of Swiss watchmakers setting a time bomb. They had left explicit instructions for Homer to check the machine and make sure it started on time. They had warned him of dire consequences if he breathed a word about the game before they watched the tape.

Plato had also left a sheet of instructions and medications for Foley's care, along with his pager number in case of emergency.

"Gotcha," Plato told Cal. "Strict radio silence."

"Anyway," she added, "there's plenty for us to talk about."

"Like what?"

"Like your theory about those skeletons." She smiled ferally, her teeth gleaming in the passing street lamps like a flickering Cheshire cat's. She oozed across the seats, sidled up beneath his arm, and purred into his ear. "Let's hear it, Sherlock."

"Hear what?" Plato asked innocently. He was studying the road, carefully piloting the Rabbit around Dead Man's Curve beneath the heart of Cleveland. Speed bumps whumped through the tired suspension, threatening to rattle the old car to pieces. The unbanked curve dragged the wheels left, and pressed Cal's shoulder into Plato's ribs.

Finally, they emerged again into city light and moonlight as I–90 wove its way east along the shore of Lake Erie. Lakefront Airport hulked in the darkness beside them; farther back, the Rock and Roll Museum glittered like a pyramid for electric Pharaohs.

Beside him, Cal stirred impatiently.

"Don't play innocent with me. *Something* put that malpractice idea into your head."

"Raw brainpower, Cal." He eased into the right lane. "Deductive reasoning."

"Lucky guessing."

"Maybe a little of both." Plato shrugged, and decided to spill the beans. Too bad there weren't very many beans.

"I hadn't heard that Lou died of aplastic anemia," he continued. "Not until you said so. Still, it's probably just a coincidence."

She lifted her head. "What's a coincidence?"

"About Albert Windgartner." He eased the Rabbit onto the exit ramp at MLK Drive. "That patient I had to see late Monday night, remember? He's on the boards of trustees at Siegel and Riverside General."

"I know." she smirked. "And his daughter's an old flame of yours, right?"

"Old flame? Erica Windgartner?" He chuckled bravely, but felt his face warming in the darkness. "Whatever put that idea—"

"Don't bother denying it, Plato. You're a *terrible* liar."

They were stopped at a traffic signal. Cal squinted at his face in the darkness. "Your *ears* are turning red. How cute!"

"It's the stop light," he protested. But the signal had already changed to green.

"Don't worry about Erica." She patted his shoulder. "You weren't the first man in my life, either. Just the best."

"Thanks, Cal." Plato eased the Rabbit into gear. "Exactly how many of us were there?"

"Oh, one or two dozen." She giggled. "I stopped counting

after Philbert Eggleston. He proposed to me during my first year at Northwestern—after three dates."

"What did you tell him?"

"I said I wanted to get my medical degree first." She sighed. "Kind of shocked him—he thought I was in fashion design. I never saw him again."

"You probably scared him off. You professional women can be pretty intimidating."

"We sure can." She eyed him critically. "Speaking of professional women, why didn't you stay together with Erica? I've met her—she seems like a great person."

Cal's voice was casual—she might have been asking Plato why he preferred steak to lobster. Weaving along the dark and winding road, he wondered. For the first time in years, he wondered.

Why *had* he broken up with Erica?

She was dizzyingly attractive—almost as pretty as Cal. Tall, lithe, and vibrant. Bright and witty, but honest and straightforward. And very intelligent.

In short, just about everything he wanted in a woman. Almost perfect.

Maybe *too* perfect. Like a beautiful, fragile ice sculpture—their growing closeness had somehow seemed to mar her perfection. And as time went on, he felt a wall rising between them—an invisible layer of Freon that kept him from getting too close.

It wasn't Erica's fault. She had seemed as frustrated, as confused as Plato. The icy wall was something neither of them had made. She had tried to tear it down, to break free. And so had Plato. He just couldn't melt her gently enough.

It was something he never really understood. But at the time, he'd suspected it had something to do with her father.

"Kind of personal, huh?" Cal patted his arm, content to drop the subject.

"Not really." Plato shook his head. "Just hard to explain. Part of it was her father. He started getting really sick, and I was his doctor, and Erica had to take over the controls at his business. She got really involved with her work and her father, and we kind of drifted apart. After a while, everything got to be kind of awkward." He shrugged. "I guess we just realized we weren't right for each other."

"I'm glad." She sat up and took a deep breath. "So. What were we talking about?"

"Albert Windgartner." Plato frowned. "He has aplastic anemia, just like Louise Higgins did."

"So?"

"So it just jogged my memory. I got to thinking about that experimental drug they're testing for aplastic anemia. It's supposed to stimulate blood cell production. Albert is taking it, and I'll bet Lou was on it, too." He shook his head. "It doesn't work very well."

"*Lots* of drugs don't work very well. You know that." Cal drew away and sat back in her seat. "That doesn't make it malpractice."

"I know, I know." Plato eased the car through another intersection and into the confusing asphalt maze surrounding Wade Park. The VA hospital squatted in the trees off to the left, while the Gothic spires and stonework of Case Western were visible just across the park. A snarling dinosaur banner flapped from a light pole, pointing the way to the Natural History Museum.

"Anyway," she continued, "no drug developer is going to come to Cleveland and steal medical charts just because his product is lousy."

"He wouldn't have to *come* to Cleveland," Plato pointed out. "Marvin Tucker—the hematologist at Riverside—invented the drug with his partner. They're just testing it locally—it's in the first phase of human trials. They're only using it on people with especially bad prognoses. People who probably won't live anyway."

Even as he said it, Plato winced. Somehow, admitting that Albert Windgartner's chances were so slim seemed to shrink the old developer's odds even further.

"If all those people were bound to die anyway, why would any doctor worry about malpractice?"

"Maybe the drug makes them worse," Plato said. "Makes them die even quicker. Or maybe the developers are fudging their results, claiming that people live longer than they do."

"I suppose it's possible. Except for one thing." As they pulled into the parking lot, Cal plucked a mirror from her purse and checked her makeup. She freshened her lipstick and snapped her purse shut again. "Tucker is a great doc, and a fine researcher."

"I know. Tucker is integrity itself." He nodded glumly. "Like I said, it's probably just a coincidence."

"Probably," she agreed. "But I still like your malpractice idea. It's worth checking into. *If* we can identify some of those skeletons."

"Too bad we don't have Sergei's master list." He parked and set the brake. "We still don't know if we have too many skeletons or too few charts."

"Exactly."

Plato climbed out of the car, darted around to Cal's side, and opened the door. She eased herself up on her high-heeled shoes, smoothed the black taffeta dress, patted her hair, and flashed a bright smile at Plato.

"How do I look?"

Her eyes shone like melted copper. Her pale skin was smooth as satin. Moonlight danced in her hair.

"How do you look?" Hands on her shoulders, he held her at arm's length and marched his eyes over her like a drill sergeant inspecting a raw recruit. "How do you look?" He beamed. "Like the first star to sparkle on a clear summer evening. Like a lonesome man's fondest dream."

She sniffed his breath. "That beer must have hit you harder than I thought."

"Like a Thaddeus Crumm Award winner." He pulled her close, careful not to muss her dress or her hair or her makeup. "You're going to dazzle them, Cal."

"Come on then, Zipkin." She held out her arm for him. "Let's go inside."

The Museum of Natural History had been transformed. A gleaming parquet dance floor had been spread across the main lobby, just in front of the tireless Foucault pendulum. An ace swing band blew easy rhythms from a corner, loud enough to set a mood, but soft enough to let conversation flow. A vast portable bar was doing a brisk trade beside the traveling dinosaur exhibit. Nearby, a dozen long tables were heaped with enough cheese and crackers and dips and fancy breads to feed a hungry stegosaurus family for a month.

Off in the Sears Hall of Human Ecology, an orchestra of

chefs and scurrying assistants were tuning their instruments between a huge tyrannosaurus model and a lounging lion family diorama. All the stuffed animals in the room—from the timber wolves and snarling bears to the alligators and the eagle—stared hungrily at the sautéed duck and broiled lamb with beady glass eyes.

The turnout was far greater than Plato had expected. Tables were scattered throughout the entire museum, from the edges of the lobby all the way back to the dimmest reaches of the earth science rooms. The front of the museum was a seething mass of medical humanity, draped in suits and tuxedoes and evening gowns.

Plato bulldozed through the crush, shaking hands, flashing smiles, seeing all the familiar faces he met every day in the wards and conference rooms of Riverside General, and marveling at their transformation. The grumpy old surgeons looked like kindly grandfathers now, and the cliquish in-crowd of internists greeted him and Cal with toasts and grins like a band of pleasure boaters welcoming a few more revelers on board. Between whispered worries about profit and loss, even the hospital administrators' faces cracked with occasional smiles.

For one night a year, at the Medical Staff Dinner-Dance, the upper echelons at Riverside General kicked up their heels, let down their guards, tossed back a few drinks, and relaxed. Monday morning, it would be turf wars and infighting and backbiting as usual.

Cal guided Plato past the tyrannosaurus and the duck, the lions and the lamb, through the room with the burial mounds and the huge dugout canoe, to the Kirtland Hall of Prehistoric Life at the back of the museum. The vast space featured the skeletons of a saber-toothed tiger and a woolly mammoth, an anatosaurus and a triceratops. But the cavernous chamber was dominated by an enormous, fully articulated skeleton of an adult haplocanthosaurus. The animal's ankles were taller than Plato. Its leg bones were as thick as redwood trunks. Its head and neck loomed like a builder's crane.

Directly beneath the haplocanthosaurus was a single table. Only four of its ten chairs were taken, tipped against the table and staked out with purses and jackets. Six seats remained.

"That's it!" Cal sprinted across the hall and tagged two of the chairs. She grinned at him. "This will be perfect!"

Standing beside her, Plato tilted his head back.

"I can see why nobody wanted this side of the table," he said. The head and neck were swaying twenty feet up, directly over their chairs. "I just hope that cable holds out for another few hours."

"Silly." She grabbed his arm and led him back to the crowd at the front of the museum. "Come on. Let's get some drinks and mingle."

Back at the bar, Plato ordered white wine for Cal and a light beer for himself.

"Nice turnout tonight," he told the bartender. "Kind of surprising, with the big game going on."

"No kidding." The bartender nodded as he poured the white wine. "Didn't want to work tonight, but I had to." He grinned at Plato and pointed to a small television tucked just behind the bar. "I'm keeping up, anyway. Ohio State's down, ten to three."

Wincing, Plato turned away in time to catch a glimpse of Cal standing near the cheese and crackers. She was talking to someone as she loaded up her plate. A tall, willowy blonde with perfect legs and a knockout figure. Cal was chatting with her like they were old friends.

Plato spun around just in time to stop the bartender.

"Hold that beer," he told him. "You got any single-malt scotch?"

"Sure thing." The bartender dug out a bottle of Macallan.

Plato nodded. Across the room, Cal and Erica Windgartner were laughing now. Cal glanced over at Plato and grinned.

"Better make it a double," Plato said. "And don't bother with the ice."

"You got a bet riding on the game, huh?" the bartender asked. "And no TV." He clucked sympathetically. "It's going to be a long night for you."

"It sure is."

He threaded his way through the crowd and handed Cal her wine.

"Look who's here," she said.

"Hi, Erica." Plato sipped his scotch. "I heard from my partner this morning. He tells me your father's looking a little better."

"He is." Erica smiled. "I was just telling Cal that I'm keeping my fingers crossed."

She looked stunning tonight—long blond hair pulled up to highlight the fine lines of her neck and shoulders, diamond earrings dangling from perfect, shell-like ears, diamond necklace plunging toward the low décolletage of her shimmering scarlet dress.

Plato pulled his gaze away and glanced over at Cal. "I didn't realize you two knew each other."

"Erica is the board's liaison with Laboratory Services," Cal explained. "We see each other all the time at Riverside General—at planning committee meetings, quality assurance surveys, and so on."

"We have lunch together almost every week," Erica added.

"How nice." Plato took a hefty swig of scotch. His eyes teared. It was like swallowing a smoldering stick of dynamite. The dynamite exploded in his stomach.

"We've gotten to be pretty good friends." Cal grinned. "We have a lot of similar interests."

"Similar tastes." Erica smiled.

They eyed Plato and chuckled together. Cal pointed at the sides of her husband's head.

"See what I mean—about his ears?"

"You're *right*." Erica stepped closer to study the glowing beacons. When she spoke, Plato could feel her breath on his neck. She glanced over at Cal. "They're so *bright*. I wonder if they glow in the dark."

"Nope." Cal sipped her wine and smacked her lips. "I can tell you for certain that they do *not* glow in the dark."

"Too bad. It could be kind of *interesting*, you know?"

Standing between them, ears flaming, a painful smile plastered on his face, Plato took another swallow of scotch. He felt like an object, an animal—the prizewinning pig at the county fair, being admired by a pair of pork-loving gourmands. Soon they would size up his haunches and hams, trade notes on his loins, admire his shanks and compare them with other boars they'd enjoyed in the past.

"Oink," said Plato.

They ignored him.

"Speaking of the dark," Erica said, "did I ever tell you about the time Plato and I—"

"Hello, dear." A tall, handsome man had appeared at Erica's elbow. He pecked her cheek and patted her shoulder with two fingers, as though to dust a speck of lint from her dress. "Sorry I'm late. You look fabulous."

His words were delivered mechanically, like lines from a ritual. Perhaps they were. Everything about the man smacked of order, precision, perfection. Each silver-black hair on his head might have been arranged with tweezers and shellacked into place. His gleaming black tuxedo was obviously not a rental—it fit him like the casing on a rifle shell. Even his smile was perfectly orchestrated, an army of teeth standing at parade rest.

The man looked vaguely familiar to Plato—the way a network news anchor looks familiar even when you've never seen him before.

He flashed the perfect smile at Plato and Cal, and fluttered a questioning eyebrow at Erica.

"Steven, this is Plato and Cal Marley," She said. "They're both doctors at Riverside. Plato is a geriatrician—he has several patients at Wyndhaven Colony."

"Yes, of course." Steven extended one hand and squeezed Plato's upper arm with the other, like a president welcoming a foreign emissary to the White House. His voice was a deep, dignified rumble. "I thought you looked familiar. I'm Steven Prescott."

"Steven is Dad's right-hand man," Erica explained. "He manages most of our nursing homes—especially Wyndhaven Colony."

Plato smiled. "It's a fine retirement center, Mr. Prescott."

Now Plato remembered why Steven Prescott looked familiar. They had passed each other in the halls at Wyndhaven a few times—usually late at night, when the poor guy was just leaving for the day. The retirement center ran like clockwork; now Plato knew why.

"Call me Steven. And thanks." He shrugged. "But I think most of the credit for Wyndhaven's success has to go to the staff. They make an excellent team."

Over the museum's speaker system, the quavery voice of

Riverside General's chief of staff announced that dinner was being served.

"I hope we can find someplace to sit," Erica fretted. "All these tables look full."

"There were a few open spots at our table," Cal suggested. "Back with the dinosaur skeletons."

"That sounds perfect." Steven Prescott glanced over to the bar. "Would you ladies like me to freshen your drinks?"

He and Plato headed back to the bar while Erica and Cal hurried off to stake out the empty places. Plato ordered another scotch. The first drink was hitting him hard; his head felt like it was stuffed with cotton. But a little more numbness would be welcome—especially if he had to sit between Cal and Erica for the whole evening.

"Do you have many patients at Wyndhaven?" Steven asked. He was resting his elbows on the bar, waiting for their drinks and glancing at the bartender's television.

"Forty or so," Plato replied. "And my partner has about ten. Mostly in the nursing home."

Steven turned away from the screen and squinted at Plato. "You're Albert's doctor, aren't you?"

Plato nodded.

"I thought so. When I came by to visit yesterday, you were walking out of his room." He sipped his drink and frowned. "How is he, anyway?"

"A little better," Plato said carefully. "Touch and go. But I think he might make it."

The administrator sighed. "I hope so. Erica is just devastated by the whole thing. But at the same time, I don't think she realizes how serious this is. If Albert dies, our company—"

"Interception!" the bartender cried. His television was propped up on the bar now. A dozen doctors, young and old, male and female, were clustered around the six-inch screen like medical students witnessing their first code blue.

Steven and Plato turned around just in time to watch a Buckeye cornerback sprint up the sideline and dance his way to the end zone.

The crowd erupted, both on screen and off. Someone jostled Plato, and he stumbled against the bar.

"You doctor types are pretty wild." Steven grinned, lifting

two of the drinks high in the air. "We'd better go find our table before we end up wearing these."

Cal and Erica were waiting for them beneath the haplocanthosaurus. Steven sat beside Erica, and Plato set his glass down between Erica and Cal. Glancing around the table, he wished he had brought the whole bottle of Macallan along.

Sitting directly across from him was Dr. Emmaus Feinstein, the former chairman of obstetrics and gynecology at Riverside. Until he finally stepped down last year, Feinstein had been the bane of obstetrics residents, and the terror of family practice and surgery residents who happened to rotate on his service.

The old department chairman had been in peak form seven years ago, when Plato had been a lowly family practice intern. Late one night, against one head nurse's advice, Plato had allowed one of Feinstein's VIP patients to give birth before the old physician arrived from his home. When Feinstein finally showed up, ten minutes after Plato delivered the baby, he was furious. Why hadn't his patient received Demerol? Why hadn't she been instructed to blow through her contractions? Why hadn't she been told to stop pushing?

Most of all, whose idea was it to wheel her into the delivery room ten minutes before the Attending Physician arrived?

Dr. Plato Marley, the head nurse had explained.

An *intern*? A *family practice* intern had delivered his patient's baby?

Feinstein was incredulous. He wanted Plato's head, on a silver platter. He wanted Plato kicked out of the family practice residency program. He wanted Plato's medical license revoked.

Fortunately, he had no power to do any of that. Especially when the chief obstetrical resident reviewed the monitor records and found that the baby's heart had shown dangerous deceleration patterns just before delivery. Patterns that might have led to brain damage or death if delivery had been delayed. The chief resident herself had been busy with an emergency cesarean section during the crisis—there hadn't even been time for Plato to consult with her.

All the same, Feinstein had kicked Plato off his service. And so young Dr. Marley had finished his obstetrics rotations at another hospital across town.

Clearly, Feinstein hadn't forgotten. He was glaring across

SKELETONS IN THE CLOSET   131

the table at Plato like a surgeon discovering a particularly nasty tumor during a routine appendectomy.

Head filled with cotton, Plato sipped his scotch and stared back. He waved at Emmaus Feinstein. He smiled. He grinned. He positively beamed.

For while mulling over their ancient feud, Plato had made an important discovery. He realized that Feinstein now had no power over him. In fact, Plato's very presence at this table was probably the former department chairman's worst nightmare come true. The lowly intern he once tried to squash was now a member of the medical staff, a member of the faculty. A fellow attending physician who could sit across from him at the annual Medical Staff Dinner-Dance and ruin his meal.

"Plato Marley," Feinstein spat. His eyes were as shiny and dark and angry as the crocodile's in the next room. "I'm surprised they let you graduate."

"Hey there, Em." Plato touched his forehead in a mock salute. "Gutted any interns lately?"

CHAPTER 13

Plato held his breath, waiting for Feinstein's response, eagerly awaiting the confrontation he'd never had the power to pursue as an intern. Waiting for the chance to finally say all the lines he'd dreamed up during those long cross-town journeys to the obstetrics department of the other hospital. Spoiling for a fight.

But he never got the chance. Feinstein simply took his wife's hand and stood.

"Come on, Ruth." He glared around the table. "Let's go eat with some civilized human beings."

As the couple walked away, Plato's fury withered like a collapsing balloon. He glanced at Cal.

"God. I never realized he was so *sensitive*."

"Believe me, he's not." Marvin Tucker, the famous hematologist, had just taken the seat beside Cal. He adjusted the carnation in the lapel of his tuxedo jacket. "I'm sure his leaving had nothing to do with you, Plato."

They watched the white-haired obstetrician wander off between the tables, his wife trailing behind him like a stray puppy. Tucker ran his hands through his thinning black hair and frowned at Feinstein's retreating back.

"I'm quite certain he left because of me." Tucker shrugged, and his voice dropped to a whisper.

"Because of you?" Cal asked.

"Yes. But that was a long time ago." The hematologist removed his Lennon-style wire-rimmed glasses and pinched the bridge of his long, hooked nose. He turned to Cal. "I understand you'll be receiving an award tonight."

Cal nodded. "The Thaddeus Crumm Award. Whatever that is."

Tucker smiled genially. "It's very impressive, that's what it is." He sent his eyes around the table. "We're all quite privileged to have the first Thaddeus Crumm prizewinner dining with us tonight."

Marvin Tucker was one of Riverside's old guard. The wrinkles and seams at the corners of his mouth and eyes showed that the black tint of his hair came from a bottle. But his smile was genuine enough. And despite his national prominence, he was one of the most personable attending physicians on Riverside's staff. Plato had spent a month on his service during his family practice residency. Tucker was the polar opposite of Feinstein.

The hematologist's quiet voice and unassuming manner tended to make listeners strain to hear what he had to say. All around the table, heads were tilted forward and eyes were riveted to Tucker's face.

"Most people probably don't remember Thaddeus Crumm," Tucker drawled. He fingered his string tie. Plato had never seen a string tie worn with a tuxedo before, but it looked natural on Tucker. The old hematologist had grown up in Wyoming; the string ties and snakeskin boots were part of his hospital uniform. Plato had no doubt that the famous boots were crossed beneath the table, and that they would look perfectly natural with the tuxedo.

"Hell, Crumm was already an old man by the time I started my residency at Riverside," Tucker continued. "But he was a great teacher. Incredibly popular with the residents." The hematologist's thin lips stretched in a grin. "His insistence on paying them a living wage probably had something to do with his popularity. And he played a big part in getting Siegel Medical College launched, and keeping it afloat. Cal Marley here will be the first person to receive the prize named after him."

He nodded to her. "I should also tell you that this award was the residents' idea. They wanted to recognize the best educators at the hospital, and encourage us all to be better teachers. All the residents and interns voted, and Cal Marley was the runaway favorite."

The entire table applauded, and Plato joined in. He was quite impressed. Despite her obligations at the medical school and the morgue, Cal still spent half of her time at the hospital—down in the pathology lab, over in the lecture hall, or up on the floors with the residents. She put in a lot of late nights preparing lectures, sorting slides, or sifting through cases for the doctors-in-training. She was a natural teacher—tireless and patient, delivering impromptu lectures on subjects ranging from how to read a blood smear to the latest research on forensic DNA analysis.

Her devotion also explained why she rarely made it home for dinner.

"Quite an achievement," Steven rumbled.

"I'm not surprised." Erica nodded. "Cal sure has taught *me* a lot." She patted Plato's arm. "Your wife is always explaining things to me at those meetings, and translating medicalese for me."

After hearing Tucker's words and the table's applause, it was *Cal's* turn to blush. Plato peered at the sides of her head.

"Look at that!" he exclaimed. "Your *ears* are turning red. How *cute!*"

Beneath the table, she kicked him in the shin.

Marvin Tucker waved to a couple standing across the room, near the wooly mammoth. Heads craned, they were scanning tables, obviously searching for some open seats.

Finally, they spotted Tucker's frantic motions and drifted over.

"Looking for someplace to eat, Phillip?" Tucker pointed to the Feinsteins' recently vacated chairs. "Here's a couple of good spots. I drove their owners away."

The hematologist glanced around the table and gestured to the newcomers. "I'm sure many of you know my partner, Phillip Andersen. And this beautiful woman is his wife, Cheryl."

Phillip and Cheryl slid into their seats and smiled around the table as Tucker introduced them to Plato, Cal, Erica, and Steven. And to the other couple at the table—a pretty young pediatrician and her husband, who had been sitting quietly on the other side of the table and holding furtive conversations behind their napkins. The pediatrician was new to Riverside General; Plato had seen her only once or twice in the hallways near the toddler floor. Yet Tucker knew her name, and her husband's name, and probably the names of their children and pets. To the hematologist, networking came as naturally as breathing. His practice thrived because of it.

So it wasn't surprising that Marvin Tucker had eventually needed a partner. Phillip Andersen had joined Tucker's practice five or six years ago. He was quite a bit younger than his partner, though older than Plato and Cal. With his longish blond hair, broad shoulders, and blue eyes, he looked more like a seafaring Norseman than a hematologist. Even sitting down, he towered over Marvin Tucker, making the older man seem small and insignificant. Andersen's wife was equally striking, with enormous brown eyes, auburn hair dangling nearly to her waist, and a petite figure cinched up tight in a short knit party dress. As Tucker introduced her, she shot him an unreadable glance.

"Phillip will be taking over my practice someday soon," Tucker was saying. "Once I retire."

Andersen chuckled. "Hopefully, that won't be for quite a while yet."

"We'll see." Tucker replied with a smile. "I just might quit while I'm ahead."

A waiter silently drifted over and motioned them toward the buffet table with all the solemnity of an undertaker herding visitors toward a casket.

Standing, Tucker turned to his partner. "I've been going through my old papers—I found some interesting data from one of our studies. Some unusual patterns."

"What kind of patterns?" Phillip asked.

"I'll fill you in on Monday."

Following several paces behind, Plato saw that the old hematologist was indeed wearing his snakeskin boots. And they actually did match perfectly with the tuxedo. Plato was sure no one else could carry it off.

"I can't decide whether to get the duck or the lamb," Cal was saying.

"Get both," Plato suggested. "That's what I'm going to do."

She frowned, pinching his waist through his suit jacket. "I can feel a lot more than an inch here."

Plato winced. "That's just the suit. Heavy padding."

"Look, Steven." Beside them, Erica was pointing ahead to the buffet tables. "They have some delicious-looking vegetable entrees."

"How exciting." Steven grimaced at Plato and Cal. "Erica's

trying to convert me to vegetarianism. It's quite a challenge, but it's worth it."

He glanced at his fiancée meaningfully. Plato wondered if he maintained his diet during lunches, when Erica wasn't around.

Standing beside the buffet table, watching Plato load his dish with rack of lamb and sautéed duck, Cal nudged him and whispered, "*Now* I know why you didn't marry Erica. You'd have starved to death."

Dutifully, Steven piled his plate with salad, spinach quiche, and steamed vegetables. Erica smiled approvingly, and grimaced as Plato topped his lamb and duck with a rich, dark gravy.

"That stuff is *full* of saturated fat," she warned.

"That's why it tastes so good," Plato replied.

Back at the table, Marvin Tucker was leaning back in his chair to study the haplocanthosaurus skull dangling high overhead. As Plato and Cal sat down, he grinned.

"At least sixty-six million years old. Amazing, isn't it?"

Cal nodded. "As a forensic pathologist, I'm always impressed that bones can last that long—even as fossils."

"I'm impressed that the *cable* has lasted that long," Plato said.

"You've got a point." Steven nudged his chair slightly to the left. "That thing could crush us to a pulp if it ever fell."

Tucker chuckled and calmly buttered a roll. "I'm sure our deaths would be swift and painless."

"It's so *huge*." Across the table, the pediatrician—whose name Plato had already forgotten—was staring at the body of the creature.

"No kidding." Erica gestured at the enormous legs. "Our ancestors could have made clubs out of this fellow's foot bones."

"And roasted his drumsticks over an open fire." Steven stabbed a piece of broccoli, forked it into his mouth, and frowned. "I wonder what haplocantho-whatever tasted like."

"No one has ever tasted haplocanthosaurus." The pediatrician's husband was shaking his head. "No *humans*, anyway. Our most primitive ancestors didn't come along until two million years ago—over sixty million years after the big dinosaurs died out. *True* humans have only been around for the past couple of hundred thousand years—an eyeblink in the history of life on earth."

"Robert teaches high school science," his wife said with a sigh. She patted her husband's arm fondly. "He's always correcting me."

"It must be an interesting job," Tucker said. "And rather challenging, I suppose."

"*Very* challenging," Robert agreed dryly. "Although I've had some wonderful opportunities. I once took a dozen advanced students on a weeklong dinosaur dig during summer vacation. We helped unearth most of a triceratops skeleton near the Slickrock Trail in Utah."

"Fascinating," Tucker said. "I would love to do something like that. Think of it—the thrill of actually discovering a dinosaur bone that's been buried for millions of years." He leaned back in his chair and crossed his arms. "I grew up out west, near dinosaur country. Used to hunt for fossils all the time. But I never found anything besides cow bones and a few coyotes."

"We got lucky," Robert said. "We had a good guide. And a great group of kids."

"*I* could never do something like that," Steven said. "Take charge of a dozen kids for a week. I have a hard enough time dealing with adults."

"Steven manages several of my father's properties," Erica explained. "Especially Wyndhaven Colony." She glanced at Steven with a sly smile. "Of course, *that's* more of a partnership."

"That reminds me," Tucker said. He turned to Erica. "I've been meaning to talk to you. I'd like to do some research—"

"Your attention, please. Your attention, please." The reedy voice of Riverside's chief of staff fluttered through the loudspeakers. "After you all finish dinner, please assemble near the dance floor at the front of the museum. The awards ceremony will start in fifteen minutes."

"They sure aren't giving us much time to eat," Plato grumbled.

"We were one of the last tables served," Erica pointed out.

"You were planning to have seconds?" Cal asked incredulously.

Plato shrugged.

"Well, *I* certainly was." Steven eyed his empty plate sadly. "I'm still hungry."

Erica lifted her chin haughtily. "A well-balanced vegetarian meal leaves you satisfied, without making you feel bloated and overstuffed."

"I *like* feeling bloated and overstuffed."

"Me too," Plato agreed. He picked up his plate. "Let's go get some seconds."

"You won't feel like dancing later," Erica told Steven.

"I don't feel like dancing *now*," he replied. But he stayed in his seat, watching enviously as Plato stood to refill his dish.

Heading back to the buffet table alone, Plato heard Erica talking about her fiancé. "Steven is an excellent dancer. But I always have to *drag* him out on the floor."

"I *try* to dance with Plato," Cal complained. "But he's always stepping on my feet. It's like dancing with a cuddly haplocanthosaurus."

"I'll be happy to dance with either of you lovely ladies," Marvin Tucker offered smoothly. "Anytime at all."

But Tucker didn't follow through on his offer. He was too busy dancing with Cheryl Andersen. And the pretty, shy pediatrician. And the chief of staff's fifth wife.

Apparently, his networking extended beyond the confines of the hospital.

But despite Tucker's preoccupations, Cal wasn't free to dance with Plato. Not long after the awards ceremony, one of the anesthesiologists had shaken Cal's hand, congratulated her, and dragged her out to the dance floor. Already, she had stayed out with him for three songs—including a slow dance—while Plato cooled his heels and nursed another scotch, along with the embryo of a hangover. And guarded Cal's Thaddeus Crumm Prize—a fancy wall plaque featuring her name, a caduceus, and a stylized etching based on Fildes's Victorian-era painting, *The Doctor*. The plaque had been presented by Marvin Tucker, who had received another award himself—his third Distinguished Researcher prize in the past five years.

Steven Prescott was sitting beside Plato and admiring Cal's prize. He handed it back and turned his attention to the dance floor.

"Is he a friend of yours?" Steven asked. He nodded toward the anesthesiologist doing the rumba with Cal.

"No." Plato shrugged. "I think he's an old friend of Cal's."

"Must be. They dance so *well* together." Steven eyed the swaying couple with open admiration. "They've got just the right chemistry, you know? Those hip movements are quite interesting. And look at the eye contact—that's really important."

"I thought you didn't dance."

"Not very often. But I enjoy the old movies, and the competitions on television. And I like watching people dance at events like this." He glanced across the dance floor again, and his grin faded. Marvin Tucker was now dancing with Erica. They were smiling, and looking into each other's eyes. Their hip movements were quite interesting. "Except when they're dancing with my fiancée."

"They look pretty good together," Plato commented wryly. "Great chemistry."

He glanced over at his companion, but Steven wasn't listening. He was studying Erica and the old hematologist, watching their every move, as though he were trying to commit each step to memory. Finally, at the end of the dance, he reluctantly strode to the middle of the floor. He took Erica's hand and led her in a decent fox-trot to an old classic—*You Do Something to Me*.

"Steven cuts a pretty decent rug." Cal had suddenly appeared at Plato's elbow. "I'm surprised Erica said he didn't dance."

"He doesn't like to," Plato replied. "But I think he was jealous."

"Of whom?"

Plato tipped his glass toward the old hematologist, who was finally taking a break near the bar.

"Marvin Tucker?" Cal smirked. "Oh, *Plato*. That's ridiculous. He's old enough to be her father."

"I know. But there was a certain, umm, *chemistry* between them." Plato shrugged. "Sort of like between you and that anesthesiologist."

Cal glanced at him as though she wasn't sure if he was serious, and apparently decided he wasn't. She giggled. "Neville Archer is just a good dancer, that's all."

Plato frowned. The name sounded familiar.

"He has a great body, and he knows how to use it," she continued. "One of those natural athletes, you know?"

Plato knew. Cal was a natural athlete, too. At a medical conference last summer, she had rubbed him all over the tennis court and practically killed his doubles partner.

"A natural," he grumbled. "Unlike me."

"What do you mean?"

"The cuddly haplocanthosaurus," he muttered into his glass. Somehow, the scotch made it much easier to feel sorry for himself.

"Oh, Plato. I didn't mean that. I was just trying to make Erica feel better." She squeezed his arm. "Come on. Let's go out there and—"

"*There* you are, Cally." Neville Archer had materialized from nowhere to appear at Cal's side. "Have you rested up yet?"

"Neville, I—" Cal seemed flustered. She glanced at the floor, at Plato, then back at Neville. "Have you met my husband? Plato Marley."

The natural athlete, the good dancer with the great body who knew how to use it, extended a hand to Plato. "Neville Archer."

Plato shook his hand numbly. He had finally remembered who Neville Archer was.

Even the best of dance partners rarely move that well together without a little practice. And Cal and Neville had surely practiced together quite a bit.

"Nice to meet you," Plato muttered.

"Ready, Cally?" Neville Archer put a possessive arm around her shoulder, and grinned at Plato. "I do hope you don't mind. It's just that Cally is awfully hard to resist. She's such a great dancer. Kind of a natural, you know?"

Plato nodded. "I know just what you mean."

Walking onto the dance floor, Cal turned and shot him a helpless, apologetic glance.

Plato merely shrugged. He was lost in his own thoughts.

Like Cal had said, Plato wasn't the first man in her life. He wasn't even the first man since Hubert Glimperton, or Rupert Muggleston, or whoever her college boyfriend was.

In fact, Cal had met Plato on the rebound, just after she was jilted by a doctor at Riverside. A tall, handsome fellow. A natural athlete. An anesthesiologist.

She had mentioned his name to Plato a couple of times. Once in her sleep, early in their relationship.

Plato tried to shrug it off. It was nothing to be jealous about. They both had skeletons in their closets, past histories that were best left behind them.

Except for one thing.

It wasn't just Neville Archer's *name* that sounded familiar. His voice did, too. It was high-pitched and hasty—a rapid-fire squeak, full of New England inflections. Like an anxious Boston chihuahua.

Glumly, Plato took one last sip of scotch, took one last glance at Cal and Neville swirling around the dance floor, and wandered off to lose himself in the dead past of the museum. He drifted through Sears Hall, paused briefly to view the burial mound and the primate exhibits, and found himself among the dinosaur skeletons once again.

The vast hall was practically deserted; even the tables had been removed. He studied the placards in front of the various dinosaurs, the saber-toothed tiger, and the woolly mammoth, and even marveled at the haplocanthosaurus again, from a safe distance. He crossed the room and gawked at the bizarre glyptodon skeleton—a bony carapace shaped like a dome and sized like a miniature tank. Eventually, he strolled over to study an odd pile of bones carefully arranged behind a roped-off corner of the room. Every piece—from the tip of the tail to the razor-toothed, predatory skull—was laid out in its proper place on the floor, as though a swarm of voracious dermestid beetles had consumed the creature's flesh and left its bones to clatter to the floor.

"Allosaurus, I believe." Robert, the pediatrician's husband, was standing at Plato's elbow and studying the odd collection. "A very efficient killer."

"Looks like he had an accident."

"They haven't assembled him yet." Robert lit a cigarette and blew smoke toward the high ceiling. "One of the curators told me about it. A work-in-progress. They brought the bones up today, and they'll start assembling him tomorrow."

"It's a wonder somebody doesn't just walk off with one of the bones."

The high school teacher shrugged. "What would they do with it? Individually, the bones are rather useless." He grinned. "Unless you're looking for a club, as Erica Windgartner pointed out."

Plato smiled, thinking of Neville Archer. "Maybe I am."

But his jealousy had mostly disappeared, to be replaced by a mild feeling of silliness. Doubting Cal was like worrying whether the sun would come up tomorrow. It was about as sure a bet as you could make. And if it didn't happen, the world would simply end, and nothing else would matter anyway.

With that happy thought, he wandered off to find her. He took the long way around the circular museum, crossing through the opposite door of the dinosaur room, passing the service elevators, and entering the earth sciences area.

The darkened rooms were a maze of glass cases full of geodes and crystals and semiprecious stones, all glowing brightly under ultraviolet lamps. Plato almost stumbled over a couple clutched in a close embrace near the volcano display. He backtracked quickly into the darkness again, but he needn't have bothered. They were too preoccupied to notice him.

He had swallowed his apology and nearly reached the doorway again before he realized that one of the pair was almost certainly Cal. He turned around and slunk closer to the pair, lurking behind a case displaying crystals of feldspar and pyroxene and magnetite.

"We've got to keep it a secret," she whispered.

"Don't worry. Your husband will never know." It was the chihuahua again. "How could he find out?"

"Oh, Neville." The woman—Cal—sounded ecstatic. "You came along at just the right time. I'm so *happy*."

"You forgive me, then?"

Cal sighed. "Of course."

There was a long pause, while Plato tried not to imagine what the couple near the volcano display was doing.

"Don't worry," he repeated. "Your husband will never know."

"I hope not. Things are bad enough already."

Plato frowned. He hadn't thought things were very bad at all. An occasional fight here and there, but wasn't that normal? And the romantic side was pretty nice. Or so he had thought.

What did *Cal* think? Had he paid enough attention to that? Apparently not.

"Tuesday night, then?" Neville asked. "At my house?"

"Fine."

"You know the way, right?"

"Of course I do, silly."

"What'll you tell him?"

Cal considered. "That I'm at a meeting, I guess. I'm always at meetings."

"Well, this will be a very *special* meeting." Neville's whisper held a smile. "Maybe I'll open a bottle of wine. There's that Mondavi cabernet we got in California—"

Cal giggled. "You still have that?"

Plato had heard enough. He stumbled away from the earth sciences exhibit, past the service elevators, and back to the dinosaur skeletons. Thankfully, the place was deserted. He couldn't bear to face anyone now. He felt sick to his stomach. He felt like someone had ripped out his heart and filled the empty hole with ice cubes. His legs quivered beneath him. Cold sweat beaded on his forehead.

Plato stood there for a long moment, taking a few deep breaths. His heart pounded in his ears. He wandered aimlessly around the room, in a state of numb shock, seeing nothing, hearing nothing.

He finally drew up in front of the tanklike glyptodon. The thing looked just as unnatural, awkward, and ungainly as before.

Even more so—because there was something especially unnatural about the two objects sticking out from beneath the shell, back near the bony tail. Two objects that almost certainly weren't part of the display. A pair of human feet, jutting from beneath the dome like the Wicked Witch of the East's after Dorothy's house falls on her.

Except that these feet weren't wearing ruby slippers. They were wearing snakeskin boots.

Near the head of the weird creature, a tiny river of blood was trickling across the floor.

Plato leaped over the ropes, scrambled to the back of the glyptodon, and burrowed underneath. He already knew what he would find.

The back of the victim's skull was completely caved in. His

misshapen face grinned at Plato with a ghastly rictus, as though he had just realized his fondest wish. The murder weapon was lying nearby. The allosaurus was still a very efficient killer.

Marvin Tucker had finally discovered a dinosaur bone.

CHAPTER 14

"Death was nearly instantaneous," Cal pronounced.

She was kneeling beside Marvin Tucker's body. The giant glyptodon shell had been carefully dragged aside to make room for a swarm of photographers, trace evidence technicians, police inspectors, a sheriff's detective, and the coroner's crew.

But it didn't take a coroner, or even a physician, to determine the cause of death in this case. The back of Tucker's head had been staved in by a fearsome blow. The old hematologist's eyes bulged from their sockets, his skin was pale and gray like fresh cement, and his thin lips were drawn back in a horrible parody of his gentle smile. A reddish-black halo of congealed blood was puddled around his head.

The murder weapon—an allosaurus femur—was lying nearby. The distal end was stained the same color as the puddle. For a moment, Cal thought back to the human femur in the excavation site at Siegel. The similarities were apparent, though this bone was stouter and longer than a human's and had an oddly curved shape.

She wrenched her gaze back to the victim.

"No sign of any other wounds," she continued. "Looks like only one blow—a good, solid one. We'll know for sure after the autopsy."

"If death was instantaneous," the police detective in charge asked, "why did he bleed so much?"

"His heart probably kept beating for a few minutes," Cal turned to glance up at the Fifth District homicide detective. Lieutenant Molly Lecowicz was a small brunette with a pinched face, intense dark eyes, and an intelligent curiosity.

"His heart didn't know he was dead," Cal continued. She gestured at the floor. "But his brain certainly did."

"His death was swift and painless," Plato said, morosely echoing Tucker's line from dinner.

Cal shot him a quick glance. Plato had been acting strangely ever since he had discovered the body. It was probably the shock—plus the fact that Marvin Tucker had been one of Plato's favorite teachers during residency.

"No kidding his death was swift." Jeremy Ames, a homicide detective with the sheriff's department, shook his head at the carnage. Cal had worked with him on several cases before, and Jeremy was a regular player at the Marleys' Saturday night poker sessions. The sheriff's detective stared at Tucker's remains with a sickly, dumbfounded expression—the very same face he wore at the poker table when he complained about Cal's shuffling technique. He was usually bluffing, then. But he wasn't tonight.

"The killer must have been incredibly powerful," he marveled.

"Not necessarily," Cal answered. She pointed over to the pile of allosaurus bones lying nearby. "Pick one of those up, and you'll see why."

Jeremy paced over to the pile and lifted the other femur— sister bone to the murder weapon. He grunted with surprise at the weight of the bone.

"Damn thing's heavier than it looks," the sheriff's detective said. He took a practice swing. "You're right—with a weapon like this, it could have been either a man or a strong woman."

He handed the bone to the police detective. Molly hefted the femur and grimaced. "They sure made them heavy in those days."

"That's probably permineralization." The words floated up from the back of the crowd. Cal recognized the voice of Robert, the high school teacher and resident dinosaur expert.

"What?" Jeremy Ames squinted at the crowd and ran a restless hand through his gray crewcut. He was a former marine and a Vietnam vet, small and wiry with a nervous energy that never quit. In his free time, Jeremy volunteered at the Boys' club, taught a police procedural course at Tri-C, and wrote alimony checks to his first three wives. And kept his ears open for interesting cases—regardless of their jurisdiction.

He stood on his toes and sent his eyes around the crowd, his long thin snout twitching curiously. "What's that?"

"Permineralization." Robert finally shouldered his way through the photographers and technicians and blithely took the bone from Molly. "Over millions of years, this bone has absorbed some very hard minerals." He straightened his glasses and squinted at the femur. "Quartz, probably amethystine."

"Who *is* this guy?" Jeremy asked the ceiling. He turned back to Robert. "You work for the museum or something?"

"He's a high school teacher," Cal explained. "He sat at our table."

"Without permineralization," Robert continued, "this bone wouldn't be so heavy. It would have shattered on impact without doing much damage. Not *that* kind of damage, anyway."

He eyed Marvin Tucker's head and swallowed heavily.

"You were at Tucker's table?" Jeremy asked.

Robert tore his gaze from the floor, handed the femur to Jeremy, and nodded. "With my wife."

"Good. We need to talk with you and your wife." He took Robert's arm. "And anyone else who was at Tucker's table."

"We're already working on it." Molly Lecowicz gently unlatched Jeremy's fingers from the teacher's arm. "It's a *city* case, remember? You're welcome to observe, if you like." She shook her head. "Though I don't understand why you'd *want* to, Jeremy. Don't you ever sleep?"

Ames nodded. "Once a week."

Molly laughed, but Cal didn't doubt it a bit. Jeremy Ames almost certainly had a thyroid condition. He had the metabolism and mannerisms of a ferret on amphetamines.

The two detectives led Robert away through the crowd. Most of the medical staff had already been screened and permitted to leave. But potential witnesses, or people who had talked with Tucker that night, or who had clear ties to the old hematologist, had been forced to stay. So several dozen physicians and high-ranking administrators were being interrogated, or napping on benches around the museum, or hanging out at the fringes of the crowd surrounding Marvin Tucker's resting place.

"The killer took an incredible risk." Homer Marley was standing on the other side of the huge glyptodon. Plato had phoned home an hour ago to tell Homer about the murder, and to release his cousin from dog-sitting duty. But rather than heading home to his apartment, the assistant prosecutor had come to the crime scene with Jeremy Ames. Neither he nor Jeremy had any official reason for being here. But Homer knew he'd probably be involved sooner or later. And Jeremy just couldn't resist an interesting case—even at twelve-thirty on a Saturday night.

Cal wondered how long Nina Ames—Jeremy's fourth wife—would put up with it.

"A horrible risk," Homer repeated solemnly. He stared at the allosaurus bone and shook his head. "He must have been desperate."

"And lucky," Cal said. Once again, she studied the faint heel marks and flecks of blood on the linoleum. Tucker was apparently felled just in front of the display and then dragged beneath the glyptodon. The hematologist was short and slight, so the movement of the body didn't require a remarkably powerful killer.

Just a remarkably lucky one. The Hall of Prehistoric Life was two hundred feet wide and featured two large entranceways. Yet none of the three hundred dinner-dance guests admitted to witnessing anything even remotely unusual.

Only a few guests admitted to visiting the hall after dinner; all of them claimed that the room had been deserted during the dance. But the lack of witnesses was still surprising.

Cal removed her rubber gloves and stood, then gestured for the coroner's crew to remove the body. She watched with Plato and Homer as the victim's body was bagged and loaded onto a gurney. The crowd quietly parted and watched the small bundle roll away. A *Cleveland Post* photographer rushed in to take one last picture of the crime scene—a blood-smeared chalk outline on the pale linoleum beside the huge glyptodon skeleton.

Off in a corner of the room, a television news reporter was holding a live interview with one of the police detectives. The camera and bright lights swiveled to follow Tucker's procession through the museum. Nearer to Cal, a pair of reporters rehashed the Ohio State game. She tried not to listen.

"Goddamned buzzards," Plato muttered. "Anything for a story."

He turned to the *Post* photographer, who was finishing his roll of film on some close-ups of the bloodstain. "Think you'll get a Pulitzer for this?"

The photographer rose from a crouch and stood, towering over Plato. The huge autowinding camera looked like a child's toy in his hands. Flashes and lenses and cables dangled from his neck like charms on a necklace. The white shirt on his broad chest could have doubled as a projection screen.

"A Pulizer?" He eyed Plato with a puzzled frown. "Probably not. One dead doctor isn't much of a story. *Two* might get me somewhere, though."

He grinned broadly, turned on his heel, and plowed away through the crowd.

"*Plato!*" Cal scolded. "What's gotten into you?"

"Nothing." His chuckle had an hysterical edge to it. "Nothing at all."

He stared at the wedding band on his left ring finger, plucked it off, and stuck it in his pocket. "Damn thing's getting uncomfortable." He glanced at Cal. "Must be all that *weight* I'm putting on."

"You feeling okay, buddy?" Homer eyed his cousin with concern, then turned to Cal. "I think he's had a little too much to drink."

"I wish I had," Plato said. He jammed his hands in his pockets and stared at the floor. "I really wish I had."

Cal frowned. Plato sure was acting strangely tonight.

Homer moved closer to Cal, and dropped his voice to a whisper. "You think Tucker's death has any connection with those extra skeletons you folks found?"

"How could it?" she replied. But then she remembered her conversation in the car with Plato, and she worried a little. About Marvin Tucker's experimental drug. And about her husband.

She frowned again. Poor Plato. Tucker's death was hitting him awfully hard.

"If it weren't for Marvin Tucker, Dr. Feinstein would still be a department chairman."

Erica Windgartner was huddled in a seat near the center of the museum's small planetarium. Jeremy Ames and Molly

Lecowicz were seated to Erica's right, and Cal was perched at the witness's left.

Curled up in a ball, heels on the seat of her chair and knees clutched in her arms, Erica Windgartner was clearly in a state of shock. She was pale, wide-eyed, and tense. Her hands clenched and unclenched the loose folds of her short scarlet dress. Her voice was barely a whisper.

But in the perfectly hemispherical chamber, a whisper was more than enough. The room's bizarre acoustics somehow amplified even the smallest sounds, focusing them at the center circle of seats. In the silence that followed Erica's pronouncement, Cal could hear Molly's gum chewing, Jeremy's raspy breathing, and each tick of Erica's gold wristwatch.

The museum's planetarium was an excellent place to question witnesses—the quiet intervals between questions and answers were almost suffocating, while the strange amplification of sounds made even *thoughts* seem audible. In the deathly hush, Cal imagined a lie would sound as discordant as the clash of cymbals during a funeral dirge.

Cal hadn't planned on joining the interrogation. She and Plato had been out in the parking lot, climbing into the Rabbit, when Jeremy had rushed up to stop them. Apparently, Erica Windgartner had asked if Cal might be present during her questioning.

Erica was nervous and upset, Jeremy explained. He didn't know why, since there wasn't any apparent connection between her and Tucker. She had declined their offer to call her lawyer. Instead, she had asked for Cal.

So Cal had left Plato out in the alcove and followed Jeremy into the planetarium. Erica seemed visibly relieved when Cal appeared. But she was obviously still nervous about something.

Now Cal believed she knew what it was, and understood why Erica had asked for her to join them. Riverside's newest trustee was hoping that Cal might act as a translator and advisor, like she had so often before, during committee meetings at the hospital. Erica had only been filling in for her father on board meetings since last December. Clearly, she didn't know how much information she should divulge to the police.

Cal patted her arm reassuringly. "It's okay, Erica. The board's actions can't be kept secret if they are relevant to the murder investigation. The police will probably subpoena the minutes from your meetings anyway."

Molly Lecowicz nodded.

Erica relaxed a little more. She loosened her grip on her knees and let her feet slide to the floor.

"You're saying that Marvin Tucker made Feinstein resign his chairmanship?" Molly asked.

"Not exactly." Erica shook her head. "As chairman of Riverside's Peer Review Committee, Dr. Tucker didn't have that authority. He just gathered evidence and made a recommendation to the board."

"A recommendation that they should force Feinstein to step down," Jeremy guessed. He sucked on a cigarette and blew smoke up into the dome of the sky. "And the board complied?"

"Yes. Eagerly." Erica leaned back to stare at the blank vaulted ceiling. Around the black rim of the hemisphere, compass points were painted in bold white letters. "The trustees had wanted Feinstein to step down for years. Before my father got sick, he had urged the rest of the board to fire him. Everyone knew Feinstein was incompetent, and that he abused his position. But he was chairman of both the obstetrics and gynecology department and the residency program. He had tremendous political power. None of the other doctors were willing to speak against him."

"I'm surprised Tucker managed it," Cal said.

"Dr. Tucker was a very patient and determined man," she replied. "He spent six months gathering evidence. He audited medical records from scores of Feinstein's patients. He interviewed nurses, technicians, and doctors who had graduated from Feinstein's program. And finally, when he had enough evidence, he interviewed other obstetricians in the department. He showed them a copy of his preliminary report and threatened them with disciplinary action if they hid anything. I think most of them were relieved to be forced to tell the truth. I know most of them disliked Feinstein as much as Tucker did."

"Tucker disliked Feinstein?" Molly asked. "So it was a personal thing."

"No." Erica shook her head. "I shouldn't have said *disliked*. Marvin Tucker was a very honest, dedicated doctor. My father had tremendous respect for him. But Dr. Tucker had very little respect for Dr. Feinstein—and for any physician who abused his authority and position. It was a professional issue, not a personal one."

"Did Dr. Feinstein see it that way?" Molly asked.

"Not at all." She shuddered. "For Feinstein, it was *very* personal. He was convinced Dr. Tucker had a grudge against him. At the meeting last December, when Dr. Tucker presented his evidence, Dr. Feinstein didn't try to defend himself, or respond to the charges at all. He simply attacked Dr. Tucker."

"Physically?" Jeremy leaned forward.

"No, verbally." Her eyebrows merged. "He called Dr. Tucker a backstabber, and a traitor to the profession. And a fraud. And a—a *womanizer*. And he threatened him."

"Threatened him?" Molly's dark eyebrows rose.

"Ye-es." Erica nodded slowly. "Yes—he said he'd make Dr. Tucker regret it, make him pay."

"Anything specific?"

"No." She shrugged, eyes closed. "After that, he stormed out of the room. "We voted him out unanimously, but presented it as a resignation. I think all the other trustees were very relieved, too."

"And tonight," Molly began. "You said Dr. Feinstein was angry again tonight. When was this—at dinner?"

"No." Erica shook her head. "It was something I saw afterward."

She glanced at Cal, but Cal pretended to study the projecting apparatus at the center of the planetarium. The maker of stars and planets squatted spiderlike on a tall pedestal, looking like a cross between a fantastically complex telescope and an overgrown lobster.

"What happened tonight, Erica?" Molly's voice was patient, gentle, understanding. "Why are you so sure that Feinstein killed Dr. Tucker?"

"I'm *not*," she protested. "I just said you should question him, take a really close look at him."

"Why is that?" Cal finally asked. "Did you see them together?"

"Y-yes," she stammered. But she nodded firmly. "Yes. I saw them arguing together. After dinner."

Jeremy leaned forward. "When? Before or after the awards ceremony?"

"Just after the ceremony," she replied. She shot a furtive glance at Cal. "I left my purse under our table in the room with the dinosaur skeletons, so I walked back there to get it. When I was walking out again, I saw Dr. Feinstein arguing with Dr. Tucker in that alcove near the dugout canoe."

Erica pointed back toward the hallway. When Cal nodded encouragingly, Erica continued. "I couldn't miss it; they were very loud."

"Was anyone else nearby?" Molly asked.

"Cal was in the room, but I don't think she could see them." She glanced at Cal questioningly.

Cal nodded again, and Erica seemed to relax.

Jeremy scribbled in a notebook. "What did you do then?"

"I walked out to the dance floor." She shrugged. "I thought about telling somebody—they both seemed so angry I was afraid someone might get hurt. But Dr. Tucker came along by himself only a minute later."

"He danced with you then, right?" Cal asked. "Did he say anything about his argument with Dr. Feinstein?"

"No." Erica shook her head. "We just talked about my father. He's one of my father's doctors."

"I see." Cal nodded.

The whole story made sense, except for one thing. Cal had indeed been standing in the dinosaur room when Erica retrieved her purse and left. On her way into the room, Cal had passed Tucker near the dugout canoe, just as Erica had said.

But Cal had been standing pretty close to the door, possibly within earshot. And she was almost certain the old hematologist had been alone the entire time.

CHAPTER 15

"Feinstein isn't the only suspect," Jeremy told Cal as they walked back toward the museum entrance. "Not by a long shot."

After the interview with Erica, Cal had told the detective how she had passed Tucker on her way into the dinosaur room and found him alone—just before Erica had come to retrieve her purse. Jeremy pointed out that Feinstein might have met and argued with Tucker while Cal was in the room. The fact that she hadn't overheard it didn't mean much—the band was pretty loud, right?

Cal nodded, but she couldn't help wondering. Had Erica only asked that she be present during her questioning in order to be sure that Cal wouldn't contradict her story?

"Dr. Feinstein doesn't have a solid alibi yet," Jeremy continued. "But then, not too many people do."

In the confusion and commotion of the party, the police were having a tough time nailing down precise times and alibis for the hundreds of attendees. That was important, because Feinstein wasn't the only member of Riverside's staff who had a grudge against Tucker. Many other doctors had plausible motives for murder, too. But few of those motives were related to Marvin Tucker's professional activities.

Cal and Jeremy found Plato sprawled on a bench in the alcove, half asleep. He sat up and rubbed his bleary eyes. Jeremy parked himself on the bench and cradled his forehead in his hands.

"We must have interviewed a dozen jealous husbands," the detective told them. "They all acted like Marvin Tucker was their best friend in the world, but none of them seemed very unhappy that he was dead." He glanced up at Cal. "Whether Marvin Tucker was really that much of a womanizer, I can't say. You wouldn't think so to look at him. But he sure had one hell of a *reputation*."

"I guess I'm not surprised." Beside him, Plato shook his head. "From what I've seen and heard, Tucker's reputation was well-deserved."

Jeremy's bloodshot eyes widened. "You're kidding."

"I've seen nurses and female residents cling to him at parties like iron filings sticking to a magnet," Plato said. "Never thought much of it. But Marvin Tucker had an incredibly smooth style."

"He certainly did," Cal agreed.

Plato scowled at her. "You're an expert, I suppose."

"As a matter of fact, I am." She sat beside him and slipped her arm around his waist. "I have a pretty smooth husband."

Plato sighed and pulled away.

"Then there's Tucker's partner." Jeremy glanced down at his notepad. "Phillip Andersen."

Cal nodded. "He and his wife sat at our table."

"Right." The detective shook his head. "Andersen snuck out of here before we could question him. Some partner, huh?"

"Loyalty isn't a strong suit for some people," Plato said, just a little too loudly.

Jeremy scratched his ear. "Including maybe Cheryl Andersen. That's the rumor, anyway."

"His partner's wife?" Now it was Cal's turn to be amazed. "Marvin Tucker certainly did get around."

"That's not the only reason we want to question Dr. Andersen. There's this drug Tucker was testing—one of the researchers on the project claims that—"

"Jeremy!" Molly Lecowicz was marching across the alcove. She stopped in front of their bench and waved her hands in the air. "I thought you said you wanted to help question that pediatrician. We've been parked on our butts for five minutes. Are you sitting in, or going home?"

"Of course I'm sitting in, Molly dear. I'll be there in just a minute." He watched her turn to go, then grumbled at Plato and Cal. "These city cops. Three hours of questioning without a break. When does the lady take a leak?"

"She doesn't *have* to let you help out, Jeremy." Cal smiled sweetly at the county detective. "Maybe you should head home and get some rest."

"Are you kidding? She *needs* me." He watched Molly disappearing down the hallway, then sprang to his feet. "Besides, this just might be the most interesting case of the year."

He trotted up the hallway after the city detective. "Hey, Molly! Wait up!"

"Finally," Cal said. "I thought he'd never let us go home."

"Who cares?" Plato asked. He leaned back against the red brick wall and closed his eyes. "I'm perfectly happy sleeping here."

He didn't *sound* happy. He sounded listless and bored, like a zombie reading a stock market report. Just hearing him made Cal depressed.

"What's wrong, Plato?" She leaned closer and pressed her head against his shoulder. "You've been acting weird all evening. Is it because of Dr. Tucker?"

He jerked away, put his hands on his knees, and stood. "Let's go home."

He was silent on the walk to the car, silent as they drove out of the city, and silent all the way down Interstate 77. At best, Cal's comments and questions were answered with a grunt, or a nod. Most of the time, though, he simply stared out the window and pretended he hadn't heard. Shouting at him didn't help. Neither did her observation that his behavior was inconsiderate, passive-aggressive, and childish.

"It's *okay* to be upset, Plato." She lowered her voice again. "I *understand* that. And I'll leave you alone, if you want. But I just think that, no matter how upset you are, you have to be considerate of other people's feelings."

"Considerate," Plato echoed. "That's a laugh."

But he wouldn't explain his remark, despite her persistent questions. Frustrated, Cal finally gave up and switched on the car stereo, hoping to fill the silence. But before she could pop a tape into the deck, a deejay shattered the silence—

"HOW 'BOUT THEM BUCKEYES?"

It was like a slow-motion sequence from an action movie— Cal scrabbled for a cassette, reached forward, and savagely thrust it toward the maw of the machine. She imagined, wished she were stuffing a sock into the deejay's mouth instead.

"THAT TWO-POINTER IN THE FINAL SECONDS WAS FABULOUS! FAKE REVERSE, AND A SHOVEL PASS TO THOMPSON!"

But all was not lost. At least he hadn't given away the final score yet. Cal leaped for the tuner knob to switch the station, but she fumbled the play. The knob came loose in her hands and fell to the floor.

Meanwhile, the Rabbit's ancient stereo was sniffing the tape, tasting it, and rolling it around like an epicure sampling a fine cabernet. Finally, the tape heads swiveled into position and the wheels started turning. But not before the deejay could finish—

"TWENTY-FIVE TO TWENTY-FOUR! WHAT A GAME!"

"Sorry," Cal said. The tape finally kicked in—Peter Gabriel's *Come Talk to Me*."

But Plato just shrugged. "Doesn't matter. I heard the score already."

"Where?"

"At the dinner. The bartender handed out game updates with every drink." He flapped a hand. "Not that anyone needed them. Half the guys had pocket radios in their jackets. The other half were carrying around those little television sets, sneaking peeks whenever their wives weren't watching."

"Of all the juvenile, unprofessional—"

"I even saw that last play." Plato signaled and drifted over to the exit ramp. "The chief of surgery had smuggled in a portable color TV in his black bag. He set it up in the men's room. About half the docs were in there watching."

"Boys will be boys," Cal scoffed.

"A few of the lady docs snuck in there, too, during the last quarter."

"I'm surprised *I* didn't hear about it," she mused wistfully.

"You were busy. Dancing or something." Plato hunched his head down between his shoulders and guided the car onto County Road 142—the half-paved highway that wound through the wooded hills and marshy valleys of northeastern Summit County.

But even this far south of Cleveland, suburbia was making its mark. Tidy little subdivisions were sprouting like ant farms, all over Sagamore Hills. As they crested the ridge near their house, Cal could see the forested hills scarred with pockets of straight little streets, uniform rooflines, and tiny circlets of light washing over perfectly manicured lawns. Farther out, the inky depths of the Cuyahoga formed a timeless, immutable barrier. The vast Cuyahoga Reserve on the west side of the river was relatively immune to development.

For now, anyway. In a few more years, the developers would finish paving over Sagamore Hills and Twinsburg and Hudson, and start greasing palms in Columbus and Washington. Then they'd push across the river like frontier families crossing the Mississippi, and gut the last big piece of wilderness between Cleveland and Akron.

Cal shook her head. She was starting to feel as gloomy as Plato. He had lapsed into silence again, bearded chin set, jaw clenched, eyes riveted to the dark road ahead as though he hadn't traveled it hundreds of times before.

"Are you angry at me?" Cal finally asked.

"Angry? Me?" His voice was sticky with sarcasm. "Whatever would I have to be angry about?"

"That's what I'm asking myself."

Plato turned into the driveway, pulled to a stop in front of the carriage house, and set the parking brake. He looked at Cal with disgust, as though he'd discovered some bizarre fungus growing in the Rabbit's passenger seat. "Maybe you'd better ask yourself again."

"What are you talking—"

"I'm going to check on Foley," Plato growled. He opened the car door and slumped out, muttering to himself. "The way things have gone tonight, he'll probably be dead, too."

He slammed the door hard enough to make the Rabbit rock on its springs. Cal sat in the car, stunned. *Ask yourself again*, Plato had said. What could he possibly be talking about? Was he still mad about the reporters at the museum? Cal certainly didn't have any control over them. Was he angry that she had danced with Neville Archer?

Despite her worry, Cal smiled to herself. She hadn't had much control over *Neville*, either.

Did Plato's anger have something to do with Foley? Did he somehow feel that Cal was responsible for the old dog's illness—and his imminent demise? Cal shook her head. Ridiculous.

But the more Cal thought about it, the more she wondered if it might be true. Foley was fifteen years old—Plato had spent half his life with the old Aussie. Senior high, college, medical school, residency, and marriage.

Foley the Wonderdog—that's what Plato's college friends had labeled him. Foley's picture was perched on Plato's bedroom dresser, beside their wedding album. The photo showed Foley—the perennial sixth player on Plato's pickup basketball teams—bounding across the path of a dribbling opponent and flicking the ball toward Plato with his snout.

Plato claimed the dog had financed half of his education at Kent State through the friendly wagers he'd helped win.

Cal was certain her husband was already grieving over Foley's looming death. And probably feeling a lot of anger along with the sadness. She had—inevitably—come between Plato and Foley, in the same way a romantic relationship usually takes precedence over other kinds of friendships. So in some crazy unconscious way, maybe Plato was blaming her for the old dog's death.

Cal shrugged and gathered up her purse. She and Plato needed to have a good long talk. A heart-to-heart discussion about Foley, about Plato's mixed-up feelings, about their plans for the future.

And she would have to make doubly sure that her meetings with Neville stayed a secret. Learning about Cal's plans now would surely break Plato's heart.

She climbed out of the car and hiked up the moonlit sidewalk. Plato was waiting for her on the sagging, weather-beaten porch. His face twisted in a rueful half smile.

"Maybe I shouldn't have said what I did. Not until I knew for sure." He slipped his hand over her shoulder—a tentative, oddly fraternal touch. "I think we need to have a little talk. It's about—"

Cal rushed into his arms. "About Foley. It's okay, I *understand*."

Plato stared down at her, his mouth open with amazement.

He was probably surprised at Cal's power of deduction, her ability to almost read his mind. Marriage was like that, though, Cal knew. Spend a few years with a person, and each expression, each inflection, revealed the inner soul beneath.

Plato shook his head and unlocked the door. Arm still over

Cal's shoulder, he tried to push it open, but nothing happened. The rickety door wouldn't budge.

"It's stuck again." He held the knob and wedged his shoulder against the door, heaved once, twice, three times before the jamb loosened and the door squealed open. "I'm going to have to fix this thing."

"Project Number 397," Cal agreed with a smile. "No hurry, though. We can always use the back door. That'll be even easier, since the lock doesn't work."

"No kidding." Inside the foyer, Plato slipped out of his overcoat and stumbled on his way to the closet. "What the—"

His voice broke off in a strangled groan. Instantly, he fell to the floor. Strange crooning noises came from his throat.

"Plato?" Cal wriggled out of her coat and rushed across the foyer. Was Plato sick? Having a seizure? The dreadful possibilities flickered through her forensically trained mind—strychnine, anaphylaxis, myocardial infarction, pulmonary embolus. And half a dozen others.

But then she stumbled, too. And instantly understood.

Plato wasn't poisoned, or suffering a seizure. He was huddled on the floor, arms encircling a large black object. The moonlight streaming through the foyer window highlighted the tears on his cheeks, on his beard, on the furry object wrapped in his arms.

Foley the Wonderdog was dead.

CHAPTER 16

November blew in three days early. Sunday morning dawned bleak and gray, like the muddy halftones of an old newspaper photograph. Somber clouds draped the treetops, and a mournful wind whistled through the bare branches. The sky oozed with that sickly mixture of rain and sleet and snow that heralded winter's arrival in Ohio.

Plato was sitting on the front porch of the old house. Watching the world drift from autumn to winter, feeling the dampness seep into his bones, and remembering.

He was alone, except for the big cardboard box sitting beside his rusted lawn chair. And the shovel leaning against the porch rail.

The cardboard box was labeled "Urinary Catheters." By some bizarre coincidence, it had been the only empty box left in the basement. Plato smiled, remembering his exasperation at Foley's complete inability to understand the paper-training process. Plato had been a high school student then, volunteering at University Hospital. He had told one of the interns about the situation, wondering if there might be a medical solution for his puppy's hopeless incontinence. The young doctor had laughingly suggested that inserting a Foley catheter would undoubtedly solve the problem—and the name had stuck.

In a few minutes now, he would take Foley for one last walk. As soon as the rain and sleet finished turning to snow. Already, the ground beneath the trees showed scattered patches of white among the green. The wind was dying down, and big puffs of snow were dropping between the branches like wads of confetti tossed by squirrels. The world was silent, save for the last few puffs of wind creaking in the trees. And the sound of Cal churning out another autopsy report on the dot-matrix printer in the study upstairs.

And the distant thrum of a motor grinding up Route 142. A pounding, rattling noise, like a jackhammer drilling through sheet metal.

The jackhammer sound died and throbbed to life again as Homer's car turned into the driveway. Between the distant pines, Plato could see the hulking black outline of his cousin's ancient Chevy Caprice threading its way up the drive.

Homer clattered to a stop behind the Rabbit, climbed out, and slogged to the porch through the wet snow and slush.

"Coming to join the festivities?" Plato asked.

Homer leaned against the porch rail and shrugged. "Sure. We'll make a regular funeral out of it."

He reached for the shovel, passed it from one massive paw to the other, and finally rested his chin on the end of the handle. He was dressed for the occasion: gray sweatshirt and flannel vest, old blue jeans, and waterproof hiking boots. A pair of work gloves dangled from his hip pocket.

He wouldn't need them, though. Plato planned on handling this job all by himself.

"Sorry about Foley," Homer said. "He was alive when I left last night."

"I know." Plato sighed. "It was bound to happen sooner or later. He was getting awfully sick."

"He looked pretty good when I left." The lawyer smiled. "He watched the whole game with me. I think he enjoyed it."

"I think everyone in Ohio enjoyed it."

Homer started. "You heard the score?"

"Yeah. Half the docs at the party were packing Dick Tracy TV sets." Plato jerked a thumb over his shoulder. "Cal still wants to watch the tape, anyway."

His cousin grinned. "Good for her. It was a great game."

"She called you, didn't she?"

"Telepathy, Plato." He tapped his head solemnly. "I sensed that you were depressed about something, so I came running. Cousins are like that."

"What makes you think I'm depressed?"

"Your face, for one thing." He grunted. "You look as gloomy as a vulture with a stomachache. And you've been sitting in that chair for hours."

"I haven't been sitting here *that* long."

"Yes, you have." Homer stepped over and brushed at Plato's shoulder. "You're soaking wet, and you've got about six inches of slush piled on your head."

"Oh." He shook his head and scraped the layer of frozen sleet from the rim of his Indians cap. "I hadn't noticed."

"Normal people notice, Plato." Homer leaned against the porch rail again. "Normal people move once in a while. They talk."

"Cal *did* call you."

Homer folded his arms and shrugged. "This isn't just about Foley, is it?"

Plato watched the snow squall swirling around the trees.

"Cal thinks it has something to do with *her*," the lawyer continued.

"I'm just depressed, Homer." He touched the cardboard box with his boot. "My dog died. My favorite teacher at Riverside was murdered last night—and it turns out he wasn't quite the guy I thought he was. My favorite patient is dying of cancer. She's refused medical treatment, and she'll probably go any day now."

"So why are you telling *me* all this, instead of Cal?" Homer raised his hands. "Not that I mind—I've cried on your shoulder often enough. Figuratively speaking, of course. But why not talk your troubles over with Cal?"

Plato looked up at Homer and slowly shook his head. "Because Cal is one of my troubles."

"Oh." Homer frowned, then stepped across the porch and brushed the snow from another lawn chair. He pulled the chair closer and sat down. "So tell me about it."

Plato told him about it—from Cal's dances with Neville last night, to their furtive embrace and clandestine conversation, to their plans for this Tuesday evening. He explained how Neville had assured Cal that their meeting would remain a secret, that her husband would never find out about it.

As he listened, Homer's expression had shifted from sympathy to skepticism to outright denial. When Plato finished his tale, the lawyer tossed his huge head like a Percheron shaking off a horsefly.

"You've got it all wrong," he insisted. "Cal would never do

anything like that. She doesn't have a dishonest bone in her body. *You* know that."

"That's probably what Phillip Andersen thought about *his* wife." Plato couldn't help remembering his own comments about Marvin Tucker last night, during the drive to the museum. *Integrity itself.*

Homer frowned. "Andersen? Oh—Tucker's partner. I heard about him." He sighed. "But Cal isn't Cheryl Andersen. She's totally honest—sometimes she's *too* honest. If she ever was going to have an affair—not that she ever would—she'd tell you first, right up front. That's the kind of person she is."

"I know." Plato stared at his hands for a long moment, then turned his gaze to Homer. " But then, how do you explain what happened?"

He leaned back in the chair and sighed. "You're sure it was her?"

"Almost positive." But Plato thought back, and wondered. The crystal display room had been awfully dark. And the couple *was* whispering.

"This guy really was her old boyfriend?"

"She called him Neville. How many Nevilles do you think there are in Ohio?"

"Two or three, at least." Homer grinned. "Neville Archer— sounds like someone from an Agatha Christie story. Pencil-thin mustache, spats, and a lisp. Certifiable wimp."

"This Neville doesn't have a mustache *or* a lisp. But he's got plenty of muscles—one of those Nautilus poster-boys." Plato sucked in his belly with a grimace. "And he dances up a storm—sort of a cross between Fred Astaire and Conan the Barbarian."

"Maybe he's giving her dance lessons," Homer suggested.

"Very funny."

"Or maybe you just heard it wrong. Maybe it's not what you think." He cocked his head. "Maybe it's some kind of meeting or something."

"Yeah—maybe Neville Archer is throwing a Tupperware party." Plato shook his head. "He's an anesthesiologist, Homer. There's no professional reason he'd be meeting with Cal—least of all at his house."

"I still don't believe it. Not for a minute." Homer sighed. "What evidence do you have—a whispered conversation in the dark? If I ever tried to convict someone with that kind of proof, I'd be laughed out of court."

"That's not all of it. There've been other things—a phone call last Saturday when he asked for Cal and hung up, some late nights at the hospital when I couldn't get hold of her, that sort of stuff." Plato shrugged. "Anyway, I'm not putting Cal on trial."

"That's right. And you're not giving her the benefit of the doubt." The lawyer spread his huge arms and huffed. "Whatever happened to 'innocent until proven guilty?' Why not give Cal a chance to defend herself?"

Plato shook his head and stared down at the cardboard box beside his chair. "I'm not sure I want to hear her try."

Homer was silent for a long moment. Finally, he stirred and scooped up some snow from the edge of the porch. "I'm glad I never got married."

Plato just nodded.

"You've *got* to talk with her about it. Either that, or pretend it never happened." He mashed the snow into a ball and watched it melt in his hands. "What if you heard her wrong? Or what if it wasn't Cal at all? Are you being fair to her?"

The front door squealed open. Cal emerged with a tray of cups and a thermos.

"Since you two won't come inside, I thought I'd bring out something to warm you up." She poured steaming hot chocolate into a pair of mugs and handed them over. She eyed Plato thoughtfully. "Good work, Homer. At least you got the snow off his head."

"I didn't want him to rust." Homer sipped his cocoa. "Give me another hour or two, and I might be able to coax him inside."

"I've got some work to do first." Plato nudged the box again. "Remember?"

"*We've* got work to do." Homer reached for the shovel and grinned. "The ground's starting to freeze. It'll go a lot faster with two of us."

"*Three* of us." Cal picked up the tray and headed for the door. "Just let me get my coat on."

She emerged seconds later with her jacket and a small piece of wood.

"Here." She handed it to Plato. "It isn't much, but I thought you'd want a marker."

The redwood board was flat and smooth, about a foot square—a scrap piece from yesterday's roofing project. Its surface was etched with woodburned writing. The block letters were clear and direct, and surprisingly neat. Foley's name was spelled out, along with his date of birth and yesterday's date.

Homer leaned over Plato's shoulder to read the sign. "That's fabulous, Cal! How'd you do it?"

"I printed the words on the computer, and traced the lettering onto the wood with a scratch awl." She ran her fingers across the surface. "Then I went over it with Plato's old woodburning pen. Summer camp in fourth grade—it all came back to me."

"'FOLEY MARLEN,'" Homer read. "You spelled 'Marlin' wrong. Did Foley like fishing?"

"That's a Y—for 'Marley'. The wood sort of caught fire there." Cal rocked on her heels and sighed. "In fact, the whole *house* smells like it's on fire. We'd better take our time burying Foley. I opened some windows, but we probably shouldn't go back inside for a while."

Plato cradled the headstone—head*board*—and ran his fingers over the letters. The sign would only last a year or two, but that didn't matter. The important thing was Cal's thoughtfulness. And how easy it was for Plato to forget his anger and disappointment.

Homer was right—Cal deserved his trust. She deserved the benefit of the doubt.

He closed his eyes and thought, hard. Pictured the scene again.

That woman in the museum last night *couldn't* have been Cal. Could it? Thinking back, he was almost certain it wasn't her. Wasn't that woman taller? Her hair was lighter, too—sort of a platinum blond, rather than Cal's butterscotch. And her laugh was different—a silly little-girl giggle that was totally unlike Cal's.

And most important of all, Cal hadn't mentioned any meeting scheduled for Tuesday evening.

Plato wondered how he had ever imagined that Cal would do such a thing. He couldn't even bring himself to ask her about it—she would be surprised and hurt by his lack of trust.

He would forget it ever happened.

At least until Tuesday.

"Thanks, Cally." He stood up and pulled her close. She felt tiny inside her huge ski jacket—a priceless jewel swathed in down and polyester. He buried his face in her hair, and she turned so her lips met his.

Homer coughed and reached for the marker. "Maybe I'll see about mounting this on a stake. You've got some wood in the basement, right? Right." He shuffled his feet. "Okay, it'll only take a minute. Don't stop on my account, you two. I'll be right back."

After a minute or two, Cal paused to catch her breath. "That was nice."

"That's just the beginning."

"I don't think Homer's going to be gone *that* long." She pulled away and studied his face carefully. "You look a lot better. Maybe Homer should have gone into psychiatry."

"He's a fine lawyer," Plato said. "Very good at arguing his case."

"You want to tell me about it?" She moved close again and nestled her head in the hollow between his chest and his chin.

"Not much to tell." He shrugged. "I was just getting depressed—about a lot of things. Foley, Marvin Tucker, Agnes Leighton."

"And me?"

He shrugged again. "It's no big deal."

"I'd like to hear about it anyway. I don't want—"

Homer emerged just then. He was carrying a sledgehammer, a wooden block, and the redwood marker, which he had mounted on a pine stake.

"Let's get this show on the road," he suggested. "I think old Foley's getting cold."

They buried him near a stand of pine at the southwest corner of the property. The forest path skirted a ravine there; a small stream at the bottom of the chasm gurgled and chattered over the rocks. At the far end of the cut, the Cuyahoga was just visible through the bare trees. A crumbling granite bench marked the spot where Plato had often sat with Foley—the halfway point on their daily walks.

After the old dog was laid to rest, Homer planted the marker and Cal delivered an impromptu eulogy. Plato said his final farewell and turned to his cousin.

"Thanks, Homer. For everything."

He shrugged. "What are cousins for?"

"When are *you* going to get married?" Cal asked the lawyer.

Homer scuffed his boots in the muddy slush, and exchanged a glance with Plato. "Maybe never."

"It's not as bad as it looks," Plato said quietly. "I'm sure you'll do just fine."

Walking back to the house, Plato wasn't thinking about Homer's marriage prospects, or Foley's final resting place, or even Cal's apparent vindication. Instead, he was realizing that he hadn't eaten anything in nearly twenty-four hours. His stomach grumbled a hollow protest.

"What was *that*?" Cal asked.

"I'm hungry," Plato confessed.

She smiled at Homer. "I think our patient is fully recovered."

"Thank goodness." The lawyer patted his stomach. "Maybe he can make us some dinner. I'm hungry, too."

"You're always hungry."

"Let's order out for some pizza," Plato suggested.

"And I'll finish off the chili," Homer replied quickly. "I wouldn't want it to go to waste."

"Hardly any danger of that." Cal led them onto the porch and opened the door. "I don't think there's much more than a few spoonfuls left."

Homer grinned. "Every molecule of Platos' chili is precious, kiddo. I'm *still* wondering what he puts in that stuff."

"Sometimes," Plato said, "I'm not quite sure myself."

Half an hour later, they were seated around the kitchen table. Homer was slurping chili a la Tupperware, while Plato and Cal ate their pizza straight from the box.

"No dishes tonight," Cal commented as she nibbled her crust. "It's a good thing, too. I have an early lecture at the anatomy lab."

"Don't be surprised if you see Jeremy there tomorrow," Homer cautioned. "He wants to have a little chat with your lab director."

"With Sergei?"

"I guess so." He shrugged. "That Russian guy—about a hundred years old?"

"That's Sergei," Plato agreed. "Why would Jeremy want to talk with him?"

"Might have something to do with those articles in the *Post* today," Homer replied. "Didn't you folks see them?"

"No." Cal shook her head. "I'm surprised you subscribe to that rag."

"I don't." He lapped up the last of the chili and set the container down with a satisfied sigh. "Jeremy called me this morning and happened to mention the articles. He wondered if there might be a connection between the Siegel skeleton and Tucker's murder. So I picked up a copy on my way here. It's out in the car."

He returned moments later with the Sunday *Post*. Tucker's murder had made the front page—a garish color photo of the body, the blood, and the glyptodon dominated the top half of the page. A pair of tie-in articles followed on page three, both printed under the headline SCANDAL, MURDER ROCK SIEGEL MEDICAL COLLEGE. The first article merely recounted last week's discovery of Siegel Woman, offering broad and unsubstantiated hints and guesses about a possible link between the skeleton and the Kingsbury Run killings. Tucker's murder was mentioned again, but the author didn't even try to guess at a connection.

The second article was more frightening. It focused almost exclusively on the old Kingsbury Run murders—and on Sergei Malenkov. The article referred to previous *Post* investigations as well as original coroner's reports and police records. Particular weight was placed on theories that the killer had been either a butcher or a doctor, that he had demonstrated an excellent knowledge of human anatomy, and that he probably had access to some type of laboratory where the gruesome mutilations were performed. The second-last paragraph again stressed the fact that the Kingsbury Run killer would now have to be at least seventy-eight years old.

The final paragraph simply stated that: Sergei Malenkov, the eighty-one year-old director of the anatomy lab at Siegel Medical College, could offer no comments regarding the discovery of a headless skeleton on the college grounds. Sources from the coroner's office report that the skeleton found at the excavation site last Monday may have been buried several decades ago. Malenkov's employee records indicate that he took a six-month leave of absence for mental health reasons in early 1939. The last known victim of the Kingsbury Run killer had been murdered in 1938.

Cal's eyes widened as she read the stories. "How can they *print* that?"

"Easy." Homer shrugged. "They're the *Post*. Printed on one-hundred-percent recycled toilet paper." He spread his hands. "Anyway, they haven't said anything that isn't true. It's just a matter of how they put the facts together."

"Poor Sergei," Cal groaned.

"The whole thing is ridiculous," Plato insisted. "How can Jeremy put any stock in that trash? And why is he investigating the Kingsbury Run killings, anyway?"

"He isn't," Homer replied. "He just happened to see the articles. He's not looking for a connection with Kingsbury Run, but the stories reminded him about that skeleton you folks found last week. He wondered if Siegel Woman might somehow tie in with Tucker's murder."

Plato sighed. He was wondering the same thing himself.

"And he's already running out of leads," the lawyer continued. "On rechecking, most of the suspects turned out to have pretty solid alibis for the exact time of Tucker's death."

"What about Dr. Feinstein?" Cal asked. "Erica Windgartner was pointing the finger at him last night."

"I know. And Jeremy thought he had a pretty good case against him, but he turns out to have an alibi, too. So they're checking into other angles."

Cal nodded thoughtfully, then frowned. "I still don't see why Jeremy thinks there's a connection between Tucker's death and the skeleton we dug up at Siegel."

Homer looked sheepish. "He's kind of curious about those four extra skeletons at the museum. I told him about Plato's theory—that maybe someone was hiding the charts to protect himself against malpractice. Jeremy got really interested when he heard about that."

"It's a good thing the *Post* hasn't found out about the extra skeletons yet," Plato observed. "They still don't know whether Alice Devon's facial reconstruction had anything to do with the medical school."

"We were very careful about how we phrased the press release," Cal said. She turned to Homer. "So Jeremy thinks those extra skeletons might tie in with Tucker's murder?"

"He sure does." Homer nodded firmly. "Tucker's partner— Phillip Andersen—is being sued for malpractice. It's not clear yet whether it was just poor clinical care, or if the problem had something to do with that new drug he and Tucker developed."

Plato and Cal exchanged glances.

"This morning, Jeremy heard from a lawyer who's representing the wife of one of Andersen's former patients." He sat back in his chair. "Seems the case isn't moving very quickly— they've had a hard time collecting evidence. Last week, when the lawyer tried to pull the patient's hospital record, it was gone."

"Which hospital?" Plato asked.

"Riverside General," Homer replied.

"I was afraid of that." Plato shook his head. "I'm checking on Louise Higgins's hospital chart tomorrow morning." He glanced over at Cal. "But something tells me we're not going to find that one, either."

CHAPTER 17

Monday morning found Plato at Riverside General Hospital, boarding the elevator to hell.

The physicians' equivalent of hell, anyway. Like hell, Medical Records was buried deep below the surface, in the bowels of the hospital. Like hell, Medical Records was blisteringly hot—the division was snuggled between the hospital's heating and electrical plants and shared a common wall with both boilers. And like hell, Medical Records was where bad physicians were sent when they broke the First Commandment of hospital care: *Thou shalt maintain thy charts in a timely manner.*

"Timeliness" had little to do with concerns over patient care or maintenance of hospital records. Instead, it was linked to Medicare and insurance requirements for reimbursement. The hospital lost millions of dollars each year because of incomplete or tardy chartwork—if enough days passed between a patient's discharge and submission of the bill to an insurer, the hospital simply ate it.

And hospitals hate eating medical bills. Riverside General, which accepted a higher percentage of charity care than any hospital in Cleveland, found unpaid medical bills especially repugnant.

Good physicians finished their chartwork on the floor, on the same day that patients were discharged. Bad physicians—those whose patient records were over two weeks past due—were branded with little pink slips and damned to hell, to track down their patients' charts and complete the paperwork. Those doctors who let too many charts go, who fed the hospital too many unnecessary bills, could lose their admitting privileges completely.

Ironically, for the first time in his medical career, Plato

Marley was completely up-to-date with his paperwork. Yet he was *still* riding the Lucifer Express down to Medical Records.

He hoped he wouldn't have to stay long.

He exited the elevators and followed the winding corridor past the autopsy suites, the hospital's small morgue, and the electrical plant, finally arriving at Hell's Gate. Sweat rolled down his temples and forehead, and tickled the tip of his nose. He felt like a stoker in a blast furnace. The brass doorknob was hot to the touch.

Just inside the door, the dictation room shimmered with heat. Only one booth was occupied: a doomed soul—an intern—was panting over a pile of charts and a Dictaphone. His white coat hung limply over the back of his chair. The sleeves of his green surgical scrubs were rolled up over his shoulders. The back of his shirt showed a dark Rorschach print of moisture. His tongue lolled. He saw Plato, nodded an eighth of an inch, and turned back to his work.

At the far end of the dictation room was the chart request area—a long, low counter where medical records were ordered up to be served by a plump, ageless woman named Mabel. Over the years, Mabel had come to know Plato quite well. Plato wasn't sure if he had *ever* dictated a chart up on the floor, on the day a patient was discharged. In terms of paperwork, Plato was a Very Bad Physician.

He pushed on through the shimmering haze, shuffled to the counter, and pressed the buzzer. The door behind the counter swung open, and a suspiciously chilly blast of air swept over Plato.

"Dr. Marley!" Mabel grinned. "Didn't expect to see *you* back here so soon. I thought you finished up your charts last week."

"I did."

"You got pink slipped *again*?" She pressed one hand against her vast bosom and flapped the other expressively. "Child, you *do* like cutting it close."

"I'm all caught up this time, Mabel. For once." He took her hand and waggled an eyebrow. "I just came down here to see you. It's been a whole week, you know."

"You missed my company."

"I sure did."

"Ri-i-ight." Her baggy cheeks molded into a smile. "You

and my husband, you're both lousy liars. You both get that twitchy thing with your lip. I can always tell when he's fibbing."

Plato touched his lip and frowned.

"Anyway, I *know* nothing but God himself or one of them pink slips could drag you down to this here inferno. How many charts you need today?"

"Just one," he replied. "*If* you can find it."

"I can find *anything*," she bragged. "Give me the name and I'll give you the chart. Who you want?"

"Lady named Louise Higgins." Plato pulled a damp slip of paper from his shirt pocket and showed it to Mabel. "They were going to pull her chart for me over the weekend—it might already be out."

Mabel squinted at the slip of paper. "Be right back."

She waddled back through the door and bounced out in less than a minute, without the chart. Instead, she handed Plato another slip of paper.

"Says here the lady died in February, ninety-six."

The note was from the evening shift supervisor. It simply stated that Louise Higgins had been a patient at Riverside until her death on February 18, 1996, and that her chart was out on loan to Siegel Medical College.

Good news and bad news, Plato thought. The skeleton had almost certainly belonged to Louise Higgins. But they were no closer to finding her chart than they had been before.

"You really *are* behind on your discharge summaries." Mabel's voice held a trace of awe. "'Course, with this lady being dead and all, you don't got much need for hurrying."

He shook his head. "This is a project for Cal. She's trying to track this woman's chart down."

"So what's the problem?" Her round shoulders lifted in a shrug. "Just go over to Siegel and borrow it."

"It's not quite that easy," Plato explained. He leaned closer and dropped his voice. "They're having trouble finding some of their charts."

"That's 'cause they don't have Mabel Rogers working for them." She mopped her forehead with the back of her hand and frowned. "Lemme see that paper again."

She studied the note for a moment, then turned back to the door and gestured for Plato to follow. "Jump over that counter and come on along. I'm thinking maybe I can get something that's almost as good as the chart."

Plato followed her through the doorway. The huge room beyond harbored the hospital's main filing system—a bewildering array of mechanical sorters and conveyers that was every bit as impressive as the Hamann-Todd skeleton collection. Wide windows in three of the walls held enormous racks of charts suspended on metal pulleys. Control panels beside the windows allowed the charts to be accessed by patient number. The pulleys dragged the charts up from storage in some mysterious, hidden space beneath the floor. Apparently, even hell had a basement.

Across the room, a bank of transcriptionists listened to headsets and tap-danced their fingers over the computer keyboards. The steady clatter of the keys sounded like a distant waterfall.

The room's climate was even more impressive. After the blazing heat outside, the filing and transcription areas felt positively arctic.

Plato sneezed.

"Bless you." Mabel nodded firmly. "I'm *always* catching colds, walking between these two rooms. So I stay in here as much as I can. Doctor says it's better for my heart, anyway."

He shook his head, bewildered. "Why isn't it hot in here, like in the dictation room?"

She shrugged. "We got air ducts in here, and you don't. This whole division's stuck right between the electrical plant and the furnace room. Didn't you know that?"

Plato nodded. "But why can't you just open our door? Then *both* rooms would be cool."

"We tried it once, last summer. It was so hot, them poor interns was dropping like flies." She sighed. "But someone from Administration heard about it, said we had to keep the door shut. To keep it cool in here. Something to do with the computers, they said."

Plato nodded. "Maybe someone could get a computer installed in the dictation room.

She checked the slip of paper again and led him over to one of the chart conveyors. Tapping Louise Higgins's patient number into the keypad, she explained. "This conveyor over here is what we call the morgue. Person dies, we take their chart out of the actives and put it in this one. Hang onto it for five years—or ten, I forget—and then we microfilm it and shred the original. Your Higgins lady's chart would be in here, if it wasn't lent out."

The conveyor pulleys clattered and clanked, dragging rack after rack of records past the window. Finally, the chains ground to a halt. Mabel walked along the full chart rack, dragging her fingers across the names and numbers of dozens of dead patients.

"Most of it's automatic, but we still have to put the charts on the rack by hand." She opened a gap in the long rack of charts and pointed to a thin folder. An index card was taped inside. "See, this card says the Higgins chart is on loan to Siegel—just like the weekend lady said."

Plato sighed. "So I guess we're out of luck."

"Maybe not." She grinned. "We still haven't checked the microfilm library."

"But it hasn't been five years yet," he protested.

"I know. But a few years back, Mrs. Travers—our director—started noticing how none of those loaned charts ever came back. Especially if the patient was already dead. So she made us start microfilming every chart that went out on loan—at least the ones from dead people."

"Fantastic! Then the chart should be on microfilm."

"*Maybe*," she cautioned. "Sometimes, folks forget to microfilm the charts before they send them out. Or they don't know we're supposed to do it—half these girls are brand-new, and they don't know a discharge summary from an H&P. But it's worth checking out."

She led him into the microfilm room, a long rectangular chamber walled with hundreds of small drawers, like a safe-deposit vault at a bank. Despite its modest size, the room held decades of patient records. Each flimsy microfilm sheet was smaller than a postcard, but held about fifty pages of patient information. Even the fattest medical charts could be crammed onto a few thin slips of microfilm.

Mabel waddled down through the years and pored over several drawers before finally lifting her head and cackling triumphantly. "Hah! I found it!"

She waved a small manila envelope in the air and read the

label aloud. "'Louise Higgins, died February 18, 1996.' That her?"

Plato studied the envelope and nodded. "That's her, all right. You mind if I sign this out, and take a look at it?"

"Out in the dictation area?" Mabel asked.

He nodded, reluctantly. One corner of the physicians' dictation area held an ancient microfilm viewer. Plato had sweated over the machine as a medical student one summer, when he had abstracted two hundred charts for a surgeon's research project on the link between gallstones and some obscure blood chemical. The link had proven to be nonexistent, and the paper was never published. To this day, the word "research" conjured in Plato's mind images of lab reports and gallstones and unbearable heat.

"Sure." He sighed. "If the microfilm viewer hasn't melted."

"Tell you what." She took his elbow and tugged him closer, whispering in his ear and pointing to a corner of the room. "Way back there, we got a nice new microfilm viewer. If you promise to put these records back in the file and sneak on out after you're done, I might just look the other way."

"Thanks, Mabel." He squeezed her shoulder. "You're one sweet lady."

"Just don't tell any interns you think so. Got to keep them in line." Grinning, she hurried out and closed the door softly behind her.

Plato sat down at the viewer and fingered through Louise Higgin's microfilmed records. The envelope was disconcertingly thick—he counted eleven or twelve of the thin plastic sheets. Six hundred pages. Praying that the patient's final discharge summary was a good one, he slipped the last page into the viewer and flicked on the light.

The tiny squares, smaller than postage stamps, were blown up to full size on the white screen. Plato quickly navigated to the last page on the sheet—two pages, really. A competent, comprehensive discharge summary. It had obviously been written by a professional:

> The patient, a 76-year-old Caucasian female, had a three-year history of severe aplastic anemia complicated by intermittent infections, severe anemia, and gastrointestinal bleeding resulting from a combination of end-stage cirrho-

sis and thrombocytopenia. This final admission followed a
week of treatment at Wyndhaven Colony for severe bron-
chitis, which appeared to have progressed to pneumonia. At
presentation to the emergency room, the patient was pale,
diaphoretic, and dyspneic, with a respiratory rate of 45 and
a pulse of 120 . . .

Plato studied the narrative carefully, jotting names and diagnoses and dates in his pocket notebook, and marveling at the
attending physician's skillful summary of a very complex
medical history. Reading the chart, Plato also experienced a
sense of *déjà vu*. Aside from the heavy drinking and cirrhosis,
her disease course was remarkably similar to Albert Windgartner's.

By the time he reached the end of the discharge summary,
Plato had discovered two very important points. First, the skull
Alice Devon had used for her reconstruction had almost certainly belonged to Louise Higgins. A note at the very end of
the chart said that, in accordance with her stated wishes, the
patient's body had been donated to the anatomy lab at Siegel
Medical College. The chart was to be sent along with the
body.

Second, the link between Marvin Tucker's death and the
missing medical records was growing stronger. For one thing,
Louise Higgins had been treated with Tucker's experimental
drug for a full year prior to her death. For another, the signature in the box marked "attending physician" was extremely
enlightening.

The author of Louise Higgins's fantastically detailed and
competent discharge summary was none other than Tucker's
partner, Phillip Andersen.

CHAPTER 18

"You are here to arrest me, then?" Sergei Malenkov, the ancient director of Siegel's anatomy lab, held his gaunt wrists before him in a gesture both pleading and defiant. He glared at the two detectives standing in his office doorway. "I will not fight you. Better to be in jail, than to remain here and face these lies."

Cal and Sergei had been sitting down to a welcome cup of tea after a very long session in the anatomy lab. During Monday morning's lecture and dissection, the old lab director had fielded countless telephone calls from newspapers and television stations asking about yesterday's *Cleveland Post* allegations. At first, Sergei's answers were calm and polite. But as the morning wore on, The Giraffe's braying could be heard from every dissecting table in the lab—even though the telephone was across the hall in his office. The crowning insult was the arrival of an entire television news crew who had somehow slipped past security. Sergei had nearly belted the attractive, obsequious reporter. Only his aristocratic Russian upbringing—and the fact that the reporter was a woman—had kept him from mussing her thick makeup with his fist.

Thankfully, Sergei's agitation had gradually dissolved as he sipped his tea and told Cal about the bewildering events that had started with yesterday's *Post* story. By the time he reached the bottom of his cup, the lab director was almost his old self again—fussing about the medical students' midterm scores and worrying whether he would have enough cadavers for next year's class.

But just then, Jeremy Ames and Molly Lecowicz had appeared in his doorway and introduced themselves, and The Giraffe's newly won composure had shattered into splinters. His hands shook, his face purpled, and his fuzzy white hairs stood up on end. He looked like a giraffe who had stuck his hoof into an electrical socket.

He rose from his chair, hands still extended for the cuffs, and shrugged. "For what do you wait? Am I not under arrest?"

"They're not going to arrest you," Cal explained patiently. "They just want to ask you a few questions. Lieutenant Ames is from the Sheriff's Department, and Lieutenant Lecowicz is with the Cleveland Police."

"They aren't here because of the *Post* story?" Sergei asked.

"No," Jeremy answered quickly. "We're investigating Dr. Marvin Tucker's murder. We wanted to talk to you about your missing charts."

"My missing charts," Sergei repeated. He dropped his arms and slumped back into his chair. "With all the fuss, I had almost forgotten about them." He gestured to the two empty chairs tucked in a corner between a stack of old atlases and a bookcase full of glass-jarred specimens. "Please to sit down."

Molly sat beside the atlases. Eyeing the jars of kidneys and hearts and tapeworms, Jeremy edged into his seat.

Sergei steepled his bony fingers under his chin and frowned. "What has Dr. Tucker's death to do with my missing charts?"

"That's what we wanted to ask you." Molly leaned forward. Quickly, she explained that a suspect in Tucker's murder was facing a malpractice suit, and that charts related to the case had apparently been stolen from Riverside General. "We wondered if your charts here might have been taken for the same reason."

"As to that, I cannot say." He spread his huge hands on the desk, palms up. "But I will be happy to help in any way I can. Then perhaps you can help with my problem."

"*Your* problem?"

"Yes." The lab director tapped the open newspaper sitting on his desk. "In thinly veiled rhetoric, I am being accused of the most heinous crimes in this city's history."

"Mr. Malenkov—" Jeremy began.

But Sergei was just beginning. He hefted a stack of telephone messages and held his reading glasses over his nose.

"My secretary has handled fifteen calls this morning, *after* I took twenty myself. Newspapers from all across the country. Television stations. Radio." He flipped through the messages. "News magazines. The *National Enquirer*. My poor wife called me from home—somebody named Herr Aldo will pay her to denounce me on television." He gritted his teeth. "*Etot sukin syn!* I never did trust the Germans."

"Mr. Malenkov—" Molly began.

"How can a newspaper get away with the printing of such lies?" he asked. "In Russia, we came to expect it. But here—I never would have believed such a thing. The proud Malenkov name, tarnished and spotted with filth. You can help me, yes?"

Jeremy was shaking his head. "Maybe if you talked to a lawyer—"

"Maybe," Cal suggested, "if these detectives find out what happened, they can help clear your name." She turned to the investigators. "Right?"

Jeremy shrugged. "We're not investigating the Kingsbury Run murders. I don't think—"

Molly nudged him. "Of course we can. Once we find Tucker's killer, people will probably forget all about this Kingsbury Run nonsense."

Slowly, reluctantly, The Giraffe placed the stack of telephone messages on his desk and slid the newspaper to one side. "Perhaps you are right. But I know very little about my missing charts. Other than that they are missing."

"Were they locked away somewhere?"

"No. Perhaps I should have locked them up." He gave a bony shrug. "But who would steal the charts of dead people? It is madness."

"A very cunning madness," Cal observed. "If the thief can avoid prosecution for malpractice."

Sergei's head swiveled from side to side. "That a doctor could do such a thing is—is—*unthinkable*."

He seemed far more upset about his missing charts than about Tucker's murder.

"We're not sure it *was* a doctor," Molly reminded him. "That's just a working theory. We haven't started making accusations yet."

"Of course, of course." He flapped a huge, gaunt hand and settled back in his chair.

"How many people had access to the charts?" Jeremy asked. "How easy would it have been to steal them?"

"Very easy." Sergei's dark eyes focused on the wall behind Cal's head. It was papered with certificates and commendations from nearly sixty years of service at Siegel. "The door to my office is rarely locked. The room beyond, where the charts were kept, never."

"Can we see the room?" Molly asked.

"Certainly." He flashed his huge yellow teeth and rose to his feet. "The detectives visiting the scene of the crime, yes? Come this way."

He opened the connecting door to the laboratory. Two fresh bodies were sprawled across the embalming tables. An elderly woman with gray hair and finely chiseled features lay on the table near the entry door. She was still fully clothed, in a prim blue dress, stockings, and blue pumps. A pair of half-rimmed reading glasses hung from a string around her neck. She looked like a librarian sneaking a nap atop a card catalog.

Across the room, a middle-aged man with a naked belly as vast as the setting sun stared glassy-eyed at the ceiling.

"My apologies." Sergei sighed. "The bodies are coming in faster than I can embalm them. Flu season, you see."

"I see." Jeremy's voice was a wheezy gargle. His face was as pale as the cadaver's belly.

"What's wrong, Jeremy?" Molly grinned. "Not used to dead bodies?"

"I've seen lots worse than this." He rubbed some color back into his thin face. "That doesn't mean I have to *like* it. Anyway, I think I'm coming down with something."

"Flu season," Sergei repeated. "The virus is quite a bad one this year."

Jeremy glanced at the tables and swallowed heavily. "Maybe it's just something I ate."

"Like your pride," Molly whispered. "It's giving you indigestion."

Sergei led them across the room and showed them the small steel door. "Beyond, that is where I kept the skeletons and the charts."

He opened the door and switched on the light. "You see, it is never locked."

The others followed him inside. Except for another week's worth of dust, it was the same room Cal had seen last Tuesday. Ten boxes were tucked into a corner, and the old file cabinet still sat beside the door.

"All the skeletons were kept in here," Sergei explained. "In boxes, stacked so high."

He held one hand up to his chin.

"And those skeletons and charts were donated to the Natural History Museum," Molly observed.

"Yes. All except for those five." He gestured to the little pile of boxes. "I kept them, for teaching purposes. And their files, of course."

He walked back to the cabinet beside the door and opened the top drawer. "All the files were once kept in here. Now I have only these five."

He led them back out again, explaining how and when the skeletons had been transferred to the museum, and how the missing charts had been discovered.

Sitting again beside the specimen jars, Jeremy frowned. "How many regular visitors do you have here at the lab?"

Sergei shrugged. "Dozens, not including the medical students. We often have visitors from the colleges, the nursing schools, and various groups coming on educational tours. We even had the board of trustees visit us last spring, when they were making plans for the new wing."

"How about researchers—regular visitors?" Molly asked. "How many people knew about your skeleton collection?"

"Sadly, very few." The old lab director gnawed his lower lip. "I had only a few visitors a month—mostly from Riverside General. I tried to stimulate the interest, but most of our young doctors are more fascinated by the glamour of the laboratories, the computers and test tubes."

"Did you keep a record of your visitors?"

"Yes, yes, of course." Sergei's had bobbed. He mined a sheet of paper from his top desk drawer. "I studied these names carefully last week, when I learned that some of my charts were missing. But I cannot believe that any of these young doctors could have taken those medical records without permission. They are all fine young men and women."

He stood and dropped the list in Molly's lap, tracing the names of his regular visitors with his fingers. "Dr. Tinelli is an orthopedics resident at Riverside—he was studying arthritis of the hip. Dr. Thomas is a rheumatologist. Dr. McGilvrey is a hematology fellow. And Dr.—"

"A hematology fellow?" Molly interrupted. "Did he work with Dr. Tucker?"

"Yes. He was researching anemia and—*Bozhe moi*!" Sergei shot two fists in the air and opened them quickly, then slapped his forehead with both open palms. "How did I not *see* this? Here is the connection you have sought, yes?"

"Maybe," Molly conceded. But her voice sounded hopeful.

Jeremy patted her arm proudly. "I *knew* I had a good reason for bringing you along."

Molly growled at the sheriff's deputy.

"What was Dr. McGilvrey researching?" Cal asked.

Sergei's tall forehead wrinkled. "Anemia—aplastic anemia. To learn whether the bones themselves changed, or just the marrow."

"I think we need to have a talk with this Dr. McGilvrey," Molly suggested.

She and Jeremy stood and thanked Sergei for his time.

The old lab director waved their gratitude away. "Perhaps you can find my missing charts. Aside from the scientific loss, it is shameful for those skeletons to be without a name, an identity."

"We'll try," Molly promised.

After they had left, Cal poured two more cups of tea. The lunch hour was shot; she barely had enough time to make her appointment at the coroner's office. During the lecture, Ralph Jensson had left a message—supposedly, he had some very interesting findings to discuss.

But she would stick around just a little longer. Even though Molly and Jeremy had left, Sergei still seemed disturbed. Another cup of tea might help calm the old anatomist down.

"Feel any better about the *Post* story?" Cal asked as she handed Sergei his tea.

"No." He shrugged. "Perhaps. Yes. Obviously the police do not believe those lies."

"Exactly," Cal agreed.

"And in my old country, the police are far more powerful

than the press." He closed his eyes. "Hopefully, the story will be forgotten, before . . ."

"Before what?"

The old lab director took a deep breath and sighed. "Nothing. It is nothing."

Cal nodded. If Sergei didn't feel comfortable telling her, she didn't want to force him.

She didn't have to. The Giraffe stared at his enormous hands as they fluttered on the desk, then cleared his throat to speak. His voice was heavy with emotion and a thick Russian accent Cal had never heard before, like the words of a ghost brought back to life.

"In the closet of our lives, we all hide our secrets."

Cal nodded again.

"Mine is not a shameful secret, perhaps." His hands danced a nervous ballet across the stacks of papers. "But one which is close to my heart."

"I understand, Sergei. You don't have to tell me."

"I *want* to tell you. I want to tell *someone*. My wife knows, of course. But no one here." He stared at the jars of specimens on the shelves. "No one but Dean Fairfax. Several years ago, he removed the details from my records. Left it as a leave of absence."

Now Cal was curious. "What happened?"

"I was once a medical student—at this very school." He smiled thinly. "Perhaps you do not believe it."

"I'm not at all surprised," Cal replied.

But she *was* surprised. Like everyone else at Siegel, Cal had assumed that Sergei Malenkov was an embalmist and a technician first, and that he had picked up his impressive anatomical knowledge through years of on-the-job training. It was astonishing that he could have kept his background a secret for so long.

On the other hand, the closet of Sergei Malenkov's life had been filling for eighty-one years. It was probably crammed with secrets.

For the first time, Cal had some notion of what had attracted her husband to the field of geriatrics.

She smiled at Sergei. "I think you have one of the finest minds at Siegel, even today."

"Thank you." His smile widened, and he brushed the compliment away. But then the smile faded away as well. "And just as anatomy was not my first career, Ludmilla was not my first love. My dearest, but not my first." His voice rose half an octave, and the Russian accent stiffened. "There was an American girl. Carlotta Watkins."

He winced as he spoke her name.

"We were engaged to be married. Her father respected me in spite of my accent and my odd Russian ways. We planned to live with her family while I finished my training." He closed his eyes and frowned, dusting away the cobwebs of his mind, revisiting places he hadn't seen in decades. "A week before the wedding, she was struck by a delivery truck. Outside her workplace near the West Side Market."

"Oh, God." Cal reached for Sergei's hand and held back her tears. The bony fingers clutched hers.

But he wasn't crying. Apparently all his tears had been shed long ago. "I left medical school, three months before graduation. I wandered for a month, ran out of money, and came back here to take a job in the dissecting lab. The people were very kind."

He pressed a fist against his forehead. "Three years I worked here in the lab. I buried myself in the anatomy books and cadavers, the death and dissection, but I could not forget." He shrugged. "So I tried to kill myself. Three failures—I was very unlucky. So I was sent to a mental institution."

"Your leave of absence," Cal murmured.

He nodded. "Six months at the Gladbrook Asylum, far south of the city. Six horrible months in a locked room."

"How *awful.*" Cal shook her head.

"Most of all, I missed the books. And the taste of fresh air." Sergei wrinkled his nose. "Next door to the asylum was a rubber factory. Even now, I can smell the burning rubber, the benzene."

"But you came back," Cal said.

"Yes. I came back." His eyes glittered. "I worked harder than ever in the laboratory. I studied anatomy at Western Reserve—not to receive a degree, but to learn. A class here, a class there. Over fifty years, I have learned a great deal."

"You certainly have," Cal agreed warmly.

"And there I met Ludmilla, and we have three lovely children, and for what is there this sadness in my heart?" He brushed the sadness away with a coat sleeve and grinned. "And the mental hospital, it has changed, too. They have made of it an elegant place for older people to live. Perhaps I should retire there." He winked at Cal. "It would add a certain irony to my life, yes?"

Cal smiled and squeezed his hand. "*If* you ever retire."

CHAPTER 19

Plato stood in the hospital room and stared at his patient in amazement. Albert Windgartner was shedding tubes and wires like a modern Lazarus casting away his shrouds. The deep ruddy color had returned to his face. The crushing strength had returned to his grip. The hard blue glitter had returned to his eyes.

Over the weekend, Albert's blood counts had skyrocketed and the infection had retreated, to lick its wounds and wait for another day. Phillip Andersen's smug note had attributed the sudden improvement to his experimental drug—though Albert had been receiving the drug for months. The ICU specialist had chalked it up to good nursing care, close observation, and careful interventions at just the right time. Albert Windgartner credited his own powerful physique, unending stamina, and vigorous constitution—the same constitution that had enabled him to survive well over a million cigarettes during the course of his life.

He was already craving another, lusting over the full carton of filterless Camels waiting on his dresser back at the nursing home.

"That's the first thing I'll do once I get out of this place," he said. "Smoke a couple of packs, in an hour or so. Two at a time."

"You're joking," Erica told him. "Aren't you, Dad?"

"Like hell I am." Albert was sitting up in bed in the PICU— the step-down unit beside Intensive Care. He glared up at Plato. "You got a problem with that, Doc?"

"It's your choice." Plato shrugged. He had stopped fighting Albert long ago. "You'll be back here a lot sooner, I'll guarantee. But you know the risks."

"Tell *her* that." Albert jerked his thumb at his daughter. "Even since I got here, she's been mooning and simpering over me like I'm a sick puppy."

Erica shot a pleading glance at her father's physician. Plato shot a helpless glance back.

What could he say? Albert had heard all the lectures before. The old developer was confident that he would die soon, no matter what. Or that he would live forever. In a way, the two attitudes were almost the same—mirror images that led to similar behavior.

More shocking was Albert's abrupt personality change—and the sudden chill between him and his daughter.

Plato had seen it happen many times before. Patients confronting death tend to soften, relent, to give up the hard edges and sharp corners they've honed and polished over the years. Defenses fall, old aggressions wither and die, and old breaches are healed.

In many patients, a brush with death leads to permanent changes. But for some, an unexpected return to health brings back a sudden rush of the old bitterness. And a wish that they hadn't been quite so relenting and forgiving, that they hadn't revealed quite so much of themselves.

They snatch up their defenses like remorseful lovers snatching up their clothes on the morning after.

"Anyway," Erica told the floor, "I'm glad you feel good enough to smoke."

"Don't get smart with me." Albert Windgartner glanced at his watch. "You've got a long-term care committee meeting here at four o'clock, don't you?"

"Steven's going," she replied, head still bowed. "They're just formalizing some appointments. It's a rubber-stamp meeting."

"There's no such thing as a rubber-stamp meeting." Albert's eyes flashed. "How many times have I told you that? You should be there, too. Networking, politicking. They're talking about putting in a new wing here at Riverside soon. They'll never take our bid seriously if you keep on skipping committee meetings."

"I've been stuck in meetings and conferences all day," Erica protested. Her eyes flashed. "Two hours at the medical school, two more with the building inspectors, and two hours of site visits. I just *got* here, Dad. I wanted to see you."

"Here I am. You've seen me." He waved a hand at the door. "Now go."

Plato shuffled his feet. "Maybe I should leave—let you folks talk this over."

"No." Albert sat up and fussed with his hospital gown. "You came here to examine me, not to hear my daughter whine."

Erica's head jerked up as though she'd been slapped. She stared at her father in disbelief, then turned and stormed from the room.

Albert Windgartner turned to Plato and smiled apologetically. "Sorry about that."

"You don't need to apologize to *me*," Plato told him. Before his patient could reply, Plato plugged his stethoscope into his ears. "Breathe."

Albert breathed. The bubbling aquarium in his right lung had faded to more of a burbling faucet. He was breathing easily despite his tirade with Erica. The Swan-Ganz had been pulled over the weekend; he was tethered to just two IVs and a heart monitor. His pulse rate had slowed to something approaching normal, and he hadn't spiked a fever in thirty-six hours.

Listening to Albert's heart, Plato heard a ghostly rumbling murmur. His patient was speaking.

"What's that?" He straightened up and pulled the stethoscope from his ears.

"I said, maybe I was a little hard on her." Albert Windgartner's fierce blue eyes were glaring at a bouquet of fresh flowers sitting by the windowsill. "On Erica, I mean."

Plato nodded. "I think you're right."

"She's just so *goddamned* like her mother." Albert shifted his gaze to the window. Outside, the sky was crisp and blue and cold. Puffy clouds drifted fitfully across the setting sun, blotting out the light and casting flickering shadows across Albert's bed and the green linoleum floor. "Just like her."

"What's wrong with that?" Plato tucked his stethoscope into his pocket and rested a hip on the nightstand.

"If you knew Cora Dentinger, you wouldn't ask." Albert grimaced at Plato and shook his head. "Iron fist in a velvet glove. Temper like a stick of cyclonite with a two-second fuse. Gentle as could be, unless you crossed her."

Plato sighed. That *did* sound like Erica. And like Albert Windgartner.

And, for that matter, like Cal.

"Fussed and frittered like the dickens," Albert continued. "Wanted everything just perfect—perfect house, perfect kid, perfect marriage. Woman tried to run *my* life, and she came pretty damned close, too." He picked at the coverlet, and contemplated the IV in his wrist. "Gave herself an ulcer and died. Leaving me with a sad little girl that's gone and grown up to be just like her mama."

"You don't have to worry about ulcers with Erica," Plato assured him.

"No kidding. She's too damn healthy—too damn *perfect* for that." The icy blue eyes swiveled over to Plato. "Why the hell didn't *you* marry her?"

Plato gulped. The question kept taking him by surprise, popping up at him like a monster in a bad dream. He tugged at the collar of his shirt. "I—uhh—I—"

Because she's too damned much like you, he was thinking.

Thankfully, Albert didn't seem to expect an answer. He was staring at the flowers on the windowsill again.

"Steven's a good enough guy, in his way. Didn't have a lot of money at first, but he had a good head for business." Albert rubbed his forehead and smiled sadly. "A little bit old for Erica, maybe. He's been with me for years—project assistant, project manager, even bought into a couple of things. He's done pretty damn well for himself."

"They seem happy."

"Yeah. Nobody's going to railroad Steven Prescott. Kid's got a fire in his belly. I like that." He grinned at Plato. "God help their kids, though. Perfect mom and perfect dad. The kids'll grow up eating fat-free grass clippings and scribbling amortization figures on their crib mattresses."

Plato chuckled.

"She's a hell of a girl, Doc. A hell of a girl." The ice in his eyes melted, just a little. "One of these days, I'll have to tell her."

Erica Windgartner was flipping through magazines in the waiting room down the hall. The television was on, tuned to

Lamb Chop's Play-Along at an inaudible volume. Shari was carrying on a silent conversation with a beagle-shaped athletic sock.

Erica had sorted all the magazines and arranged them alphabetically in piles on the coffee table. She flapped a *Newsweek* at Plato when he walked in.

"This is the most recent one—only a year old."

"Careful aging," Plato explained. He sat beside her on the sofa and riffled through the contents. "Think how smug you can feel, looking through these articles. Like this one on the federal budget. A year ago, you wouldn't have known Congress was lying."

"I would have only *suspected* they were lying."

"And this one about computers. Pentium!" He fluttered the page. "Makes them look pretty silly, huh?"

Erica leaned over and peered at another headline in the business section. "'CONSTRUCTION INDUSTRY BOOM PREDICTED.' Well, they got *that* right."

"Your company is doing pretty well, huh?"

"So Steven says." Erica frowned. "Too bad Dad isn't around to enjoy it."

Plato set the ancient magazine on the coffee table. "He's doing a lot better."

"For now." She shrugged. "But what about next time?"

"Maybe there won't *be* a next time," he replied. "Not for a while, anyway. Your father's blood counts have—"

"Doubled? Skyrocketed? I've heard *that* before." She shook her head. "And a week from now, a month, two months, it'll happen again."

"Erica—"

"And when it does, for a day or two, he'll let me be close. He'll act like a real father, instead of a business partner." She shook her head and stared at Plato with glistening eyes, then turned her gaze back to the floor. Long blond hair waved forward to frame her face. "I feel like one of those paddle-balls on a string. Every time I start to get close to him—*slam!*—he bats me away again."

Plato remembered the feeling—from the months he had dated Erica.

"Sometimes," she began in a hollow voice, "sometimes I wish he'd stay sick just a little longer."

"He said he was too hard on you. Just now." Plato squeezed Erica's arm. "He said you're an awful lot like your mother."

"He did?"

"And he said you're a hell of a girl."

"He did?"

"Twice."

Erica shook her head again, and her voice dropped to a whisper. "Then why can't he tell *me*?"

"I think he's trying," Plato replied. "He's calmer now—maybe if you went in and talked with him again . . ."

"No." Erica Windgartner squared her shoulders and sat up, tossing her heart back into the freezer again. Her face was calm, composed, determined. Like a news reporter at a crash scene. "I'll just wait here until Steven's committee meeting is over. We're going out to dinner—to celebrate. Steven's gotten final approval on his rehab hospital—it's going in just up the road from Wyndhaven. On property that the partnership already owns. He's been working night and day for months to push the deal through."

"Congratulations."

"I wanted to tell Daddy, but he wouldn't let me." She smiled thinly. "Step-down rehab is the wave of the future. And even though it's a small hospital, we stand to make a major killing on the construction alone. The long-term revenue projections look very, very good. We outbid two HMOs and the county hospital for the certificates of need, but we *still* have potential for a huge profit margin."

"It sounds wonderful."

"Windgartner Industries is having a *fantastic* year. Wyndhaven Colony is turning in record profits this year." Erica rubbed her hands together. "Of course, that's mostly Steven's, but our other two luxury communities are doing almost as well."

"Huh."

"We're growing by leaps and bounds. Masterson's chain of nursing homes was our biggest competitor in this market, but we're leaving them in the dust." She grinned happily. "Keep this under your hat, but *someone* said they're about to go under."

"Great."

"Their management system is positively Stone Age. And

they don't know how to milk the system, to bring in the high-paying patients. They're living mostly on Medicaid, and you know what that means."

Plato shook his head. "Bad news, huh?"

"Not for us. Of course, Steven deserves a lot of the credit for our success," she conceded. "I came in here last year with hardly any experience. I'm *still* feeling my way around. Steven showed me the ropes."

"He seems like a great guy."

"He is. A great salesman, and really good at buffing the company's image—volunteering for fund-raisers and all that." She sighed again. "Our best year ever. Dad should be impressed with *that*. If he lives long enough."

A few minutes later, Steven appeared and took her off to dinner in a flurry of handshakes and smiles and nice-seeing-you-agains.

Buffing the image. Milking the system.

Sitting alone in the empty waiting room, Plato tried to remember what had attracted him to Erica Windgartner. And wondered where it had gone.

CHAPTER 20

"So. What do you think of our pretty pictures, Cal?"

Coroner Ralph Jensson was standing before a pair of X-ray viewers in the main autopsy suite at the County Morgue. Eyes sparkling happily, he puffed his pipe to a cheery red glow. He tapped its mouthpiece against the glowing screens.

"On the left, we have the film taken last week from the bones you found at Siegel." Puff, puff. "And on the right, we have Kate Shirvesky's last X ray, taken shortly after her cast was removed. Just a week before she unpacked her apartment and disappeared from Case Western."

Cal was impressed. After leaving the anatomy lab, she had grabbed a quick bite of lunch and dashed across town to the morgue. Ralph had called that morning to say he had a bit of interesting news, but she had never suspected that they might finally have a shot at identifying Siegel Woman. The bones had seemed so ancient, brown-stained and pumice-light from demineralization.

Apparently, the skeleton of Siegel Woman wasn't quite as old as it seemed.

"Ms. Shirvesky was a skier, they tell me." He tapped the film on the right. "Cross-country, mostly—and those skis don't release if you fall. That's how she got this."

Cal studied the two images closely. The X ray on the right, taken last spring, actually showed two bones—the tibia and the fibula—along with a ghostly whitish glow from the muscles of her leg. The X ray on the left, taken last week, simply showed the long white shaft of the tibia they had found in the excavation site. The trabeculae—fine white striations of dense bone that form along the lines of pressure and tension—were less obvious, and the center of the bone appeared nearly black.

"Obvious demineralization in the film on the left," Cal began. "The trabeculae are difficult to see, and much of the bone marrow appears to have leached out."

"Quaite." Puff, puff. "And we took that X ray using the lowest possible power."

Cal looked closer. Luckily, the two films had been taken from almost identical angles, making comparisons much easier.

"From what I can see, the trabecular patterns are similar, if not identical."

"Very good." Jensson's chubby fingers traced the road map of whitish lines on both films. "As you know, the trabeculae are different in each individual, forming something of a bony fingerprint. Like webs woven by different spiders—similar, yet distinctive."

Cal finally turned her attention to the fracture itself—visible in both films as a jagged band of white crossing the middle of the femur. Both films were taken before the bone had completely healed. Although no crack was visible on X ray or examination, the bony callus—a calcium-rich scar responsible for healing the bone—was still present. The calcium in the healing scar blocked more X rays than the surrounding bone, and caused an apparent white band on the film.

The direction and width of the callus were virtually identical in the two X rays. Cal finally lifted the old X ray and placed it over the autopsy film. The angles of the two shots weren't quite exact enough to show a perfect alignment, but the similarity was obvious.

"Looks like you've got a match," she concluded.

"Quaite." Jensson studied the X rays thoughtfully, then nodded. "I wanted your unbiased opinion before I told you what *else* we found."

"You found something else?"

"Not me *personally*. More correctly, the Summit County Coroner." His feathery eyebrows fluttered. "Or, to be brutally precise, Fratiano's Landscaping Services."

"Oh, no." Cal shook her head. "Don't tell me—"

"Oh, yes." Jensson crooked a finger and led her to a corner of the room. There, on a plain blue towel, was a complete human skull. Grinning, as though it was happy to join in on Jensson's little suspense play.

"Dr. Cal Marley, meet Kate Shirvesky. Or what's left of her, poor lass." Jensson patted the skull sadly. "We've got a positive dental ID. Now you see why I wanted your opinion on the leg films before I showed you the skull."

Cal nodded. If she had known that the skull had been found and belonged to the missing student, she might have been more likely to identify the tibia as belonging to her as well.

"As you can see, we have a possible cause of death, but not necessarily a manner of death." He traced the lines of a star-shaped fracture that started at the center of the skull in the back, sending five jagged lines up toward the parietal bones and down toward the base of the skull.

Cal nodded. The fracture could have been homicidal or accidental—the result of a fall. It might even have happened while the skull was being dug up or transported to the landscaping project. But the fracture pattern matched others she had seen in victims of fatal falls.

The skull showed no telltale indentations or other signs that a blunt instrument had been used to perform murder. But even if Kate's death had resulted from a fall, the manner of death could still be homicide—she might have been pushed. And the fact that the body was buried certainly pointed to foul play. Cal frowned. "Where was the skull found?"

"In Hudson. From what I understand, the landscapers were installing a new lawn in one of those ritzy new developments down there," Jensson explained. "Though why anyone would throw good money away on sod is a mystery to me."

"A lot of Hudson is like that," Cal said. "Turf wars—they weed their lawns with Agent Orange and trim them with precision lasers. The neighborhoods look like putting greens with houses on them."

"Quaite." Puff, puff. "Apparently this homeowner was no exception. She complained about the quality of the soil they were trucking in. Too many rocks."

"Oh, dear."

"So the landscape designer suggested she build a rock border for her garden. The workers gathered all the rocks and piled them beside her garden. Apparently they were in quite a hurry, so they didn't notice that one of the rocks wasn't a rock at all."

"You're kidding."

"Nay." Jensson shrugged. "Packed with clay and muddy as it was, the skull was easy to mistake. The jawbone hadn't been found yet, of course."

"So when did the homeowner notice?"

"This morning. After yesterday's rain and snow had melted away. She was putting in her neat little garden border when she noticed a pair of eye sockets staring at her from the rock pile." Jensson shook his bald head sadly. "After the initial shock, she assumed it wasn't a real skull—just a Halloween prank. Until she found the jawbone under a nearby bush."

"The fill dirt came from the excavation site at Siegel?"

"As far as we know." Jensson leaned on the countertop and crossed his arms. "Several truckloads were needed to bring this woman's yard up to grade. The dirt came from two places—the Siegel site, and a distributor of screened topsoil."

"I suppose that explains it, then." Cal remembered Plato's joke that the missing skull would be found in Medina County next spring. He wasn't too far off. "We know the identity of Siegel Woman now. At least we have one question answered."

"Aye, but at the expense of several more." Jensson's freckled dome furrowed. "For starters, if poor Kate died only a few short months ago, why do her bones look so old? The extent of demineralization and discoloration might indicate a watery grave, yet these bones were found buried in the soil. How did they get to Siegel? Who put them there?"

Cal nodded. "And I'm wondering what the connection is between an unstable grad student at Case Western and a bunch of missing charts at Riverside General Hospital."

"Exactly. And, of course, we have one more very important question." Jensson seized the skull in both hands and showed it to Cal. On the roof of the cranium, near the right side, one distinctive white spot was visible. An odd shape—a pale triangle with two straight sides joined by a convex curve. It stretched from the peak of the skull down toward the opening where the right ear had been. "What caused this pattern of bleaching on Kate Shirvesky's skull?"

Cal nodded. She had heard of similar cases in the past. A

distinctive white pattern—most commonly caused by sun bleaching—could indicate where a bone had rested over the past few months. The rays of the sun filtering through a hole in a roof or a car's trunk could leave a distinctive mark on the bones and lead to the trail of the killer—even after the bones had been moved or buried.

"How did the leopard get its spots?" Jensson's eyes glittered. "When we can answer that question, we just might have the key to all the rest."

That evening, Cal bumped into the prime suspect in Kate Shirvesky's murder.

Not that it was necessarily a murder, of course. After all, they still weren't even sure about the cause of death. But someone had certainly gone to great lengths to hide the body—and the skeleton.

Walking out of Riverside General that evening after checking up on a few things in the pathology department, Cal was thinking about the odd bleaching pattern on Kate Shirvesky's skull. Re-creating the shape in her mind, and trying to imagine what could have made it. The outline had seemed too regular to be a simple hole in a roof or a trunk.

Lost in her thoughts, she collided with Phillip Andersen on her way out of the main lobby.

"I'm sorry," he said. He was standing directly in her path, but he didn't move. He just stared at her with wild, pleading eyes—like an escaped convict hearing the baying of distant bloodhounds.

"That's okay. Excuse me, please." She turned to move around him, to avoid further conversation, but it was no use. He stepped across her path again and gently touched her arm.

"Cal Marley? You may not remember me. I'm—"

"Phillip Andersen. I know."

"Can we talk?" The hunted eyes darted over to the door of the physicians' lounge and back to Cal's face.

"I really shouldn't be—" Cal began. She watched the flicker of hope in Phillip's eyes dim. He dropped his hand from her arm and shifted his gaze to the floor. She shrugged reluctantly. "All right. Let's just say you're consulting me about a problem with the lab's blood smears. Okay?"

"Sure." Phillip's relief was almost palpable. He hurried to

the physicians' lounge and peered inside. This late, it was almost always empty. Today was no exception.

He perched on the edge of the wing chair and Cal took the sofa. For a long moment, he just sat staring at his hands.

"The police think I killed Kate." His voice was low and hollow, like an echo from a dry well.

"Kate?" Cal asked.

"Kate Shirvesky." He stared up at the ceiling. "A student at Case Western. Did some research with me last year."

He stared at his hands again and tried to speak, but managed only a rasping croak. He cleared his throat, swallowed heavily, and tried again. "She's dead. That skeleton they found at Siegel. The police think it was hers."

He looked a question at Cal.

She nodded. "I think they're right."

"Oh, God." His mouth was a thin red slash. His jaw muscles worked as he fought for control. "I thought she had just *left*—because of me. I didn't know—"

Tortured words and phrases spewed out in an angry torrent of regret and self-recrimination. Finally, he closed his eyes and drew a deep breath.

"It's been over between Cheryl and me for a long time. We've just been going through the motions, I don't know why." Phillip shook his head slowly. "I knew about Cheryl and Marvin. God knows he wasn't the first, though I thought I knew my partner better than that." He sighed. "But when I met Kate, for the first time I could forget about my wife. I could—"

He broke off and buried his face in his hands.

In a voice muffled by fingers and tears, he asked the timeless question. "Why would anyone *kill* her?"

Cal stirred on the sofa, moved by his grief. She would have made an awful cop—she was a lousy judge of character. Too trusting, too gullible. All the same, she couldn't imagine that Phillip Andersen was putting on an act.

She reached out and touched his arm. "You heard from the police today?"

"This afternoon." He nodded. "Those two detectives came by, while I was in my office seeing patients. They said it was urgent." He stared at the ceiling again and bit his lip. "They sat there in my office and told me Kate was dead. Real casually, like they were talking about the weather."

His hands clenched into fists. "Lieutenant Ames told me how they found my name—and Marvin Tucker's—as coauthors on one of her research projects. He said one of the nurses here saw us leaving together a few times last spring. God! Kate's own *roommate* didn't even know about us. We were really careful, but not careful enough." Phillip Andersen shook his head. "And then he sat there watching me like some kind of angry Doberman, waiting for me to make a move so he could get me by the throat. I *hate* that guy."

"But you told them the truth?"

"Everything. I told them everything. About me and Kate, about how things really were with Cheryl. How I knew about Marvin and my wife." He took a deep breath and sighed. "I came clean this time. Talked for an hour. But it didn't matter."

"They still suspect you?" Cal wasn't surprised. Jeremy Ames could be pretty single-minded. The fact that Phillip Andersen hadn't been truthful the first time he was questioned undoubtedly counted against him in Jeremy's book.

"They're sure I did it—killed them both."

"Why?"

"To protect myself from a malpractice suit. Or to cover up fraudulent research on our experimental drug. Or something." Andersen gave a dazed shrug. "I don't understand it all myself. I guess some medical charts are missing, and my name was on at least a couple of them. And then Kate was doing some research with Marvin. But her project had nothing to do with Marvin's drug—and very little to do with my research or patients."

"What *was* Kate researching?" Cal asked.

"What *wasn't* she researching?" Phillip gave a wry smile. "She wanted to be an epidemiologist. You know how *they* are."

Cal knew. Epidemiologists studied the distribution patterns of disease, and factors that influenced their spread. Their specialty areas covered virtually every branch of medicine—from studying risk factors for premature birth to hunting down patterns of Alzheimer's disease in families, from learning how the common cold is spread in a small town, to investigating

how the Ebola virus could jump from Zaire to the United
States.

"Anyway, Marvin was really helping her with the project,
not me. And Kate and I didn't talk much about our work
when we were together." He sighed. "But she spent a lot of
time researching at Riverside—we even found a vacant office
near ours where she kept her things. She studied the hospital's
medical charts on-site, so she didn't have to copy everything."

"Did she have any particular research interest?"

"Cancers—especially blood cancers." He smiled slightly.
"That's how she got hooked up with Marvin. And aplastic
anemia—she was really interested in that. Of course, blood
diseases and cancer are often related."

"Of course." Cal nodded. Cancer and blood problems were
so often related that hematology and oncology—treatment of
blood disorders and cancer—were generally combined into a
single specialty. Andersen and Tucker were both hematolo-
gists *and* oncologists.

"Kate had some interesting theories about that—about the
link between cancer and immune cells in the blood. And the
environment." His face fell and his eyes glazed over, as
though he'd just realized again that she was gone. "I kept
some of her papers, the few that she'd left in my office. Kate
was very intelligent. I never bought the line that she had just
disappeared."

"She'd done it before," Cal pointed out.

He nodded. "She had some problems at other schools—bad
relationships, a problem with drugs. But she'd gotten all that
straightened out. *I* thought she left because of me."

He stared blankly at Cal. "They're going to arrest me,
aren't they?"

The hollow echo had returned to his voice. He didn't really
seem to care what the answer was.

"If you're innocent, you don't have anything to worry
about." She sighed. "Even if they arrest you."

Phillip's slumped shoulders rose a quarter of an inch, then
fell again.

"It doesn't matter." His eyes were two dull blue marbles,
seeing nothing.

Cal realized that she had misread Andersen's motives for

confronting her in the lobby. The hematologist wasn't afraid of being arrested, or hoping for her help. He was afraid of the truth. And hoping for an answer Cal couldn't give.

The flicker of hope had faded from Phillip Andersen's eyes.

CHAPTER 21

"It looks like the police are going to arrest Tucker's partner," Cal told Plato later that evening.

They were huddled around the propane grill in the ramshackle courtyard of Marley Manor, roasting porterhouses and waiting for the opening kickoff of Monday Night Football. The Monday night routine of steak and football had become a tradition during their off-call weeks. The mingled aromas of grilled steak and baked potatoes, the taste of an icy cold bottle of beer, the roar of the crowd as modern gladiators battled under the lights all made Mondays vastly more tolerable, even as winter was closing in.

So did Cal and Plato's other Monday night tradition: the after-dinner exercise. They rarely stayed downstairs to watch the second halves of the games.

"The cops *already* arrested him," Plato noted casually. After searing both sides of the steaks to seal in the juices, he cut the gas to medium. "Just as a material witness, but Jeremy's hoping for an indictment."

"You talked to Jeremy?" Cal was surprised. She hugged her thick ski jacket tightly around her and shivered.

"Yeah. He called, just before you came home." Plato shifted the steaks again and warmed his hands over the burgeoning flames.

The cheap Sunbeam could produce a bonfire from a single spot of grease. In a kind of nuclear reaction, the grill could turn dripping fat into pure energy, with black carbonized steaks as the only by-product.

"All the evidence is stacked against Phillip Andersen," Plato continued. He pulled a squirt gun from his coat pocket and zapped the flames into submission.

"All *what* evidence?" Cal asked.

"Remember how I told you about Lou Higgins's microfilmed charts? The folks down in medical records were able to trace all the missing charts that way."

"Every one?"

"Every single one. Mabel is pretty slick." He flipped the steaks again and blew into his hands. His breath was a foggy cloud in the bright moonlight. "She spent all afternoon making a list of Andersen's patients, finding out which ones had died, and then figuring out which of *those* had donated their bodies to Siegel. She came up with four names, including Lou Higgins."

"To match the four missing charts." Cal nodded. *Now* she understood why Phillip Andersen was so sure he would be arrested.

"She was able to get microfilm records for all four patients," Plato continued. "All of them had aplastic anemia. And every single one had been treated with Tucker and Andersen's experimental drug."

"Oh, dear." She frowned.

"And of course, Phillip Andersen was the primary doctor on all four cases. Tucker only did a few backup consultations on those patients." Plato shook his head. "So whether it's research fraud or malpractice, everything points to Andersen. I even heard he was involved with that Shirvesky girl—the one you and Ralph identified in the morgue today."

Cal nodded. But she still couldn't believe it. She told Plato all about her meeting with Phillip—about his troubles with Cheryl, his relationship with Kate Shirvesky, Kate's research, and his grief when he finally realized for certain that Kate was gone.

"Phillip was *really* upset, Plato." Cal shook her head. "No matter what Jeremy says, I think he's barking up the wrong tree."

"You're too gullible, Cal. Too trusting." Plato shrugged. "Not that it matters. Wrong tree or not, you know how Jeremy is. He'll just keep barking until something happens."

She considered a moment. "What about Dr. Feinstein? He sure had plenty of reasons to bump Tucker off, even if his alibi looks good."

Cal had already told Plato about Erica's testimony in the

planetarium—the whole story about Tucker's investigation and the dismissal of the chief of obstetrics at Riverside.

"Yeah—Jeremy looked into that." He moved the steaks to the center of the grill. They sizzled and spat, surrounded by a solid sheet of flame. He crouched down and turned the burners off, then closed the lid. "Funny thing—he talked to other members of the board, and their story doesn't quite match with Erica's. Tucker *did* present the evidence, much like Erica said. But only one of the trustees remembered Feinstein making any threat, and he didn't take it very seriously. Sort of a 'you'll hear from my lawyer' kind of thing, and it seemed to be directed at all of them, rather than at Tucker alone."

"Strange," Cal mused. Erica had been so certain that Feinstein had threatened Tucker.

"Feinstein was six months from retirement, so they let him finish out his year."

"Swept it under the rug," Cal observed, but she wondered. *Had* Erica exaggerated the facts? Why would she?

She didn't want to think about the answer.

"Riverside politics as usual," Plato agreed. "Anyway, Feinstein has a really solid alibi now. Some guy at a gas station out in Willougby identified his photo. Twenty miles away from the crime scene, half an hour before Tucker was found."

"I guess that rules him out."

"And rules Phillip Andersen *in*." He lifted the lid and watched the flames flicker and die. "They really don't have any other clear suspects."

"But if Phillip really killed Kate and Marvin to cover up his malpractice, how did he get those charts from Sergei's office?" Cal challenged. "He's not on faculty at the medical school—is he?"

"He certainly is," Plato replied smugly. "He teaches the hematology section to the sophomore students."

"Oh."

"They're covering hematology this month." He crossed his arms. "Phillip Andersen has been lecturing at Siegel for the past couple of weeks, since right around the time that the first charts were stolen."

"Oh." Cal frowned again. "But what about Kate's skeleton? Why would Phillip have buried it in the excavation site? And how?"

"Maybe he used those awful dermestids of Sergei's to clean the bones." Plato grimaced at the thought. "Like Alice Devon said, it would only take a few weeks. He might have been hoping to clean the skeleton and hide the bones in Sergei's collection, just like we thought. Except the skeleton collection was moved."

"But how could he be sure Sergei wouldn't check his colony and find Kate's body?" Cal asked. "I'm sure he has to feed those bugs once in a while. Besides, dermestids wouldn't explain the changes in Kate's bones. A lot of calcium was leached out, and they were stained deep brown, like they had been buried for a long time."

Plato thought for a long moment, listening to the pop and sizzle of the steaks.

"Then maybe it wasn't dermestids after all," he finally replied. "Maybe the body was resting in water. That could explain the changes, right?"

Cal started, surprised at his insight.

"Maybe," she agreed with a nod. "That's what Ralph Jensson suggested. Iron or tannin in the water could stain the bones, and the calcium would leach out much more quickly— so the bones would look much older than they are."

"But could a body turn into a skeleton, in just a few months?" Plato asked.

"In the summer? Easily." Cal shrugged. "I've heard about some bodies that turned to skeletons in just a few days, or a couple of weeks. If the body were partly covered with water, the process would go very quickly." She pressed a finger to her lips and considered. "Depending on the rate of decay, and the predators in the area—"

"Predators?" He chuckled. "In Cleveland, Ohio?"

"Scavengers, then. You know—mice and rats and bugs and so forth. They're very quick and efficient, and they don't mind a little water. There's a whole subspecialty in forensics—dating deaths according to the amount of work the little creatures have done." She pressed her thumb and index fingers together and made little nipping motions. "We found some chew marks on Kate's bones. Rats, most likely. Hungry little devils. Ralph Jensson told me this story about when he found—"

"I'd *love* to hear all about it," Plato interrupted. He lifted the porterhouses onto a platter. "But the steaks are done."

"Fine. I'll tell you Ralph's story after dinner." She eyed the steaks hungrily. "Those look *wonderful*. Cooked just right, and dripping with juice. I'm so hungry I could chew mine right down to the bone."

"Just like a mouse." He grimaced. "Or a rat."

"Or a bug," Cal added. "Don't forget the bugs. Very tidy scavengers, insects are. Nature's cleaning service—you don't really need dermestids. Take the Wroblanski case last summer, for starters. . . . Plato? Plato?"

He had disappeared into the house.

Halfway through dinner, Cal decided to broach the subject again. Plato had recovered his appetite and attacked the porterhouse and baked potatoes and sweet corn and garlic bread with reckless abandon. He was slowing down now, savoring the last few bites of fillet and watching with a glazed, happy smile as the Bears pummeled the Cowboys.

"I still don't get it," Cal said thoughtfully. "Even if Phillip Andersen dropped Kate's body in a culvert or something, why did he bother moving it? And how did he get her skeleton into the excavation site? It's surrounded by a barbed-wire fence."

"Not completely," Plato pointed out. "The fence stops at the rear entrance of the medical school. Two of Siegel's doors open into the construction site itself."

She nodded slowly. "And one of them is the emergency exit from the anatomy lab stairwell."

Plato speared the last bite of fillet and washed it down with a swallow of beer. "As for *why* he moved the bones, we can only guess. Maybe Andersen had put the body someplace incriminating—like on his property. Maybe in a well or a storm sewer or something. He was probably afraid of discovery. Maybe he thought Tucker had guessed what had happened. So he bundled up the bones, lugged them in the side entrance, and tried to hide them in Sergei's collection."

"Only to find that the collection was gone."

"Right. So he took the next best course. By burying them in the foundation of Siegel's addition, he could be sure they wouldn't be discovered for a long, long time."

Cal sighed. It still sounded pretty far-fetched.

"Of course, he didn't know that the building inspector would insist on deepening the foundation by another two feet."

"That's *right*!" Cal agreed. She sat up quickly. "So Kate's skeleton must have been buried just before the excavation was deepened."

"Exactly. And guess who was at Siegel the night before we found the skeleton?" Plato set his plate and glass on the coffee table, stretched, and paused for dramatic emphasis. "Phillip Andersen. Signed in late that Sunday night, and spent three hours there. He *claims* he was working on slides for a lecture—using the Internal Medicine department's computer. But nobody else was around to confirm that he stayed in the office."

"I take it he doesn't have a good alibi for Tucker's murder, either?"

"Nope."

Cal sighed. "With all that evidence, I'm surprised the police haven't charged him yet."

"They will." Plato nodded confidently. "Jeremy and Molly are just getting all their ducks in a row."

And it was quite a flock of ducks, Cal mused. The impending malpractice lawsuit. Phillip's connections with Kate Shirvesky, Marvin Tucker, and the patients whose charts were missing. His presence at the scene of Tucker's murder, and his close ties to Kate. The timing of the theft of the charts. Motive, means, and opportunity.

Balanced against that gaggle of evidence was only one factor in Phillip Andersen's favor—Cal's stubborn conviction that he was innocent, that his shock and dismay at Kate Shirvesky's death were genuine. And perhaps one other factor.

Ignoring the half-time show—another propaganda piece about the NFL—Cal grabbed a piece of paper from the end table. Digging a pencil from between the sofa cushions, she absentmindedly sketched the roof of Kate Shirvesky's skull, carefully tracing the lambdoid and parietal suture lines and reconstructing the oddly triangular bleaching pattern at the right upper portion of the skull.

Sitting beside her, Plato peered at the drawing and frowned. "What's that?"

Cal told him the saga of Kate Shirvesky's skull, the poor Hudson homeowner's unsettling discovery, and the peculiar bleaching pattern Ralph Jensson had pointed out.

"Ralph thinks this might have come from a manhole cover. Like for a cistern."

"Great," Plato said sourly. "Now all you have to do is check every manhole cover in the county."

"Maybe not." She traced the markings with her finger. "Jeremy's going to check the area around Andersen's house. There were some bones missing, remember. If they find anything—the missing sternum, or one of the finger bones—that would seal the case against him."

"I think they've got a pretty solid case already." He turned back to the television. Crowd scenes showed a few Bears fans in Halloween attire: caricatures of Frank and Al and Dan, a few shaved heads painted to resemble football helmets, and an amazingly realistic grizzly bear costume. The bear suit seemed like rather sensible attire for a snowy, blustery evening at Soldier Field.

"That reminds me," Plato continued. "Tomorrow's Halloween. You'd better pick up some candy on the way home from work."

"Oh, I forgot." Cal sighed. "I've got a meeting after work tomorrow. General surgery—morbidity and mortality review. Only a couple of hours or so, but I'll probably miss the little trick-or-treaters."

"A meeting?" he asked softly.

"Yes." She turned from the television to glance at her husband. Her eyes widened with dismay. "Plato! Are you all right?"

He looked like he had seen a poltergeist—an early Halloween ghost—playing peek-a-boo from behind Cal's right shoulder. His jaw sagged, his face paled, and his green eyes bulged from their sockets.

"Plato!" Cal reached out and squeezed his arm. He swayed unsteadily on the sofa, as though at any moment he might tumble to the floor. "What's *wrong*?"

"I—uhh—" He swallowed heavily.

At least he wasn't choking. Instinctively, Cal reached for Plato's wrist. His pulse was strong and steady, if a bit fast.

"What's the matter? Are you sick?"

"No, no. Not that." He swallowed again. "I just remembered something, that's all."

Slowly, Plato wrenched his gaze back to the television. A

wide receiver for Dallas had just let a beautiful forty-yard pass slip through his fingers. The play was reviewed in slow-motion, from three angles and the blimp.

"I have a lecture to give tomorrow morning," he muttered.

Cal eyed him with concern. "Are you sure that's all?"

"Yeah. I have to get my slides together." He leaned over to fuss with the dishes on the coffee table, avoiding Cal's gaze. "Thank goodness I remembered in time."

He glanced up at her for just a moment. A disbelieving look, as though he wasn't quite sure Cal was really there. As though Cal herself was the poltergeist.

She frowned. Maybe it was time to drag Plato to their family doctor again. The pressure at work was probably getting to him. Or maybe last winter's pneumonia was coming back. Nathan Simmons had warned Plato that he would be more prone to pneumonia in the future.

"Are you sure you're not sick?" Cal felt his forehead.

Plato pushed her hand away irritably. "I'm fine."

He piled the dishes up and carried them into the kitchen. The rest of the evening was passed in virtual silence—cleaning up the kitchen, watching the second half of the football game, and heading up to bed. In keeping with the Monday night tradition, Cal slipped into some exotic sleepwear—a gauzy blue teddy gown she had ordered from a *Frederick's of Hollywood* catalog. It had come with Saturday's mail, while Plato was up on the roof with Homer. She had been saving it for tonight, hoping to surprise him.

Plato was already on his side, seemingly asleep. She slipped under the sheets and pressed against him. No response.

"Plato?" she breathed.

"Huh."

"Are you asleep?"

"No." He sighed. "Just thinking. About my talk tomorrow. And all that."

"Oh." Reluctantly, she slid away and stared at the ceiling. The trouble with gauzy blue teddies was that they were constructed with only one function in mind—and it wasn't sleep.

She sat up, got out of bed, and walked across the room to get her novel from the bookcase. Plato opened his eyes for just a moment, glanced at her, and closed them again. She leaned closer and kissed him on the nose.

"Everything all right?"

"Yeah. Just fine."

She strolled back around the bed and sat up beside him. Noisily, she opened Elmore Leonard's *Get Shorty* and leafed through the pages.

"Good book, this."

"Huh."

"Even better than the movie."

"Huh."

"Of course, I *could* be persuaded to set it aside." Cal chuckled softly. "For the right reasons."

"I'm kind of tired."

"It wouldn't take *much* persuading," she said.

He rolled over and gave her an apologetic smile.

"It's after midnight, Cal. I've got a lecture tomorrow." He rolled over again and folded the pillow over his head. "Good night."

Cal closed her book and frowned. She slid out of bed once more and climbed into her comfortable jammies. Hanging the teddy gown up again, she eyed it critically. The sheer, gauzy skirt framed her figure perfectly, and the outfit featured an assortment of interesting ribbons and ties and stays. The last time she had worn an outfit like this, Plato had reacted like an angry bull sighting a matador's red cape. Cal had hoped for a similar response tonight.

Fever or not, Plato was *definitely* sick, she decided with a nod. There was no other possible explanation.

CHAPTER 22

"Hey, good-looking."

Plato glanced up from his Dictaphone to see Cal in the doorway of his office. She was smiling happily, without a single glimmer of deceit showing in her soft brown eyes.

"I thought I'd drop by and cheer you up. You were awfully gloomy this morning." She picked her way across the environmental disaster zone that was Plato's office and perched on the arm of the sofa. The couch itself was covered with papers and charts and textbooks and medical journals. "How'd your lecture go today?"

"Okay." Plato shrugged. "Not bad."

"Had lunch yet?" Cal asked brightly. "I thought maybe we could risk the cafeteria together. Safety in numbers, you know." She grinned. "Tom Brunelski said he found a piece of real meat in the chicken surprise. Not *chicken*, of course, but it's a start."

"Guess I'll have to pass." Plato's voice sounded flat, even to himself. He patted the stack of charts beside the Dictaphone. "I had a really full morning here, and I haven't dictated a single chart yet."

"So I'll bring something up, and get ready for *my* next lecture." She shrugged. "I'll keep you company—I've got plenty of free time today."

I bet you do, Plato thought. Aloud he muttered, "No, thanks. I'm just not very hungry."

He flipped through the first chart, pretending he couldn't feel her concerned gaze.

What did *she* care, anyway? Why was she making such an effort to cheer him up? Would it make her feel less guilty tonight, knowing her deception was complete?

Across the room, Cal shifted on her perch. She sighed. She cleared her throat.

"Plato?"

Finally, he looked up—and was surprised to see lines of emotion etched on her face.

"I have a confession to make." She was staring at the floor, eyes shining wetly.

Here it comes, he thought. Faced with the final, horrible confirmation of his worst fears, Plato felt his heart drop out again. His throat shrank to the diameter of a cocktail straw. His pulse throbbed dully and distantly, a sad ocean sound from somewhere far away.

"This past week or two, I've been keeping something from you." She looked up at him. Her face was racked with guilt. Tears welled up in her eyes.

As hurt as Plato felt, he couldn't fight the wave of sympathy that washed over him.

"I thought it was for the best," Cal continued in a broken voice. "But I can't hide it anymore. I've been seeing Neville—"

"Hi, folks!"

Homer burst through the doorway with the unexpected suddenness of a lightning bolt blasting through a cloudless sky. Plato rocketed from his chair. Cal's head jerked up. She stood quickly and mopped her eyes on her sleeve.

Homer glanced around the tableau and frowned. "Sorry. I guess I should have knocked. But the door was open, and I thought—"

"It's okay," Cal interrupted quickly. "We were just chatting about medical stuff. You didn't interrupt anything."

The big lawyer's frown slowly faded. "Good—because I've got a favor to ask."

For the first time, Plato noticed the bulging briefcase in one of his hands, the grease-stained paper bag in the other.

"Oh, no," Plato said.

"How would you guys like some free lunch?" Homer asked with a grin.

"No way, Homer." Plato shook his head firmly. "I've got a stack of charts to dictate, a ton of paperwork to fill out, and I was hoping to stop by the nursing home tonight—if I ever get out of here. Enn-Oh. Not a chance."

"Too bad for you," Homer replied. He set the briefcase on

the floor and riffled through the paper bag. "A whole assortment of rare delicacies, as prepared and served by that street vendor over on Ninth Street, by the Rock Museum. The guy's an artist—a *genius*—I swear. The Jacques Cousteau of submarine sandwich makers."

He opened one of the wrappers and sniffed daintily. "Italian sausage, marinara sauce, and a sprinkling of raw onions. Just the way you like it, Cally." He shrugged. "Such a shame. I suppose I'll have to eat them all myself."

"Hold on a minute," Cal interrupted. Her eyes were glued to the sandwich in Homer's paw. Her nostrils flared. "Exactly what do you want us to do?"

"Nothing too strenuous." He planted the bag and sandwich on one of the bookcase shelves, just beyond Cal's reach. The aroma of sausage and onions and tomato sauce washed across the room. He opened his briefcase and dragged out an imposing stack of papers and manila folders. "Just glance through some of these records. They're copies of the microfilms from those stolen medical charts, along with a few papers from Andersen's or Tucker's offices that mentioned Kate Shirvesky. Research stuff, mostly."

Plato's stomach grumbled impatiently. Cal edged closer to the sandwich.

"What are you looking for?" Plato asked.

"We're not sure." Homer shrugged. "Patterns. Something that might look like a trend of malpractice. Anything that might point to what Kate Shirvesky knew—and what got her killed. We've got plenty of circumstantial evidence, but we need to tie up the motive. I'm going to talk with that girl's research advisor this afternoon, and see if he can give us any ideas."

"You've got nine medical charts there," Cal observed. "I thought only four were missing."

Homer nodded. "We found a list of patient names in the Shirvesky girl's handwriting. Four of them matched up with the missing charts from Siegel. The other five belonged to some of Andersen's patients who *didn't* donate their bodies to Siegel—including the lady whose husband is suing Andersen."

"All of the patients had aplastic anemia?" she asked.

"Yeah." He spread his hands. "And all five charts were missing from Riverside's Medical Records Department. Lucky for us, someone microfilmed all the charts before they lent them to Kate. I guess it's their policy."

Plato frowned. "Nine charts, huh?"

"Maybe it's too much to ask." Homer shrugged. "We need some kind of opinion by tomorrow, or Thursday at the latest."

"What about McGilvrey—that hematology fellow?" Cal asked. "Have you shown the charts to him?"

"Of course. He's looking over some copies right now." Homer's eyes narrowed. "But chances are good that he was involved in at least some of the cases."

"That's right," Plato agreed. "He's not exactly an impartial witness. Even though he's just a fellow, a malpractice case could spill over onto him."

"Exactly." Homer wrapped the tantalizing sausage sandwich up again and stuffed it back into the bag. "Too bad you folks are so busy. I suppose I'll have to find somebody else. Maybe a couple of residents would be hungry enough to give me an opinion."

"Nonsense." Cal had been watching the sandwich disappear again like a hungry dog watching its master tossing a plateload of scraps into the trash. She stood and grabbed the sandwich and the files. "We'll be happy to help you out, Homer. Besides, the residents don't have time for this sort of thing."

"And we do?" Plato asked.

She pointed at the bag. "What else is in there?"

"Two soft pretzels with that hot mustard Plato likes—for an appetizer." He stared at the ceiling. "Another sausage sandwich, with green peppers and onions. A meatball sandwich. Oh—and a corn dog."

"A *corn* dog?" Plato breathed.

Homer nodded. "I told you this guy was an artist. How he keeps them hot and crispy, I'll never know. Trade secret, probably. Oh, and lots of cheddar cheese sauce."

The aroma of the food was overpowering. And somewhere within the bag, a corn dog had Plato's name written on its crusty shell. It was calling him. Despite Cal's guilty admission, Plato's stomach was writhing like a python after a forty-day fast.

No reason to be miserable *and* hungry. Besides, Plato owed Homer more than a few favors.

"All right." Plato sighed. "Cal and I can split the charts up.

We'll look them over today— and compare notes after her *meeting* tonight."

Cal shot him an odd look. Homer's eyes widened. He glanced from Cal to Plato and back again, then shook his head.

"Whatever you say, Plato." His voice softened. "I'll be around tonight, if you need me."

"Sure, Homer." Plato glanced over at Cal. "I just might."

Homer packed up his briefcase and left the sandwiches and papers behind.

After he was gone, Cal stared at the doorway curiously.

"He sure left in a hurry."

Plato shrugged.

"And what was all that stuff about 'if you need me'? Are you in some kind of trouble, Plato?"

"Hardly." He shook his head. "*I* haven't done anything wrong. Now, what was it you were going to tell me?"

Before Cal could reply, her pager twittered. She plucked it from her pocket and stared at the window. Her face fell.

"Damn! Some kind of emergency down in pathology."

Plato's eyebrows rose. "An emergency in *pathology*? What kind of emergency? Everyone down there is already *dead*."

"Whoever paged me punched in a number '1', and that means it's an emergency." She bundled her sandwich up again. "Probably some surgeon doesn't trust the pathology resident's reading on a frozen section."

"Oh." Now Plato understood. During surgery, tumor samples were often sent to pathology for quick freezing and mounting so that pathologists could interpret them as benign or malignant. The pathologist's verdict could spell the difference between a simple or radical procedure, but a misjudgment could be fatal.

"I've got to go." She counted out five of the charts and tucked them under her arms. "I'll take these along and check over the rest with you later. Okay?"

"Fine."

She hurried to the doorway, paused, and turned around.

"And we'll talk about the other thing tonight, okay?" She peered at him with a concerned frown, as though Plato were a malignancy on a frozen section. "It's going to take a little time."

"Sure, Cal. Whatever you say."

She turned and dashed through the door, white coat and blond hair sailing behind her. The ache in Plato's heart returned with a vengeance, an emotional riptide sucking all animation from his body. He sat for several minutes, staring at the Dictaphone, the piles of charts, the bag of sandwiches, and the telephone.

Finally, he lifted the receiver and dialed the surgery department.

"Hi, this is Dr. Marley. No, *Plato* Marley. I was wondering—are you folks holding a Morbidity and Mortality meeting tonight? Oh. Only on Saturday mornings? Uh-huh, that's what I thought. Thank you. No, nothing's wrong. I was just curious, that's all."

Plato settled the receiver back into its cradle and slowly closed his eyes.

An hour passed before he woke up again. Plato hadn't planned on falling asleep. But he had stayed up half of last night, tossing and turning, wondering and worrying. Trying to fit Cal's carefree attitude with the obvious lie she was living. Toward morning, he'd finally decided—again—that he must have made a mistake, that there really *was* a meeting tonight.

But he was wrong.

Dictating charts was the very last thing Plato felt like doing. Leaping from the helicopter pad on the roof of Riverside General seemed like a better use of his time.

But Mrs. Cummings was very sick, and Julio Cisneros needed his medical forms filled out before his disability checks would start coming again, and Olga Ingelmeier would be coming back for a follow-up visit on Friday. If he didn't get the charts dictated, he would have to write them out by hand later this week—if he didn't jump off the helicopter pad first.

Gradually, he slogged his way through the pile. The work had a mind-numbing effect, like plunging his emotions into a vat of liquid nitrogen. As he sorted and filed and dictated, Plato was conscious of a dull ache in his chest, a sadness that lurked at the edge of his awareness. Whenever his mind started to wander, the ache began to grow, the feelings threatened to thaw—and he redoubled his efforts.

It was three o'clock by the time he finished the charts and paperwork. And when he was finally done, it was a simple thing to reach for Homer's pile and sift through those charts as well.

Hilda, his nurse, poked her head in at four-thirty to say she was leaving, and received only an impatient grunt for a reply. Outside Plato's window, the sun settled behind Riverside General as he worked his way through the stack of Homer's charts—reading Phillip Andersen's painstakingly thorough notes, decoding the scrawled consultations from other physicians on the cases, studying lab values and test reports, and following medication records and nurses' notes. On a separate sheet of paper, he listed any findings that seemed even remotely significant.

He finally turned the last page of the fourth chart and placed it back on the pile. Leaning back in his chair, Plato studied his notes.

Homer was sure to find the results disappointing. If Phillip Andersen had stolen the charts and committed murder in an elaborate cover-up, Plato couldn't understand why. He had found no evidence of malpractice. Like his discharge summaries and progress notes, Andersen's clinical work was thorough, conscientious, and scrupulously detailed. He was an excellent physician, and it showed. He wrote notes on his patients every day and often twice daily, depending on their condition. In emergency situations, his telephone orders were prompt and incisive. He occasionally quoted recent journal references in his progress notes, chapter and verse, to justify his rare digressions from standard clinical protocol. Allowing for the fact that Plato wasn't a hematologist, the few apparent flaws in patient management had all been committed by other consulting physicians rather than by Andersen himself.

Oddly enough, Plato even recognized the names of two of the four patients. One of them had been a patient of Dan Homewood's, and the other had been a roommate of one of Plato's own patients. And of course, Lou Higgins—whose chart was apparently in Cal's stack—had lived at Wyndhaven.

He flipped to the first page of the top chart in the stack—the sheet that listed demographic details like age, sex, and place of residence.

That patient had been a resident at Wyndhaven Colony. Plato leafed through the other three charts. All four patients in the stack had indeed lived at Wyndhaven, though one had been sent home shortly before he died.

Plato frowned. Any connection with the nursing home itself was ridiculous. All four patients had died natural deaths. And the fact that they all had come from Wyndhaven really wasn't so surprising. The nursing home was affiliated with Riverside, after all. And Andersen and Tucker had probably divided their caseload geographically, just like most groups did. Dan Homewood—Plato's partner—covered several dozen patients in a West Side nursing home, while Plato handled most of the group's patients who lived at Wyndhaven Colony.

So the common feature was probably Phillip Andersen, rather than the nursing home.

Plato eyed the meager stack of papers linking Andersen to Kate Shirvesky. A few telephone messages, a seemingly innocent birthday card signed simply "Kate," and the first few pages of a rough draft of a research paper. The project was entitled "Putative Etiologic Correlates of Blood Dyscrasias in Northeastern Ohio, 1950-1995." The paper's title page listed Kate Shirvesky as the primary author, along with Marvin Tucker, Phillip Andersen, and a couple of Ph.D.'s from Case Western. The text itself was vague and rambling—mostly a literature review giving details and statistics from other studies.

It sounded amazingly dry. Plato tried to imagine how romance could flare over conversations about putative etiologic correlates, but he gave up.

At the bottom of the scanty collection, a handwritten note from Kate to Marvin Tucker detailed the charts she had borrowed and stacked in her office. The strikingly incriminating document listed all nine cases whose charts subsequently went missing. She noted that four of the charts were on loan to Siegel and would have to be retrieved later. In the margins, Homer had scribbled a note saying that this was a copy of the sheet they had used to track down the nine missing charts. All five charts missing from the hospital had last been signed out to Kate Shirvesky. And all nine were, of course, Phillip Andersen's former patients.

It was getting dark. The hospital-issue clock on Plato's wall reported that an hour had passed since Hilda's departure.

Cal had probably already left for her 'meeting.'

Plato felt a rising tide of sadness, depression, and anger

welling up inside him, like a sulfur bubble surfacing in a pool of hot lava. His hands, clenched into fists, had bent his ball-point pen into a pretzel shape.

He forced himself to take a few deep breaths. After all, it wasn't the end of the world.

Not *yet*, anyway.

He rubbed his eyes and tried to concentrate again on the charts, on Phillip Andersen, on the baffling circumstances of Kate Shirvesky's death. The red-hot anger slowly dimmed, fading to a faint ripple just beneath the surface.

The whole thing was so confusing. After looking over his four charts, Plato had to agree with Cal that Andersen was probably innocent—of malpractice, at least. As for the nebulous possibility of research fraud or some tie-in with the experimental drug, Plato could see no likely connection with the murders. Tucker and Andersen's drug was an established flop, a last-ditch treatment that seemed to provide no clear benefit to patients with aplastic anemia. But based on Plato's brief study of the charts, the drug didn't seem to *harm* anyone, either.

Though unfortunate, the experiment's failure certainly wouldn't destroy Andersen's reputation or threaten his career in any conceivable way.

But if Andersen didn't kill Kate Shirvesky and Marvin Tucker, then who did? And why would the killer steal medical records that seemed to hold no incriminating evidence whatsoever? Why would he—or she—risk almost certain exposure to bury the skeleton from a murder victim whom the police had already forgotten?

Each new fact made the picture even more confusing. Plato tossed his white coat onto his chair, donned his heavy winter jacket, and grabbed his notes and the stack of charts. He couldn't help wondering whether the five charts in Cal's stack would show some pattern, some clue, some detail he had missed.

If Cal were really at the hospital, the charts would be in her office. She certainly wouldn't lug them off to a legitimate meeting.

On the other hand, if she had actually left the hospital and didn't plan on stopping at Riverside on her way home, she would have brought the charts along with her.

Ten minutes later, Plato found himself outside Cal's office, with no recollection of crossing the street or descending in the hospital elevator. He couldn't even remember whether he had entered through the lobby or the doctors' entrance.

It didn't matter. Very little mattered, now.

The door was unlocked. Plato opened it, flicked on the lights, and nodded. As he'd expected, the other five charts were gone. So were Cal's coat and briefcase and purse. Crossing to the telephone, to try calling home in the vain hope that his wife might actually be there, he noticed a light flickering on the answering machine.

Plato's hands trembled as he flipped the switch to PLAY.

The voice on the tape was smooth, calm, and confident. Almost gloating.

"Hey, Cally. Neville here. In case you haven't left yet—how about bringing along something to eat? My fridge is empty again. And they're doing construction work along Willis Road, so you'll have to come the back way. Take I–77 down to Route 32, head east, and my street'll be the third one on your right. And listen, hon—this is the right thing to do. Don't worry about Plato. You'll feel so-o-o good when we—BEEP!"

Standing in the center of the office, Plato thought of several dozen endings to Neville's last sentence. He felt his face growing hotter, his heart pounding like a pile driver as the sulfur bubble finally burst, sending up a thick choking cloud of jealousy and anger and bitterness.

He spun on his heel and left the room and Cal behind.

CHAPTER 23

After taking I–77 to Route 32, heading east, cruising down the third street on the right, and verifying that Cal's rusty silver Corsica was indeed parked in the long driveway of a palatial mansion, Plato headed home to pack.

Now that his worst suspicions were confirmed, Plato found that he really couldn't feel much of anything at all. He sorted through his emotions like an accident victim checking himself for broken bones, but he found nothing. The anger and resentment had disappeared, for now. The sadness had dwindled to a dull empty feeling, like the ache from an amputated limb.

He had felt it before. Whenever his patients passed away, succumbing to disease and old age. When his father had finally surrendered to lung cancer and emphysema, drawing his last labored breath even as his hand went slack in Plato's desperate grip. When his mother had left them long, long ago, just before Plato's sixth birthday.

It was happening all over again. And maybe that explained why Plato couldn't feel anything this time. Sergeant Jack Marley had taught his son one very important lesson: if you don't show it, you don't really feel it, either. At least, not as much.

After she left, Jack Marley never mentioned his absent wife again. He merely picked up his life and went on without missing a step, like a shell-shocked soldier who doesn't notice a bullet wound in his chest.

Plato piloted the Rabbit around the chuckholes in County Road 142 and stared out the window with glazed eyes. In the little subdivision just up the road from their house, white-sheeted ghosts and black-robed witches and ponderous fat pumpkins were tripping from house to house and cavorting beneath the street lamps. Doubtless many of the more intrepid goblins would hike through the woods to trick-or-treat at the Marley home again this year. Last Halloween, several dozen had made the daring trek, to Plato and Cal's surprise.

Tommy Jorgenson, their paper boy, had explained that the Marley mansion was the closest thing to a haunted house in all of Sagamore Hills. And having a real "dead person doctor" handing out candy was an added attraction. Some of the younger kids at school even thought Cal was a witch, Tommy explained. But he had assured them she wasn't, because he'd seen her reflection in a mirror.

The kids would be disappointed this year, Plato mused. The dead person doctor was out practicing her witchcraft on some-one else, and Plato planned to leave again just as soon as he could find and pack his suitcase.

Which turned out to be harder than expected. He and Cal hadn't taken a vacation since the fiasco at Chippewa Creek last fall. The suitcases weren't lurking among the dozens of boxes and packing cartons lining the walls of the basement, nor were they hiding in the dark and dusty corners of the attic above their bedroom. Plato finally found them tucked away in a dry corner of one of the servants' rooms.

As he retrieved the two largest suitcases, a pair of bats brushed by his face. Or maybe just one bat, flapping wildly enough for two. It didn't really startle him—Plato had gotten used to the creatures, who seemed to have built a luxury con-dominium in the eaves over the east wing. Once he and Homer finished working on the roof, they would—

Plato shook his head stubbornly. The old money pit was *Cal's* problem now.

He turned and lugged the suitcases back to their bedroom. Plato's packing method was simple: pull out three of his draw-ers from the dresser, invert them over one suitcase, and squash the contents inside. In the bathroom, he slid his toothbrush and shaving kit into the side pocket of the bag. Finally, he grabbed twenty hangers-worth of slacks and jackets and shirts and folded them into the other suitcase. He would come back for the rest, some day.

Plato was dragging the bulging suitcases across the floor of the foyer when the doorbell rang.

"*Damn!*"

Vague shapes were visible on the other side of the living-room window, peering inside.

No chance of avoiding them, of pretending he wasn't at home. They had almost certainly spotted him.

"TRICK OR TREAT!" they shouted through the closed door.

Reluctantly, Plato dropped his suitcases, switched on the porch light, and opened the door. Waiting just outside were three grotesque figures—a zombie with suspiciously ketchup-like blood dripping from a nasty head wound, a black-hooded executioner with a hangman's noose in one hand and a gore-stained plastic ax in the other, and a grinning twelve-year-old who looked remarkably like Tommy Jorgenson, except for the greenish goo dripping from his clothes and face and hair, the extra set of arms, and the third eye in the middle of his forehead.

"TRICK OR TREAT!" the trio shouted again.

"Sorry, guys," Plato said. "I don't have any candy. I was just stopping home for a minute."

The zombie's shoulders slumped. The executioner made threatening motions with his ax.

"I thought you said they'd have something *good*," he muttered from beneath his hood.

"*I* didn't," the zombie protested. "*Tommy* did."

Tommy Jorgenson's face fell. "Sorry, Alex."

The executioner thumped his ax on the porch. "We tromp *all the way* through those woods in the dark, I lose my hood *three times*, and they don't have anything? You're a real turkey, Tommy."

The zombie dabbed a finger in his head wound and daintily licked it clean. "It's not Tommy's fault. They had good stuff here last year. Nestlé's Crunch and peanut butter cups and those little bags of M&M's. You got to take as much as you wanted."

"*Can* it, Ben." The executioner waved his noose at the zombie.

The zombie shrugged. Tommy stared at the floor.

"Wait a minute, guys." Plato held up his hands. "I didn't say I wasn't going to give you *anything*. I just said I didn't have any *candy*."

He pulled out his wallet and prayed for ones. He fingered through a twenty, a ten, two fives, and one-two-*three* singles.

"I've got just one condition," Plato warned as he doled the dollar bills out. "Tell everyone else you see not to come here. I'm about to leave again, and I don't want kids hiking through these woods for nothing."

"Sure, Dr. Marley!" Tommy Jorgenson's goo-spattered face had lit up. He reverently placed the dollar bill in the half-full pillow case at his side.

"Before you guys go," Plato asked him, "tell me one more thing. What are you three supposed to be?"

"I'm an executioner," said the executioner.

"I'm a zombie," said the zombie.

"And I'm a mutant," said Tommy. "Of course."

"I thought so." Plato nodded sagely. "But what's all that greenish stuff? Smells like lime Jell-O."

"It *is* lime Jell-O," the executioner muttered.

"It's *toxic goop*," Tommy insisted. He gave a pair of shrugs and pointed to the *faux* eyeball. "That's how I got this way."

"I *told* you to use real Slime instead," the executioner scoffed.

Ben the zombie—ever the peacemaker—stepped in. "Lime Jell-O smells even worse than Slime. It smells like *real* toxic goop."

The trio drifted off the porch and back toward the woods, arguing the virtues of various toxic goop substitutes.

But Plato wasn't listening. He was standing in the open doorway, staring at the full orange moon rising in the east, and thinking.

Like the zombie, he was thinking about *real* toxic goop. The kind that might not cause extra arms and eyeballs to grow, but might cause a funny smell at a retirement center—an odd, constant scent of soap and cleaning solvents. Toxic goop might also explain a wave of rare illnesses at that same nursing home. And lead a promising young epidemiology student to write a paper about the causes of blood disorders in northeastern Ohio.

Plato stumbled back inside, past the suitcases, and into the living room. Sprawling into the battered recliner, he closed his eyes to think.

All four patients from Plato's stack of charts had lived at

Wyndhaven Colony. And all four had died of aplastic anemia—in a span of less than four years. Some, if not all, of the patients in Cal's stack had lived at Wyndhaven, too. And those patients had also died of aplastic anemia.

And of course, Albert Windgartner had aplastic anemia.

Good God! The retirement community housed only three hundred and fifty people. Aplastic anemia was a relatively rare disease. Ten patients in four years might not seem like a huge number, but a 3 percent incidence was probably quite high.

Probably high enough to spark an epidemiologist's interest.

But what had Kate Shirvesky found? Was someone at the nursing home *poisoning* the residents, to cause apparently natural deaths? Ridiculous—most victims had survived for several years despite their illness. That didn't fit with murder.

Not poisoning, then. But what about environmental factors? What about toxic goop?

Plato paced over to the bookcase and dragged out his copy of *Harrison's Principles of Internal Medicine*. The book was over four inches thick, with flimsy onion-skin pages. Like a sorcerer's apprentice studying the Great Book of Spells, Plato had worked and sweated over the tome during medical school, residency, and fellowship. He had read and reread its chapters on the nights before board exams. Its initially bland pages had been underlined and highlighted and starred and checked until they resembled the abstract dabblings of a mad painter.

Like a mountain climber facing an impossibly difficult peak, Plato had always both loathed and admired the text. He lugged *Harrison's* back to the recliner and settled in.

The chapter on aplastic anemia—like most of the entries—was long and imposing and delved into the subject with far more detail than Plato would have ever desired. Still, he read the entry carefully. As in Albert Windgartner's case, many occurrences of aplastic anemia were never traced to a cause. On the other hand, the disease did have a number of *known* causes. Many cases were linked to drugs and toxins.

Plato glanced down the list of causes. The possible toxins weren't limited to the typical, familiar poisons. Environmental causes—air and water pollutants—had been linked to the disease as well.

Benzene and arsenic were very high on the list of environmental toxins. So were insecticides.

Benzene and arsenic were common industrial chemicals, Plato knew, but there were no factories anywhere near Wyndhaven Colony. Likewise, insecticide use was carefully monitored at the nursing home. And the place was so clean that pesticides were rarely needed—if ever.

None of it made any sense. Plato snapped the book shut and slid it back into its place on the shelf. This trail, like all the others, seemed to have played out to another dead end.

Until Plato remembered his visit with Marietta Clemens last Friday. And the beautiful view through the vast windows of the reception area, marred by what she had thought was an ugly building next door.

What if that building wasn't simply Marietta's imagination—her re-creation of a memory from her old home? What if there really *was* an ugly old building perched just beyond the trees? What if the building was a decrepit factory, or a toxic waste dump?

Plato's heart quickened. Even as he was dismissing the idea as ridiculous, other pieces were falling into place. Erica Windgartner's ruthless attitude about the nursing home's record profits. Her ability—as a member of the boards of trustees at both Riverside and Siegel—to enter Riverside General and steal the charts from Kate Shirvesky's office. And to enter the medical school, to plant Kate's skeleton and take Sergei's four missing records.

A disclosure that Wyndhaven Colony was tainted with benzene or some other industrial waste would have completely destroyed the nursing home's spotless image. No clean-up, however thorough, would restore its tarnished reputation. Few patients would want to stay there, regardless of how cheap Wyndhaven became. The sprawling retirement community might even go under, along with its record profits. The Windgartners' other two luxury nursing homes would probably be hurt as well. And the promising plans for a new rehabilitation hospital would simply fade away.

So would Erica Windgartner's dreams of finally satisfying her father, impressing him and getting his attention. Instead, Albert's last days would be spent battling some very vicious—and very expensive—lawsuits.

Motive, means, and opportunity. Erica Windgartner had them all. She was certainly strong enough to wield the allosaurus femur. Her story about Feinstein had proven to be an exaggeration. And according to Jeremy, she didn't have a solid alibi for the time of Tucker's murder.

Planting the bones in the construction site would have been tricky, of course. Erica certainly couldn't have buried them during the day. But even as a trustee, she would have needed to sign in to enter the medical school after dark. Why hadn't anyone noticed her name on the list of visitors on the night the bones were buried?

And then Plato had it. Windsor Construction. That was the name on the sign at Siegel's construction site.

Windsor Construction. Wyndhaven Colony. Albert and Erica Windgartner.

All of the Windgartner' many Cleveland-based enterprises began with some variation of the word "Wind"—even their chic downtown restaurant was called "Windy City East." Plato had been a fool not to link Windsor Construction with the Windgartners. But back when they were dating, Erica hadn't been as closely involved in the family business. And Plato was never very good with names.

He nodded firmly. Erica didn't *have* to sign in at the medical school on the night she buried Kate Shirvesky's skeleton. Yesterday, she had talked about visiting construction sites; she almost certainly had a key to the barbed-wire enclosure surrounding the excavation at Siegel.

The only questions were, why had Erica let her father continue to stay at Wyndhaven once she realized the dangers? And where had she hidden Kate Shirvesky's body the *first* time?

Plato didn't want to think about the first question. But he thought he might be able to answer the second. He found the drawing of Kate Shirvesky's skull—the drawing Cal had made just last night—and stuffed it in his pocket. He grabbed his suitcases and wrestled them out onto the porch.

And finally, after one last look at the sad empty house, he hurried out to his car.

CHAPTER 24

"*You* sure are pulling a late night."

Steven Prescott was leaving the nursing home just as Plato was walking in. Standing in the reception room, briefcase and overcoat in hand, he frowned a question.

"Or is this an emergency?"

"No." Plato shrugged. "I was going to come out earlier, but I got backed up with paperwork."

It was true enough, he supposed.

"*I* wanted to be a doctor, once." The administrator shook his head and grinned. "For about a month. That's how long I lasted in pre-med. You guys work too hard."

Steven Prescott looked like *he* had been working too hard. His smile was strung tight across his face. His eyes shone with an almost feverish intensity. He clutched his lizard skin overcoat like it was an angry crocodile.

Plato smiled. "You're keeping some late hours yourself."

"Paperwork." He tapped his briefcase. "That's the name of the game for all of us, I guess."

"It sure is." Plato nodded, expecting Steven to leave.

But he didn't. The administrator just stood there, fidgeting and staring at the mirror glint on his brightly polished shoes. Finally, he lifted his head.

"How's Albert doing?"

"Much better. He'll probably come back here tomorrow." Plato spread his hands. "It's an amazing thing. He goes into the hospital at death's door, and he comes out looking tougher than ever."

But thinking about it, Plato wasn't really surprised. There wasn't any toxic goop at Riverside General. More than ever, he noticed the cloying scent of the air here at Wyndhaven. A strange, organic chemical scent. Or was it just his imagination, coupled with a little Murphy's Oil Soap?

"Erica had a nice long talk with her father last night," Steven said. "After I took her out to dinner."

"I'm glad." Plato nodded. "It's been a long time coming, I think."

"She's been kind of jittery lately. Under a lot of pressure." He frowned. "She's working too hard—with the medical school addition, and the proposal for our rehab hospital here. And keeping track of Albert's shopping malls and office buildings and everything." He gestured back to Albert's wing. "It's amazing how much work her father still does, from his rooms here."

"I know." Plato nodded. Even though he had technically handed over the reins of power to his daughter, Albert still had a large office and a full-time secretary here at Wyndhaven. And once a week, if he was feeling well enough, he visited the company's main offices up in Beachwood.

Steven shook his head. "When Albert's not around, it puts a lot of pressure on Erica."

"I'm sure it does," Plato agreed.

Steven Prescott was obviously feeling that pressure, too. Perhaps he suspected that something was wrong. Or maybe he was just concerned for Erica. Either way, the administrator practically hummed with energy and tension, like a high-voltage wire in a thunderstorm.

"I think she can handle it," Plato assured him. "Erica's a tough gal—at least as tough as Albert."

"No kidding." He shrugged. "But I still worry about her. Pinch-hitting for her father—that's a tough position to be in. And someday, she'll have to play the position for good."

Plato couldn't help feeling sorry for Steven as he shuffled out the door with his briefcase and his worries. He had no idea how tough Erica's position really was.

Plato was certain that Agnes Leighton had died. Her skin had the ghastly parchment texture of a freshly embalmed corpse. Her eyes and cheeks were deep hollows, her mouth a thin red slit. Her skull was clearly visible beneath the papery skin of her face. Resting atop the blanket, her arms and hands were

frail and gaunt and skeletal. Her ribs threatened to poke
through the thin fabric of her nightgown.

Cancer and starvation had wasted every ounce of fat she had
left, and burned away much of her muscle tissue as well. She
reminded Plato of Cornelius Updyke, the tuberculosis victim
whose bones and photos were on file at the Natural History
Museum.

Until she drew a deep breath, winced, and opened her gray
eyes. They were instantly alert, fixing on Plato and widening
in surprise.

"What are *you* doing here, Plato?" Her voice was a throaty
rasp, like a file on a dull steel blade. "What time is it?"

Plato glanced at his watch. "About eight o'clock."

"At night?"

"Yes."

"Good." Agnes gave a satisfied nod. "I was planning on
dying tonight. I was afraid I'd missed it."

"You're planning on *dying* tonight?" he asked. "Why?"

"Why not?" Her shoulders rose and fell—a shrugging coat
hanger beneath her nightgown. "It's Halloween. I think that's
a pretty good night for dying."

"I think you've had a little too much pain medication." Plato
frowned and reached for the clipboard at the foot of her bed.
"How much are we giving you, anyway?"

"Nonsense. I'm perfectly rational." She patted a spot on the
bed. "Come sit down."

Plato sat.

"I'm just planning on checking out tonight," Agnes continued. "I can feel it."

"Oh."

Plato could believe it. From a closer vantage, she seemed
even more gaunt and frail than before—if that was possible.

"What's wrong?" she asked suddenly. "You look like
you've just lost your best friend. Somebody else here die already? Is that why you're here?"

"No." He shook his head. "I came here to check up on
something else. And I thought I'd drop in to see how you
were."

"*You* look like you could use a drink," Agnes said. She
rested her head back against the pillow and took a deep breath.
Already, the conversation seemed to be tiring her. But she

flashed her crooked smile. "You look like Harry always did after we had a fight."

Plato grunted. "It's that obvious, huh?"

"To the trained eye, yes." She nodded. Her speech was slowing down. "You forget, I was a detective. One of Cleveland's Finest."

"I'll never forget that," Plato said. "That's part of why I'm here. I think I figured out the story behind that skeleton we found."

"Some case. I've been following the news. Crazy." Agnes closed her eyes and patted Plato's arm. "You just stay right here and tell me the whole story, doc. I want to hear all about it."

"I don't know, Agnes." He clutched her hand. "I think you'd better get some rest."

She opened her eyes. They were just as sharp and clear as ever.

"Give the lady a last request." She gave that bony shrug again. The muscle fibers were visible beneath the skin of her neck. "Tell me a story. You're not gonna be able to tell me tomorrow."

Plato sighed. "Okay."

For the next twenty minutes, he filled her in on the details of the case—the murder of Marvin Tucker, the identification of the skeletons, the link between the missing charts and Phillip Andersen, and the identification of Kate Shirvesky's bones. Finally, he told her how most or all of the patients had lived at Wyndhaven Colony—and explained his theory about a connection between aplastic anemia and a possible toxin in the area.

While he talked, Agnes seemed to be in a trance, or asleep. Her eyes were closed to slits. Her breathing was deep and infrequent, like the unnatural sighs of a mechanical respirator. Her body was completely immobile and limp, except for the fingers clutching Plato's hand.

But every so often she would open her eyes, back him up to retrace a tidbit of information or explain parts she didn't understand. Once he finished, she spent several minutes digesting the information, then nodded.

"I know that smell you're talking about. Always thought it was soap or something." She grimaced. "And all the buildings

are on well water out here. Too damn far from the city pipe-
lines."

Plato nodded.

"So maybe you're right about that." She raised a quivering
hand as though she were delivering a benediction. It fell to the
bed again. "Only trouble is, I've seen that building Marietta's
talking about. Back when I used to take walks around here. It's
not a factory—it's an old hospital or something."

"A *hospital*?" Plato frowned. "You're sure?"

"I'm sure." She stared at the ceiling. "I remember reading
the sign. Glenville or Grandview or something. Damn, I've
lost it. Some kind of hospital, though."

"Not a factory."

"No." She closed her eyes. "No way."

"I guess that shoots my theory, then."

"One way to find out." The fatigue and starvation were taking their toll on Agnes. She fought to keep her eyes open, but
they kept drooping closed. Her speech was starting to slur. She
sounded like a sleepwalker, or a fortune-teller in a trance. "I
know someone who might have seen that Shirveskowitz girl,
what's-her-name. If she really came here and got herself
killed."

Plato frowned, puzzled. "Who would remember all the way
back to last May?"

Especially here, he thought quietly. Eidetic memory wasn't
a strong suit among the residents of Wyndhaven Colony.

"Eliot Ness," Agnes Leighton said. "He'd know. F'r sure."

Plato frowned. Poor Agnes. Now she was hallucinating. Her
fantasies about the legendary cop had finally come alive.
"Ness?"

She nodded slowly.

"Maybe you're right," he agreed. Gently, he patted her
hand. He continued in a half whisper. "Only trouble is, Eliot
Ness is dead."

Agnes's eyes shot open. "Not *Ness*, idiot! *Nestor*! Elroy
Nestor!"

"Elroy Nestor. Of course!"

"'Eliot Ness,'" Agnes repeated to herself. "You think I'm
senile or something?"

"Never, Agnes." Plato patted her hand. "Never."

"Sure. Thass what they all say." She scowled at him. "You

better hurry and see Elroy. He's a big baby about getting his eight hours. He's prob'ly already in bed."

"Maybe I should." Plato stood up. "Is there anything I can get for you, Agnes? Anything I can do?"

"Go home and make up with your wife." She closed her eyes and brushed him away with her hand. "And lemme know how the story ends—if I'm still around."

Make up with your wife, Plato thought as he followed the long corridor to Elroy Nestor's room. That was rich. And about as likely as Foley's ghost coming back to play one last game of basketball.

Getting a glimpse of Elroy Nestor's black book seemed just about as impossible. But at least the retired stockbroker was awake when Plato arrived. The television was tuned to an old western, but Elroy flipped it off as soon as he spied Plato in the doorway. He furtively slid the remote beneath his wheel-chair, as though it were a cache of cocaine.

"Mr. Nestor?" Plato stood in the doorway and smiled reassuringly. "I'm Dr. Marley. Remember me?"

"Of course I remember you." He squinted through the thick glasses and frowned. "You were here last week, I think."

"Yes, I was."

"What do you want?" Elroy Nestor pulled his lap blanket up to his chin.

Plato thought hard. He could see that this was going to be tricky.

"Just thought I'd say hi." He nodded to the television. "You like Audie Murphy?"

Elroy shrugged, reluctantly. The hands clutching the lap blanket relaxed, slightly.

"He's not bad. Better than John Wayne, anyway."

"I think so, too." Plato smiled. "Ever seen *Kansas Raiders*?"

Elroy nodded, hairy ears flapping vigorously. "Sat through three showings of it. At the old Hippodrome, downtown near sixth and Euclid."

"*Three* showings?"

"After I got back from Europe. Fought in France, and spent five years in Vienna after the war." The blue blanket receded into his lap like a wave drawing back from the shore. "Didn't get back again until nineteen-fifty. *Kansas Raiders* was the first movie I saw in the States."

Elroy Nestor stared at the blank television as though it were the old Hippodrome screen and he was waiting for the movie to start just one more time.

"Audie Murphy fought in the war." Plato eased inside the doorway.

"No kidding." Elroy swiveled the cataract glasses toward Plato again. Grinning, he looked more like a bat than ever. "Most decorated soldier in World War Two."

"My dad was stationed near Berlin. Military police."

"Was he really? I was in the Supply Corps. That's how I got my job in Vienna—connections." Elroy Nestor was positively beaming now. He nodded at the vinyl-upholstered chair across from his. "Sit down, sit down."

Over the next half hour, Elroy told Plato most of his life story—from his life in Vienna after World War II, to his return to Cleveland and his work for Cyrus Eaton, to the launching of his own trading firm. He had been happily married, and now he was unhappily widowed. He had three children and sixteen grandchildren, scattered across the United States like so many dandelion seeds.

Nobody cared, nobody came to visit. Not that he expected them to, they lived so damn far away.

As the old man talked, Plato realized that Elroy wasn't so much paranoid as he was lonely. Accosting every visitor to Wyndhaven and keeping his little black book were probably just excuses to meet people, to get some attention, to have someone to talk with. And maybe the practice expressed a hidden wish that one of those visitors was coming to see him.

Plato gently led the conversation back to Wyndhaven itself. Elroy admitted to being reasonably happy with the nursing home. The food was good, and the staff was almost as nice as a real family. But he didn't have much use for most of the residents. Too snobby, he said. Too private. Never want to talk about anything but their families—what their kids do, how many grandchildren they've got, who's coming by to see them tomorrow afternoon. Like they didn't have a life of their own, here.

"You keep pretty good track of the visitors, huh?"

"Sure do. Tell you something." Elroy leaned over conspiratorially and whispered. "People think I'm crazy. I like that."

"You do?"

He nodded firmly. "Gives me a chance to watch them. See what's going on. Nobody pays you much attention if they think you're nuts."

"I bet you've met some interesting people."

"Interesting people. Crazy people. One guy tried to belt me when I asked him his name. I hit the switch on my chair, almost ran him over." He nodded to a bookshelf in the corner. "They're all in my books, over there."

"You have more than one book?" Plato feigned surprise.

"'Course I do." He drew himself up proudly. "Been keeping them ever since I got here."

"So if I just picked a month out of the blue—say, last May—you could pull out a book and tell me everyone who's been to Wyndhaven?"

Plato held his breath.

"Just about. Daylight hours, anyway. Wintertime, I come inside the reception room and park by the door." He flipped a switch and wheeled across the room to the bookshelf. "Back when I retired, Dr. Homewood told me to find myself a hobby. Thelma Czedniak collects leaves. Ed DeWitt collects old birds' nests, God only knows why. I collect people."

He reached for one of the notebooks on the shelf. "Yep. Here's last May. Lots of good stories. See for yourself."

Plato took the notebook and tried to steady his shaking hands. He leafed through the pages slowly, casually, pretending to listen to Elroy's running commentary.

". . . and once the governor came here. The governor. No entourage, no nothing. He was looking for a place for his mother. I took his name just like everyone else . . ."

Nothing in the first week. The volume of Elroy's output was enormous. Not just names and times, but descriptions, clothing, mannerisms, accents, and odd behaviors. And a crude classification scheme that ranged from "sweetheart" down to "moron" and worse. All written out in Elroy's spindly fine-point scrawl.

". . . take breaks for lunch and dinner. Sometimes I see them out my window, though . . ."

Kate Shirvesky was one of the "sweethearts." May 17th, at

12:20 P.M. Wearing a Cleveland Indians warm-up jacket, jeans, and red tennis shoes. It was a rainy day, so Elroy had been camped inside the common room. Kate had answered his questions, sat beside his wheelchair, and chatted for a few minutes. Then she went on inside.

She didn't stay very long. She left at 12:55 P.M., headed for the nature trail and woods to the east despite the pouring rain.

But to Plato's surprise, Kate hadn't come to see Erica Windgartner. She had come to meet with somebody else. A person Plato knew.

A person Elroy had seen leaving Wyndhaven Colony at 12:57 P.M. A person who hadn't given a name or stopped to chat. But it didn't matter. Elroy Nestor had written a perfect description.

CHAPTER 25

The full moon was riding high now. Plato almost didn't need a light. But he walked out to his car anyway, to pick up his flashlight and take a good look at the detailed street map in his glove compartment.

It didn't show much. The property around Wyndhaven was represented by a vast shaded area labeled "Wyndhaven Colony R.C." The property stretched for over a mile along the southern edge of Cuyahoga County. To the west, it was bordered by a road leading to a small subdivision. To the east, the property ended at a set of railroad tracks. The tracks slanted up toward Cleveland and sent off a tiny spur just east of the Wyndhaven property line. But there was no sign of any factory or hospital or *anything* bordering the Wyndhaven grounds themselves. According to the map, the edges of the property seemed completely undeveloped. There weren't even any large creeks or rivers nearby that might have carried toxins from a factory upstream.

Disappointed, Plato shoved the map back into the glove compartment, moved his car closer to the nature trail entrance, and dragged out his flashlight. And asked himself what the hell he was doing. Why not just tell the whole story to Jeremy Ames? Or to Homer? He could be on his way over to Homer's apartment right now, to have dinner and explain his suspicions.

But that was just it. Right now, they were still only suspicions. And with no evidence of any factory or dump site on the map, he could only walk the grounds and try to retrace Kate Shirvesky's steps, hoping to find the building that Agnes claimed was hidden in the woods east of Wyndhaven.

Besides, Plato wasn't ready to think about his *other* problem. Not yet, anyway. And he sure wasn't hungry.

The nature trail was a perfectly paved ribbon of asphalt that circled the entire Wyndhaven grounds, winding over and around grassy knolls and hollows, passing through patches of pine and spruce and poplar, and curving into the eastern woods only briefly before ducking out into the open again. The wheelchair-accessible trail was nearly two miles long, marked every tenth of a mile with small plaques describing the nearby scenery, offering encouraging or inspirational quotes, or suggesting exercises for Wyndhaven's more ambitious residents. It was a cross between a par course and a walking trail. The *Plain Dealer* had featured it in a Sunday Magazine spread last summer.

Back in his more athletically ambitious days—last spring, in fact—Plato had tried running the trail every other afternoon. For a whole week. He had gained four pounds, developed shinsplints, and twisted his ankle hopping through one of the par course obstacles. After rounds the next afternoon, he watched as one of his seventy-year-old patients breezed around the course like a wizened Edwin Moses. Plato had hung up his running shoes for good that evening.

But he still remembered the course well enough to navigate its curves and ripples under the bright moonlight. Plato hurried his stride, glancing back over his shoulder and trying to ignore the butterflies doing laps around his stomach. His ankle ached with remembered pain.

The forest loomed ahead like a black curtain. The stiffening breeze stirred the trees, setting their bare branches clacking like so many bones. Small animals skittered through the carpet of dead leaves. The thick woods finally closed overhead to swallow the moonlight and the path and Plato. Where the trail curved back toward the west again, Plato left it and continued on through the forest to the east.

After tripping twice, stumbling into a tree trunk, and nearly losing an eyeball to a spiky branch, Plato decided it was safe to switch on his flashlight. Obviously nobody was following him.

He still wasn't sure what he was looking for. He only knew that Agnes had seen some kind of ruined hospital out here. And Elroy Nestor had watched Kate Shirvesky disappear in the rain on the afternoon of May 17, headed in this direction. Apparently, Elroy was the last person to see Kate alive.

Except for the murderer, of course.

Plato glanced over his shoulder again. Something was moving through the leaves. He switched off his flashlight and tried to silence his breathing.

Rustle. Rustle. Skitter-skitter-skritch.

He flicked the light back on, just in time to spy something darting behind a tree. Another chipmunk—the forest floor was alive with them.

He swung the beam eastward again and picked his way through the trees. The nature trail was far behind him now; even the lights of Wyndhaven had faded in the distance. Plato was alone, except for the chipmunks and tall trees and fallen trunks. *Lots* of fallen trunks—despite the flashlight, Plato stumbled and fell again.

Still, there was very little undergrowth to block his progress. Surprisingly little. And just a hint of a whiff of a scent, carried fitfully on the breeze. The barest trace, like the lilac scent that wafted through their bedroom window on warm spring mornings.

Except that this wasn't lilac, or anything like it. The odor carried Plato back to the organic chemistry lab at Kent State. Bunsen burners and beakers, hydrochloric acid and acetone. Plato was always screwing up, breaking pipettes and cylinders and making horribly impure mixtures, incurring the wrath of his Saudi lab instructor, who moaned at him in English and cursed under his breath in Arabic.

Plato's compounds had sometimes smelled like this. *Another of Marley's witch brews*, Abdel had always complained while pouring the ghastly concoctions down the drain and fretting over the damage to the laboratory's plumbing system. Plato wondered what Abdel would think of this brew.

But the breeze soon swung east again, and the smell faded. The moonlight faded as well; fleecy clouds were scudding in from the west, shrouding the bright moon and draping the forest in shifting shadows. Plato stumbled down a short incline, nearly losing a shoe as he crossed a muddy creek bed. Just up the opposite bank, a pink-flagged marker was jabbed into the soil. The writing on the stake offered no insights; it merely read "E127."

Beyond the marker, a narrow dirt road led up from the south, from the main highway that led to Wyndhaven's entrance. The road had been carved quite recently; huge Caterpillar treads were still sharp and fresh in the damp clay. Nearby, trees on both sides of the road were marked with blood-red Xs.

Plato followed the dirt road north for a while, but it led nowhere. Perhaps it would eventually lead to the rehab hospital Steven and Erica had mentioned.

He turned east again and hiked another quarter mile before deciding he'd had enough. He halted in a small clearing and considered. In the fickle moonlight, he might easily have passed within a hundred yards of a ruined hospital or factory without realizing it.

Plato could see no alternative but to drive over to Homer's apartment and tell him the whole story. Early tomorrow morning, they could come out together and search the area by the light of day. If there really *was* anything to see out here, Plato would never find it in this darkness. Besides, there was safety in numbers—especially when one of those numbers was Homer.

Just as Plato turned around to retrace his steps, the flashlight beam glanced across another marker stake. Or so it seemed. But as he moved closer, Plato realized that he had found a rusted iron post. He hurried over and found another post nearby.

Aiming his flashlight beam along the line between the two posts, he picked up the ruins of a heavy stone gate just fifty yards south.

He hurried along the line, stumbling over ancient hunks of rusted iron, and finally coming to the gate itself. He was standing on the face of a gentle hill that sloped up toward the east. Beneath the carpet of leaves and dirt was a crumbling brick roadway that wound along the hillside from the north and continued on out through the gate. The shattered brick pavement was covered with shards of ruined, rusted metal. A wrought-iron gate, by the look of it.

Most of the posts and cross braces had rusted to powder. The left-hand column of the gate was ruined as well, just a pile of stone and rubble. But the column on the right was still standing. And halfway up—at eye level—Plato saw that one granite square had been finished smooth. He brushed the surface clean, tracing the writing with his fingers and the flashlight beam:

GLADBROOK ASYLUM FOR THE INSANE
1909 A.D.

Plato stared at the writing for a long moment, then flicked his flashlight off and paused to think. Had Kate Shirvesky stumbled across this very sign five months ago? What was the connection between an ancient asylum and Wyndhaven Colony?

He shook his head. None of it made any sense. He hadn't found the source of the elusive smell. Certainly an *asylum* couldn't represent a source of toxic waste. Maybe there was an old factory farther on, where the map had shown a railroad spur. Even so, that search would have to wait until morning.

The moon drifted out from behind its cloudy pall, splashing the forest with silvery twilight. And through the gates, Plato caught his first glimpse of the Gladbrook Asylum. Or what was left of it. The building reminded him of the ruined castles he had seen in Europe. One enormous wall was still standing, leaning downhill at a crazy, impossible angle. The center portion of the building resembled a graveyard for giants— columns and buttresses and granite corners standing like so many monuments and markers. Uphill, the eastern section was mostly intact.

Plato followed the buckled brick roadway north through the gate and along the hillside toward the asylum. Huge oaks and maples linked their branches into a lacy canopy over the drive. The main entrance to the asylum itself was marked by a broken granite stairway and seven stone pillars. The eighth pillar lay in pieces along the steps.

Beyond the asylum—down the hill to the west, the brick roadway continued on toward a smaller building. An old brick house, by the looks of it. Probably the residence of the asylum's director, Plato guessed. Even after several decades, it seemed to be in far better repair than the main building. At least it had a roof.

He turned his attention back to the asylum itself, mounting the front steps and climbing over the broken pillar to peer at the wreckage beyond. Most of the first floor walls were still standing. But the jagged upper stretches of granite and brick were stained black.

Now Plato remembered. He had heard about the Gladbrook Asylum disaster—probably read about it in school. During the early 1940s, a fire had broken out at the asylum. Thirteen psychotic patients—locked in their rooms and unable to escape—had perished in the flames. Their horrible fate had helped launch a movement toward safer, more humane treatment of patients in mental hospitals and prisons.

Unwilling to risk venturing inside the ruined structure, Plato circled eastward and studied the outside walls. Despite the dilapidated condition of the building, most of the bars on the first-floor windows had stood the test of decades. Each window's bottom crossbar bore the institution's initials, carved in fancy wrought-iron letters: **GA**

Wide square wells led down to basement windows, which were also covered with bars. As Plato continued east, the ground of the ridge rose gently until it nearly reached the level of the first-story windows. Plato turned the corner and followed the eastern face of the rectangular structure until he came to a side entrance.

This section of the building still had all three floors; apparently the fire hadn't quite reached this far. The entrance featured a small courtyard, with stone benches facing out toward the east. Most of the larger trees had been removed long ago, leaving a clear view of the land to the east. Up the gentle rise, Plato could see the railroad tracks from his map, along with a ruined semaphore. And just beyond the tracks lay the probable source of the elusive smell.

Plato swung his flashlight eastward, pointing its powerful beam uphill. Off in the distance, four tottering smokestacks rose from a vast brick building like arthritic fingers stretching up from a giant palm. In the faint glow of flashlight and moonlight, the building looked almost as dilapidated as the Gladbrook Asylum. Stacks of barrels framed a ramshackle warehouse nearby. Huge rusted tanks lolled in the yard beside the railroad spur like a herd of humpback whales washed up on a beach.

The place seemed to have been abandoned decades ago. A faint aroma rolled down the hillside toward the asylum and

Wyndhaven beyond. A nasty, organic smell, like rotten eggs steeped in lacquer thinner. And a hint of that cleaning fluid odor that was so common around Wyndhaven.

Plato had found his factory.

He grinned to himself and turned to head back to the front of the asylum. But he stopped dead in his tracks when he heard the sound.

Not a skitter. Not a skritch. It was a firm, uncompromising *crunch*, followed by another, and another. The same sound his own shoes had made when he had walked up the crumbled brick driveway.

Plato flicked his flashlight off and crouched in the shelter of the site entrance, praying that the beam hadn't been seen.

He eased around the side of the building again and peered at the front entrance. His visitor had paused there, flashlight in hand, to peer down at the ground.

Plato held his breath and watched as the flashlight turned eastward to sniff along the side of the building, its owner following close behind.

Heart pounding, Plato tiptoed back to the side courtyard, scrabbled for a loose piece of stone, and heaved it away to the southeast. It fell into the brush near the railroad tracks with a satisfying and very convincing *crunch*!

Rather than continuing along the side of the building, the flashlight and owner hurried up the slope to the southeast, toward the sound. Plato stood at the side doorway and sighed with relief.

But what to do now? Apparently, he *had* been followed after all. Could he find his way back to Wyndhaven, quickly and silently, without using his flashlight?

He would have to try. Once his pursuer's flashlight moved out of sight, Plato turned and eased along the side of the building again. He would sneak along the front of the building and hurry back toward the gate. Once he got his bearings, he would break into a sprint. Running through the woods, his pursuer would be just as handicapped by the darkness as Plato.

But just as Plato reached the front corner of the building again, a flashlight beam swept across his path.

He froze. The beam flicked away as its owner hurried back toward the asylum. Down in a crouch, Plato darted back to the side entrance and ducked into the darkness.

Had he been seen? In the eerie stillness, Plato's frantic heart sounded like a booming kettle drum. He was standing inside a small and very dark foyer. He slid his hands along the walls and crept through a doorway to his left. Panting, he peered outside through a large front window. His pursuer hurried past, heading toward the main entrance again. Plato sighed with relief. Hopefully, it would seem that he had made a break for Wyndhaven.

He was safe, for now. Plato waited for his eyes to adjust to the darkness. The moon cast just enough light through the window for him to make sense of his surroundings. He was standing in a small square room littered with carpet shreds and paper and bits of cotton wool. The shelves lining the walls were filled with hundreds of shredded books. The skeleton of an upholstered chair sat beside an enormous wooden desk. The legs of the desk tapered to oddly irregular points. Plato knelt down to brush his hands against the wood and shuddered.

The wooden legs were knobbled and scratchy, as though they had been chewed. Glimpsing a large, dark, scurrying object from the corner of his eye, Plato realized that they probably had.

Rats. That explained the chair, and the books, and the carpet. Apparently when they got hungry enough, the little beasts chewed on the desk itself. Or maybe that was how they sharpened their teeth.

Plato shivered, and glanced out the window again. The flashlight hadn't moved off, as he had hoped it would. It was still sniffing around the front of the building. Plato needed a better place to hide.

He hurried back into the dark corridor again, blundering into a closet that turned out to be a stairwell. He realized his mistake almost instantly, barely managing to plant his foot on the first step and grab hold of the handrail. Still, Plato stumbled halfway down the stairs before he finally recovered his balance.

And instantly lost it again. The step beneath his feet gave way with a sickening and very loud *crack*! Plato plummeted down into the darkness, praying that the basement floor wasn't too far away.

It wasn't. Knees bent, Plato smacked into the floor just a few feet below the broken step. He tucked and rolled, then crawled out from beneath the stairway to take a careful inventory. No scrapes or bumps or bruises. Except to his pride.

A lighter, slimmer person—like Neville Archer—probably wouldn't have broken the stairway. A more graceful, athletic person—like Neville Archer—would doubtless have caught himself before ever falling down the stairs.

But in the asylum's near-total darkness, how was Plato to know that the damned closet was really a stairway? And why had the step broken, anyway? Surely Plato wasn't *that* heavy.

He risked flicking his flashlight on for just a moment, to get his bearings. And he instantly understood why the old stairway hadn't survived the passage of decades. Unlike the floors in more modern basements, this room was paved with fine gravel. The ground beneath the gravel was damp and squishy, and the entire basement was awash with a sickly sweet odor, like the stuff sitting in those tanks on the hill. The rickety stairs were stained with dry rot and wet rot and patches of fungus.

Plato glanced around the wide room. Only two of the four crude masonry walls were pierced by doorways. The small doorway to the south probably led to a room directly beneath the rat-chewed office upstairs. To the west, a much larger doorway seemed to open onto a corridor leading toward the center of the building.

Plato switched off his flashlight again and considered. He was playing hide-and-seek with a confirmed killer who seemed quite willing to play all night. He was trapped in a basement with no apparent way out aside from taking his chances on a rotten stairway that had already broken once. Or exploring the dark corridor that led toward the center of the building—looking for a sturdier staircase, but possibly getting trapped.

The sound of footsteps on the floor overhead simplified Plato's decision. Apparently, his fall had been overheard. Flashlight still off, Plato dashed across the gravel floor, bumped into the far wall, and felt his way along until he reached the central corridor.

And not a moment too soon. Just as he ducked into the hallway, a flashlight beam split the darkness of the room behind him. It shone down on the broken step, hesitating for just a moment before the owner began easing his way down the stairs.

Hands pressed to the rough masonry, Plato felt his way

down the long corridor, bumbling into walls, stumbling over bits of wreckage on the floor, nearly losing his head to a broken beam that had fallen across part of the passage. And hurrying, always hurrying.

It was like going through one of those haunted houses sponsored by the local high schools or Jaycees. Where you fumble blindly through a maze of plywood walls, waiting for the next ghost or goblin or monster to pop out from a hidden passage. Enjoying the surprises, the scares, the fluttering waves of fright, laughing all the while because you know it's not real.

Only this *was* real. Very real. The person behind him was almost certainly a killer. And if Plato couldn't find another stairway, he would never leave this haunted house alive.

Four times, Plato's searching hands found gaps in the walls on either side of the corridor. But each of the doorways only led to small rooms or storage areas or closets: dead ends. Plato considered hiding in one of them, but guessed that his pursuer was checking each room as he tracked his prey along the passage.

Finally, the walls of the corridor disappeared completely. Plato found himself in a cavernous space. Moonlight filtered down through windows in three of the walls. It also filtered down through a gap in the ceiling nearby—the other stairwell. Plato hurried closer, and risked flicking his light on for a moment.

Unfortunately, the stairway itself had rotted or burned away. Not a single step remained. The square gap in the ceiling was charred. Many of the joists nearby were blackened as well. Plato was apparently standing in the western half of the building now, the section most thoroughly consumed by the flames.

But oddly enough, the far wall of the room held another doorway. Had Plato lost his bearings? He was certain this was the end of the line, the western wall of the building.

Flashlight off again, he crossed the room and felt his way along the wall. If nothing else, the doorway might hold another closet, a hiding place where Plato could wait to surprise his pursuer.

But it wasn't a closet. It was another long corridor, lit by a window well on the right side. It was also very, very damp. Following the hallway, Plato felt the gravel beneath his feet grow soggier and soggier. Finally, the putrid water formed into puddles and then a small lake that gradually rose to his ankles, his calves, his knees.

Plato was slogging through a pool, a river, of toxic waste. The narrow passageway smelled like a crematorium for skunks.

When he passed a second window well, this time on his left, Plato knew for certain that he was in a tunnel. The underground passage apparently stretched from the basement of the asylum to the basement of the house up the road—the director's quarters, or whatever it was.

If Plato could only make it to the house, he would almost certainly escape. Surely the windows in *that* basement weren't barred. Plato hurried to a jog, splashing noisily through the poisonous lake. He passed two more window wells. Already, the tunnel was curving upward again; the water had receded back to his calves.

And just as he began to relax, to breathe easier, to think he had a chance, Plato felt the floor rise sharply beneath his feet, heeling up from the water into a soft mound of dirt and clay and broken timbers.

Sometime long ago, the ceiling had collapsed. The tunnel was a dead end.

Stunned, Plato clambered up the little hill, digging his feet into the soft earth, searching for a passage through to the other side or to the surface, and finding only more wreckage, more clay, more muddy earth.

He slid back down again, feeling the chilly poisoned water rising over his feet and ankles and calves. Catching his breath. Watching the flashlight—at the tunnel entrance now—begin to sniff its way along the passage. Struggling with the bars on the window well nearby, hoping they were loose enough to allow him to escape, to run for home base before he got tagged.

They weren't. The iron was as solidly anchored as the day the asylum was built. Plato slumped down against the mound of dirt. And stared at moonlight slanting down through the window well to shoot a pattern of shadows onto the far wall. A very familiar pattern. The pattern he had seen Cal draw, just yesterday evening.

GA

The inner portion of the "G" perfectly matched the oddly curved triangle on Kate Shirvesky's skull.

The flashlight beam continued its slow, measured pace up the tunnel. Desperate, Plato plunged his hand down into the water, crabbing along the gravel floor for some kind of weapon—a rock, an old scrap of iron, *something*.

The floor was bare, except for tiny bits of gravel and a small flat piece of stone or rusted metal. About the size of a hair comb. Flat and relatively smooth. Maybe he could throw it at his assailant.

Plato pulled it out and held it up to the moonlight.

Even though he wasn't a forensic pathologist, even though he couldn't tell a bear femur from a cow femur to save his life, he recognized the object in his hand. Long and flat, with small indentations along the sides. It was supposedly shaped like a broadsword, but it wouldn't be much use as a weapon. Except in a murder trial.

It was a breastbone—Kate Shirvesky's sternum.

Just as Plato realized what he was holding, the flashlight shone on his face. Behind it, a figure was visible in the moonlight from the window. A familiar figure. With a perfect face, perfect hair, perfect clothes.

Steven Prescott's perfect teeth gleamed in a satisfied smile.

"Alley-alley-in-free."

CHAPTER 26

"Hello, Erica?"

Cal Marley was barreling down Interstate 77 after a wonderful evening with Neville Archer. Her companion was sitting beside her in the front seat of the Corsica. She glanced over at him, struck again at how handsome he was. Graceful and powerful and handsome.

"Sorry to bother you so late." The receiver hissed with a shower of static. She was borrowing Neville's cellular phone. "I just had a couple of questions."

"Questions?" Over the airwaves, Erica Windgartner's voice sounded very, very small.

"Just general things." Cal tried to sound reassuring. "About the nursing home."

"About Wyndhaven?" Erica's voice shook.

"Yes. I tried to reach Steven, but—"

"I don't *know* where Steven is. I'm very worried."

Erica didn't sound worried. She sounded scared.

"I know." Cal felt like a parent soothing a frightened child. "I'm sure he's all right. I just wanted to ask you about the nursing home. You folks are building an addition out there, right?"

"Right. A small rehabilitation hospital." Erica's voice slowly gained strength. "For all kinds of rehabilitation—strokes, injuries, even addictions. On land that my father bought way back in the seventies." She sighed. "Steven is very dedicated to the project. He's very excited about it."

"I'm sure he is," Cal agreed. "After all, he owns part of Wyndhaven, doesn't he?"

Erica didn't answer. The other end of the line was silent for so long that Cal wondered if she had lost the connection. She exited Interstate 77 and turned down the winding country road toward Wyndhaven Colony.

"Erica?"

"Yes." Her voice was a high-pitched flutter. Clearly, she was crying.

"I'm sorry to be asking you this. But I thought you'd rather talk to a friend."

"I know. I—I appreciate that." She sniffled. "But just give me a minute. Okay?"

While Erica coughed and sniffed and blew her nose, Cal thought about the case. Looking through her pile of charts that afternoon, she had quickly noticed that all five patients had come from Wyndhaven Colony.

Not that it necessarily meant anything. The charts might have been sorted according to patient address, so that Plato's four charts had come from other locations. Or perhaps all of Phillip Andersen's malpractice cases had been limited to Wyndhaven patients—but that would have been a remarkable coincidence.

Even more remarkable was the high incidence of aplastic anemia.

The fact that Andersen himself hadn't picked it up wasn't surprising. Few doctors paid close attention to where their patients lived. According to his notes in the charts, Phillip had seen his patients in the hospital or his office, but had never actually visited the nursing home. For his patients' general medical care outside the hospital, Andersen tended to refer them to a variety of internists or family physicians or geriatricians.

None of them had picked up the high incidence of aplastic anemia, either. But Kate Shirvesky had. And so, apparently, had Marvin Tucker.

"I've been so scared," Erica faltered.

"I understand." In the darkness, holding the cellular phone, Cal shook her head. She really *didn't* understand. How would it feel to suspect that the person you loved most in the world was hiding a horrible secret?

"I didn't really want to think about it," Erica continued. "I thought if I ignored it, it would just go away."

Cal sighed. *This* secret certainly wouldn't go away. Guilty secrets never did. Cal wondered how she would feel if she found out Plato was hiding this kind of secret.

It was inconceivable, unfathomable. He wouldn't be Plato anymore, he would be someone else. Some monster in human form. She would feel betrayed, angry. It would destroy her faith in others, her faith in herself.

But Plato had always been honest with her. With an almost childlike innocence, a complete inability to fool her, even with his dumb jokes and teases—that twitchy thing with his lip always gave it away. And of course, she had been completely honest with him.

Well, maybe not *completely*. She glanced at her companion in the passenger seat and grinned. He smiled back.

"Steven bought into ten percent of Wyndhaven when my dad first built it." Erica's voice was low and controlled. "He had inherited some money. And he was making a very good salary with my father's company. I think my father *encouraged* Steven to invest, because he knew it would make him a better manager."

"Steven must have done very well."

"Oh, he *has*." Erica was emphatic. "Well enough to increase his share to fifty percent."

"Steven owns *half* of Wyndhaven Colony?" Cal tried to hide the surprise in her voice.

"Yes. He mortgaged his shirt to buy another forty percent."

"When was that?"

"Five years ago. Of course, my father has full ownership of the other two luxury centers, and the smaller homes in the chain." She sighed. "Steven has his half of Wyndhaven nearly paid off, but now he's using it as collateral for the rehab hospital. *That* project is really Steven's baby. My father had very little to do with it."

"It sounds like he's taking a big chance," Cal noted.

"Steven likes taking risks," Erica answered quickly. "He says you never get anywhere without taking chances."

Cal pulled into Wyndhaven's parking lot. Plato's battered Rabbit was parked near the entrance to the nature trail. She had tried calling him at home, but nobody answered. Apparently, he had reached the same conclusions as Cal.

She parked her car beside Plato's. Off in the distance, in the woods to the east, a light flickered dimly. Maybe it was just her imagination. But the old map she'd found in the hospital library had shown a factory just east of the Wyndhaven grounds.

"Cal?"

"Yes?" Sitting there in the darkness, staring at Plato's car, she had almost forgotten about Erica.

"I'm scared. For Steven." She drew a deep, shaky breath. "I think I understand why you're asking all these things. But you're wrong. You *must* be."

Her protest had a hollow ring, as though she were trying hard to convince herself that one plus one equals three.

"Steven is very gentle. Very caring." She was sobbing again. "He wouldn't hurt anyone."

"I'm sure he wouldn't." Cal glanced at the empty Rabbit and hoped that Erica was right.

"He's been under so much pressure lately. He's putting everything he owns into the new hospital. He hasn't been himself."

Cal couldn't help wondering why Steven didn't just ask his future father-in-law for a loan.

"He's very proud," Erica seemed to sense Cal's unspoken question. "He doesn't want Daddy's money. He hasn't wanted us to get married until he launches the new hospital."

"I understand," Cal lied.

"He would never hurt anyone," Erica insisted again.

"Dr. Tucker talked to you on Saturday night," Cal said. She had vague memories of Marvin Tucker dancing with Erica— along with half of the other women at the dinner-dance. "About the nursing home, I think. Right?"

"Just hints and theories," Erica replied. "Crazy allegations about toxins in the water. Rumors like that could damage our company."

"Is that what Steven said? You talked with him after you danced with Marvin." She remembered Steven taking Erica's hand and leading her away from the hematologist. Plato had chalked it up to jealousy. But he was wrong.

Now she understood why Erica had overplayed Feinstein's possible guilt. Consciously or unconsciously, she had been shielding Steven. And her father's company.

Steven likes to take risks, Erica had said. Cal shuddered. The bludgeoning of Marvin Tucker, out in the open in the vast Hall of Prehistoric Life, was certainly a big risk. But it had paid off, so far.

"Did you tell Steven what Dr. Tucker had said?"

"He's really a gentle person," Erica whispered. "You must be wrong."

"I hope I am." Cal sighed, and glanced at the empty Rabbit once again. "I really hope I am."

She hung up the phone, locked the car, and grabbed a few things from the trunk of the Corsica. Finally, she hiked to the nature trail and followed it toward the eastern woods, her companion pacing beside her.

She smiled at him once again. He was so handsome and strong and graceful. Despite Plato's absence, Cal felt safe. Almost.

CHAPTER 27

"I didn't kill Kate Shirvesky."

Steven Prescott stared at the crowbar in his hands. He was standing very near to Plato. He had carefully folded his lizard skin overcoat and placed it on a fallen timber, then propped his flashlight beside it. All of his motions had been careful, deliberate, vigilant for any quick moves on Plato's part.

Such things were very far from Plato's mind. Right now, listening to Steven Prescott's confession, he was thinking about Marvin Tucker. Picturing the old hematologist lying on the floor of the museum, his head caved in from a fearsome blow.

Plato was wondering if, ten minutes from now, he would look exactly the same way.

"She called me at my office last May," Steven continued. His voice was tight with indignation. "Over the telephone, she blabbed something about toxic benzene levels near Wyndhaven. In the water, in the soil." He shook his head in disbelief. "I figured she was one of those environmentalist nuts. But I said I'd meet with her—at the nursing home. I'd let her show me what she found."

He glanced up at Plato and shrugged.

"That was reasonable, don't you think?"

Plato didn't answer.

"Well, *she* sure as hell wasn't reasonable. She came to my office that afternoon and started shooting her mouth off about cancer rates and some kind of anemia and saying it was my fault." His mouth tightened. "She said she had come out the day before and found a big factory uphill from us. She wanted to get our drinking water tested at a special lab, to see if there were any weird chemicals floating around."

He slapped one palm with the curved end of the crowbar.

"I got mad. I lost my temper, told her she didn't know what the hell she was talking about."

"Your rate of aplastic anemia is several hundred times normal, Steven." Plato tried to keep his voice calm, cool, reasonable. "God only know what your cancer rate is."

"We've got *old* people here," he answered. "Of *course* they're sick. That's what I told her, but she wouldn't listen. She just got madder. Another goddamned environmental crusader—looking for toxic chemicals behind every bush and tree."

"If you didn't believe her," Plato asked, "why didn't you just go along with the tests?"

"I couldn't risk it. You can see that." He glanced up at Plato. "Wyndhaven's reputation has been spotless—that's how we get our paying patients. And I'm using Wyndhaven collateral to put up a hundred-bed rehab hospital. Any questions about safety would sink the whole deal."

Plato nodded slowly. He had guessed that Steven Prescott owned a big share of Wyndhaven Colony. And he already knew that Steven was heavily involved in the rehab hospital project.

"And there would *be* questions, I know that. No matter what the tests showed." He grimaced. "The whole world is full of toxins, right? I went to Yellowstone last summer and they wouldn't let us drink the stream water."

"I think that's a little different," Plato said. "Contamination from—"

"All it would take is *one* little molecule of benzene or chloro-whatever to show up on those tests. Our reputation would be sunk. I'd lose my shirt." He slapped his hand with the crowbar again. "So I put a little pressure on her. I said I'd call her advisor at Case Western and say I was being harassed by one of his students."

Steven smiled.

"*That* put the fear of God into her. First time she shut up during the whole interview. I guess she was kind of on the rocks, academically."

Plato was staring at the wall behind Steven. The full moon had risen higher in the sky, and the outline of the asylum's initials had already sunk into the water. Only the shadow of the bars remained on the wall.

"She left after that, but I saw her from my window, heading toward these woods." His jaw clenched. "I figured she was going to take a sample—maybe from the ground here on our property, or from one of those barrels up the hill. I ran out to stop her, to tell her she couldn't do that without permission."

Steven shook his head.

"She spotted me coming. She ducked into the asylum, right into the front entrance." He rubbed his hand over his mouth and sighed. "I guess she was scared. She must have thought I was going to hurt her."

He spread his hands helplessly. The crowbar flashed in the moonlight.

"I wouldn't have hurt her. I never hurt anyone. It was dark and rainy. I ran in here after her, calling her. I didn't want her to get hurt." He pointed back to the origin of the tunnel. "You know how it is there. All burned out. No roof over the western half of the building."

Plato knew.

"She saw me coming. She knew she was trapped." He stared at the crowbar in his hands, genuinely upset. "I waved my hand, told her to stop, that I wouldn't hurt her. But she backed right into that open stairwell. The one without any steps."

He swallowed heavily.

"I hurried around to the eastern entrance, down those other stairs, and rushed along through the basement. But she was already dead. I think she hit her head on the floor."

Plato believed him. He had almost met the same fate himself, in the other stairwell. Steven wouldn't have needed the crowbar.

"I felt terrible," Steven said. "Didn't sleep for days."

"But you took advantage of the situation."

"What choice did I have?" he protested. "If I told anyone what happened, they would have asked what she was doing out here. Everything would have come out." He shrugged. "I dragged her body into the tunnel down here—I didn't want to risk moving it somewhere else. I took her keys and cleaned out her office and apartment. I drove her car to Pittsburgh and left it down by the river without the plates."

"And tracked down those patients' charts," Plato added.

"Yes. She had a list of all nine patients in her purse—and a note saying that four of them were at Siegel's anatomy lab." He caressed the crowbar. "Lucky for me, she already had the other five charts in her office at Riverside. Getting into Malenkov's office was tricky; I tagged along with Erica during an evening board meeting last June and snuck downstairs. I thought I was *never* going to find those charts—and then I had to pull the ID stickers off the boxes, too."

Thank goodness Kate had made a copy of her list, Plato reflected. At least *somebody* would figure out what had really happened. Someday.

"Why did you move Kate Shirvesky's bones?" Plato asked. "That was a big risk."

"I *had* to. The new hospital is going up just a quarter-mile away. We've already started building an access road. I couldn't risk having one of the workers blunder in here and find her." He smiled shyly. "I was going to move the body, bury it somewhere else, but when I got here, only her bones were left. I couldn't believe she was a skeleton already." He swept his crowbar back toward the asylum. "Of course, that old place is *full* of rats and bugs."

Plato shuddered, remembering the office, the skeletal chair, the whittled legs of the wooden desk. And he remembered Cal's assertion about rats and mice and bugs. Very efficient cleaners.

"So you decided to plant her bones in Sergei Malenkov's skeleton collection," Plato guessed.

"I *tried* to. I took Erica's key and snuck in the back way. I remembered all those boxes of bones in his office, and I figured he wouldn't notice one more. But when I got there with the sack of bones, practically all the boxes were gone." He grinned. "Lucky for me, we were just about ready to pour Siegel's footers. I snuck out to the dig site and buried her."

"Only to have her dug up the next day."

He grimaced. "I couldn't *believe* it. I thought it was all behind me. It was an accident—nothing else."

Plato shook his head.

"And Marvin Tucker—was that an accident?"

"In a way." Steven glanced up at Plato and shook his head. "See, he found out about that girl's work. Somehow. I think he was helping her with a research project. He must have found some of her papers in his office."

Plato thought back to the dance, and Tucker's comment to his partner that he had dug up some old research papers. And his discussion with Erica out on the dance floor.

"Tucker said something to Erica about it on Saturday night," Steven continued. "Just that he had some concerns about Wyndhaven's anemia rate."

"So you killed him."

"I didn't have any choice." He shrugged helplessly. "If Tucker's story came out, if they started checking over Kate Shirvesky's data, everyone would assume that I killed her."

Plato shook his head. The conversation's twisted logic was confusing him. Right and wrong seemed to be very relative things for Steven Prescott.

"It was too bad," Steven continued. "Tucker seemed like a decent guy. I really didn't want to kill him." He shrugged. "I don't want to kill you either, Plato."

"I'm not crazy about the idea myself."

"But what else can I do?" He stood with his feet shoulder-width apart and clutched the crowbar behind his back. "Nothing."

Doing nothing sounded very, very good to Plato.

"I have to think about what's best for everyone. It would *kill* Erica if she found out what happened."

It wouldn't kill *Cal*, Plato knew. His death would be a fortunate coincidence. Once Plato was gone, Cal could have her graceful, athletic anesthesiologist without any real guilt.

"Now, then." Steven grinned. "This won't hurt a bit. Isn't that what you doctors always say?"

Midsentence, without breaking the cadence of his words, Steven Prescott swung the crowbar out from behind his back and whipped it around in a smooth rounded arc toward Plato's left ear.

Plato spun away and leaped back as the crowbar whizzed by, barely missing his left arm. *Almost* missing, actually—it nipped his shirtsleeve just over his left bicep. And tore the skin there; Plato felt a warm trickle of blood seep down his arm.

Steven feinted a backswing, pivoted, and spun the crowbar straight at Plato's forehead.

He ducked just beneath the blow. The heavy iron rod

cleared his head by millimeters, flashing past with a ghastly, powerful *whoosh!* like a semi roaring down a freeway.

Before Steven could recover his balance, Plato darted beside him, around him, almost making a break down the tunnel before the killer whirled to block his path. He stared at Plato with open admiration.

"You're awfully quick, Plato." Despite his deadly ballet, Steven Prescott wasn't even breathing hard. "Good thing I brought this crowbar along, or I'd have a fight on my hands."

Plato doubted it. He hadn't hit anyone since second grade, when Ricky Bosconi had stolen his book bag and stomped on his lunch. That night, when Plato had tearfully told his father about the incident, Sergeant Jack Marley's solution had been simple. In one evening, he gave his son a few quick lessons in life. How to fight clean, how to fight dirty. How to use words to avoid a fight altogether. A few basic boxing moves—blocking and jabbing, keeping your head down and leading with your right. Moving your feet. And most of all, the uppercut. It was Jack Marley's favorite punch.

The next day, when Ricky Bosconi stole Plato's book bag again, Plato was ready. When reason failed, when Ricky stomped on his peanut butter and jelly sandwich once again, Plato landed a picture-perfect uppercut on Ricky's chin—and felt more pain in his hand than he would have imagined possible. He had broken his middle finger, and Ricky Bosconi had needed seven stitches—in his *tongue*. They had shared the same emergency room cubicle. Each stitch was more agonizing for Plato than it ever could have been for Ricky.

Plato had never hit anyone again. He doubted if he remembered how.

Not that it mattered, anyway. Plato stumbled into the wall of the tunnel, shaking and panting as the sick weight of fear and despair settled on his shoulders. He couldn't see much point in even *trying* to escape. Even if he made it out of the tunnel, outran Steven to the eastern end of the building, Plato doubted he could climb the rotten stairway before the steps collapsed beneath his feet. Steven was far too agile, quick, and powerful to let him escape.

Besides, who really cared if Plato lived or not?

He crouched low as Steven confidently moved in for the kill. The murderer gripped his weapon tightly in both hands, holding the crowbar high over his head like a batter poised to hit a home run. Plato held his breath and readied himself for another leap.

Once again, Steven slammed the crowbar at Plato's head, and once again his target sprang away at the last possible moment. But this time, the bar glanced off Plato's left shoulder, sending a searing wave of pain down to his hand and up to his neck. It would probably be the last thing Plato ever felt.

Steven waved the crowbar back once more and watched Plato jump free. He seemed to be enjoying the challenge.

"Neat move. I thought you didn't dance." He grinned. "You should have been out there with your wife Saturday night—instead of that anesthesiologist. I think she's got the hots for him."

Catching his breath, panting, staring at Steven Prescott's smirking face, Plato felt the hot sulfur pool of rage seething and bubbling again. Just as the killer took another short backswing, he ducked inside the arc of the crowbar and slammed his fist into Steven's belly, his knee into Steven's groin while grabbing for the crowbar with his left hand.

And he would have had it—if only his left arm had worked. But it dangled uselessly at his side, nerveless and limp after the punishing blow to his shoulder.

Plato struggled anyway, pushing Steven back toward the wall and throttling his throat with his right hand. But the crowbar slashed up again, barely missing Plato's chin and sending him dancing back to the wall.

"Too bad this wasn't an allosaurus bone. I'd have had you."

With a satisfied grin, Steven advanced toward Plato. Panting and shaking and sick with pain, Plato shambled along toward the entrance of the tunnel. Behind him, Steven followed confidently, barely hurrying his stride. He caught Plato at the entrance to the tunnel, grabbing his bad shoulder and spinning him around like a rag doll.

Plato stared up into Steven's face, Steven's eyes as the killer wound up for the final blow. He was smiling surely, confidently. Rather than aiming for Plato's head, he brought the heavy bar around and down toward his victim's chest. Plato had no time to duck, no room to dodge free. He turned slightly, sacrificing his useless left arm to shield himself from the mortal wound.

And just then, from the corner of his eye, he sensed a sudden movement, a black furry blur that hurtled up from the tunnel entrance to connect with Steven Prescott's arm.

Foley's ghost.

The Australian shepherd had timed his leap perfectly, hurtling his body into Steven's forearm, slowing the momentum just enough for Plato to duck under the swinging crowbar.

Steven Prescott stared down at the animal frantically growling and nipping at his heels, his pantlegs, his knees. "What the—"

Drawing on Jack Marley's playbook, Plato stood, planted his feet and brought his right fist up in a picture-perfect uppercut that connected with Steven Prescott's jaw.

It hurt Plato just as much as it had twenty-five years before. Steven tottered and swayed, eyes rolling back in his head, feet doing a crazy little shuffle on the floor. The crowbar clattered from his grip. For a moment, Plato was sure the killer would join it on the floor.

But Steven was far more durable than Ricky Bosconi. While Plato was still shaking the feeling back into his hand, Steven swooped down, grabbed the crowbar, and spun to his feet. And instantly passed out again, toppling over like a falling redwood.

Well, not *quite* instantly. First had come a flash of silver, a metallic thud like a pumpkin hitting a sidewalk.

Cal was standing in the doorway, her trusty twenty-six-inch Easton aluminum T-ball bat in her hand, a satisfied smile on her face.

"Terribly sorry," she said. "Did we interrupt you?"

"What?" Plato stared from Cal to the dog, and back to Cal again.

"That was some punch." She twirled her bat like a cheerleader's baton. "But I thought you needed a little help."

Plato nodded, and glanced down at the body on the floor. Steven Prescott was clearly down for the count. Plato unbuckled his belt and tied it around the killer's hands before turning to confront his wife.

"What the hell is going on?" He shook his head. "I thought you were at a *meeting*."

"No." Cal shook her head slowly. "I wasn't at a meeting. Not exactly."

"I didn't think so." Down on the floor, knotting Steven Prescott's belt around his ankles, Plato felt a warm tongue lapping his face. "And who is this fellow?"

"Gophe. Short for Gopher."

"Gopher?"

"Yeah." Cal knelt to pat the dog. "He's always digging holes in Neville's lawn. And fetching things out of Neville's basement. Like 'go-fer,' you know? Kind of a play on words."

"Neville's lawn?" Plato blinked. "Neville's basement?"

"Neville Archer." Cal grinned. "The guy I was dancing with Saturday night—remember? He raises Australian shepherds."

Gophe rolled over so they could scratch his belly.

"Neville raises Australian shepherds?" Plato asked, confused. A minute before, he had been waging a life-and-death battle with a killer. Now he was talking with his wife about Australian shepherds.

"Yeah." Cal smiled. "That's why I spent so much time with him at the dance Saturday. I wanted to surprise you and get a puppy from Neville. He was all excited because his prizewinner had another litter Saturday evening."

"So you were going to meet with him tonight." He frowned. Cal had wanted to surprise him. With a puppy.

"Yeah." She leaned over to check for a pulse in Steven's wrist, then nodded. "We planned it all out on Saturday night. I wasn't sure if it was a good idea—if you would resent my trying to replace Foley, but Neville thought it would be all right. Still, I wanted to surprise you."

Plato remembered the conversation in the dark.

Don't worry, Neville had said. *Your husband will never know.*

You came along at just the right time, Cal had answered. *I'm so happy.*

"I'm surprised, all right." Plato shook his head. Cal had no idea just *how* surprised he was. All the doubts and suspicions, the jealousy, the anger suddenly seemed ridiculous. A silly game he'd been playing with himself.

He needed some time to sort everything out. "Thank you."

"You're welcome."

"Neville's puppies grow awfully fast." Plato pointed at Gophe. "What does he feed them?"

"Oh, Gophe isn't a puppy. Not really." Cal patted the

Aussie fondly. "He came along last spring, but Neville hasn't found a buyer for him. He was going to give us one of his new puppies—pick of the litter—as a kind of belated wedding present. But I asked if we could have Gophe instead. Since he looks so much like Foley."

"He sure does," Plato agreed. And he *acted* like Foley, too—catching Steven's hand with his body just as the crowbar was slashing toward Plato. Just like Foley used to do with the pickup basketball games at Kent State.

"And besides, he's already potty-trained," Cal added. "No need for any Foley catheters."

"I'd keep him even if it took a year to train him." Plato scratched the Aussie behind the ears, under the chin. His tongue lolled from the side of his mouth. "I owe him a big favor."

"I thought you'd like him. He really does look like Foley, doesn't he?"

Plato nodded, struck again by the resemblance. Even from close up, he could hardly tell the difference.

"I hope he was a little easier to paper-train."

Gophe licked Plato's hand fondly.

"We'll have to change his name, though." He shook his head. "I can't really see him as a gopher. I don't want him to see *himself* as a gopher. We have enough gophers tearing up our lawn, and eating our garden."

"Better pick something that rhymes," Cal suggested. "Something that sounds reasonably close. So he doesn't get confused."

She pulled a portable phone from her purse, lifted the antenna, and dialed a number. "Cuyahoga County Sheriff? This is Dr. Cal Marley. We need police assistance and possible EMS support immediately. . . ."

Plato watched as Gophe assumed a watchful position beside Steven Prescott. The dog seemed remarkably intelligent. Even so, Cal was right—he needed to pick a similar-sounding name.

But what rhymed with "Gophe"? Loaf? Oaf?

How about something that just sounded similar—doe, go, low, doze, pose, most, roast . . .

Cal finally hung up the phone and slipped it back into her purse just as Steven Prescott began to stir. Gophe growled firmly.

Watching his adversary coming back to life, Plato remembered that final deadly swing, the black blur leaping up from the darkness like Foley coming back to life for one last basketball game. And he remembered his prediction after talking with Agnes—that making up with Cal was about as likely as Foley's ghost coming back to play another game of basketball.

"Ghost," Plato said aloud.

"What?"

"That's his new name. *Ghost*."

The Aussie glanced up at him quickly. Plato patted him on the head. "Good dog."

Cal nodded her understanding.

"The police should be here any minute," she said. She frowned at Steven Prescott. His eyes slowly opened to slits. He groaned like a man with a toothache. He probably had *several* toothaches. And a whopping headache, courtesy of Cal's T-ball bat. "They're coming up the access road."

She moved closer to crouch beside Plato and sucked in her breath. "Plato! What happened to your *hand*?"

He lifted his left hand. It was covered with dried blood.

"Nothing. Our friend here just nicked me in the arm. Up here." He pointed to his tattered, bloody sleeve. "And whacked my shoulder. I think he hit a nerve or something. My whole hand is numb."

"Poor dear." She leaned closer, poked at the hole in his shirt and squinted at the wound. "Does that hurt?"

"*Yes!*" Plato yipped, pulling away. "How about if we leave it to a specialist, Cally? Someone who deals with *live* people."

"Okay," she answered meekly, then glanced down at the killer. His eyes had fluttered closed again. "You sure hit him *hard*."

"So did you."

"It's all in the wrist." Cal grinned. "That's what our hitting coach always said. A firm wrist, and lots of follow-through."

Sirens sounded in the distance.

Minutes later, Plato and Cal were standing in the parking lot of Wyndhaven Colony. The sheriff's deputies had packed Steven Prescott into the back of a police cruiser and ferried the Marleys back to their cars. Cal leaned into Plato's good arm and shivered.

"I was so worried about you. When I saw your car parked

here, I got really scared. I don't know why." She looked up at him, eyes shining in the moonlight. "I knew you were out here, in trouble, somehow."

"I was." He shrugged, and winced at the sudden pain in his shoulder. "I think when couples are really close, they get this kind of sixth sense about things."

"Like *I* did—about you and Foley. That's why you've been so upset, acting so strange lately. Isn't it?"

Plato glanced down at her and frowned. He considered carefully, then decided on the truth. After all, he would eventually have to explain the two suitcases of clothes stashed in his trunk.

"Foley wasn't the *whole* reason I've been upset," he began.

"You've been under a lot of stress," Cal agreed. "We both have. I wish we could just go home and pack a couple of suitcases and take a week's vacation."

"That's kind of what I wanted to talk about. You see—"

His new pager squawked, like an anxious hen looking for a lost chick.

"Don't tell me you're on *call* again," Cal moaned.

"No. I'm not on call." He glanced at the display. It showed the number of Agnes Leighton's ward. "But I need to run inside for a few minutes."

"Why? Is there an emergency?"

"No." He led her toward the entrance of Wyndhaven Colony. "I just have to say good-bye to a friend."

CHAPTER 28

"So what are we doing tonight?" Lying on the bed, Plato riffled through the Friday *Plain Dealer*. "Seeing another drive-in movie?"

"Nah." Cal shucked off her white coat, blouse, skirt, and nylons, frowned at the pile of clothes, and sniffed. She had spent most of the afternoon in the anatomy lab at Siegel. "First thing *I'm* doing is getting out of these clothes. I smell like a cadaver."

"Better than smelling like a toxic waste dump," Plato observed.

"Not by much." She stuck out her tongue and made a face. "Sergei's special recipe. Guk!"

Cal finished undressing and slid onto the bed beside Plato. She undid his tie and pulled it off. "Maybe I should help *you* undress, too, hmm?"

"Not a bad idea." He dropped the paper to the floor.

She unbuttoned his shirt and nuzzled his chest. "Just what the doctor ordered."

"Exactly." He slid his arm down her bare back, pressed his face into her hair, and wrinkled his nose. "On the other hand, maybe we should have dinner first."

"Dinner?" She frowned up at him. "*That's* never happened before. You must really be hungry."

"No—it's not that." He wrinkled his nose again. "Let's just say you have a certain *atmosphere* about you."

She gave a skunklike waggle of her eyebrows. "Ahh, zat ees just the aroma of love, cherie."

"Sorry, Pepe. Zat ees the aroma of formalin." He patted her bare derriere wistfully. "Not terribly romantic, I'm afraid."

She twirled a hank of hair under her nose and sniffed. "*Eau de Cadaver*, huh?"

"Precisely. I'll take a rain check."

"Aww, come on." She slid closer, nuzzled his neck, nibbled his ear, and gave him a long, passionate kiss. She opened her eyes suddenly and drew away.

"You're holding your breath."

"Am I?" he asked innocently. "I hadn't noticed."

Actually, he *had* noticed. Sergei's special embalming recipe had a very distinctive aroma, one that was difficult to ignore. And Plato's memories of anatomy lab were not very pleasant. After flunking anatomy during freshman year of medical school, he had been required to repeat the entire course. He was painfully familiar with the aroma of Sergei's special embalming recipe.

Cal frowned sympathetically and brushed her lips across his forehead. "Just give me ten minutes in the shower. I'll smell like a live person again, I promise."

She bounced off the bed and hurried into the bathroom. While she showered, Plato scanned the entertainment section of the newspaper. The pickings were pretty bleak. The summer movies had disappeared from even the second-run theaters, and the holiday releases hadn't started showing yet. They had a choice between two sappy romances, a Stallone shoot-'em-up, and a Van Damme beat-'em-up.

Cal poked her head around the bathroom door as she toweled her hair. "Anything worth seeing?"

"Nope." Plato sighed. "Looks like another boring evening at home."

"We'll see." She gave an impish grin and ducked back into the bathroom. "Heard any more news about Wyndhaven?"

"Not really." Plato flipped to the front of the paper. Two weeks after the story broke, Wyndhaven headlines were still making the first page. "Looks like the county's getting a pile of Superfund money. Probably enough to clean up the mess, if the state kicks in some cash."

Tomlinson Chemicals, née Tomlinson Rubber and Plastics, née Jas. Honneker Rubber, had declared bankruptcy in the 1950s and abandoned their factory near Gladbrook Asylum. Their manufacturing processes were notoriously sloppy and unsafe even for their day, which helped explain why they had built their plant twenty miles from the city itself. After declaring bankruptcy, they had left hundreds of barrels of waste—benzene and a toxic soup of other dangerous organic chemicals—stacked near the unused siding and in the abandoned plant itself. Even worse were the huge holding tanks scattered around the old factory. Most of the tanks had rusted and leaked their contents into the soil and the water table beneath—the same water table tapped by the residents of Wyndhaven Colony.

Needless to say, Wyndhaven Colony had immediately begun trucking in city water while arranging to tap a recently installed pipeline leading down from Cleveland.

"I talked to Erica this afternoon," Cal said. "She's taking it better than I would have expected."

"Really?"

"I think she's burying herself in her work."

Plato nodded. "I'm not surprised."

The day after Steven's capture and confession, Albert Windgartner had quickly stepped in to buy back the other half of his flagship nursing home. With the proceeds from his share of Wyndhaven Colony, Steven Prescott would be able to cover his legal fees and clear his debts in canceling the rehab hospital project. Not that it mattered much, though. According to Homer, Steven would probably spend the rest of his life in prison.

But Albert would keep the nursing home open so that he wouldn't have to move.

Oddly enough, most of the Wyndhaven residents felt the same way. Though the Tomlinson Chemical dump had contaminated the aquifer beneath Wyndhaven Colony, the nursing home and surrounding lands were found to be otherwise quite clean and safe for habitation—provided that an outside source of drinking and bathing water was used. Most of the residents viewed Wyndhaven Colony as their home. Few wanted to leave—especially when they saw that the nursing home's owner was staying on as well.

But Steven Prescott and Albert Windgartner and their insurance companies would probably spend years battling claims filed on behalf of residents who had developed anemia or cancer during their stays at Wyndhaven Colony. Albert Windgartner was generally perceived as an unwitting participant in the disaster—after all, he, too, had developed aplastic anemia while living at Wyndhaven. So far, he appeared to be free of any direct blame or knowledge of the incident. His other nursing homes had continued to thrive. Albert would probably emerge from the crisis smelling like a rose.

Unlike Cal's clothes. Plato climbed off the bed and tossed the offensive garments into the laundry chute.

"You're still dressed," Cal complained. Behind him, she had emerged from the bathroom.

"So are you," Plato shot back. But he didn't mind it at all.

Evidently, Cal wasn't planning to go out to dinner, or to the movies, or anywhere outside the bedroom. She was wearing dark stockings and garters beneath that shimmery blue dressgown thing she had worn Monday night. In the heat of anger and jealousy Monday, he hadn't bothered to do more than glance at Cal.

But even then, it had taken a lot of willpower to close his eyes and ignore her.

Now, he stood gaping, drinking her in with his eyes. Five feet two inches of heart-stopping curves and shadows wrapped in a gown of satin and lace and ribbons. Honey-blond hair, a turned-up nose, and an elfin smile. And a pair of copperbrown eyes that shone for him alone.

Plato smiled. He would never doubt her again, he was sure of that.

Hips cocked, Cal shot him a come-hither look.

Plato came hither.

"How do I look?" She spun in a neat pirouette. The gown swirled about her hips like a dark ocean wave.

Plato gulped, feeling his own tide rising. "How do you look?" He spread his hands. "Like the first star to sparkle on a clear summer evening. Like a—"

She pulled his face down and stopped him with a kiss. "Hush."

"Yes, ma'am."

"You're overdressed." She helped him free of his clothes. "Here—isn't this more comfortable?"

"Yes, ma'am."

She slid her arms around his waist and pressed her head against his chest. He leaned over and buried his face in her hair. And sniffed.

"Better?"

"Much." He untied one of her ribbons and smiled. "This is some outfit. Did it come with an instruction manual?"

"Just a map." Cal giggled. "You've got to find the buried treasure."

"I'll take my time looking. Check every square inch." He crouched and hefted her into his arms, carrying her over to the bed. In two weeks, the shoulder had healed pretty well. "Now, let's see." He untied another ribbon and moved down. "Should I check here?"

"Sure. That's a good place to check. Mmm. You're getting warm."

"I know." He moved to the other side. "How about here?"

"Warmer still." She helped him untie the next ribbon and sighed. "Hot. Very hot."

"'X' marks the spot," he muttered.

Just then, a frantic barking sounded from somewhere in the house. Plato ignored it, but the sound came again. A tortured yelp.

Cal pulled away. "You'd better see what it is."

Plato nodded reluctantly. Ghost and Dante hadn't quite become friends yet. Ghost thought the cat was far too bossy and aloof, and Dante couldn't quite understand why Ghost didn't smell like Foley. Or act like him. The first time Dante had tried to cuddle up with the dog who looked so much like his old friend, Ghost misunderstood the gesture and nipped his right ear. Their relationship had been touch-and-go ever since. Quarrels were common and occasionally led to brawls, which Dante usually won. Cats fight dirty.

Apparently, another squabble had developed.

Reluctantly, Plato slipped out of bed and into his terry cloth robe. Ghost's barking and Dante's shrill calls continued.

"You'd better hurry," Cal urged. "They may have found your pager again."

Plato rushed into the hallway and down the stairs. Behind him, Cal slipped a flannel nightshirt over her disheveled outfit and followed.

The commotion was coming from the basement. For some odd reason, Ghost loved the dark corners and chaotic mess down there. He spent most afternoons nosing around the junk and boxes and ancient furniture, occasionally ducking back upstairs to show Plato and Cal his latest discovery—a brass doorknob, a tattered blanket, the stuffed orange dolphin Plato had slept with as a child.

Ghost bounded up the stairs just as Plato and Cal reached the doorway. The Aussie was holding a small white object in the corner of his mouth, and Dante was in hot pursuit. Apparently, the object was quite popular.

Cal wrestled the prize from the dog's mouth and gawked at it. "Oh, my God!"

Plato took it from her hand and examined it carefully.

"What?" Smooth and pale in color, it looked like an ordinary pebble. "It's just a rock."

"It's a *wrist bone*, Plato. The scaphoid bone. From a human hand."

"Very funny, Cal." He eyed the object again and smiled to himself. "Don't tell me you think we have *bodies* buried under our basement. Steven Prescott didn't build this house, remember."

"Have *you* ever been in the crawl space under the servants' wing?" she asked pointedly.

"No."

"Well, apparently Ghost has." She grabbed a flashlight from the countertop and started down the stairs. "We don't have the slightest idea what's down there. We could have a whole *graveyard* under our house. What's so funny?"

"You." Plato tossed the scaphoid bone up and caught it backhanded. He held it up to the light and motioned for her to take a closer look.

She did. "What the—"

Engraved on the narrowest portion of the bone were four letters: HHAC.

"Harold Hawkins Anatomical Company," Cal read. She shook her head. "But we don't have a *hand* model yet. Do we?"

"Your next installment came in the mail today," Plato confessed. "The human hand. It was addressed to 'Dr. Marley.' so I opened it. When I saw what it was, I took it down to the basement."

Cal rushed downstairs to examine the package. This model included a complete, dissectable left hand and the skeleton of a right hand. Ghost had dragged the skeletal hand onto the floor and toyed with the contents. Fortunately, none of the bones were damaged.

"Wow! They're *magnetic!*" Cal started fitting bones together. In seconds, the entire skeletal hand was reassembled. "Whatever will they think of next?"

She turned her attention to the realistic Plaskin hand and smiled. She pulled at the skin and peeked at the tapestry of muscles beneath. "This is *fabulous*."

"Yeah." Plato sighed. "Sure."

Cal glanced up from her prize. "Why didn't you *tell* me this came? And why were you hiding it in the basement?"

"I thought I should put it next to Harold's head." He gestured to the other model resting on a nearby shelf. The eyes *still* weren't straight. "And I knew you'd spend all evening fiddling with it, instead of—"

"Instead of fiddling with *you?*" She smirked and put the hand down. "No way. Harold Hawkins is a fascinating man, but I happen to prefer the real thing." She moved closer and undid his robe. "And you're very, *very* real."

He pulled her close and kissed her. "I *was* kind of in the mood for a quiet evening alone with you."

"Me, too." She turned to gaze wistfully at Harold's lifelike hand. Every wrinkle, every hair, even a *mole* near Harold's left wrist, was depicted in a perfect replica of plastic and rubber. "Looks like an absolutely *splendid* reproduction."

"You're sure you don't want to dissect it now?" Plato offered. "I can wait."

"No. That's okay." She grinned. "Let's go practice a little reproduction of our own."

"That's the spirit."

"And then we can have some dinner." She nodded firmly. "Shooter's shouldn't be too crowded—and I can bring Harold's hand along." She picked up the replica and gazed at it fondly. "We can dissect it while we eat."

Plato groaned, picturing the swath of empty tables surrounding them, the averted gazes, the disgusted looks. After their last experience, he'd be surprised if they were ever allowed into Shooter's again, with or without teaching materials.

He gently pried the model hand from her grasp and set it on the high shelf beside Harold's head. "I think takeout might be nicer."

She waggled her eyebrows meaningfully. "More private, huh?"

"Exactly." He glanced at Harold's head. With its left lid partially closed, the model was giving a crooked wink. And the lifelike hand—mounted palm-out on its stand—seemed to be waving farewell. Or bestowing a blessing. "A nice, quiet evening alone. Just you and me."

They headed back upstairs together, leaving Harold and Dante and Ghost behind.

AUTHOR'S NOTE

Like Plato Marley, many doctors have trouble listening to or carrying out their patients' final wishes, for a variety of reasons. Doctors and other medical professionals are first taught to preserve life, and the subject of death is often treated as an afterthought. Physicians and patients and families are often uncomfortable with the subject of death, and so patients' wishes are seldom sought or discussed. Our medical, legal, and insurance systems all emphasize acute hospital care for critically ill patients, but they offer few resources or alternatives for those patients whose illnesses have progressed beyond reasonable hope of recovery.

Agnes Leighton knew her own mind, and made her wishes clear in no uncertain terms. Unfortunately, such situations are relatively uncommon. Many people who reach the end of the health care road are unconscious, too sick, or too debilitated to describe their wishes to their doctor. Decisions are then left to doctors or to the patients' families, who must struggle with indecision and conflict and guilt. A landmark Robert Wood Johnson study found that two-thirds of critically ill patients were never asked about their wishes regarding "heroic" life-sustaining measures, and less than half of those who asked *not* to be resuscitated actually had their wishes obeyed.

We all must face death sometime, but we can exercise some control over the event by planning ahead—making living wills to let doctors know our wishes and expectations for life support and resuscitation, asking for information about certain situations and procedures so we can intelligently weigh the benefits and risks, exploring insurance plan options for home and hospice care, and possibly designating a power of attorney *before* one is needed. The American Association of Retired Persons offers several helpful pamphlets covering issues of medical decision-making, powers of attorney, and living wills.

Here's a preview of the next mystery featuring Cal & Plato Marley, *Ten Little Medicine Men*.

Chapter 1

INTEROFFICE MEMO

From: Lionel Wallace, Ph.D., Chief Executive Officer, Riverside General Hospital
To: TREND Task Force Members (All Division Chiefs)
Date: Friday, March 27
Re: Planning Retreat at Camp *Success!*

Please remember that the retreat for the Team-Related Education of Nurses and Doctors (TREND) at Camp *Success!*
takes place this weekend. Attendance is mandatory for all
clinical department chiefs. Training in team building will
be a major theme of the retreat. Major reductions in funding among the various departments will also be discussed.
Attached is a list of equipment required for the trip.

"I'm going to kill him," said the Chief of Obstetrics and Gynecology.

On a cold and windy Friday afternoon in March, the Council of Chiefs was gathered in the lobby of Cleveland Riverside
General Hospital. Oddly enough, not a single white coat was
visible in the small cluster of doctors and nurses and division
chiefs. Not a single stethoscope or suit jacket or Rolex watch.

Instead, most of the chiefs were bent double under the load
of heavy frame backpacks, sleeping bags, canteens, and duffle
bags. All eight members of the party were staring dolefully
through the hospital lobby's front window, huddled together
like a litter of puppies born in an animal shelter.

Decked out in their jeans and nylon jackets and camping
gear, the Council of Chiefs looked as alien as a chamber orchestra playing Mozart on the moon.

"I'm going to kill him," the obstetrician repeated.

"How?" asked the Chief of Nursing Services.

"Poison," guessed the Chief of Internal Medicine.

"Slow torture," suggested the Chief of Psychiatry.

"The Death of a Thousand Scalpels," grumbled the Chief of Surgery.

"Hardly," sniffed the Chief of Obstetrics and Gynecology. She smiled ferally. "I'm going to scoop his heart out. With a blunt speculum."

"Won't work." The Chief of Pediatrics shook her head sadly. "Our dear hospital president doesn't *have* a heart."

Two young chiefs hovered silently at the edge of the crowd, cautiously noncommittal. Plato Marley, the acting Chief of Geriatrics, fingered his backpack uneasily.

"Tough crowd," he muttered to his wife.

Cal Marley, the Chief of Pathology, nodded. The oversized backpack dwarfed her tiny frame like a cabin cruiser hitched to a Volkswagen Beetle. But her back was unbent; she stood perfectly upright despite the heavy load.

"Good thing Lionel Wallace isn't here," she agreed. "I think we'd have a riot on our hands."

Lionel Wallace, the newly appointed president of Riverside General, was unaccountably absent. So was his vice-president. Perhaps they were already at Camp *Success!* Better yet, maybe Wallace had read the weather report and canceled the weekend trip.

Plato Marley sighed wistfully. That was too much to ask.

He turned to his wife. "I guess we shouldn't tell anyone this whole trip was *your* idea."

"*My* idea?" Cal tossed her blond head and glared at her husband. "What are you talking about?"

"Don't you remember?" He spread his hands. "Last December, just before Wallace was appointed. You talked with him at the medical staff Christmas party."

Cal gasped. She remembered now. The president-elect had lamented the poor relations between the various clinical departments at Riverside. He worried over the need for cost-cutting measures. He asked Cal if she had any suggestions for improving teamwork between the teaching programs.

Cal had agreed with him—turf battles were always blazing between surgery and internal medicine, between pediatrics and obstetrics, with all sides jockeying for more funding and greater flexibility. Unfortunately, she didn't see any obvious solution. Turf wars were a part of every major hospital, and always would be—especially when budget cuts were looming.

Cal had jokingly suggested packing all the department chairmen up and sending them off to Camp *Success!*, Northern

Ohio's corporate boot camp. She had just seen an article about it in the *Plain Dealer* on the morning of the Christmas party. Camp *Success!* was the latest fad in business management—sending top executives out into the woods for encounters with nature, in order to build teamwork.

She and Plato had shared a good laugh about it over breakfast that morning, imagining fat accountants and lawyers and executives waddling through the Geauga County forest on scavenger hunts for buried notebook computers and cellular phones.

It had seemed hilarious at the time.

"I was just *kidding*," Cal insisted. "I never thought he'd really—"

"You don't kid around with Lionel Wallace." Plato sighed. "He has utterly no sense of humor."

"I know."

A large black minibus slid up to the hospital entrance with all the quiet dignity of a hearse. Its side panel was emblazoned with the Camp *Success!* motto: BUILDING TEAMWORK—ONE CHALLENGE AT A TIME. Beneath the motto was the camp's logo—a colorful abstract smear that might have been painted by a team of emotionally disturbed orangutans. The driver, whose black nylon jacket also bore the Camp *Success!* logo, jumped from the swing door and strode purposefully into the lobby.

He halted just inside the door, stood at attention, and fixed his gaze on the backpack-laden group. With his jet-black hair, dark sunglasses, and clean-cut good looks, he might have been a Secret Service agent eyeing a particularly suspicious crowd of White House visitors. Finally, his face softened and he stood at ease—feet shoulder-width apart and hands folded behind his back.

"Benjamin Disraeli once said that 'the secret of success in life is for a man to be ready for his opportunity.' " He smiled shyly at the floor, shrugging off their gratitude for this great pearl of wisdom. He looked up again. "My name is Claude Eberhardt, and I'll be your guide this weekend. I hope it will be a great opportunity for all of us."

He turned and led his charges outside.

Several chiefs groaned.

"A great opportunity," the surgery chairman echoed. "Opportunity for *what*?"

"For murder," the obstetrician replied with a grin.

"You brought your speculum?" the psychiatrist asked quietly.

"Of course." She patted her backpack. "Never leave home without it."

The guide started loading their backpacks into the luggage compartment of the bus.

The Chief of Internal Medicine handed his pack and sleeping bag over, then turned back to the group and shook his head. "I just don't understand it—Lionel Wallace sending us on this trip."

"Why not?" asked the Chief of Nursing Services. "You know what Wallace is like."

"I know." The internist's eyebrows were heavy and seamlessly joined—like a long woolly bear caterpillar. The caterpillar marched up his tall forehead. "But it's too innovative, too crazy—even for *him.*"

"I agree," grumbled the Chief of Psychiatry, a short, dapper type with enough skin for two faces. The wrinkles deepened. "Lionel Wallace could never have dreamed up this scheme alone. He's as single-minded as a locomotive on a railroad bridge."

"All too true." The Chief of Surgery nodded sagely. "Someone must have put the idea into Lionel's head."

"I'd like to know *who,*" grumbled the Chief of Obstetrics and Gynecology. Her sharp, perfect teeth glinted in the morning sun as she strode toward the door of the bus. "I'd yank *his* heart out with a pair of blunt forceps."

Plato glanced down at Cal and winked.

"Don't," she pleaded in a harsh whisper. "Don't even *think* of it. Not a word. Not a syllable."

"Never," he pledged solemnly. "She couldn't *torture* it out of me. Not even with a blunt speculum."

"She won't *need* torture." She sighed, patting his arm fondly. "You're about as secretive as a Dictaphone. All she has to do is push the right button."

"Are you implying that—"

"Shh." Cal led her husband to the rear of the line. Discreetly, wordlessly, they lurked at the fringe of the crowd and handed their backpacks to the driver.

Just then, a plump blue-jeaned figure poked its nose out through the doors like a timid groundhog tasting the weather on a cold winter day. Lionel Wallace's long, sparse mustache twitched and his feeble eyes blinked in the chilly afternoon sunlight. Apparently, the president had come along for the ride.

He glanced with polite surprise at the Council of Chiefs gathered on the sidewalk, as though he was meeting a party of trick-or-treaters on Halloween. His eyes flicked over the obstetrician's shoulder, past the other members of the party, and finally settled on Cal.

"Ah, Dr. Marley!" he said happily. "You must come ride up front with me. After all, this little excursion was really *your* idea."

Cal gasped. Six heads turned from the hospital president to the two chiefs lurking at the edge of the crowd.

Before Cal could reply, Plato suddenly nodded and threw his shoulders back with a grin. "Thanks for remembering me," he told the hospital's CEO. "I'm sure we'll all enjoy this weekend together."

Lionel Wallace glanced from Plato to Cal and back again, blinked five or six times, then nodded slowly. "Yes. Yes, of course, Plato. I'm sure we will."

Cal followed Plato through the gauntlet of chiefs, feeling six pairs of eyes sear the back of her neck as they stepped into the bus. Behind them, the obstetrician growled softly at Plato, like a Doberman marking a plump, juicy burglar.

Once inside, Cal sat between her husband and the hospital president. The Chief of Obstetrics followed, sitting directly across the aisle from the trio.

"An absolutely *splendid* idea," Wallace repeated. "Don't you think so, Dr. Oberlin?"

"Yes-s-s," the obstetrician hissed through her teeth. Her dark eyes flashed at Plato. "Thank you *so* much, Dr. Marley."

He smiled generously. "You're welcome, Dr. Oberlin."

Beside him, Cal clutched his arm, leaned closer, and whispered ever so softly, "My hero."

"Accept the challenges, so that you may feel the exhilaration of victory."

On television screens scattered around the bus, smartly dressed actors were delivering inspirational quotes. The Council of Chiefs was bouncing along a narrow winding road somewhere in the hills of Geauga County, about thirty miles outside of Cleveland. Most of the campers were asleep—lulled into a stupor by the vapid ramblings of the video monitors.

"Here we are." Cal pointed out the window of the bus.

Across the street, a wide wooden sign dangled over a rutted dirt road. The sign read TEAMWORK IS THE GATEWAY TO SUCCESS.

Plato glanced out the window and sighed. "Homey, isn't it?"

"I think this is going to be even worse than we imagined."

Cal didn't bother lowering her voice. Beside her, Lionel Wallace was curled into a fetal ball and drooling into his overcoat—probably dreaming of big insurance contracts and record profits and new hospital wings.

On the television monitors, an actor vaguely resembling George C. Scott frowned earnestly. *"Never tell people* how *to do things. Tell them* what *to do and they will surprise you with their ingenuity."*

Across the aisle, Mark Inverness shook his head. The internist had stayed awake and chatted with Plato and Cal during the long ride.

"Patton." He sighed.

Another actor wearing dark glasses and an old fedora filled the screen. *"Winning isn't everything, but wanting to win is."*

"All these slogans." Cal made a face. "I think I'm going to be sick."

"Barfing isn't everything," Plato intoned, "but wanting to barf is."

"Patton and Lombardi." Mark Inverness rolled his eyes. "They're quoting army generals and football coaches—to a busload of doctors."

Beside him, Marta Oberlin stirred and stretched. "Role models for the health care profession, I suppose. Decimate the competition." She glanced across the aisle. "Do you find General Patton inspiring, Plato?"

"Very." He winked at Cal. "I read him to my sick patients."

"It's a wonder they don't all die."

"They all do—eventually." He spread his hands. "That's the beauty of geriatrics."

"He's just kidding, Marta." The internist stirred in his seat. Mark Inverness hated controversy. The caterpillar crawled up his forehead again. "Aren't you, Plato?"

"Of course." He nodded.

"I know all about *Plato's* sense of humor." The obstetrician chuckled. "He was the hit of the house staff party last weekend. I wondered why you weren't there, Cal."

Plato's jaw dropped. The party. The St. Patrick's Day party. *Oh, my God.*

"I didn't know about it," Cal replied slowly. "I was out of town last week."

She flashed Plato a puzzled look. He shrugged innocently, burrowing his chin into the collar of his coat.

"Too bad." Oberlin turned to the internist. "You remember Plato's little exhibition, Mark. Kind of a Chippendale motif. And in the middle of March, yet."

"Chippendale?" Cal dropped Plato's arm and sat up. *"Plato?"*

"Not at first." The obstetrician chuckled again—an ominous sound that differed little from her Doberman impression. "He had more than a couple of drinks before the tuxedo finally came off. That's what I mean by his sense of humor—it was the *way* he took that tuxedo off that was funny."

"I bet it was." Cal eyed Plato like some sort of dangerous alien life form: the Andromeda Strain in human shape.

"It was a—*swimming* party," he sputtered. "At the health club. I—I had a cold, and I really didn't want to go in, but—"

"But Terri Lynn Jones convinced you," Oberlin noted helpfully.

"Terri Lynn Jones," Cal echoed.

"You've seen her, I'm sure." The obstetrician stared at the ceiling of the bus. "Psychiatry resident. Blond and gorgeous. More curves than the Cuyahoga River. Anyway—"

"Terri Lynn Jones had nothing to do with it," Plato insisted.

"Then maybe it was those two surgery nurses." Oberlin shrugged. "The ones that kept dunking you in the pool."

Plato frowned. "I don't remember any surgery nurses."

"The ones in the string bikinis."

"Oh." He buried his chin farther inside his coat, like Beaker on *The Muppet Show*.

"You told me you were *sick* all week—that you didn't go out at all." Cal glared at Plato, dark whirlwinds looming in her brown eyes. "You said you lived like a *monk* last week."

Marta Oberlin chuckled. "One of *Chaucer's* monks, maybe."

"It was all perfectly innocent." Mark Inverness squirmed in his seat, obviously uncomfortable. "Really."

The obstetrician shrugged, oblivious to Cal's storm signals. Maybe it was just her sense of humor, which—as Plato recalled from the party—was even more bizarre than his own.

Or perhaps she was getting back at him for supposedly plant-ing the Camp *Success!* idea in Wallace's head.

"He had this skimpy green swimsuit on under his tuxedo," Oberlin continued. "And he did this little dance at the side of the pool."

"It was hardly a *dance.*" Inverness shook his head. "Plato's shoelaces got stuck, and he hopped around trying to get them off. So we all started teasing him."

"And he started this little striptease." Oberlin giggled—*giggled!* "It was cute."

"Don't listen to Marta." The internist glanced over at Cal. "It was nothing—Plato was a perfect gentleman."

Oberlin shrugged, finally silent. Cal harrumphed. Plato glanced at Inverness and sighed thankfully.

But that was just like Mark—always the peacemaker. At council meetings, whenever tempers flared or arguments erupted, Inverness always began soothing, temporizing, com-promising. He was allergic to conflict, squirming and wincing at harsh words and angry comments, as if they wounded him personally.

"I wish my ex-husband could have danced like that," Ober-lin mused softly. "We'd probably still be married."

Inverness patted her arm and shot her a warning glance.

The residents called him Dr. Congeniality, and they were right. But like any nice guy, Inverness was prone to finish last. He never said "no" to his patients or his residents. His practice had the highest proportion of uninsured patients in the entire hospital. He haunted the floors day and night, caring for his sick patients personally while backing up his overworked resi-dents. Even after he became Chief of Internal Medicine, he re-mained the most personable, most approachable physician in all of Riverside General Hospital, seeming to have time for even the most trivial complaints or problems.

His wife and children had left him years ago.

Cal was still fuming, making those little chuffing noises under her breath like she did when she was angry—like a well-mannered cat quietly working out a stubborn furball.

Plato's heroic gesture—rescuing Cal by shouldering the blame for the Camp *Success!* idea—was apparently all but for-gotten.

"Anyway, I'm sure we all know about Plato's sense of humor," Marta concluded.

"We certainly do," Cal growled. She glanced at the obstetrician. "Maybe you could lend me that blunt speculum of yours."

"Any time, dear."

Beside her, Mark Inverness squirmed in his seat.

The bus lurched and careened down the dusty dirt road into Camp *Success!* On the screen, the actors were still delivering their quotes and slogans and words of inspiration.

"Some men see things as they are and say 'Why' " the television noted smugly. *"I dream of things that never were, and say, 'Why not?' "*

Across the aisle, Mark Inverness winced.

"Three bedrooms, ten occupants—and one bath," Cal griped. Standing in the common room of the Henry Ford Cabin, she shook her head sadly. "I guess we're going to learn teamwork, all right."

The bus had jounced and rattled along the dirt road for nearly half an hour. They had crawled past the John D. Rockefeller Lodge, the Harvey Firestone Trail, and the Cyrus Eaton Challenge Course. Each landmark had been proudly described by their guide as the bus went by.

Finally, they drew up at the Henry Ford Trail, a mile-long winding path marked with brass plaques bearing more inspirational slogans and quotes. As the pack-weary hikers slogged up the trail behind their guide, Claude Eberhardt had paused to read each signpost aloud, like a priest reciting the Stations of the Cross.

Just as the campers were threatening to rebel, the guide had led them over one last hill to the Henry Ford Cabin. The sprawling pile of rotting planks and cedar shingles and rough-hewn logs made Plato and Cal's decrepit century home seem like the Taj Mahal.

"Rustic" was how Claude Eberhardt had described it. Marta Oberlin had used a less kind word.

"Do you *seriously* expect us to spend a weekend here?" The obstetrician's dark eyes flashed from their guide to Lionel Wallace and back again.

"Perhaps Claude can suggest some more suitable lodgings," Inverness suggested. His voice was calm and soothing, like an animal trainer caged with a lioness.

The Council of Chiefs had formed a half-circle around Wallace and the tour guide. Backed up against the crude stone fireplace, the CEO glanced at Eberhardt.

"They do have a point, Claude." During the walk, Wallace had chatted amiably with the guide, pointing to plants and trees and birds and quizzing Eberhardt about them. In deference to his companion's age and rank, Eberhardt had carried the CEO's backpack. The two already seemed like old friends.

Oddly enough, Wallace sometimes had that effect on people. Like the Board of Trustees, for instance. Unfortunately, mere friendship wasn't going to provide a solution this time.

Claude Eberhardt stared at his feet and shrugged. "Uh. Er. The other lodgings—Harvey Firestone Cabin and Rockefeller Lodge—are both full this weekend."

"Then you have no other place for us." Cy Kettering, the Chief of Psychiatry, unslung his backpack from his small shoulders.

"I'm afraid—"

"You must be aware that these quarters are completely inadequate." Kettering folded his arms and stared at the tour guide. Although he was hardly taller than Cal, the psychiatrist had a marvelously abrupt and confrontative style which put other physicians—and his patients—off guard. He puffed his saddlebag cheeks in disgust. "It's a miracle that this building hasn't collapsed. The floors are moldy with rot. The roof almost certainly leaks. The bedrooms smell like an old flophouse." He shook his head. "I wouldn't let my *dog* sleep here."

"We're not *asking* your dog to sleep here," Lionel Wallace pointed out. "I believe there is a rule against pets, anyway. Isn't there, Claude?"

Plato bit back a laugh. Beside him, Cal's eyes were bulging.

At his left, Marta was whispering to Inverness. "He didn't just say that. Did he?"

Inverness closed his eyes and sighed.

"They're remodeling the buildings one at a time," the guide explained lamely. "They just didn't get to this one yet." He gave a weak smile. "Camp *Success!* used to be a Boy Scout campground."

"Perhaps we should just head back," the Chief of Surgery suggested gently. *"After* we rest a while."

Andre Surfaire had barely survived the hike up to the cabin. He had done plenty of hiking in his youth, outrunning Papa Doc and the Tontons Macoutes across the hills of Haiti. But that was several decades and a few hundred pounds ago. At fifty-something years of age, and well over three hundred pounds, the surgeon got winded every time he blinked.

He turned to Wallace. "How about it, Lionel?"

The president turned to Godfrey Millburn, his vice president and Chief Operating Officer. Millburn had the dour, sad face of an undertaker, mounted on the body of a half-starved basketball center. He shrugged his bony shoulders under the backpack.

"We paid in advance. Nonrefundable." He glanced around the cabin. "Believe it or not, this outing cost us several thousand dollars."

"We have a dozen trainers on staff," Eberhardt hastily explained. "You'll meet them tomorrow. Between the team-building program and the food, Camp *Success!* spends quite a bit of money on a typical training weekend."

"Must be some great food," Plato muttered.

"If the rats haven't already eaten it," Cal replied grimly.

"Rats?"

She traced a plump rodent shape in the air. "I saw a big fat one in our bedroom."

The vice president leaned closer to Wallace and whispered something about a photo opportunity.

Wallace had seemed tempted to call the weekend off, but he nodded quickly. Turning to Claude Eberhardt, he stared at the guide for several seconds, then smiled. "I think we should give Camp *Success!* a chance. Eh, Claude?"

"Yes, sir." The guide nodded happily. "I'm sure you won't regret it."

"I'm sure he *will* regret it," Marta Oberlin said quietly. She gave her Doberman growl again, then flashed her teeth at Plato. "And you too, my friend."

On his other side, Cal was glaring at him with silent rage. He recognized that look, the way a weatherman recognizes thunderheads looming on the horizon. At the very least, Cal's glare forecast a long, stormy conversation, with a steady downpour of choice words like "inconsiderate" and "thoughtless" and "dishonest."

Plato shuddered. He was *already* regretting coming here. Sandwiched between a jealous wife and a slightly unbalanced obstetrician, he felt like a mouse in a pit of vipers. It was shaping up to be a dangerous weekend.

But Plato had no idea just how dangerous the weekend would prove to be.